COPING WITH ASH

COPING
WITH ASH

a novel by

MICHAEL SCOTT CURNES

Cover and interior design by Masha Shubin | Inkwater.com
Cover Photo: Evan Sharbonneau
Author Photo: Bernard Sauvé
Ash images © arsen merc. BigStockPhoto.com
Back Cover Image of a traditional Nez Perce twin bag woven from cornhusk and dogbane, cour-
tesy of the museum collection at the Nez Perce National Historical Park Spalding Visitor Center.

This is a work of fiction. The events described here are imaginary. The settings and characters
are fictitious or used in a fictitious manner and do not represent specific places or living or dead
people. Any resemblance is entirely coincidental.

Author's Notations:
The following works appear in this text:
"First Fig," written by Edna St. Vincent Millay.
"Grease" written by Barry Gibb, recorded by Frankie Valli (RSO, 1978).
"Afternoon Delight," written by Bill Danoff, recorded by Starland Vocal Band (RCA, 1976).
"Material Girl," written by Peter Downs and Robert Rans, recorded by Madonna (Warner
Brothers Records, 1984).
The story "How Coyote Lost His Penis" is used with author's permission from the reference
book titled Linguistics Volume 104, *Nez Perce Oral Narratives* by Haruo Aoki and Deward E.
Walker, Jr., University of California Press, ISBN-10: 0520096932

Paperback ISBN-13 978-1-7772988-1-4

Printed in the U.S.A.

1 3 5 7 9 10 8 6 4 2

CONTENTS

THE END

AS CREMATORIUMS GO, I SUPPOSE THIS ONE IS ON THE TIDY side of the *dead don't mind anyway* continuum.

That's me—well, the former me—inside the highly flammable white body bag on the stainless and slotted gurney being guided toward the rails of the incinerator. This bag, I have to say, makes a mockery of the Federal Code of Regulations, Part 1615, which set the standard for the flammability of sleepwear. But for once, I am silent. Gone are the days when a skillfully raised point of order—you know, the out-of-the-mouths-of-babes sort that left parents smacked down and examining their childrearing skills—gained me free range to sleep and dash about naked lest my Sears and Roebuck PJs should spontaneously combust and start a three-alarm house fire.

Well, gone are the days, period.

The gurney transfers onto a pair of rails as a whoosh of natural gas rattles everything. This is quite likely about to get messy, not to mention noisy, so let's focus on the other business of the day—the nitty-gritty byproduct of what's about to occur.

Ashton Taylor, *Last Will and Testament*, page 1

I, Ashton Bernard Taylor (a.k.a. Ash), of Seattle, Washington, being of sound and disposing mind, do hereby make, publish, and declare the following to be my *Last Will and Testament*.

I declare that I am partnered with Rich "Limping Rabbit" Dreadfulwater, whom I have herein referred to as my squaw . . . [Oh hell, I'd better change that to spouse or someone's likely to get his arrow bent out of shape] . . . whom I have herein referred to as my spouse and executor, and that I have no children now living.

I direct that my executor pay all of my cremation costs, all state and federal estate, inheritance, and succession taxes, administration costs and all of my debts subject to statute of limitations, except mortgage notes secured by real estate, as soon as practical. I give, devise, and bequeath all of the rest and remainder of my estate, of whatever kind and character, and wherever located, to my spouse, provided that my spouse survives me. Given my rather peculiar medical afflictions, the odds are certainly in Limping Rabbit's favor.

As for my remains, I have always leaned toward the fatalistic side of living, reinforced by personal lessons early on—my quick cha-cha with cancer in the early 80s, my gastro-intestinal and asthmatic issues, and the deaths of too many intimate friends and lovers during this AIDS pandemic, which of course ravages on in its third decade. These have taught me to prepare for the eventuality of death. I want, therefore, to take this opportunity, while I still have your attention, to list a few items that will hasten my departure from this realm and hopefully minimize your grief and anguish at my passing.

The following instructions detail how I wish my body to be handled. Not that I was overly picky about how or by whom it was handled when I was alive. [A little levity. LAUGH, dammit!] In order to preserve my precious family history—which ends with childless me, incidentally—I would like to have a simple but permanent grave marker installed in my family's plot in Coeur d'Alene, Idaho. You'll have to coordinate with my father on this, but the marker should record my date of birth—April 4, 1962—and not a date of death but the total number of days my heart beat. For example, today marks 13,954 days.

My sister teaches third grade. She'll get a kick out of bringing her class of nine-year-olds to the cemetery to figure out how old her brother was. The third graders need the fresh air anyway. That was my problem, if you ask me. Not enough fresh air.

Plain and simple, I wish to be cremated. And here's a note to Limping Rabbit on this matter: while I'm sure you could come up with some entrepreneurial way to do it cheaper, I wish to be cremated professionally, so don't be a tightwad.

That's my husband down there—Rich "Limping Rabbit" Dreadfulwater—exotically dark and handsomely tall, trying to explain to the funeral director why he doesn't need an urn or a casket or a floral spray or a formaldehyde spritzer. It's not that he can't afford those things. He's a very successful, even celebrated Seattle defense lawyer. It's just that these trinkets and gadgets aren't necessary to carry out my wishes, plus if he can save a buck . . . well, enough said. My suddenly liberated, off-the-hook life partner doesn't completely grasp what has just happened to me, to him, or to us—but he is trying. Bless his full-blooded Nez Perce Indian heart.

If you hadn't bothered to do the research, like I did, you might not have realized that cremation gets selected less than a third of the time from the menu options pedaled by the funeral industry in North America. That means more than two thirds of the US dead are still—in this (you'd think enlightened) day and age—getting pumped full of toxic formaldehyde and interred in caskets buried in the crowded ground to leech into the drinking water. My death was just one of about 2.5 million that will occur in the United States this year. It has been calculated that close to 30 million board feet, 104,000 tons of steel, 2,700 tons of copper and bronze, and 1.6 million tons of reinforced concrete get buried in this ritual every year. I wasn't about to leave that footprint. True, the two hours it is taking for my body to be vaporized by natural gas at 2100° F does release a dainty dose of carbon dioxide into the immediate atmosphere—but scarcely more than I would have released myself if I were still breathing.

That's about it for the former me; just twenty minutes to go in the cremulator—a *Cuisinart* for bone fragments—and I'm pretty much good to scatter.

Wait.

Oh, dear.

This isn't good.

It looks like Limping Rabbit is about to faint. The funeral director is trying to hand him the plastic-lined cardboard box with what remains of my corporal self. My lover for the past 7,235 days reaches for the back of a chair to buttress his six-foot frame, but opts instead to sit down. The funeral director places the half-size shoebox on a round, doilied side-table and says "when you're ready" before taking his leave from the oppressive maple wood-paneled receiving room.

Through moist, puffy, bloodshot, and late-autumn chestnut-colored eyes, Rich stares down at the box for several minutes, struggling to comprehend the rendering my body has undergone. He needs his analytical brain to figure out how the body of the man he shared the past nineteen and a half years of his life sleeping and laughing and arguing and walking with, went from one hundred and eighty-seven pounds—my weight when he delivered me to the emergency room a little more than seventy-two hours ago—to this: a fair bit less than what I weighed at birth.

How about we give him a few minutes?

ASHTON

My candle burns at both ends
It will not last the night;
But ah, my foes, and oh, my friends—
It gives a lovely light!

Edna St. Vincent Millay

BY WAY OF PRELUDE, YOU'LL NEED TO UNDERSTAND THAT
the "candle," in my case—in shape, length, endurance, and practical
usefulness when things started to go bump in the dark—was a shame-
less euphemism.

I was born on a Wednesday, April 4, 1962, at Lake City General
Hospital in Coeur d' Alene, Idaho, at 7:44 in the morning.

John F. Kennedy was president of the United States, the Cuban
Missile Crisis was still five months away, John Steinbeck had just won
the Pulitzer for Literature, and Marilyn Monroe had a measurable
heartbeat beneath those breasts—not that I would have ever noticed.

My father, Gerald Leroy, was twenty-seven, and my mother, Carole
Jean, was twenty-three when I survived that fortunately unmem-
orable ten-and-a-half-hour journey to get some fresh air. I weighed

seven pounds and seven ounces and was nineteen inches long. But size doesn't matter—less so now, in the after-world, than ever.

Five days later, on April 9, 1962, my candle was circumcised—the mutilating, un-anaesthetized surgical trauma for which I blame everyone and everything that has happened since.

From birth, Carole Jean had attempted to breastfeed me—without success, of course. She gave up trying entirely on the day of my circumcision—likely accepting that the mother-son bond was about to be sliced and diced anyway. I had shunned her, so she shunted me. I guessed we were even. Female breasts weren't my thing. *My* thing had just been amputated. I would grow up to lament the larceny of my foreskin, removed ostensibly to "aid the boy to maintain cleanliness," according to the *Better Homes and Gardens* Child Care and Training Department. Well, screw Better Homes! Studies have since indicated that there are five erogenous zones on the uncircumcised penis that are removed during the procedure, leaving just one sensitive location on the circumcised penis, which happens to be the circumcision scar itself. Little and lame consolation prize, Monty Hall.

Unfortunately for me, this was a truly American fad, with over three quarters of the boys born in hospitals in 1962 undergoing a scalpel within two weeks of birth, almost always without anesthesia. In the 1970s, genital mutilations finally began to diminish, when hippies started to question everything that had anything to do with lovemaking. When, ultimately, no medical evidence could be produced to support the necessity of the procedure, and when the practice of circumcision was revealed to be an overzealous attempt to keep boys not hygienically but morally clean—that is, not as likely to masturbate or derive unnecessary and non-procreative pleasure from sex—all bets were off, and foreskins began staying on. Too late for this shorn clubber.

Was it any wonder that I never trusted a woman with my penis again?

Seven-four-four (time) on four-four (date) and seven-seven (weight). If I had been Chinese, these numbers would have signified death, anger, and abandonment—and since they happened to me in pairs, at least doubly so. But I was not Chinese. I was born in the Chinese Year of the Tiger, though, and we all know what that means, or can at the very least google it. One search suggests that Tigers are rebellious and impatient. They are both vibrant and spontaneous. Their boundless energy and lust for life are inexhaustible. They adore being center stage and never wander out of the spotlight. Tigers are anxious and seek action at all times. They do not conceal what they feel, especially when it comes to emotions, and they treat everything and everyone with a guarded suspicion.

Though known to have quick tempers, they are also affectionate, protective and generous. Behind their odd stripes and snarls, Tigers have fantastic senses of humor. They live to show off and entertain, and have a need to be involved with and surrounded by others. Their dedication to fairness and overcoming challenges is fierce. Tigers can sniff out adventure, and have a tendency to act out and even rebel. Tigers are so brave and daring that they collect affection and admiration wherever they go. Even those who might disapprove of a Tiger's actions will secretly admire a Tiger and wish they could be that brave.

When Tigers get hurt, they need loads of sympathy. Rational and logical thinking will not appeal to them when they are down. They want to be coddled. While they may listen to advice you give, they will more likely do the opposite as it pleases them. With unlimited energy, they are not defeated, and can recover and rebound in an instant. Tigers are experts at reinventing themselves; when one tactic fails, they switch to another with unparalleled dexterity.

People born during the year of the Tiger tend to be egomaniacs. You'd be wise to give them space and walk cautiously around them without frightening or angering them. Tigers have a tough time forgetting or forgiving if they have been wronged. Tigers are playful. They are teasers and crowd pleasers. Prone to passion, they can be jealously—even possessively—romantic. Tigers are known to have difficulty controlling their emotions, and still they hunt for those emotional situations that allow them to live and love their lives away.

Now, if I were the lazy sort of post-mortem memoirist, I could easily end my life's explanation on that note. Those of you who thought you knew me are probably nodding your heads pretty enthusiastically about now.

But you don't know this Tiger; at least not yet.

We're circling back now to check on Limping Rabbit's progress. I'd say he's doing a fair bit better. I don't weigh enough now to make the seatbelt sensor go off, but he's seatbelted my box of cremains next to him in the passenger seat of his BMW Z4 Roadster for the drive home. Adorable. I am safe. I am sound. We are heading through downtown Seattle on 99, then onto Fifth Avenue, past the Space Needle, toward our condo home on the top of Queen Anne Hill.

He is consumed by retrospection that eats him alive from the inside out, like a starfish that has inserted its stomach into the shell of its prey. He learned all about echinoderms at the Seattle Aquarium while on a weekend date with his boyfriend—me, now riding in a plastic-lined box in the passenger seat. It had been early in our almost two-decade long relationship together when I had declared it a *Be a Tourist in Your Own Town* weekend. Rich the lawyer had tossed out a rash of intervening arguments for why the Experience Music Project and the Museum of Flight and the SAM and the Aquarium would all represent a drain on our take-home salaries; but they were hollow, since he made great money and wanted for nothing. When the weekend was over, Rich had been that wide-eyed, A-minus-average student on a school field trip that had a blast learning about sea cucumbers, finding out that the very first Air Force One was a Boeing 707, and discovering that John F. Kennedy started the 1962 World Exposition by illuminating the Space Needle using a remote control. He also learned enough about his boyfriend, now just dust in that box next to him, to fall even deeper in love than he thought he was capable. And this is the cruelest part of this new reality—that all the early investments and pronouncements and hope-bursting promises still brought him to this empty place, this catastrophic loss, this life-stopping heartbreak.

Rich is understandably puffy from bawling and not getting enough sleep, and he probably shouldn't be driving in his condition, but somehow he gets us there. He gets us home. This is the best place for us right now until he figures out the next part, the what-in-this-hell comes next, which of course I have already spelled out for him once he summons the strength to consult my wishes. He'll get there too. If I learned anything in my fifty-four years, it is to have faith in Limping Rabbit.

Now, not a lot should be said about my childhood but perhaps something should be written about the two humans who brought me into this world.

Born in Indianola, Iowa, on January 29, 1935, the sire of my seed, Gerald Leroy—or "G.L.," since he preferred to abbreviate things like details, feelings, emotions—smothered me with attention and affection during the first two years of my life. That was my entitlement as the first progeny—and male, to boot. Curious, really, how that would change with the birth of my sister, and how I would later grow up to misunderstand and even blame him for being physically out of touch and emotionally absent.

Born on Friday the 13th of June, 1938, in Moscow, Idaho, my incubator, Carole Jean, is also a Tiger, but of the more docile zoo variety, thanks to my zookeeper father, who was born in the Year of the Dog. Dogs are loyal. They will do anything and everything to protect themselves and those they love. Calculating and calm, they can be mistaken for being cold and indifferent. Preferring only black or white, Dogs have no time or tolerance for gray. Rule-abiding, and always with an eye on the ball, they pant for what's fair and just. They wield authority as they shepherd their flocks. They will put themselves between you and danger—even at their own peril—time and time again. Their bark may deafen, and their howl may be piercing. But their trust will protect you, and it cannot be stolen away. Dogs are the saints among us. They suffer no madness in the world, guarding us from ourselves and other dangers. Dogs cannot be deceived, with their keen senses of hearing and smelling and seeing. They can't be distracted from their duty to love and obey and protect. People born during the Year of the Dog are bound by loyalty and oath to patrol the boundaries between right and wrong.

I was raised—not by my parents (don't worry, they are likely not taking credit for it either) but by the letter of the *Better Homes and Gardens Baby Book: a Handbook for Parents—Fifth Revision*. In a bestselling, companion, fill-in-the-blank journal book from the

University of Chicago Medical Center, titled *Our Baby's First Seven Years*, my mother meticulously recorded the details of my birth: due April 2 (which meant I was conceived on July 1, 1961—my parents' first wedding anniversary); onset of labor occurred naturally at 9:18 p.m. on Tuesday, April 3; birth occurred—no pain killers required—in the head-down normal position the following morning; respiration occurred spontaneously. At birth, my eyes were blue, my hair was black, my eyebrows and eyelashes were brown. (Of autopsical note: at death my eyes were bloodshot and green from oxygen deprivation, my eyebrows had thinned, and my three-day gray head and face stubble was embarrassingly only three razor swipes shaved on the right side).

My mother remarks on an early page that no birthmarks were detected at birth—however, at six weeks, she discovered an inch-long mark on my lower back. Truthfully, it was at the very top of my ass crack, which was to cause me immeasurable grief once I reached showering age in junior high physical education class. "Taylor over-wipes his ass! Taylor over-wipes his ass!" You can just imagine the taunting.

I had my "first professional haircut" on November 21, 1962, according to my mother's label on the window envelope pressed between the pages of the aforementioned baby book; the envelope contained clippings cut by a barber named Leo Frazier, in Indianola, Iowa. It must have been during my first cross-heartland visit to the Iowa grandparents. Her envelope label always caused me to suspect that I had experienced at least one prior, *un*professional haircut—likely at my mother's hands, as she had already proven herself to be so good at getting things snipped. The insinuation here—that she had to turn matters over to a professional—was not surprising. My hair was to present a challenge to every barber, stylist, makeup artist, and hairdresser who foolishly thought they might be the one to finally tame it. In the 80s, chemotherapy gave the etch-a-sketch a shake, causing my hair to fall out and then mutate into a curlier tangle when it finally grew back. But by the time it began thinning in the late 90s, my hair had gone from Prince Valiant to Chernobyl to Howie Mandel to a day I could see approaching when it would just be gone, period, I reluctantly decided my new look would be Mr. Clean. So I began daily shaving my head bald.

Some people have a limp or stutter. Others struggle with dyslexia, dialysis, or diabetes. I was cursed with unmanageable hair that dogged me 'til the morning I died, in the middle of the daily noggin shave—just to tie things up in one nice, big, thematic hair ribbon.

Again, referencing my mother's beautifully handwritten notes in the "Physical and Mental Development" sections of the baby book, I can pass along the following highlights: eyes and head follow slow-moving objects at three weeks; turns head or makes other response to human voice at six weeks; puts objects in mouth at twelve weeks (no mention of what said objects were); begins teething at three months; pulls self to standing position at seven months; walks alone at nine months. Added in the margin of that last page: *dances* at fourteen months. Of course, the lab rats in the Child Care and Training Department hadn't thought to include *artistic* movement as one of their prescribed stages in development.

Around the one-year mark, my first word was "Daddy," followed by "thank you." I'd previously mastered the very useful automobile and donkey sounds by five months, and my mother recorded my first sentence of more than four words as "Eddy Peak, Eddy Peak—this is home set." A quick spin on Google reveals that Eddy Peak was a US Forest Service fire lookout tower, about a dozen miles east of Thompson Falls, Montana, where we had moved shortly after my first birthday. My dad, who worked for the US Forest Service, was away for weeks at a time during the summer, fighting wildfires—and, in later years, coordinating the government's response to them. Each year around May, before the season flared up, he'd monitor emergency radio communications from home. If that was my first spoken sentence, I likely mimicked what I'd heard him repeating into a two-way radio from his pre-season base station in our living room.

Gosh, I must have completely idolized the man in the beginning, during my take-off years—just as I would again shortly before my engine conked out and I started to plummet toward my crash landing.

It was the blasted middle where our father-son relationship experienced the greatest, rivet-rattling turbulence.

My sister, Krista Mardel—who was also an abbreviator (call her "Kris")—arrived on April 26, 1964, during the Chinese Year of the Dragon. This was both unsettling and oddly welcome. After two years, I was growing restless and bored with G.L. and Carole Jean. This helped set the boredom barometer that I would faithfully apply to the rest of my life, as I tended to lose interest at or around the two-year mark of anything. That is, of course, until I crossed paths with Limping Rabbit.

But back to my sister. People born in the Year of the Dragon use fire, stature, and every possible device to impress and intimidate. You will not win a battle or a debate with a Dragon. They do not take kindly to challengers or outsiders. Once enraged, a Dragon takes a long time to cool down. They do not forget an affront. They are stubborn and calloused and scaled—this protects them and those they care about from the elements. Dragons swoop in for the rescue with a solution to any problem, choosing their moment to prevail and boast. They are competitive, and they take credit for each win and save. Dragons want to be loved and revered, but aren't overly romantic. Their emotions can get away from them—and given their capacity for fire-breathing, they often say things that they immediately regret. But there is beauty inside these beasts.

I don't want to belabor the sibling blame game, but my sister's birth was likely the first time I experienced rejection from a man—my father. The pain was so unbearably intense that I would live the rest of my life paying every cost—emotional, psychological, physical, medical, spiritual, and retail—to avoid it again. Hell, it's a hypothesis.

Fast forward sixteen years to contrast and compare this hunch to an emotional survival tactic I would steadily perfect: reject men first, usually within two years, preemptively and awkwardly. No matter how handsome, kind, or innocent the victim, I made sure that either their warranty ran out, or I self-recalled somewhere inside forty-eight months. For more than a dozen years, this warped record had spun, sometimes slower at 33, sometimes speedy-quick at 78, but most usually at a respectable 45 RPM that was sure to give others the impression I hadn't rushed to my prophetic conclusion.

That record that spun me right round, baby, right round, would be revolving still if the turntable hadn't been knocked off its pedestal when all my issues, habits, and hang-ups crashed headlong into an eighteen-dysfunction pileup the day I met my beautiful Indian in 1996. Only Rich Dreadfulwater had been able to stop the dizzying revolutions of my cyclical behavior in a way that cured me of everything—well, everything but my death, which had always seemed to be speeding toward me, like one of those Japanese electric bullet trains. And it seemed that way because, at something like 300 kilometers per hour for the next 7,235 days, it was.

RICH

HE IS SITTING THERE IN HIS WHITE BMW ROADSTER INSIDE the parking garage of our condo building in parking space #325 next to my black Saturn Vue in space #326 with both hands, white knuckles up, on the steering wheel—scared of death to let go. The automatic garage gate clangs and cymbals to a close and then there is silence and car fumes—but not nearly enough of either to let him slip the surly bonds of his grief. I can tell that he is trying to pull it together by talking to himself. He does that all the time; before confrontation, before entering a courtroom, before calling his father (which he stopped doing about seven years ago), and before forcing himself to do something he doesn't want to do, like go on living one more hour without me. Counting the voices in that boy's head from one moment to the next would keep a statistician working overtime. He says they are his ancestors—which is funny, coming from Rich, who works overtime to camouflage his heritage with white boy trappings, like his Beemer and his law degree and this ridiculously expensive condo in the old Queen Anne High School.

Sometimes I think if it hadn't been for my excessive boasting of the beauty of our mixed ethnic relationship, and maybe Limping Rabbit's unbreakable tether with his baby sister, V'ronica (who wasn't a baby anymore but still lived on the reservation near Lapwai, Idaho), Rich would have had zero ties back to his Nez Perce roots, and likely would have preferred it that way. The *raison de guerre* for this estrangement with his dad was that Lil' Chief (his father's nickname for him, and a way of reminding him that he was next in line) had declined his pop's 2004 invitation to head the legal team representing the Nez Perce in the adjudication of their treaty-granted water rights in the Salmon and Clearwater river basins. It is through the heart of the traditional Nez Perce territory (where both Rich and I grew up, only sixty miles apart but in entirely different cultures) that these wild rivers flow. If you were a salmon, which neither of us were in this life—nor apparently for me, in the one after—you could swim from the Pacific Ocean into the Columbia River, then into the Snake River, then into the Clearwater River, then into the Salmon River. These rivers flowed through our hearts too.

Rich was raised along the banks of the Clearwater, in quasi-traditional but increasingly modernized Indian ways. My character and identity were formed and informed by my Dog Father, who was an historically sympathetic civil servant raising his family on an agricultural plateau about 1,800 elevational feet above the Salmon. It was known as *The River of No Return*, so after graduating high school, I didn't.

Though we wouldn't meet each other to share a nod or a bed for another fifteen years, I bet if we were to retrace the potholed lanes of Idaho State Highway 95 that ran between our towns, re-conjure the regional and state scholastic and athletic events where our teams must have competed against each other, flashback to the fall and spring class registration sessions at the U of I in 1981 and 82, and then overlay the hopelessly barren, oxygen-starved isolation that could only be recognized by teens growing up gay in rural Idaho, it would eliminate all doubt that we were mates of the same soul—suckers of a common geographic bosom.

Conflicts of interest aside and in proper context, Rich's father's legal request had been an unappetizing dish served with hefty side plates of authority and familial expectation that his son would meet this tribal duty and that he would work practically pro bono. As DNA would have it, both men happened to be directly descended from the legendary Chief Joseph, who lived in the late 1800s. Limping Rabbit's father, named

Moses by second-generation Christian missionaries, is the first, by eleven minutes, of two surviving twin brothers, both of whom claimed ascendancy as hereditary chief—and either of whom will be passing that distinguished lineage on to my widower, whether he likes it or not. When making what he thought would be the closing argument in his decision to not take on the treaty fishing rights for the tribe, though, he had said: "Whether or not it is Rich Dreadfulwater's desire or destiny to become chief of the Nez Perce is immaterial. The truth is that you can't afford this lawyer and this lawyer can't afford to work pro bono."

So now, if he never gets around to reconciling with his father the chief—or his son-less uncle, in the event the latter survives his father—Limping Rabbit will have succeeded in thumbing his unpierced nose at the one hundred centuries of Nez Perce that came before him. (I make the point of saying "unpierced" because what makes this historically ironic is that the name *Nez Percé* is an exonym given to Rich's ancestors by French Canadian fur traders who visited the area with some frequency in the late-eighteenth century; a name meaning literally "pierced nose." There is no evidence his ancestors ever pierced anything beyond arrows through the soldiers of a marauding cavalry. Still, the French name stuck. In modern times, the Nez Perce self-identify more often as *Niimíipu*, which simply and more accurately means "the people" in their traditional Sahaptin dialect.)

Now that I'm on this side of the flat line, I need to lobby those ancestors—including Joseph—whose voices Rich says are in his head. Someone needs to be telling Limping Rabbit something like *Warrior Dude, fight your world no more forever, and get real with your Indian self!*

Now, what is he doing? I'm not sure why he is taking the stairwell instead of the elevator, but at least he is out of his car. He never takes the stairs on account of that slight developmental hitch in his step that gave him his native namesake. Maybe it's because he doesn't want to be alone with me in an enclosed, windowless space, reduced as I am to grit. Maybe taking the stairs is metaphor for everything that has changed for him—for us—in the past seventy-two hours. Believe me, this Tiger—once accustomed to the adoration of center stage, and the glow of a spotlight—has some adjusting ahead as well, in this new supporting role as offstage narrator. Please bear with us. We're all just coping at the moment.

Our home—*his* home (that isn't so much a distinction resulting from my vacated post as much as it was always his home)—feels empty. Not like a moving-truck-came-and-packed-everything-away empty, but more like "soul empty," if I may state the obvious.

Rich had been renting an apartment in the old Queen Anne High School when we met at an AIDS fundraiser in 1996. It was an about-to-burst housing bubble and I didn't know it yet, but I was on the path to losing my sub-prime shirt on a home in nearby Edmonds. Since we had both been born in 1962 and so were both Tigers, we lived separately for the first decade of our relationship, taking advantage of both homes as it suited our schedules and tax regimes. Rich preferred to stay in the city during the week for ease of access to the courts and his law firm's office in the Columbia Tower, so I joined him there most weeknights. We'd weekend in Edmonds, where we'd garden and renovate, courtesy of a second mortgage that encouraged such nonsense. We'd flirt with the notion of growing old and making it our retirement home.

In 2005, when the residents of Queen Anne High School were notified that the building was about to undergo conversion to condominium units (read: "evicted"), Rich raised the stench of a lawsuit, but didn't follow through, eventually moving his things to Edmonds. He didn't reveal to me at the time that the developer, wanting buyers and not lawsuits, had offered the brash, young, and ballsy lawyer with the Indian last name his pick of the complex, and first-purchase rights on any unit in the hundred-year-old building. Though he had been living on the second floor above the main entrance without much view facing Galer Street, he marched the developer up the wide staircases to the fourth floor, and apparently laid claim to what would become the premium space in the building: a 1,432 square foot, one-bedroom-plus-den corner unit with 1.75 bathrooms and two floor-to-ceiling Palladian windows with views of Elliot Bay, the Space Needle, downtown Seattle, and Mt. Rainier. It was next to the top floor, above an enclosed courtyard with a topiary-ringed three-tiered fountain. Tailored to the new owner's specs, with lots of built-ins, a walk-in closet, heated floors, and a state-of-the-art entertainment system, it would have been the first time Rich had used legal intimidation for his own gain.

He had financing and papers in place within two weeks, but still hadn't told me. I had either been so completely under his influence or tipsy on my own new relationship Kool-Aid, but I honestly thought we would live out our days in the sleepy bedroom community of Edmonds. I thought his demanding career required a separation between courthouse and home life; that the fifty minutes he'd spend each way commuting forth and back would be therapy between two worlds he had said he wanted to keep separate.

Suburban life was grand, in the beginning. He was so convincing at it, he fooled himself. All the while, his city dream home was coming together. If he could only find a way to break the news to me. In 2008, when it looked like Wall Street was starting its meltdown, I had to face and then reveal that I had been carrying a secret of my own. After four years of home ownership, I had zero equity in our Edmonds house. My bank had not only encouraged but incented me to leverage everything I'd put into it to fuel a completely unnecessary renovation mortgage. Rich had talked to a few investor friends who were already forecasting that suburbia would bleed most in the letting that would be needed to purify the toxic marketplace—and of course, this prophecy was realized in the tsunami of foreclosures that came next. We were lucky to sell early without a gargantuan loss, and even though our alternative housing option smelled Pike Place fishy, I allowed my partner to play the superhero and swoop in with a readymade shelter that sparkled like a diamond atop the crown of Queen Anne.

The new home didn't have a yard or even a balcony, but it was spacious and exclusive, and when the windows were open on a spring or summer day, there was no home like it anywhere. Hooked on the concept of adaptive reuse, we tricked it out with vintage classroom things, like wall-mount pencil sharpeners, a pull-down world map, and giant chalkboards in the living room and open kitchen. Upright, graffiti-tagged lockers lined one side of the entrance hall and served as the coat closet. A pair of student desks from the 20s became nightstands on either side of the master bed, and an old porcelain drinking fountain was plumbed to hang on the wall outside the guest bath-room—a facility that would have had a matching urinal if I hadn't objected to the excessive dedication to theme.

Even with all of this stuff, the place seems gutted now.

The sun has come out and plunges its glorious rays deep into the old classroom, through windows that students like L. Ron Hubbard must have gazed out of, daydreaming away the boredom of a 1926 curriculum when the building was still a high school. The sun reveals dust on every flat surface, since the housekeeping hasn't been tended since Wednesday, when the housekeeper croaked. The chalk hearts and the dozen *I love you's* (which I'd clacked onto the kitchen chalkboard last Valentine's) arrest Rich's gaze, and he drops to one knee on the recycled gymnasium flooring. He hasn't taken either hand off the box he is carrying, and I can see him forcing his brain to decipher how he could have possibly left here with me in one physical state, to return with me now in quite another.

The comforts of this refuge—Rich's made-to-order man cave—should reach out meaty arms to wrap a welcome home around my widowed lover. But the comforts hang there, limp and lifeless. We are home. Still, the place—his place—is touched-by-death different. He can't or won't rise off the floor. He is sobbing. The afterlife is so not what I imagined. There he is, holding me in his shaking hands, and I can't find any fucking way to squeeze him back.

Rich! Hey, Rich! I am right here with you!

Yeah. Nothing. He doesn't hear me. What I wouldn't give for one more moment to tell him how much I love him, to prepare him somehow for his life without me, to feel his grip and his warmth and his razor stubble, to let him let me go. So much left undone; too much that will never be reconciled—this is my hell.

"How could you leave me, you fucker!" Rich screams, shaking the box in his hands like a medicine rattle. His whole being quakes involuntarily on the floor. His face is puffy, sorrow streaming through tangled lashes out of those chestnut eyes from a hidden spring plumbed so deep—a spring neither he nor ten generations of his ancestors could have known existed. "I can't do this without you, Ash."

He sets the box on the floor in front of his knees. Each of his fingers stretches open along the painted boards, slow and deliberate, like blood leaving an exit wound to pool around a victim who has been cut down in the movies. It is obvious that every cell of his being, every molecule he can engage in this moment is imploring the floor, the building, the earth to open up and swallow him whole. "I don't want to be alone!" is the wail that comes out of the rocking body that tips over to lay curled on its side like a thumb-sucking fetus around the box that embodies his heartbeat inside his womb—which is his apartment. "I'm not finished loving you" he slobbers, barely speaking.

My soul—and that's nearly all that's left—absolutely aches for that broken man on the floor. There is a multitude of things I can't do anymore, but the inability to change this for him kills me all over again. We went from being together every day, holding hands in the car, tangling up limbs in bed every night, shaving next to each other every morning, reading each other's minds, growing older, making the other an after-work, after-trial, after-deadline, after-review, after-disagreement cocktail, to never, ever being able to touch or see or hear or smell or taste each other again. Where's the sense in that? I don't get it. What became of that meteor that was supposed to take us both out at once? That was our exit strategy. All my life I'd been told to believe it would make sense in the end. Well it fucking doesn't—not to me, and not to him.

In one second, Rich sucks back a strand of drool before it can fuse to the floor, and in the next, one of the casement windows pops open with a whooshing thud, sending him quite nearly out of his skin. In the jolt, the box with my cremated remains tips on one side and the lid releases the tiniest puff of ash dust.

You would have thought it was weaponized anthrax, the way Limping Rabbit has just lurched back and away from it. I am laughing with the angels at this one. In another second, he is laughing too, through tears that haven't stopped. Clearly unable to deal with me at this moment, Rich musters his composure, takes the upset box o' boyfriend into the open bedroom closet, and puts it on the shelf high up. He turns off the lights and returns to the living room.

He thinks he has left me in the dark. "Hey!" I want to shout, without lungs, vocal cords, or lips. "You can't leave me in here. This isn't in the plan!" And just like that, the closet light comes back on, he removes the box with one hand and is rooting for something toward the back of the shelf with the other. He finds it—a ceremonial mat that was once a food storage bag in the Nez Perce weaving tradition, about the size of two bandanas. He walks it to the bookshelf-lined den where he uses his hand to iron the mini-tapestry on the top of his home office desk. He centers the box on it, satisfied with the reverence of the display. He sits in his chair and folds his arms into a pretzel on the desk. He clears his throat, sore from days of dry sobbing.

"Look here," he says with authority. "I need to come to terms with this new reality. Eventually, I will . . . I promise." He sniffles. "But I can't do what you expect me to do. I can't." He continues to cry, shaking his head. "I know you had this plan"—his chest heaves with two rapid intakes of breath—"this plan for me to take your ashes and divide them up. But I can't do it." He reaches with a finger to pull the mat closer to him; he encircles the box with his arms and torso. "I've already lost too much of you to lose one particle more." He slobbers, stammering to get the words out.

I cannot comfort or debate you, I tell him. *There are too many things I cannot do now. I cannot touch you or make you hear me, but if you sense me at all—my presence or my spirit or whatever—please know that I am right here with you. I never left. That's something else I cannot do.*

"I feel so abandoned by you," he suddenly blurts out, as though we are actually having this conversation, and it might actually resolve something.

Listen to your argument, counselor, I shout. *It was not my choice to leave you.*

"Shit, of course you didn't abandon me." He wipes his face with the back of a hand.

Maybe I am getting through to him. I try again. This time I shout louder.

People die from natural and unnatural causes, every minute of every day, Rich—all around the world. Evidence will show, once the paperwork is finished, that it was just my time—7:27 a.m. last Wednesday, in the middle of my weekday morning routine, nineteen days before my fifty-fourth birthday. I lived 19,691 days before that left ventricle of mine exploded. Write that down—you're going to need that number. Life is random. Death is not.

Oh for shit's sake! What does it matter, all this counseling? My widow has been distracted by something dried, white, and flaky on his jeans. He takes his thumbnail to the task and tries to remember the last time he did laundry. He will struggle with this one, since he doesn't do laundry. Rich Dreadfulwater does dry cleaning, and not the indigenous beat-your-hides-on-a-river-rock-and-flop-them-over-a-teepee-pole method; more the fully chemical, in-by-ten-ready-by-five drill. I honestly don't know how this one will cope. There isn't a self-reliant molecule in his body.

The dried stuff on his jeans, by the way, is shaving cream, from those frantic moments barely seventy-two hours ago when he cradled my half-shaved head in his lap as he waited for the EMTs to arrive. It takes another few seconds for him to make this connection, and he relapses into sobs with new abandon. He suffocates the box with his above-desk body like an emperor penguin surrounds a single egg with his brood pouch—abandoned for the toughest bit by the partner that gave them both life. Except I'm not coming back with a gut full of krill, and this is beginning to dawn on him.

Oh, dear. It doesn't look like you are going to pull it together for your first day back in court tomorrow. You had better call in broken, and figure out how you are going to deal with this brand new and fucked-up reality.

TAYLORS

GEOGRAPHICALLY, THE TAYLOR FAMILY HAD COVERED SIG-
nificant territory in my first four years in the world, and some of it
more than once. To briefly review, my parents married in 1960 and I
was born in Coeur d'Alene two years later. The US Forest Service transferred my father and his zoo of tigers to a ranger station in Thompson
Falls, Montana, around my first birthday. My sister was born in nearby
Missoula, weeks after my second. Shortly thereafter, the Forest Service
bounced us back to Coeur d'Alene—909 Homestead Avenue—where
I learned to extract optimum advantage of the parental diversion my
swaddling sister had handed me.

Earliest memories of time with my sister mostly revolved around
the suffered indignities of being dressed in matching clothes. The aunt
on my father's side, though completely blind from retinitis pigmentosa,
fancied herself quite the knitter. Please, take a moment with that and
then consider her output and our matching inventory: 1) red sweaters
featuring a pattern of intricate white snowflakes; 2) Christmas stock-
ings with realistic beard hair on Santa's face and our birth years knit
into the jingle-belled borders though the six was backwards on mine;
3) winter hats complete with pom-poms; 4) slippers, also with pom-
poms; and 5) gloves—because mittens could have been a crapshoot of
extra fingers, and thumbs that didn't oppose.

Not to be outdone by her sister-in-law, our Tiger mother, a budding DIY seamstress in her own right, decided one Halloween to make us identical orange-and-white polka-dot clown costumes, oversized to fit over the top of winter jackets and snow pants, and jovially constructed from an improvised *McCall's* pattern. When she wasn't catalog shopping direct from the latest issue of the Lane Bryant catalog, mother was creating her own plus-size wardrobe, followed in later years by a prom dress, a bunny costume, vacation ditty bags, a two-person cow costume (complete with ball sack *and* udders—only in Idaho), and a nifty series of stuffed whales and dinosaurs for the grandkids she'd never have.

But mostly Sis and I wore matching pajamas and windbreakers, T- and sweatshirts from the US Forest Service, and Smokey Bear lines of trademarked logo wear, and powder-blue University of Idaho (or Montana) sweatshirts with puffy raised white collegiate lettering—depending on which side of the Idaho/Montana border the USFS had my father logging his professional time. (The forestry pun is of course intended.)

We weren't twins. In fact, we weren't at all alike, as our first bath together shockingly revealed. But we had matching clothes, so that complete strangers would know we somehow belonged together, part of a set not to be sold separately on the child slave market—my mother's personal salt-and-pepper shakers for show-and-tell, if you will. My sister was the only girl I had ever seen naked in the flesh, thanks to some bizarre water conservation measure instituted by my father during the weekends he was home. This memory, like a tattoo emblazoned on my frontal lobe with a contaminated needle, would hold sufficiently fast and recallable as a flashcard, until my early forties, when I was coaxed into a sleazy strip club on a dare, after wings at *Hooters* proved too tame for my visiting straight friend Lars, from Germany. There, at Deja Vu Showgirls on First Avenue across from Pike Place Market, I was confronted by the adult version of my sister from the bathtub—with fully extended limbs on a voluptuous body that seemed to spring from a hearty ornamental shrubbery that quivered and popped and shimmied to the music like some beaver puppet that had escaped off the hand and out of the miniature forest tableau of a Chuck E. Cheese puppet theatre. It was this forced, front-row observation of a naked woman who was not, but who certainly could have been, my adult sister that I could not un-observe. And this somehow reawakened the sleeper-psycho-chain-mutant-reaction-cell that had possibly turned me homosexual in the first place, and so I recoiled. My dare with Lars— that I could stomach a strip club—had backfired on me.

Now, where was I going with this?

Oh yes. So, on schedule, and surely according to either a *Better Homes and Gardens* recommendation for proper pacing between offspring—or, more likely, a Christian-scribbled prescription for calculated and non-pleasurable procreation—G. L. and Carole tried to have a third child in 1966. But after weighing its survival options, the little embryo decided it just wasn't ready for Planet Taylor. The couple would wait the requisite two years before trying again.

That Christmas, it was back to Iowa—just four of us, this time by train, with the intention, I'm sure, to show off the expected and heralded third child to the Jesus-loving, scripture clinging, Hawkeye State grandparents. It's only now that I stop to consider the unbelievable pain and difficulty this trip must have presented my mother on the heels of her terminated pregnancy—traveling through Middle America in a vastly hopeless winter, to waiting in-laws who would attribute the epic failure to her inabilities as an incubator, mother, wife, and Christian. Aside from wishing I were still alive, I wish I could have better supported my mom in this moment of awkward recompense. But like she always did, my mother the Tiger eventually found her own growl and got the jungle dirt back under her paws to succeed with childbirth once again—two years later, with the delivery of my younger brother. I hope I somehow managed to take some of the Christian pressure off her during this visit to Iowa, though, by agreeing to a spontaneous seventeen minute and forty-eight second *a cappella* concert of my entire repertoire of Sunday School songs from memory—a concert that was emceed and recorded live by my Year of the Dog Father on my grandparents' stereo console reel-to-reel tape recorder. It wasn't noted anywhere, but I think it is safe to say that I commanded that stage, holding my own microphone.

A year later, at age five, I was enrolled briefly at Merry Melody Musical Kindergarten (my preparation for gay life was unstoppably underway at this point). On the topic of kindergarten, my mother notes in *BH&GBB* that despite being picked on by other kids, I "enjoyed this [kindergarten] so much—anxious to perform and show off his new songs." Such a Tiger.

I'm sure deemed too developmentally advanced for Merry Melody, I had been quickly transferred across town, where I successfully graduated from the Zepp-Montague Musical Kindergarten Course, and progressed immediately to the Jack-n-Jill Kindergarten, under the tag duo of Mrs. Fawcett and Mrs. Anderson. Later that year, I received a record player for Christmas from my blind Aunt Charlotte-the-knitter, along with my first album—the story of *Ferdinand the Bull* on one side, with two or three sing-along songs in Spanish on the flip side. Oddly, I picked up the Spanish songs with ease. This raised more than one eyebrow, and cemented a lot of developmental bricks together for me. It also warrants a review and perhaps a paragraph of analysis here, since it was omitted, redacted, or simply not accommodated by *BH&GBB*.

But first, let's drop in on Ferdinand. In the story by Munro Leaf, Ferdinand is this drop-dead gorgeous bull of the Iberian heterogeneous cattle variety, coming of bullfighting age in the Spanish countryside. While bulls in other pastures snort and paw the earth, trying to intimidate each other, Ferdinand is content lounging in the ample shade of a cork tree (*Quercus suber*), delighting in the smell of the nearby meadow flowers. His mother begs him to imitate the other bulls—to get off his hind quarters and run and play. But nothing can convince Ferdinand that this will lead to a better life than he already commands.

In my case, credit a long tap dance with vanity, complete with biannual dance and piano recitals; a stint modeling in a local department store fashion show; afterschool drama camp in fourth grade; singing live onstage in a small, hand-picked-by-Karen children's choir with *The Carpenters* on May 12, 1973; a mail-order Bowflex in high school; a Polaroid camera for taking early, mostly naked selfies, and so on.

Ferdinand grows up to be a big, handsome, virile, ball-swaying bull nonetheless. When the matadors from the city come to the countryside to pick the biggest and fiercest bull for the bullfight in Madrid, they spot him. Just then (probably while preparing to spiral-arrange the flowers he so fancies), Ferdinand sits on a bumblebee which launches him into a fit of fury and dramatics. It takes him a good twenty minutes to work the sting out of his system—but by then, the matadors from the city have witnessed the characteristics they'd come shopping for, and Ferdinand is loaded onto a wagon bound for the bullring. Back in Madrid, hundreds of Spaniards push and shove their way into the ring for the bullfight of the decade. It is a bullapalooza of dancing and singing and flowers; in fact, more flowers than Ferdinand has ever seen before. He gets pushed into the ring and finds himself at the center of attention, with people shouting and clapping for him, throwing buckets of flowers at his four hooves. With a fanfare of trumpets and yelling, a matador arrives in the ring, blood in his eyes. But try as he might, he cannot get Ferdinand to react, or to budge, or to fight. Enthused by the crowd's adoration, Ferdinand could not be happier than he is in that moment, just sitting there and smelling the flowers.

So let's see. Uncompromising individuality . . . unlike the other bulls . . . a mother who tries to push him to conform . . . a misunderstood ethos . . . a tendency to gravitate toward center stage . . . a disappointment to others . . . a preference for flowers over fighting. What was I to do with this recorded account of the bovine me but play it over and over for the rest of my life?

As for the Spanish language songs on the flip side of this longplaying record—after generations upon generations of really white ancestors and living, as we did, on the unofficial border of Idaho's Aryan Nation, I was born a somewhat inexplicably brown-skinned baby. Even my mother noted this in my Baby Book.

So because of this and my aptitude with Latin rhythms and lyrics, I later developed an alter-ego-driven fantasy that had me the byproduct of my mother's tryst with a migrant Chicano, while her husband was away from the casa fighting fires. This fantasy grew some *cajones* the older and more cynical I became about my white dad and white siblings, to whom I couldn't relate. If only the math had worked out, or

I'd ever found proof I was maybe one year older than my birth certificate indicated, or if my mother had opted for the gestation period of an elephant—well, then my Mexican jumping bean spermatozoa origin theory might have held some *agua*. For you see, just before getting married, my mother had taught school in Southern Idaho, which was really one giant potato field that stretched from Nevada to Wyoming and spilled over into Utah. Between the Basques and Mexicans who outnumbered Caucasians and drove the agricultural economy there, my *padre* really could have been anyone. Four decades later, I was still sort of waiting for the other *zapato* to drop when all of a sudden I dropped instead, and on the bathroom floor half-shaved—which is where this story began some pages earlier, didn't it? Come to think of it, I never did get around to mail-ordering that DNA-swab test kit. But I bet my DNA is pretty cooked now.

The second highly questionable surgery of my life, also part of a larger healthcare fad sweeping the nation—and this time with anesthesia that smelled like black licorice—was a tonsillectomy on July 5, 1967. Though medical professionals question the need for this procedure today too, I prefer to think it cleared the way for me to become really great at oral sex. So thanks for that, Mom!

My sister and I came down with chicken pox right before my brother Jeffrey William was born on July 27, 1968, in the Chinese Year of the Monkey. I like to think my contracting that affliction was just another way of acting out against the looming birth of another attention-stealer. Under the column labeled *severity* in the *BH&GBB*, my mother writes: "168 pox," and that I "itched—not sick at all. Able to play outside most days."

Enter stage right: Jeffrey William (who oddly never goes by "Jeffrey"; only "Will"). Born in the Year of the Monkey, he is clever and cheeky and nimble. There is no puzzle Monkeys cannot solve, and no prize they will not claim. They are charmers and romantics and lovers, just as they are thieves and connivers and conjurers. They can wait a whole day before springing a surprise. They are inventors who love gadgets and are masters at games. People born in the Year of the Monkey are smart, humorous, and entertaining. They go about life in a practice-makes-perfect kind of way. They revel in their accomplishments, and are fastidious with their housekeeping. Monkeys are thinkers and problem solvers. They can be their own best company, and can get happily lost in a crowd. There isn't anything they won't try. Monkeys are doers, and they are never idle. Monkeys can fool anyone if they want to. And nobody can stay mad at a Monkey.

Parents again distracted, I entered first grade at Coeur d'Alene's Borah Elementary School. Remarkably, given the demands of another mouth to shake a breast at and another penis to circumcise, my mother had time to scribe one last set of remarks under the *Parents' Notes* page of my baby book: "Very anxious to please. Begins to argue and ask 'why.' Talks continually. Much better appetite; quite a good eater. Very excited with company. Anxious to help but not willing as a rule to spend enough time on a project. Often forgets duty or job halfway through. Moves and thinks fast. Very active. Rarely walks. Anxious to please [she wrote this twice] and loves praise. Wants to be loved whenever Krissy is getting attention. Prefers writing and coloring and learning projects. Rides bike well. Walks to school and around block by himself. Shows some improvement so far as entertaining himself. Plays piano and sings. Dances around to music."

Tiger. Tiger. Tiger.

My first-grade teacher, Mrs. Torkelson, wasn't exactly an egg-salad and crunchy dill pickle picnic for two (or twenty-three, for that matter). Being minutes away from retirement and tasked with a couple dozen illiterate upstarts, she couldn't possibly provide me the attention I required. She had the audacity of suggesting on the back of my first report card that "extra reading at home would help Ashton read smoothly with expression." It was just as well then that the USFS decided early in 1969 that it was time to yank my father by the roots back to Montana. This episode: 1821 Dixon Avenue, Missoula.

So I finished the last quarter of first grade with Miss Baker at Charles M. Russell Elementary School. I remember walking to school that first day in a new city, the stench of the pulp mill wedged in the Bitterroot Valley like a shimmy in a door jamb as I retraced the steps along the route practiced in advance a couple times with my fairly impatient father, who had to cram all of his parenting into a weekend maybe twice each month.

I'd lost my front baby teeth and my ears seemed suddenly more pointed than ever. I had a stupid cowlick where I should have sported bangs like every other boy in "Big Sky Country" (the yellow-lettered tagline on the blue background of Montana license plates). I was about as alien-looking as transfer kids come. Plus, I was arriving after the middle of the school year, and certainly after everyone else had chosen their friends and forged their alliances for the year—maybe for life. I didn't know anyone. For days, I'd stared out the front and back windows of our new home, at the barren, completely kid-less landscape. It might as well have been the moon, except by now there were even humans there too, I think Miss Baker had told me one afternoon coming in from recess. [Note: That's not quite true or chronologically accurate. After years of crash-smashing unmanned spacecraft into the moon, it wasn't during this particular school year but the early weeks of the summer that followed when NASA apparently put men on its surface—July 21, 1969 to be precise.]

At this new school in those first few weeks, I was teased by the other kids for just about everything—from being a "transfer retard" to having girl-long eyelashes (which, by the rationale of my peers, meant that I was supposed to be a girl). I couldn't do anything about being a transfer retard, but surely I could alter my appearance to be more boyish. I took my mother's good sewing scissors—the ones with the green handles that we absolutely weren't allowed to use—and cut off my eyelashes as close to the eyelids as I could get. My mother was reported to have sobbed nonstop until they grew back—and twice as long as before, she'd swear, so I wouldn't attempt the stunt again. It would not be the last time I changed the way I looked or acted to please and snag the attentions of those around me—nor would it be the most drastic thing I would do in the next forty-eight years either. But I was just starting out in the shape-shifting business.

It wasn't long after this incident that I showed the world just who could "read smoothly with expression." I'd learned how to charm my way into my first crush, and the evidence I'd succeeded was there on my final first grade report card, dated June 9, 1969, in a teacher's perfect penmanship: "I enjoyed having you in my class this last quarter, Ashton. You were such a nice addition. Have a nice summer. Miss Baker."

I should jog backwards to interject that first grade had been interrupted a second time by the unexpected death of my paternal grandfather, Clarence. You might remember the Iowa grandparents as the Christian limbs on my family tree. It was explained to us at the time by our father—who was reticent at the best of times—that my grandpa had died of a heart attack in the bathtub of the Indianola, Iowa home he shared with my grandmother. Half marks for accuracy, G. L. It seemed Clarence indeed died in a bathtub full of water. But curiously, the autopsy, when I requested it during college research on my own genealogy, listed barbiturates in his system. In later years, this got me wondering. Unless you counted lovesickness as the cause of his heart attack, the man may have died from an intentional overdose, possibly brought on by depression and perhaps the discovery that his wife might have been having a clumsy affair with his best friend and co-worker—a husky, horse-loving guy named John Rex.

Awkwardly, the latter couple married quickly, possibly even before the flower pinned to the suit that my dead grandfather had been buried in lost its last petal in the bottom of the casket. I, of course, would never know for certain if there had actually been an affair or if he'd overdosed himself or if he had been drugged by someone else. As a perceptive child and a Tiger, I did pick up on the confusion of the adults around me at the time, so I never took to or trusted my step-grandfather. The event did bring me a bevy of new step-cousins— many of them boys older than me, so nice to observe. This made subsequent visits to Iowa a bit more interesting. Still, I was suspicious. Iowa, already odd enough, became more so when my grandfather died.

So I was pulled from Miss Baker's class for a week, and my sister, baby brother, and parents boarded a Northwestern jet airplane that looked like it had been painted using a PAAS Easter Egg Coloring Kit (my first plane) to attend a funeral (also my first). When you are nearly seven years old, there are plenty of firsts ahead of you. For example, this trip also marked the first time I threw up on an airplane. When there is a first, there is a second—and, when it comes to choppy jet stream malfeasance, also a third and even a fourth. There is some confusion on my mother's part over which of us started this chain reaction, and whether it was during the outbound or return flights. But I remembered watching my sister barf her scrambled egg breakfast all over the back of the seat in front of her—a seat occupied by a nun. Across the row, where I sat with my mother behind a priest and another devoted bride of Jesus, I was rather inspired by my sister's high-flying commentary on organized religion—enough that I felt it necessary to puke on the priest. There was an oft-told version of this story that included an emergency landing to change aircraft at an airport in North Dakota, but I am certain I made that part up as an early storyteller.

The second time I tossed cookies on a plane, in case I forget to mention it chronologically when I get there, was sixteen years later, over the state of Georgia, en route to Venezuela for the first time. Again, where there was a first, there was a second and third, and in my case a fourth excursion to that remarkable country on the Caribbean. Holy Virgin of Coromoto, how I loved Venezuela—or, more accurately, the Venezolano men. Anyway, I had over-everythinged at a going-away party in my honor the night prior; it was a mildly successful night if you count the de-pants-ing of Steve Suazo, a campus stud I'd been stalking the whole previous semester. The night took its toll at 35,000 feet.

The third time I orally erupted on a plane occurred twenty-three years after the second incident, and thirty-nine years after the first—this time over the Amazon River Basin on a flight from Buenos Aires to Caracas (a city in the aforementioned country, to which I was returning for the fourth time). The events heaving up to this episode of epiglottal horseplay had included a week-long, round-the-clock cycle of sputtering diarrhea in Patagonia, followed by four emaciated days in Buenos Aires, where I managed to pass nothing but time. Fortress-constipated from pressurized air travel, and suffering from low-grade carbon monoxide poisoning to boot—this came from living in a hotel room with about a dozen floor-to-ceiling windows one *piso* above the eighteen-lane *Av. 9 de Julio*—I thought surely I might be coming down with Yellow Fever. I had clutched my stomach and this theory with much bravado as I taxied to the Ministro Pistarini International Airport. It wasn't until my fellow passengers and crew were about one and a half hours into a violently turbulent flight over the Amazon that had kept the fasten seat belt sign ablaze since takeoff that I began to realize it might nearly be broomstick for this piñata. Once the plane finally leveled off—I'm guessing we were over Cochabamba—and I was free to move green-faced about the cabin, I can report that sliding my fingers down my throat to relieve the abdominal pressure, was not my only maneuver at 38,000 feet. [For more details on this Buenos-Aires-to-Caracas nonstop toward the end of an exhausting five-country South American itinerary, let's hope I remember to footnote the celebrity psychic named Douglas Bernal, who was seated and flirting across the row from me on this flight, when I refer to the final statistics of my *1996 Brown Uncut Research Tour* (See *B.U.R.T.* in the appendix). Okay, there's no appendix here—nor, incidentally, was there one in my body at the time of death, thanks to appendicitis in 1982, which marked surgery number three of my lifetime.]

While we are on the theme of queasiness and a nervous tummy, there was a fourth and final case of barfing on the wing. That one happened aboard a seventy-seat de Havilland Dash-8 Q400 turboprop, after an ill-chosen versatainer of sushi—purchased at the airport, but made offsite and who-knows-when. Trust the storyteller: you do not want to have wasabi-laced imitation crab forced cut through your nostrils at any altitude.

Having nearly cleared the fifty-four-year hurdle, after spewing the indigestible the indigestible from both ends for as many years (that's upwards of 23,700,300 grams, according to one website that estimates the average human fecal output at about 1,300 grams per day)—you'd think vomiting and defecating would no longer be remarkable memoir material. But the body is a complex, unsung factory of convulsing parts until it craps out. Trust me and Joni Mitchell. You just don't know what you got till it's—or make that *you're*—gone. Take my word for it—or don't, and be sorry. It's never really up to you to say *when*, and there's nothing like the constipation of eternity. So treasure your cookies and seize your toilet paper over the top of the roll firmly with both hands, and be damn grateful for every last puke and wipe—because these are the signs you are alive!

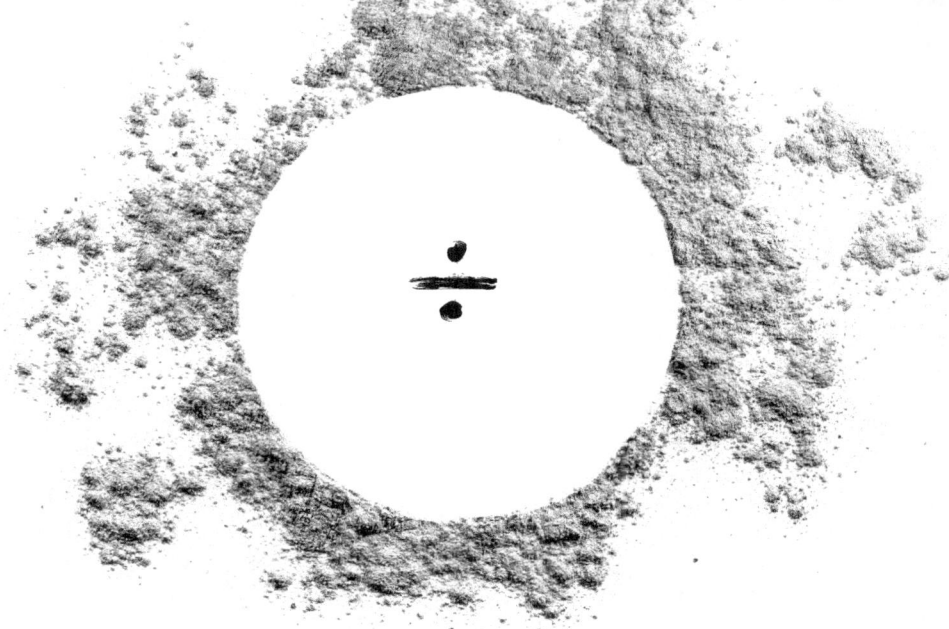

TO THE DAY, IT HAS BEEN A MONTH OF BARELY COPING FOR
Rich Dreadfulwater. His eyes are so puffy and bloodshot from chain-
crying every chance he steps off his public stage that I'm surprised he
can see out of them at all. The mirrors in our house are the hardest for
him to navigate and reconcile. They hurt him physically each time he
passes or faces one of them, because he knows that for years they had
reflected my image, but now they defiantly refuse to reveal a trace of
the ghost that had loved him. Yes, mirrors are by far the hardest.

The box containing my ashes still sits atop the Nez Perce mat on
his home desk—untended to, despite the instructions he hears me
saying over and over again in his head:

Ashton Taylor, *Last Will and Testament*, page 2

I would like my ashes to be divided into nineteen 35-mil-
limeter film canisters, which can be found empty and
labeled inside a shortbread cookie tin at the back of my
personal file cabinet. You'll find other instructions that go
with each of these canisters there, too.

He hasn't brought himself to check for the cookie tin or consult my

wordy will and last testament. He hasn't cancelled any of my subscrip-
tions (*Vanity Fair*, Netflix, Shave Club for Men, Wine of the Month
Club, *Up with People* International Alumni Association newsletter),
so these reminders of me will keep arriving and reminding him of his
loss. His clumsiness conspires to convince him that I am haunt-nag-
ging him to take care of my remains. Tuesday, he stubbed his toe and
will probably lose the big nail. Wednesday morning, he sliced his chin
open, shaving without the mirror he can't bear to use. Today, after
reopening yesterday's shaving wound, he got a nasty shock trying to
knife-liberate a chubby bagel from the plugged-in toaster. So with a
wad of toilet paper blotting the gusher on his chin, a double Band-Aid
on his big toe, and a burned bagel that could have killed him had he
been standing in a puddle of water, he makes his way to the closet
where our side-by-side file cabinets have been dry humping each other
since we moved them here from the burbs. He slides one half of the
mirrored closet door to the side, with his eyes shut.

When he opens them, out of habit he checks the Komplement
LED slim track light system from Ikea—the one I had to have—to see
if today would be the day, after months of never working, that the
motion/light sensor eyes would automatically illuminate the closet as
advertised. Making it do so would have been a wicked nice trick to
play on him if I had the means, but the damned thing still doesn't
work. In case you're wondering, the toe, chin nick, and bagel weren't
my nether-meddling either. I'm apparently out of tricks. I have no
method or special angelic powers to answer or signal this man I loved
as much as I loved life itself.

He reaches up to manually click the closet lights on, reciting under
his breath the universal Ikea curse—probably in unison with hundreds
of thousands of consumers around the globe who were simultaneously
experiencing a similar malfunction as penance for buying cheap.

The lungs in his hairless chest expand slowly as he moves his arm
in slow motion to open his lover's file-cabinet drawer. He steps back
to give me room to escape into the room, as if he were thinking this is
where my spirit had been hiding all this time. Silly, spooked, supersti-
tious Indian. He reaches toward the back and pulls the hanging files

forward. There it is—the octagon-shaped black tin, with roses of all colors decorating the top and sides. He places the macabre box on his desk, where the gold foil label catches a halogen and blinds him for a moment. There is a slight tremble in the fingers as he fiddles with the lid of the container that once held "Carr's Famous Assorted English Biscuits," according to the label. His face reddens as the lid frees.

The blob of bloody toilet paper gives in to gravity, and falls into a crevice between the empty film canisters inside the tin box. Whether in search of answers or the TP with his DNA, Rich extracts the nineteen empty black film canisters one at a time and lines them up so the white, Avery 5160 labels are facing him—except for one that doesn't have a label. On each label is printed, in Arial Narrow, the first and last names of those who will become his accomplices.

Ashton Taylor, *Last Will and Testament*, page 2

> My final wish is that these canisters are filled with my remains and distributed as per the following instructions.

Except for the desk swing-arm halogen and the closet Ikea light he has left in the *on* position, this part of the apartment is dark. Trademarked Seattle sheet rain runs down the Palladian windowpanes in streams through which the skyline and Space Needle can be vaguely made out if you are familiar with the view.

> To my partner, RICH. Since I'm likely to precede you in death, the task of doling out my remains likely falls into your hands. As I can count on you above anyone else I have ever known to do this task in a calculated, no-nonsense manner—and God knows, at the cheapest possible cost— you become my obvious choice.

Rich heads into the kitchen and returns momentarily, pulling on a pair of bright blue dishwashing gloves. He scoots the ceremonial woven mat and the box of ashes into the center of the film canisters he has arranged into a semi-circle. He sits at the desk and stares at the box until his eyes water—which takes no time at all since the taps have been left in the *on* position since I passed. He positions a white plastic funnel next to the box and pauses, unable to break his stare.

> My calculation of the volume of ash for someone my size is that you will have more ash than canisters. Here's what you do. After all the canisters are filled, place the last of my ashes into the black tin that held the canisters. I'll tell you what to do with this later. And Limping Rabbit, don't be a sissy and think you have to wear gloves. Buck up! I may only weigh four-and-a-half pounds now, but it's still just me.

Rich looks at his hands and instantly removes the rubber gloves. He takes a deep breath and opens the flap of the cardboard box. He gasps at the sight of the ash, even though he knew all along it was inside. The shock of that moment paralyzes him, but then a peace visibly falls over him. He plunges his bare hand into the box and lets it rest in the ashes. His second hand joins the first in this strange marination, as tears begin to burst from his face like a garden hose suddenly unkinked.

By hand, he begins filling each of the eighteen labeled canisters to the same level, which is almost full. Uneasy, and feeling like he may have been too generous in this division, leaving not nearly enough for himself, he measures a rough tablespoon of powdered me back into the box I came in. He snaps on eighteen lids. His face registers that he is unsure what to do with the nineteenth unlabeled canister, so he leaves it empty. There are ashes on his hands, stuck there and darkened from his tears, which haven't stopped falling. Ashes adhere to his upper lip where his nose has been running, and on the nick of his chin—like glitter to Elmer's Glue in Miss Baker's classroom just before Valentine's Day. Despite the care he thought he was taking, particles appear to be escaping and suddenly seem to him to be scattered everywhere. Analyzing the messy scene before him and squaring this with the unbelievable task he has agreed to undertake, Rich breaks into laughter—hearty, uncontrollable laughter—not

÷

immediately recognizing that this is the trickster of emotions when you are grieving, and that the sinister aftertaste of this deception will plunge him deeper into his dark self. A crying hiccup starts sideways in his esophagus, snapping him sober. He is washed in panic that there are parts of me—my essence—that have gotten away from him.

Acting a bit like a distraught Jackie Kennedy scampering onto the back trunk of the Lincoln Continental convertible to retrieve parts of her slain husband's brain, Rich begins scooping the arrant ash into a pile on the desktop, like a snowplow goes about clearing a parking lot. He adds this to the leftover me in the plastic-lined box he'd received at the mortuary, and then lifts the plastic bag like a crane from this box, to be deposited inside the biscuit tin. During the transfer, it seems like Rich is calculating a few things and all at once he tries to rationalize the first of his thoughts out loud.

"Since my name doesn't appear on any of these containers, am I supposed to take this to mean this cookie tin must be for me to keep," he chokes on his words, "the rest of you in?"

He is partially correct in thinking this. What I didn't realize when he began speaking his question out loud, is that he must be trying to reach me in the Beyond or the Afterlife or wherever he thinks I am, to provide him the answers he craves.

I *am* no longer.

This is nothing like I could have imagined.

It is not anything Liming Rabbit had allowed himself to anticipate, ever.

We are both of us lost in this.

He measures the volume of the remaining contents of the plastic bag against the size of the biscuit tin. Needing to be the majority shareholder of my cremains, Rich selfishly levies an additional tax—a symbolic sprinkling from each film canister back into his plastic bag. Just before sealing it with a hot-pink Ikea potato chip bag clip, he spots and then fishes out the blood-wad of toilet paper from the bottom of the tin. He examines the crimson proof of his living essence beneath the halogen, and then contrasts it against the colorless lifeless ash inside the plastic bag. He ponders this a minute as though he might neutralize the finality of death by adding a teaspoon of life. He pops the bloody toilet paper into the bag and gives it a swirling half shake until it is swallowed by the ashes. He clips the bag, places it in the tin, and affixes the lid—just as snug and tight as the two of us had been in our cozy, loving lives together.

Twin orchestras that had been momentarily warming up in the pits of each tear duct, waiting for the next uptick of the grim conductor's baton, gush into a slobbering overture that suddenly crescendos to rival the drumming waterworks assaulting the windows just beyond his desk. Limping Rabbit cannot stop this funeral procession from marching deep, muddy ruts across his soul. He tries to pull himself together, to focus through his tears, to make out the city of Seattle that is very much alive and glistening on the other side of the double-pane argon glass that separates him from his eventual salvation and this immediate torment. These are early hours in the Land of Grief. Not nearly ready to abandon this suffering, my earthly lover folds his torso at the waist to press the heart in his chest against the flowered biscuit tin that contains all that's left, in a scene so very sad it's enough to make a newly minted angel cry.

I shouldn't imply that I have been made an angel. At least as far as I am able to perceive, I am still very much in newcomer's limbo. There's been no orientation or official welcome at the pearly gates. In fact, there have been no gates—or wings or trumpeted proclamations or reckonings. I've seen no balance sheets indicating what I achieved, what I've won or more obviously lost. I haven't come across any golden tablets that engrave for me what is yet to come, or what's left of me, which I'm only assuming must be my soul. I haven't been presented my own personal planet or received my thousand virgins or been tormented by the flames of anything. If you think Rich Dreadfulwater is lost, just try to imagine how helpless and in need of a decoder ring I am right now. Sure, I can see him in his suffering, but he cannot see me in mine. Perhaps this truly is hell then; what I've earned and deserve. It is certainly cruel and not something I would wish on my worst, freshly dead enemy; to watch all the people in my life receive the

÷

news that I am no more, that my heart beats no longer, that I am—as they knew and loved me—kaput!

Lost.

Gone.

And now, how soon forgotten?

Only the time, emptiness, and incomprehensibly vast space of eternity will tell.

But so far, no one's revealing and nobody's talking.

It sucks, really.

POSTAGE

BECAUSE I AM FURTHERMORE NO MORE—AND NOT AT ALL because Limping Rabbit is ready for it—comes a critical moment for both of us.

Ashton Taylor, *Last Will and Testament*, page 3

Now this is the tricky part.

I know, I know—the ashes weren't exactly pleasant as smelling daisies in a meadow like you were Ferdinand the Bull, but the US Postal Service does not knowingly handle human remains unless, according to its hazardous materials policy 462.2-b, they are packed in sift-proof containers, identified on the outside of the box and sent registered mail with return receipt service. That's a pain in Limping Rabbit's cottontail, so I've simplified matters.

You lie.

Rich is waiting in a long line at the post office, perhaps too dramatically clutching a reusable grocery bag from Metropolitan Market containing eighteen identical square packages tied with string. The crush of pre-work errand runners eventually delivers him to the counter. One by one, he presents his computer-labeled packages on the countertop for posting. For anyone other than this robotic, unionized, government employee, it would be obvious that this man is struggling not to cry, struggling not to appear guilty or up to something suspicious, struggling to let go. A tear escapes. He wipes his eyes, blaming allergies.

The attendant takes the eighteen boxes, attaches postage (calculating three of the boxes for international destinations), and then tosses them casually into a bin behind her. Rich inserts his credit card into the chip reader and squeezes his eyes closed. Other tears escape now. He opens his eyes and mouths the word *goodbye* as he presses his PIN. His attempts to dramatically botch the transaction have failed. The credit card approves. The US Postal worker says "have a nice day," looking past him—or perhaps through the fragile parchment of the person he's become—to the next person in line.

LATER THAT SAME EVENING, back at home after a sideways collision of a day in appellate court, Rich assembles an eighty-five minute iTunes playlist of perhaps the fifteen saddest pieces of music ever recorded. Seriously, grab a pen and notepad, 'cause Limping Rabbit has done all the grieving homework for you. Here it is: Mahler's *Symphony No. 5*; Evanescence's "My Immortal"; Ray LaMontagne's "Be Here Now"; Samuel Barber's *Adagio for Strings—Opus 11*; Delerium's "Fallen" (performed by Rani); Henryk Gorecki's *Symphony No. 3: Symphony of Sorrowful Songs*; Shakira's "La Pared"; Vladimir Godar's *Ecce puer*; "Into the West" by Annie Lennox; *Operá* by Emmanuel Santarromana; "Glacier" by James Vincent McMorrow (featuring Arto Lindsay); Bon Iver's "Holocene"; the BBC Scottish Symphony Orchestra's recording of "Ae Fond Kiss" by Robert Burns; Candice Glover's *American Idol* performance of "Lovesong," and the heart-demolishing clincher—the Carpenters' "Say Goodbye to Love."

While this set-to-repeat soundtrack of sorrow and irresolvable despair fills his home with despondency, he rests his chin on the flowered Carr's Biscuit tin, still lying in state atop the Nez Perce cornhusk and dogbane woven mat on his desk. Like this soundtrack, he keeps replaying over and over the moments in his life that delivered him to this very sad place, to see if there might possibly have been a different path he could have taken. But of course, there wasn't. And no matter the prevailing emotion, Seattle could always be counted on for a precipitation accompaniment; and so it has again begun to rain on top of Queen Anne Hill. Low clouds tumble in from Elliott Bay to shroud the upper third of the Space Needle in turquoise moodiness—right on his downbeat.

Despite what appears on the surface to be an oxymoron, Rich Dreadfulwater has been a privileged Indian, the first and only son of a hereditary chief—the first in a two-century lineage to get a university degree, and the first, according to his father, to turn his back on the dwindling *Nimíipuu* (the 3,600 people of the modern-day Nez Perce tribe). Well, that just wasn't true. Rich cross-examined his conscience on a daily basis, and he hadn't turned his back. This was only a hiatus he was taking, technically. He looked at it as his personal vision quest to walk in two worlds, uncovering what was most relevant about the *Nimíipuu* and finding out what it meant to be a "modern Indian." Limping Rabbit always knew he would return to North Central Idaho to lead—that it was his destiny and his obligation. There was just no possible way he could manage this while his obstinate, all-Indian-all-the-time father was still in the leadership picture. The 1,195 square miles of tribal lands that their treaty had afforded them in 1895 simply wasn't an expanse big enough for the two chiefs to keep from destroying each other ideologically. But he would return when it was time.

In the silence between tracks, Rich wills his hand to jar the wireless mouse that brings his sleeping iMac (but nothing else) back to life so he can read the upcoming track title and memorize the order of this perfect-for-mourning playlist. On cue, the *Adagio for Strings* begins with a sustained B-flat. He syncopates his own slide show to the mournful, cathartic strings, summoning the memories of his dead

---

companion from iPhoto, and commanding them to fill his grand emptiness. Of course, they can't, and he knows that—but for the same reason he forces himself to listen to sad music, he navigates through the photos anyway, in atonement and disbelief. Rich Dreadfulwater is normally a rational, analytical man, but grief—like vodka—makes him mean and angry at the world. He knows it won't bring me back, but maybe it won't let me get completely away either, as long as he constantly feeds this vigil of his. Tired of clicking, he sets the display in iPhoto to auto-run, and decides this scene needs candles, lots of them—and just maybe every Sarah McLachlan song he owns.

It was a mistake that Rich regretted almost instantly—and is regretting still—to have shipped parts of his companion off in eighteen directions. It cramped every muscle in his body as he turned to walk out of that post office; the deed has left him with a cavity in his heart and a boulder his lungs cannot lift off his chest. Not just physically, but symbolically—and perhaps metaphysically—his life partner's presence here has been diminished by the postal exercise, and Rich sits there, knowing now that he's been played. His grief takes on a special panic that in the sinking days to come he might become even more empty than he is now. Photo after photo reveals a mountain of evidence that he loved and was loved, that life has been beautiful and fulfilling and wonderful—and that he has so foolishly taken most of it for granted. Rich would give anything to have the opportunity to undo all the times he'd said *no* to me—all the times except that moment after a pointless argument that capitulated with the question of whether he would ever leave. The answer then had been *no*. He meant it when he said it. He had proved that now, hadn't he?

His computer screen fades to black and heads into sleep mode. He gets up from the desk, walks to the bedroom closet, and immediately changes every item of clothing he has been wearing into its equivalent from my side of the wardrobe. He adds the sea-foam colored hoodie lined with polyester-simulated sheep's wool that I never took off at home and always said was my smoking jacket (even though I never smoked). With tears swamping his eyes, Rich returns to the open living and dining rooms to huddle in front of the windows that normally overlook the Space Needle, Elliot Bay, and downtown. Between the tears in his eyes and the rain streaming down the windows, it's like he is looking through the windshield of his BMW, sitting inside an automatic carwash. He tucks the hoodie's unzipped flaps into opposing armpits, with arms crossing under his chest, and tries to control the quaking that will surely render his soul into two pieces that will not survive dissected.

After lighting the only three candles he can find, and bombing his butt into the chair, his leg bumps the desk, jarring the mouse that restarts the slide show on his computer screen. He can't watch it again. He closes iPhoto. He has stuffed his brain and broken heart full of enough data to stoke the fire of his grief, and he now sits swaddled in his dead lover's clothes—waiting, wanting to be consumed. He sees his candlelit, hobo-like reflection in the window panes as Sarah is razor-blading her way through "Ben's Song," and he thinks that frankly it could not get anymore pathetic than this—could it? He deciphers the scene as though he were looking down on himself from somewhere up above—like where I am, or, as I've already tried to explain, where the residual me still inhabits. He aches in heavy wonder of what will become of him. My university-educated Indian is intelligent enough to know that life ultimately will go on; that grief can't prevent him from living. But right now he is stuck and paralyzed and hurting. Whether he will love, laugh, smile, risk, trust, believe, or feel happiness again hasn't been worked out for him yet. He is pretty certain the answer will be another *no* that he'll have to live with and never have the chance to undo.

The comparison that comes next is probably natural. He wonders for a moment if he felt this angry, abandoned, and hopeless when his mother was killed after a night of playing bridge with her lady friends, as she traveled home between Lewiston and Spalding in the early spring of 2003. Of course, he had cried, and he had hurt. His anger would have been more focused had the drunk driver survived crossing the double line, slamming into his mother's Oldsmobile and plowing them both over the bank and into the Clearwater River. But he drowned too, leaving Rich no place to deposit his fury.

This loss isn't the same. This new emptiness is an unfair megaton worse. In this grave, almost oxygenless reality of his, it makes sense to blame himself for not tuning in to what had been going on with his partner the past few months: the general lethargy in me that he'd misread as depression, and lately the dreams where I'd be sleep-talking—having full-on conversations, out loud, with dead boyfriends. There isn't much he can do about it now except to blame himself for not appreciating me more than he did every single, beautiful day we'd shared together; so that's what he does. Now, the props from our double decade *pas de deux* are scattered about the stage, making it impossible for him to think he could ever dance again. Itemed among this debris field: the toothbrush in the bathroom cabinet that was last used in my breathing mouth; the dirty clothes (including those he has on now) that he can't bear to wash, because I last wore them; the sheets on our bed that he refuses to change because they still contain the essence of my night sweats in those last days; the Visa statement and quarterly newsletter still getting mailed to my attention; the fruity Greek yogurt in the refrigerator that only I would eat; the toilet paper placed in the holder my way so that I could always find the end in the dark; the three-quarter read Christopher Bram novel (*Lives of the Circus Animals*) on the nightstand on my side of the bed; the hula hoop (of all things) hanging off the Jurassic-sized Bowflex that only I used in order to maintain my physique/vanity; and the arsenal of creams and concealers and cleansers forming their own skyline on my side of the bathroom sink for those ongoing skirmishes with aging.

Then there are the rituals now cancelled, like kissing me on the birthmark at the top of my ass-crack every night as I turned over on my stomach before sleeping—that was always good for a wrestle, since I didn't like anyone getting anywhere near my precious rosebud. I'm sure Rich already misses the morning bathroom stench that lingered after the smelliest poos (I blamed pharmaceuticals and couldn't bring myself to use aerosols—the ozone, you know), and the what must have been sweetly entertaining though usually out-of-tune concerts that I blared from the shower stall. Then there were the last words I spoke to him, as we became separated from each other forever, just as we had made it inside the emergency room at Swedish Medical:

"To be honest, I'm a little scared this time."

And Rich's words back to me, through tears he couldn't hold back then or now:

"You are not permitted to leave me, ever."

Rich Dreadfulwater swivels a quarter-turn in his chair. He cannot distinguish where his watery eyes end and the rain-streamed windows begin. He stares his path through this double gloom, refusing to bring anything but his sorrow into focus. Wearing his remorse like his dead lover's clothes is a nifty exercise in compunction, but it neither lets me go nor brings me back.

When his mom was killed he had me right beside him, to help him pull out of the tailspin. He has no one now to slap him out of this funk and end the funeral in his heart. Well—that isn't entirely true. He has his baby sister, V'ronica—twenty-nine years his junior. But he hasn't yet found the courage to tell her that I am gone. Still ridiculously protective of her though she is technically an adult, he knows she will hear the news and disintegrate, just like he had. And then what good would either of them be for the other? He'd have to tell her this shocking, unbelievable new truth in person. That might be a step forward, he realizes. It might somehow transfer the pressure from the quick-hardening cement about to encase and crush his heart to a possibility in which he might break out to do something other than mope and listen to Sarah McLachlan.

Just thinking about scheduling a trip home to Idaho, though, seizes his intestines in a granny-knotted cramp he can't take on at the moment. He's at his limit.

V'ronica—or "Ron," as I had talked her into abbreviating her name when she began abbreviated mine—and I had been enviably close. Sometimes she acted like she were closer to me than she was to her older brother. She was the one who dubbed me "Ash," a pet name that seemed to stick with others too. The two of us got on like the Hardy Boys; sleuths at solving stuff small and large, which was of course the opposite of the reaction Rich had been anticipating when he told his sister all those years ago that he was gay, and introduced her to his white boyfriend. Ron was tickled to have a new brother who was funny and sensitive and great looking and not nearly as stuffy as the lawyer-one. Rich managed to set jealousies aside when I suggested and his sister agreed to leave Spalding and the Lapwai Reservation to live with us occupying the Edmonds spare bedroom for a year. Travel and off-reservation exposure had done a world of good for the Indian lawyer, and he wanted the same doors opened for his sister—but after a semester at Seattle Community College, Ron announced she was *res*-sick (same as homesick but for the reservation) for their culture and her school friends. She returned home, but not before the duo of Ron and Ash teamed up our superpowers to stretch Limping Rabbit's boundaries and recalibrate the course his life would take.

It didn't make sense to Ron or me—and we suspected not to Rich either—for him to pretend he wasn't Nez Perce. So it had been our first brainchild, now four years ago, for the chief apparent of the *Nimíipuu* to establish a website and blog to coalesce the next generation of tribal decision-makers around his virtual leadership. Together, we had collaborated on its design. We handpicked—even staged—some of the photos that depicted him in action. One featured Nez Perce actor Chaske Spencer's shirtless arm over Rich's shoulder, during a break on the set of the *Twilight* series, at Silver Falls State Park in Oregon. In another, he got a kiss on one cheek from Nez Perce actress Elaine Miles (of *Northern Exposure* and *Smoke Signals* fame) and on the other from her *Smoke Signals* co-star, Evan Adams—this was at an international conference on indigenous rights they were all attending in Victoria, British Columbia. In one particularly dramatic photo from the family archives, he was a teenager dressed in traditional powwow regalia. In his day he had been considered one of the best Duck and Dive dancers maybe of all time. (The Duck and Dive was a traditional warrior dance that depicted the 1877 Battle at Big Hole in Western Montana, where almost one hundred Nez Perce were killed in a brutal attack that came at three in the morning, under the cowardly command of US Army colonel John Gibbon, and 200 of his soldiers.) Limping Rabbit loved this photo most, as it helped him recall how much he loved to lose himself to find himself in this dance.

Rich Dreadfulwater had been so deliberate in his upward mobility and infiltration of white privileged society that he could stand to lose himself—his current self—all over again, if you asked me or Ron. He could make good use of a trip back to Spalding for a brisk encounter with his wandering spirituality, but I'm sure he thinks his caseload won't allow it. I am certain he believes in his heart that ramping up his workaholism, and not his inner Indian, will deliver him from this grief, just as it had all but erased everything he had been running away from since busting out of the Lapwai Reservation more than three decades ago. I can just tell by the way he is prepping for his work day tomorrow—laying out his suit, shirt, and tie on the stuffed chair in the bedroom; scribbling notes in his planning agenda; and packing his brown leather Coach legal briefcase to full-bulge—that he plans to plunge himself into the deeper end of his workload and that he will convince himself he has the room to take on two or three more clients.

He stands up. He gives his head a rapid shake and takes fists to his eyes. *It starts now*, he proclaims to himself and to the ghosts of the historic old high school building—a cohort that now includes me, his beloved Ashton Bernard Taylor. (ABT: Amazing But True; America Ballet Theatre; Amateur Bowlers Tour; Atomic Buffalo Turds; Autologous Blood Transfusion; Academy for Business Technologies; Aryan Brotherhood of Texas; Alcohol, Beverages, and Tobacco—I used to come up with names for my initials as a cure for recurring insomnia).

Like an owl, Rich slowly swivels his head around the condo, and spies the Bartell's plastic bag on the kitchen island. He remembers his earlier mission, and goes toward the bag. He extracts a container of black pushpins—they had also been available in festive multi-colors, but that didn't seem to hit the note he was after for this somber project. Also from the bag, he removes a package of No. 2 pencils. He opens both packages, dumping the pushpins onto the countertop. He has to herd a few of the errant ones along the granite slab and back into a pile.

Next he removes the erasers from the ends of the pencils. Using a steak knife—a very odd implement, given that ours (make that *his*) is a mostly vegetarian household—he plucks them out, then cuts them in half. He carries a pushpin and an eraser button toward the wall, where the giant pull-down world map dangles next to a chalkboard and a single stack of library shelves crammed with antique volumes. There, with his index finger, he searches out a little town called Cubero that he remembered was situated somewhere near Albuquerque. It isn't on the map, of course, because it was too small and abandoned a place when the map was made—and likely even more so now.

Thumbing through the memories in his cranium, Rich remembers being there—or at least very near there. It had been that time I surprised him with a trip to Las Vegas, a handful of Thanksgivings ago. We only went to Vegas because it was cheap flying in and out, and there had been a new *Cirque du Soleil* show I'd wanted to catch. Rich had never been out of the Pacific Northwest—or Cascadia, really since this included British Columbia—and I had long wanted to introduce him to the American Southwest, and especially the Native American history and culture that stretched over the mesas and down the canyons and across the desert expanses, like familiar skin.

The morning after *Zumanity* we had rented a car and driven through Arizona to Albuquerque, to pay homage to the adobe-hallowed halls of UNM. This is where I had done my level best, over the course of six years in the 80s, to tackle an elusive undergraduate degree in poli-sci; communications and Spanish; Western occult traditions; or, at one point, Russian studies. For a number of reasons, which were transformed into excuses phoned or postcarded home to my parents, I never did complete that degree. I imagine I'll come back to this in some detail a little later, but in case I don't, here's where I decided to place the blame: I found it impossible to focus or stand still following the astounding year I had taken between high school and the start of university to join an international musical troupe on an eight-country tour. I was a singer and dancer.

Okay, it was the *Up with People* show, so not exactly the big time, but it was a big deal for me. Yes, thanks be to Merry Melody Musical Kindergarten, *Ferdinand the Bull*, and particularly the state of Idaho for the get-the-hell-out-of-jail-free card. But this exposure to the world beyond the Panhandle made it ridiculous to think I could ever go home to stay.

Still, I'd promised my parents I would try the U of I, since both of them had graduated from there and they were paying my tuition. As predicted, it was ridiculous. Two miserable semesters later, I transferred to the University of New Mexico, where I was immediately enchanted to be surrounded by darker-skinned people like me, who spoke Spanish, liked green chili on everything, and had great hair. I was bound to finally succeed at university, right? Incorrecto. After part of the summer and only one semester in the mile-high desert, I had to return home to Idaho for surprise surgeries number four and five, with four months of chemotherapy sandwiched in between, to beat back the testicular cancer and malignant teratoma I apparently had been cultivating in my gut. By the time I got back to ABQ post-cancer, minus great hair and down a testicle, gay cancer was creeping not so gingerly into the news in New York and San Francisco. This was 1983. Of course I couldn't help but wonder if that is what I had had, and whether it was lurking still. For a gay man, any cancer that attacked the genitals was insidious, and in my fractured frame of mind, surely it would handicap my odds for successful boyfriending.

I returned to university scarred and feeling self-consciously amputated. It was a good little while before I felt like being sexual or took my clothes off for anyone who couldn't point to a framed medical degree. I'd only just turned twenty-one, but had already begun that long tango with mortality. Paranoia pushed my legs in a forward motion, while my head was locked and looking back over my shoulder for whatever would ambush me next. Even more than before, university studies were at the very bottom of the satchel of concerns I lugged around. Instead, I concentrated on putting myself back together. The New Mexico sun was what healed me, baking me pure. Turned out I didn't need a testicle, a college degree, or even a boyfriend. What I needed was a tan.

Rich is remembering New Mexico more clearly now; the Pueblo Indian culture, the adobe, the tastes of a corn-based cuisine, the colors of the earth and the pottery and the pervasiveness of native culture stamped on everything from buildings to the raw landscape. I understand how this gets him thinking about things, and how he has already worked out something in his head for the trip he will need to make home to reconvene with his own native culture at some point in his future. What I don't understand is how this leads him to go searching for my iPhone, and how, while the spent battery is recharging, Limping Rabbit figures out my password and manages to discover my shirtless *Grindr* profile, and with that, my semi-occasional penchant for public sex in Kinnear Park. So much for orchestrating every detail of how I would be remembered.

Hey! Now what is he doing? He's reading my profile, of course, thumbing through my online, mostly dink photos. How does he know how to use *Grindr*? Look at all those green dots—and a few of them within 500 feet, too! One of the user profile pics about a mile away gets a blue border and a chat message is delivered.

Hey, Sexy Stranger! Haven't seen or slurped you in a few months. Heading to Kinnear in about twenty. Can you break away?

Rich is thumbing through *happyhungnhorny's* pics which don't include a picture of his face. Then he starts messaging him!

Sure. I can be there in twenty, he texts, with his long, nimble, dark-skinned fingers.

What the hell?

ARMELINO

Ashton Taylor, *Last Will and Testament*, page 4

These are my ashes. I am at long last dead. Please take me on horseback to the place you called el Picacho, east of Cubero, in the shadow of Mount Taylor. Pour my ashes into a crevice at the top of this dormant volcano, so I can be at the centerpiece of the most magical landscape you ever shared with me.

IT'S NOT THAT ARMELINO SALAZAR HAS GOTTEN TO A PLACE in his life that he is beyond being shocked by some scheme I contrived. There had been a crazy number of moments in our almost three years together—now some thirty years ago—and a few odd occurrences since that had convinced him nothing was beyond the scope of possibility when it came to the first man he had really allowed himself to fall in love with. He actually wasn't even that surprised to learn from his mother that I had died. In organizing the compartments of his brain, Armelino—who lied to me the first time I met him when he told me that his name was "David"—had for the most part released me a long time ago, and was comfortably reconciled to the idea that we wouldn't (and didn't need to) speak again—which was a bit like acknowledging that I was dead to him already, right?

If there was a measure of surprise in learning from his mother over the phone about the contents of the small package mailed to their post office box, he didn't show it. If he interpreted my gesture as a reckoning that in taking stock of my life, I must have at long last realized the impact that our "affairship" had on me, he would be the first to say it still didn't change any of the outcomes. (Immaturity was just one of a host of impediments preventing us from ever achieving a full relationship.) Indeed, he had grown up and moved beyond there being any purpose in reconciliation. If he was touched or in the least bit flattered that he ranked high enough to register a footnote—much more a command performance in the achievement of my final wishes—well then, he didn't act it. There had been this long-distance silence after he had encouraged his mother to open the envelope and describe to him what she found. What was anyone supposed to make of a plastic film canister that contained a part of the man who . . . what? Secretly longed to return to him? Needed to experience New Mexico again? *Just what is the reason?* he wonders still. *You need to come home for this one, Mijo,* was all his mother had been able to say to him.

He talks his partner into opening the store, saying he isn't feeling too well. That seems apropos, since he and I had pretty much been willing to deploy any excuse (from a 24-hour flu to bloody diarrhea) for a chance to skip town to ride horses all those years ago. He doesn't divulge, to his life- and business-partner of these past twenty-four years, the subject of the brief phone call in Spanish he had with his mother, Carmen, last evening. Nor does he mention the errand that has him playing hooky so that he can drive out to Cubero today. When it comes to matters involving Cubero, his mother-in-law, Spanish, and horses—since none of these had ever really been of much interest to Armelino's partner who had grown up white and privileged in a sprawling Albuquerque Heights mansion—he doesn't ask questions. The way he saw things, he was just a pawn in the cultural divide that had always seemed too wide to span with any sincerity, so he didn't even try. Waiting a good thirty minutes after his partner leaves for work that morning, David jumps in the car, idles a couple minutes in a McDonald's drive-through, waits for a rub-bery egg McMuffin, and then continues west on Interstate 40, climbing through the petroglyphed lava mesas and across the beige-and-sage-col-ored desert toward home.

His mother barely looks up from the crossword book she is working on, to receive a kiss on the forehead from her only son, whose birth name was *Armelino Jr.* before it occurred to him that he might just be able to pass as Anglo, and so changed it to "David." He was her precious little boy who had been forced prematurely to become a man—the result of having been shipped off to a Roswell military school at age fourteen by Armelino Sr. She'd always regretted this, but it had seemed the only way to save him from becoming another version of his father. Armelino the latter had been born smack in the middle of a flush of four daughters; the older two were half-sisters, one of whom had died earlier that spring from undetected ovarian cancer. The younger two were twins, and had since married and moved away.

"It's over there on the counter, and I packed you some fresh torti-llas for the ride," Armelino's mother manages to get out while tapping her pencil on the magazine. "*Mijo*, what's a five-letter word for public transit that begins with M?" she hollers after her educated boy as the screen door slaps the piñon jamb of the mint-green adobe house she has lived in for sixty years. Then there is silence—the theme and soundless track of her mostly solitary existence. No children, no dogs, an old husband who disappears in his pickup to who-knows-where all day most days, an occasional breeze to toss up bits of desert against the glass if she is lucky. But for the most part, her hours are passed in cool, un-electrified quiet. She traces a section of the floral pattern on the sofa with an index finger, as the red dust of her life levitates into the sun that streams through her living room window.

"*Metro!*" David yells back from the horse outside the house. He lowers the Ray-bans from his thick graying hair and onto a maybe-too-large-for-his-face nose, and lines up the old horse's ears so that Mount Taylor rises between them. He chuckles to himself, recalling how honored I had pretended to be when I learned that Cubero was so forward-thinking that they had already named a mountain after me—and a volcano to boot! David knew that Ashton Taylor was corny that way.

Almost instantly, the plastic canister in his front pocket needs to be adjusted inside his Wranglers so as not to rack his balls when the horse eventually finds gallop. When he had inspected the package on his mother's kitchen counter, reading the accompanying note written by someone he'd never met, he peeked inside the gray lid to confirm its contents. *This mission is definitely up there on the crazy scale with all of Ashton's other schemes,* he thinks as he gains some distance from the house.

He slows then stops the horse for a moment at the grave of his beloved blue heeler, Jigger, who had been shot twenty years ago by a piss-drunk cousin lugging some family grudge around like groceries he could never seem to put down. David was already living in Albuquerque at the time, and couldn't have a dog where he was staying, so Jigger had stayed behind in Cubero. His father and namesake, Armelino Sr., with his mysterious disappearances and his alcohol-tempered Spanglish, had most likely been the provocateur, reigniting old family dynamite. Jigger's only mistake had been the company he chose to loyally follow.

David and the horse are as still as statues. The rider's brown eyes suddenly flood, and a breath seems to snag on a jagged bone inside his ribcage. It isn't just the memory of burying Jigger. It's the loss of his older sister, Laura. It's the vertical creases that have left parentheses on his face from a decade of taking AZT. It's the shock of growing older. It's the upset of being home. It is the act of carrying the ashes of a dead boyfriend he once loved, from a distant careless time before AIDS. It is his mother sitting alone with her crossword puzzles. It is the little that has changed, and everything that hasn't. It is full-blown melancholia that has dispatched these tears, and what in his world has equipped him for dealing with that?

His tennis shoe heels startle the horse into a body-jarring trot that seems to take twenty minutes to smooth into a gallop they can both live with. He worries that the aging horses aren't getting enough exercise, and that they had been retired long before necessary. The twins, Melodia and Harmonia, had been champion barrel racers before moving away to cities in Texas he could never keep straight, but they now had young children of their own who weren't yet old enough for horses. Plus, according to Carmen-the-jilted-grandmother, they didn't visit near often enough to suit her or the horses' needs anyway.

A good five-mile ride northeast from Cubero, *el Picacho* looks like a hitchhiker's thumb made of earth and rock. It is five hundred feet tall, sticking out of the desert floor. From the angle of David's approach, you could imagine a crooked banister left over from some dilapidated staircase that may have once led the recently departed to heaven—or some far-fetched Pueblo Indian legend like that. Geologically, the formation is a remnant of a 4.5 million year old volcano that has eroded away, leaving behind only the lava-clad throat that stretches to a height of 6,759 feet above sea level. David told me that in Spanish, *picacho* means throat. I don't think it does.

David can't recall the number of times he's been to the peak, but he always remembers spending one night in particular on mescaline, floating like an astronaut, tucked inside a sleeping-bag-lined crook near the top. And of course he remembers hiking up there once with a fellow named Ashton Taylor, who he had met a weekend earlier, when their sweat had mingled magically on an Albuquerque dance floor, during the extended version of Madonna's "Holiday." He slows the horse to walk it across Indian Service Road 46, and then follows the artery of a shallowly buried waterline another quarter mile or so until the thumb begins to elongate. Now, *el Picacho* looks like a petrified Spinosaurus sinking in the sand. David dismounts at the last tree—a short piñon not tall enough to cast a smidgeon of shade in the midday blaze. He pulls one of the two water bottles from the sling bag around one shoulder, and cups a hand near the horse's mouth to create a drinking basin. The move is more psychological than functional, but at least the horse's tongue gets wet.

David hitches the horse to the tree trunk—another act taking advantage of the horse's small brain, since with its size and strength the animal could have uprooted the shrub with minimal exertion. Satisfied that the horse isn't going anywhere, David again adjusts the canister in his jeans pocket before beginning the ascent on a path that in places quickly becomes only wide enough for two feet that are smaller than his. The stubble of grass cover gives way to columns of lava rock that once must have erupted from the surface like baby teeth through bleeding gums. The columns run parallel—first vertical, then horizontal, then diagonal to each other, just as they had flowed and pushed inside then out of the earth millions of years ago. Reaching the first hump before the serious climb commences, David pauses to examine some scat with the toe of his running shoe: sun-bleached fur, small skeletal fragments. It's either Western screech owl or red-tailed hawk—or maybe it's a golden eagle that had crapped out these remains of small desert mice.

He fancies himself a self-taught naturalist and anthropologist—his predilection for the outdoors is the result of being raised in a house full of girls. About the time this interest might have germinated into something more serious, he had been shipped off to the New Mexico Military Institute by his father, who couldn't live with the defeat that his son was becoming under the influence of all those women. Before this four-year Roswell exile, his secretive amateur digs had unearthed some impressive pueblo pottery in the area behind his Cubero home. David suddenly recalls that during a visit he and I had made to introduce him to my family in Idaho, he had presented my mother with one of his larger finds—an intact vessel about twelve inches tall and about as wide, with either Acoma or Laguna flourishes in earth-orange, and black geometrical patterns. He wonders if she still has it. (She doesn't—it had been re-gifted to me on my request years ago, and still forms the focal point of a ten-set collection of Pueblo pottery sitting on top of a halogen-lit bookshelf in the Seattle condo that, until recently, I shared with my beloved Indian.)

David takes a deep breath and shifts his calves into a more vertically-oriented gear. My instructions for him, printed on a slip of paper that Rich had sliced from a photocopy of the original document using a paper cutter at his law office, and then rubberbanded to the canister for mailing, were to "take my ashes to the top of el Picacho and add them to the basalt sections of rocks that rise toward the heavens on ancient hydraulics."

"The top? Seriously?" David asks out loud as he powers upward. It is going to take equal measures of muscle, resolve, and stubbornness—accompanied now by a flood of memories—to get this job done. David exhales all his breath in a laughing burst and pauses, steadying his balance and feeling just a little light-headed at an altitude he calculates is nearly a mile and a quarter above sea level.

This latest parcel isn't the first indication David has received since our university days that he still meant something to me after all those years. There had been my first novel, *VAL*, published in 1996 around the same time I met Rich. The central figure—the book's narrator, a character named Dominick Veneziano—seemed to be way more than loosely based on Armelino Salazar and the childhood he'd spent in Cubero. I had sent him a signed copy via his parent's post office box. He'd read it, but never wrote or spoke to me about it—not even twelve years later, when I all of a sudden materialized in the flesh again, standing with my by-then husband, in the middle of La Casa Bella, the home-decorating store that David and his partner own and operate near Albuquerque's Old Town. It shocked me then to see how much he had physically changed after years on AZT—especially in the face, where ditch-deep parentheses framed each corner of his uneasy smile. He had not revealed to me that sometime after our university days he had become HIV-positive, so in the awkward minute that followed my shout of "surprise!"—when it was plain to see that we both were—I figured this must have been why he hadn't sent me a photo at any point during the preceding decade.

But the two of us had recognized each other in a flash of each other's smiles, and we embraced warmly next to a ridiculously large candle and silk flower retail display. There had been the introduction of our for-real-for-life boyfriends at an impromptu dinner that followed later that evening, but we didn't really get to fill in many of the blanks of what had become of our lives through the years. We were like two-by-fours that got carpentered into a framework that kept us apart.

After a few more limb-stretching and crag-pulling maneuvers, David is at the top of *el Picacho*, panting for oxygen. A persistent hot wind blows his hair into his eyes, so he gingerly adjusts his position on the pinnacle to create a windshield with his body, trying to decide how to empty the contents of the canister without losing them to the wind. Since his instructions sort of run out the moment he reaches the top, David needs to improvise. He lowers the small backpack and extracts his water bottle, feeling for it between a windbreaker and the foil-wrapped ration of fresh tortillas his mother had contributed to the ceremony. A tortilla! That's it. This is a more organic solution as a final resting vessel—and is especially appropriate since he knows how I had loved his mother's fresh tortillas, hot off the stovetop and slathered in butter. He instantly feels better about this. He won't just leave me behind in the plastic canister on the top of this rock formation. He will create a new container that along with its contents will become part of the rock and matter of this dormant volcano.

He balances the water bottle in a rock holder and removes the foil package from his bag. He liberates a brown-speckled disc of his mother's flatbread. He reaches into the front pocket of his Wranglers with the other for the film canister, but his index finger quickly reveals the cap has come off, during either the ride or the climb. Now the canister is more than half empty. His middle finger confirms that the inside of his pocket is indeed gritty.

His face goes flush. He feels momentarily dizzy, and again takes note of his elevation. He hasn't really paused a moment to think about the remnants of his former lover inside the canister—and now they are outside of the canister. He carefully removes his fingers from his pocket. He examines the end of his middle finger. Through his aviator sunglasses, he can see there are bits of gray matter under his fingernail. Rather than freak out, he resigns that he is into this mission too far to abandon the assignment now. He undoes the buttons on the fly of his jeans to give more play around the waistband. He needs his second hand, so he places the end of the tortilla between his dry, clenched lips. He grabs the pocket from the inside of his jeans, holding the canister and the spilled contents in a tight pouch. He then begins to slowly turn the pocket inside out.

A bit of ash is caught by the wind, which races off with it. David further angles his body so that the extruding pocket is more out of the wind. He removes the tortilla from his mouth, cups it like a taco salad bowl in his open fist, and begins to force the pocket contents into the tortilla. He removes the black plastic canister, now emptied, from the small mound of ash that has been deposited in the bottom of the tortilla, and he sticks it inside the band of his briefs for the moment. He next folds the pliable tortilla like an enchilada—or maybe more like a taquito—around the filling that had once been his beefy mesomorph of a college boyfriend. He seals the ends in an expert wrapping procedure that he has probably known since shortly after birth. He takes the package in both hands and looks for a chink in the basalt where he can wedge it. He finds a spot and works the tortilla pillow into the grip of protruding rock. David then turns his jean's pocket completely inside out and slowly pivots into the wind to purify his jeans.

"I hope this is what you wanted," he says out loud to the spirit of—well, the spirit of all things, he supposes. He removes the canister from his underwear, fishes for the lid, and tosses both, refastened, into the bag. He does up his jeans and begins to look for the route of his descent. He turns back to plant a kiss on the exposed flank of tortilla, already re-baking in the late May sun. He is pretty confident he has done right by me, that this is what I had intended when I set the plan on paper and arranged for the distribution of my cremated body. He has, and it is.

David has moved maybe twenty or thirty feet below the top of *el Picacho*, when he sees a shadow through his sunglasses. He raises a hand to his forehead, searching the sky to see what has passed between him and the sun. It is a red-tailed hawk circling low, just above him and the mountain. David hears it screech, and recognizes the same call that has been used in Western movies for as long as he can remember, whenever a bald eagle is part of an outdoor landscape scene.

He continues down a few steps, and when he looks back, he sees the hawk has landed and is working at the tortilla with his beak. "Hey!" David yells. But that doesn't scare the bird. He waves his arms and yells again, but the raptor isn't giving up. David begins to scramble back up the rocks, and the hawk becomes more persistent, working faster. The next second sees a misplaced foot that shotguns David's left knee—the one he injured repeatedly during orienteering in military school—into jagged rock. He gasps. A puff-explosion of gray grit is illuminated by the sun as the hawk spreads its wings, escaping with the opening tortilla on an updraft, leaving behind an impressive comet tail of ash.

Whee! Look at me! I must be an angel now! I just got my wings!

ORDER!

IN THE DARKNESS OF THE TOP-FLOOR CORNER APARTMENT
in the old Queen Anne High School, a ringing phone has been arrested by
an answering machine and the voice of the recently deceased—yours truly:

> You've reached Ash and Rich's modest hovel atop Queen
> Anne. Sing us your message. Messages left unsung will
> not be returned with any urgency.

In the middle of this outgoing announcement, the front door
opens. Hearing his dead lover's voice on the answering machine, Rich
rushes through the apartment in the dark. His shoulder clips the bookcase, causing him to rebound then veer off the regular traffic pattern,
driving his leg into the back of the leather sofa, where he unburdens
himself of his suitcase and the pilot-sized briefcase he lugs everywhere.

"Shit! Hold on! I'm coming."

The answering machine beeps and a male voice begins singing, to
the tune of "Hello Dolly."

"Well, hello Richie, oh hello, Richie. It's so nice to have you back
where you belong."

Rich jabs for the speaker button in the dark. "Wait. Bret! I'm here.
I just got home." He pants, nearly out of breath.

"Hey. Welcome back from Aruba!"

There's a wicked audio feedback from the answering machine, as it is still recording. Rich can't see the button to stop that, so he endures it, apologizing.

"I got your message a little while ago," Bret says. "I guess I just missed you when you stopped by the court house on your way home from the airport. Sandy said you'd been by."

"Yeah, about that. Listen, Ash has me jumping through a thousand hoops, getting his remains stashed everywhere he wanted to end up."

"Like Aruba, huh?"

"No." Rich flicks on the desktop lamp. He wants to punch the button to stop recording the conversation, but he can't find the right one and then becomes distracted anyway with an examination of the newly minted tan on the back of his already brown hand. "Aruba, I'm afraid, was selfishly just for me. Anyway, Ash has this notion—" He stops himself. "*Had* this notion that I can just drill out a core in the wood of Judge Patella's gavel, fill it with ash, and plug it with wood putty or something like that."

Bret begins to laugh. "Judge Patella's gavel—seriously? The very same conservative asshole who refused to marry the two of you the morning same-sex marriage was legalized in Washington?"

"Yes, the very same. So anyway, I just stopped by the courthouse to nab it, figuring I could do the deed and get it back inside the court-room before his—make that *our* first trial tomorrow morning." Rich moves within the radius of light to retrieve the implement from his brief case. "I have it with me now, but I haven't a clue how to core it and get the ashes inside."

"Judge Patella's gavel?" Whether Bret repeats this to irritate or clarify, Rich can't make out. His buddy, Bret, is a lawyer too—petty crime and small claims. They play racquetball together sometimes.

"Yes, yes. I stole it. It barely registers as mischief, maybe mis-demeanor. You know how Ash loved to see me defending my downtrodden, Pioneer Square clients at the bench, especially when I get carried away. I guess he figured this way he could have a hand in keeping me in line."

"Yeah, a hand . . . maybe a foot. Who knows what part of his remains you're actually dealing with?" Bret must have thought for a millisecond how distasteful that comment sounded, because he next apologizes for being crude. "Hey, sorry, man."

"Well, that's enough on that technicality. I'm trying not to think about the exact source of the material I'm dealing with here, so I can get on with things. Are you going to help me with this or not?"

"Meddle with justice? Are you kidding? I'm on my way over." The phone double-clicks as Bret disconnects and the machine signals the end of the message with a beep.

Rich stares at the answering machine. He presses the outgoing message button.

> You've reached Ash and Rich's modest hovel atop Queen Anne. Sing us your message. Messages left unsung will not be returned with any urgency.

Raising his open hand to cover his mouth and cradle his chin, he pushes the button again.

> You've reached Ash and Rich's modest hovel atop Queen Anne. Sing us your message. Messages left unsung will not be returned with any urgency.

Rich sniffles, wipes his nose with the sleeve of his shirt, and presses a new button on the machine. "Record message," the machine says. "Press the stop button when you are finished recording." There is a beep.

"Hi," he says. "It's just *Rich* here. You don't have to sing anymore, but please leave a message. I'll get back to you as soon as I can." He pauses. "And hey, thanks for the call."

Ashton Taylor, *Last Will and Testament*, page 5

One of the things I think I'll miss most is watching you argue your client's cases in the Second Appellate Courtroom of sitting Judge (and resident fat-ass) Leon Patella. I don't know if I ever took the opportunity to tell you how proud I am of you and your gift for debate, and your compassion for the homeless and luckless. I don't think there is a more profound moment in the entire judicial system than when you—an exotically handsome and GQ-dressed Native American defense lawyer—are representing fellow Americans, be they Native, African, Korean, or just plain-Jane white trash. You sing in the courtroom, Limping Rabbit. I want to be there to hear you sing. So I need you to swipe Honorable Fat Ass's gavel. Drill a large core out of the middle, pour my ash inside, and then seal it back up with fast-drying wood putty. I figure it will make the gavel lighter, less authoritative, so it will bang more softly and give you longer to sing.

Not even one week later, Rich Dreadfulwater approaches the bench in one of his two-thousand-dollar tailored Harry Rosen suits. It cuts a flattering line, revealing his exquisitely proportioned and genetically-blessed body. His thick, black hair is gelled back, so as not to conceal a single raised eyebrow, the narrowing of his brown eyes, or the lift of his dimpled grin. His stride, with the slight hitch in the left leg from falling out of the back of a moving pickup when he was five, is a deliberate swagger that owns the space and punctuates the objection he is about to deliver. Because Judge Patella, criminally overweight beneath that tent of a robe, runs hot under the collar—not to mention the waistband, and surely around the Great Perineal Horn as well—there is a strained circuit-breaker-load of portable fans that oscillate papers, contempt, and verdicts around the nearly one-hundred-year-old courtroom. The morning's hearing has resumed post-lunch, and the early summer afternoon sun streams through the third floor windows on the Elliot Bay side of the King County District Court building on Third Avenue. US and Washington State flags are placed on either side of the judge, with a framed photo of a cheeky, rightly satisfied President Barak Obama in the background.

"I object to this general line of questioning, Your Honor. My colleague on the prosecution team would have you believe my client sold the undercover officer drugs because he didn't know better, because he lacked anything more than an eighth-grade education, and because his social status does not permit him to rise above the level of petty misdemeanor and thievery. The facts before us prove that my client was set up and my client was entrapped. Your Honor, it's not that I make this argument because my client is Native American and I get my legal kicks out of defending"—he pauses to make quote marks with his fingers—"my people."

The judge interrupts him. "That's enough, Mr. Dreadfulwater. I will record your objection and overrule it so Mr. Rissman can get on with his closing remarks. It will be your turn soon enough."

"Your Honor, I will offer that my client is Shoshoni. My family's clan is Nez Perce. Our tribes have not historically gotten along. Truth is, I could care less where my client comes from, what color his skin happens to be, or what his people believe, and I suggest this court should care the same, as it pertains to his rights and this trial."

The prosecuting attorney turns toward the bench. "Your Honor— if I may resume? I promise not to refer to the defendant's race or *his people* again, if that would satisfy the Defense."

Rich Dreadfulwater raises a tanned hand—courtesy of Aruba— looking even more exotic than usual. "The charges against my client are trumped up and they are being exaggerated here based on his race, and I will object again and again and again . . ." His voice crescendos, provoking a supporting hoot and holler from the spectators in the courtroom—several of whom are waiting and named in the day's docket.

That is all Patella needs to be provoked. He raps the gavel tersely on top of the judge's bench. "I'm warning you, counselor. You are walking a very fine line." He raises his voice. "And this will serve as my first notice of the afternoon to the spectators in this courtroom that you are to observe the court proceedings in silence."

Limping Rabbit is in his element, and he is *on*—not even thinking about the gavel he'd rigged. It was on deliberately constructed momentum like this that a defense case was hinged, and often could be won, if he could keep the pressure building. "I still object, Your Honor, to Your Honor not allowing my objection to stand"—he pivots his face slightly so that his voice will carry—"on the grounds of racism!" There it is, the *r*-word, lobbed like a Molotov cocktail. More cheering explodes behind the defense attorney.

Patella bangs the gavel hard, striking the hammer sideways on his desk. "Order!" he bellows. He bangs the gavel again, this time even harder, entirely dislodging the wood-putty plug, which flies off, leaving the judge enveloped in a cloud of ash that sends him scrambling up out of his swivel chair, sputtering.

In this moment, Rich loses the tan from Aruba along with much of the Indian in his face.

Judge Patella stands up, waving his arms through the dust cloud. "Bailiff, clear this courtroom! This court is in recess until we determine the source of this . . . this dust! I want to see both counselors in my chambers immediately."

In the terrorist-age panic that ensues, the two dozen or so members of the public clamor for the exits. Conveniently swept up in this evacuation is Rich Dreadfulwater's defendant, who has been un-hand-cuffed during his court appearance and who no longer feels compelled to participate in the Washington State criminal justice system. Outside of the courtroom and into the vestibule, the defendant tugs at the nearby fire alarm pull station, sounding a full building alarm. Other courtrooms and washrooms and offices empty their human contents into the stairwells. From there, people spill onto the sidewalks of Third Avenue. The suddenly emancipated Native American defendant makes a beeline to Pioneer Square, where he knows he can track down the bastard who owes him ten bucks.

OH, BROTHER

WHEN DID YOU KNOW YOU WERE DIFFERENT?

If I could be given back one upright, intact, twenty-four-hour day for every time I was asked that question, I would, I suppose, still be alive. Everybody is different, of course. DNA, fingerprints, and irises used to distinguish me from you and everyone else on Earth, but I always knew what was meant by the word "different." The narcissistic truth for me was that I didn't ever really see myself as different from everyone else as much as I was convinced everyone else was different from me. I didn't see this as a bad thing or something that needed to be corrected. But I did find it odd, even sad—for them.

What folks who aren't homosexual probably think they are asking when they string together the words "When did you know you were different?" is "When (or sometimes how) did you know you were gay?" That's what people not like me always seem fascinated to know. Gay men never ask that question. Instead, gay men ask *When was the first time you had sex?*, like your answer is automatically fused somehow to precisely the same day you realized you were gay and had to do something about it—but not all gay men are that lucky in the epiphany and fulfillment departments. Some need to wait and while away the hours masturbating their brains out before these two instances get connected. And some, like me, settle the unnerving debate with the calming contentment of just accepting their very special selves just the way they are.

Okay, but seriously, when did I know that I was gay and really different and super special? Well, consider this: in 1969, G.L. had been transferred to Missoula, Montana, moving the family smack in the middle of officially nowhere—not even five months into my first year of elementary school. I was about to turn seven years old, and surely, by then, I was already Greco-Roman wrestling with my character and my identity. One grandfather had been found dead in a bathtub from a drug overdose, and the other one didn't speak to children. I had outgrown my tap shoes. My only father figure spent the better part of the year fighting forest fires—instead of my demons and dragons and premature urges to discover everything in my world naked. I had a four-and-a-half-year-old sister who didn't have a penis, and an almost one-year-old brother who might as well have not had one, since I wasn't about to go gardening in that perpetually poopy diaper to find out. My mother sewed or altered just about all of her own clothes, and—horror of horrors—even some of mine. We hadn't yet lived any place within an hour's drive of an ice arena, where I could have at least started figure skating lessons.

And let's face it. I had already made a living mockery out of *Better Homes and Garden*'s criteria for textbook-perfect development, thanks to my only role model—Ferdinand, who was a cartoon bull. My parents hadn't found a single kindergarten in the entire Pacific Northwest that could feed or contain my creative spirit, and now that I had been circus-cannon-catapulted across the Idaho-Montana state border, how else could I be expected to leave a dimple-sized crater in that vast, cultural wasteland, without becoming the very opposite of what was expected of me?

I think I reported earlier that for the first lonely days after the Mayflower moving truck had dumped us on the southwest end of Missoula, there hadn't been a single sighting of another child-aged human being on either side the street, for as far as my green and about-to-get-eyelash-mowed eyes could see. Given the trauma of having been uprooted again, it was so very easy to mope around and emote like I had been deceived. Toss in an extra dash of precociousness and I could hardly be blamed for feeling maudlin to boot.

Then, the wind stopped one day, idling tumbleweeds for a moment and trapping the pulp mill stench right there where I stood on the sidewalk of Dixon Avenue. There was complete stillness. Eerily, even the robins, who started their songs each day before I woke up, and kept singing until after I was in bed, had all of a sudden stopped chirping. In the following seconds, the day turned to night and the sun disappeared in the middle of what had been a clear, blue, big Montana sky. My mother appeared on the front porch and hollered with pitched urgency for me to come into the house right that minute. I stood there on the front lawn, not moving a six-and-a-half-year-old muscle like I'd landed that pose in Swing the Statue. I could make out a thin outline of light where the sun had been before God took a Pink Pearl eraser to it. I thought a moment about getting vacuumed up into that black hole in the sky—like maybe this was where my grandfather had gone off to in the middle of his bath, and maybe I was next.

"Ashton! Bernard!"

My mother punctuated both of my names, which could only mean one thing if I didn't snap out of it—but something was wrong with my snapper. A dog started barking maybe a block away, and the sun began to spill out of that black hole in the sky. I had raised a hand to shield my eyes, just as Carole, with the strength of Hercules in a Lane Bryant smock dress, plucked me off the grass with a fist full of shirt. The wind picked up again, but was blowing in the opposite direction, and I could see song-robbed birds scattering for higher trees.

And then, lo and behold, the neighborhood around me had been celestially transformed, magically revealing the blessed brotherhood. It was precisely at that moment during the annular and total solar eclipse when my fascination with boys and men emerged from thorny bud to horny blossom. Across the street and one house west, stepping onto their porch to stare at the mischievous sun, were the LeBray Brothers. Mark would become my best friend for the next two or three years. We even had matching red Flash Gordon T-shirts at the height of our friendship—the symbolic equivalent of going steady, I figured.

Mark's older brother Mike would pursue high school and then college football—you sort of had to in that U of M Grizzly football-obsessed family of theirs. Purely for the physical contact it gave me with the LeBray Brothers, I would try really hard to get into football too, decked out in the teal-and-tangerine Miami Dolphins ensemble I received at my very next birthday. Though brave, those colors never really worked together, and sports that required extra layers of protective clothing never really took with me.

Something else happened at the height of the eclipse. Two houses across the street to the east, the Donaldson Brothers emerged, blond and tall. The older of the two would end up giving me shoulder rides back and forth across Dixon Avenue if I ran around the MacDonalds's garage without my clothes on while the MacDonalds were away on vacation. That's probably the first erection I can remember. The friction against the back of that long neck and at that dizzying height off the ground was insupportably addictive—so round and round that garage I sprinted until I was the best kind of *nekkid* dizzy.

But the porch revelations in the neighborhood that morning didn't end with the LeBray and Donaldson boys. The first to explain the solar eclipse were the MacDonald brothers, next door to the west, sons of astrologist Mac and wildlife biologist Chloe. I walked away from their explanation thinking the astronauts were lucky to get off the moon when they did, before its run-in with the sun. The McDonalds turned their backyard into an ice skating rink every winter (hockey only—since, sadly, figure skating was for girls) and kept reptiles in their laundry room that had to be tweezer-fed mealworms while they were away on long summer expeditions in their truck camper. On the far side of the MacDonalds's house lived the Graves family, with maybe a dozen kids—easily half of whom were boys—and whose parents owned and operated a sizeable fleet of mobile snow cone wagons each summer. The Graveses had a swimming pool, though I have no recollection of ever being asked over for a swim. I don't remember seeing any of them in the pool either, even when I climbed the giant cottonwood tree in our back yard to surveil the hood or watch the drive-in movie screen that was about five unobstructed miles away. Perhaps what I thought was a pool was actually where they emptied the snow cone melt at the end of each day.

I apparently wrote a dirty word once with a green Bic Banana felt marker on the low stone wall that retained the Graves's front yard. I say "apparently," because I do remember getting caught and having to scrub off the word. I don't remember the word and I don't remember if I was co-opted with promises of a Donaldson shoulder ride—but the MO and the timing would have synced with my then-permanent state of arousal at the start of second grade, and perhaps a new, Miss-Flynn-inspired focus on cursive penmanship.

We had landed in the same class, Mark and I. Miss Flynn was our teacher and the reason for the two of us locking horns in an after-school contest where we used folded-up lilac leaves to speed-write our last names on the side of the Tate family's light-yellow house. After a dozen dead heat draws, Mark and I got caught leaf-handed by Mr. Tate right in the middle of a disputed tie-breaker, during which we'd called the Donaldson brothers over so we could climb onto their shoulders to reach new writing space. Our autographed vandalism was not something we could convincingly pin on any other perpetrator, so Mr. Tate, mostly winking at me the whole time, made me and Mark clean the whole side of his house—which wasn't even fair, as we hadn't written on the whole side.

The point of all this—and what apparently took standing in the moon's umbral and penumbral shadows so that the seven-year-old me could come out and come of age at the same time—is to answer the question: when did I know I was different, gay, and special? I can tell you precisely. It was September 11, 1969; the day the sun had to disappear to reveal the light of my truth.

That was the day I figured out several things. First: I wasn't living in a neighborhood without kids. When you counted me and my little brother, Jeffrey (who we called Will), and our sister, Kris (a tomboy at the time), there were fourteen boys growing up—and at least one of us *out*—in that Dixon Street neighborhood. Second: I didn't really need a full-time father figure, since there were so many other boys and even a next-door man to emulate (Mr. Tate—more about him soon). And third: I was old enough to embark on my first ever crush and unleash a seven year-old's infatuation on an unsuspecting Mark LeBray.

As for my early willingness to do just about anything for hyper-sexualized gratification—that is, if we aren't going to blame the rogue moon for getting in the sun's way—I suppose it all came down to just feeling damn good to me. And feeding that feeling would swallow up the next several decades as I mastered my particular suite of clandestine manipulation skills to score anything from shoulder rides to top-secret sex—as long as it felt good. To be fair and accurate from second to fifth Grade, it was not sex yet, though I found the set-up as heady as the friction, and the getting away with it more thrilling than the feeling itself.

And in Idaho or Montana, you *had* to get away with it, or you could die. That's what being different from everyone else meant to me: I could die for just being me. With stakes like that, my early dedication to applying the sciences and arts of espionage and counter measures should have caught the eye of MI6 or the CIA or the KGB or the Miami Dolphins—but of course, to nobody's surprise ever, there was zero interest in anything going on in Montana or in next door Idaho in those days. With the face and re-sprouting eyelashes of an angel, I could have been a prepubescent serial killer and no one would have suspected a thing.

With the six-year age difference, you wouldn't have thought I had anything in common with my younger brother, William. But one afternoon a few years after the eclipse, he went missing. For hours— maybe more like minutes—our mother was apoplectic. My sister and I were dispatched to canvass door-to-door, likely while the milk cartons were being printed and distributed across town by the First Baptist Church ladies. We couldn't find him. Our father, I'm sure, was away fighting forest fires, and you didn't just call the sheriff in those days without a deceased body to report.

I don't remember how we discovered that he'd been locked in the MacDonalds's garage, but I do remember seeing the older Donaldson brother leaving from that general vicinity a little earlier that afternoon. How do I remember this? I asked him for a shoulder ride, that's how—but for the first time since mounting this gig, he wasn't in the mood. Somehow, while discovering my by then ten-year-old capacity for mounting a jealous rage, I managed to put two and two together, and deduced that my little brother must have been earning his own shoulder passage on *my* giraffe by streaking around the empty garage next door. I'd been double-crossed by a Donaldson and outsmarted by my own flesh and blood. It would have never occurred to me then that I had just grown too big to pack around.

William took a much different path with his life. The day he accepts that he's different too doesn't seem to have happened yet. But as he palms a black film canister in his left hand and with his right finger and thumb pinches his lips together as he strategizes his task, William is coming to terms with a whole lot of stuff right now. Normally he's juggling doubts he carries about his decision thirty years ago to go into the Navy out of high school, his need to marry early when he miscalculated another need to use a condom, and whether now the timing made sense to leave his wife, the mother of their only child now grown up and off to military school. On top of this, today is the day he has decided to tackle my request. He has his hands full.

Ashton Taylor, *Last Will and Testament*, page 6

To my ultra-conservative and inexplicably Republican brother, William . . . Pardon me, First Lieutenant Corporeal J. William Ashton, United States Navy, blah, blah, blah . . . I have one final request.

You and I didn't see eye to eye, fist to fist, or brain to brain on anything while I was alive, so I don't expect a breakthrough here. Like it or not, I happened to be your older brother, your blood, your kin. I have no doubt you're still attempting to deny any chromosomal linkage to a professed homosexual like myself. I expect you are still denying a lot of things, but that's your circus.

I was never in the navy like you or our father before us . . . well, not in the navy per se, but there was this one

sailor on leave from his ship that I managed to get inside
while I was in San Francisco one wild summer night, if that
can count as my contribution to the fleet. My pound of
flesh for the military cause, as it were. There isn't so much
as an ounce left of me, now, I imagine. But what there is,
you'll find in the enclosed film canister. I would like you to
take these ashes of your brother to a favorite bar of mine
located on the corner of Twelfth and Harrison Streets in the
Castro, on any Friday. Here's a survival hint: Go in the late
afternoon—say, between five and seven. That way you can
avoid the crowd. Walk straight in, like only you can, past the
main bar. Underneath the Harley Davidson hanging from
the i-beam is the men's room. Inside and against the far
wall you'll see a trough filled with crushed ice. That's not
a punchbowl. That's the urinal. Sprinkle my ashes over the
top of the ice and then get out of there. That's your mission. Be brave, Soldier.

From the onset, when I devised this last will and testament, the
odds were he wouldn't do it. There was also a chance he'd be hurt and
pissed off forever if I didn't include him in the scheme. There was a
suspicion that he might discover a curiosity in a task that involved a
gay bar. And there was a possibility that he'd blab to his fellow sailors,
turning this into a gang affair to make sure that William could get in
and out unscathed. What I couldn't have possibly banked on was that
my brother would choose to wear his full navy uniform, drive into
the Castro in the middle of Pride Week, and march through the front
doors of The Eagle—completely missing the outdoor reader board that
read "All Day Happy Hour: 2 for 1 cocktails for anyone in uniform."

Inside, he allows his eyes to adjust to the darkness of what must
surely be his nightmare: a packed room of men comes into focus, with
everyone dressed in uniforms ranging from police to military to lab
rats to *Star Wars*. Taller and more handsome than average, his arrival
is duly noted. Large group body dynamics churn and gyrate like gears
to grind the naval officer in the direction of the bar. To look shorter

and less conspicuous, William takes off his hat, where he had stashed the film canister. It deflects off his shoulder and tumbles end over end onto the concrete floor, where he instantly drops to retrieve it from a forest of black boots. This also has not gone unnoticed.

"Those party favors, Sailor?"

"Pardon me?" my brother asks over the percussion pushing out of speakers that double as supports holding up the service bar, and directed toward patron crotch level. He tucks the canister inside his breast pocket, but the Boy Scout-uniformed man has moved on to lock lips with a California Highway Patrolman, who is a dead ringer for Erik Estrada.

The bartender reaches a meaty forearm across the bar and arrests my brother by the wrist. "What can I getcha?"

"No, I'm good. Thanks."

The black-bearded bartender smiles, revealing a bank of paper-white teeth. "I don't doubt that for one second," he flirts. "Tequila's what I'm pouring. Join me?" He nudges an over-filled shot glass toward quite possibly the only legitimately uniformed dude in the joint. My brother has conflict written all over his ice-cutter face. He could use some liquid courage, and he adores tequila. The bartender raises his shot glass. My brother's reluctant clinks with his, and the two slam back shots like their moves were choreographed. What is about to come next—to my post-mortem delight—is also choreographed.

William thanks the bartender by just using his eyes and eyebrows—some Morse code he must have learned in the navy—then scoots the empty glass back within reach. He can now address the mission. The booze burns in his gut, begging him to lower his guard, but that would take guy wires, a boom crane, and possibly a lobotomy. He spies the Harley suspended from the ceiling, and ducks through the entrance, finding himself in a darkened hallway and not a bathroom at all. His determined momentum in crossing the bar takes several steps into the backroom maze before he can stop—and by then, of course, it is too late. He allows his eyes to adjust to the new darkness, surprised to encounter so many men waiting to get to the john. There is too much body contact for his heterosexual taste, but initially not too much to make him abandon the moment out right.

He thinks I must have lived for corporeal moments exactly like this. That this darkened, seedy, testosterone- and alcohol-fueled atmosphere had been my scene, my oxygen. That's what he's thinking right now. He doesn't have the insight about his own brother to know that I had been to this bar, this cliché, exactly once—or that I stayed maybe fifteen minutes before hightailing it to The Stud which was not nearly as pretentious. I have of course perpetuated his misconception by sending him here, and lying to him too about this being my favorite bar in San Francisco. But my intention in staging this treasure hunt wasn't malicious or vengeful. It was to advance my theory that while this scene didn't appeal to me, there was a better-than-nothing-chance it would tantalize his curiosities and stir his demons. Stopwatch running, Lieutenant Corporeal J. William Ashton has already spent more time inside The Eagle than I ever did.

Another man, about my brother's height and also in a navy uniform, cups a meaty hand around my brother's crotch, and squeezes it while delivering a sinister facial expression, full of authority and bravado, less than an inch from my brother's nose. He has crossed a line. My brother grabs the offender, with two fists on the lapels of his cheap and second-hand uniform. "You're going to show me where the men's room is. Then you're going to fuck off. Is that clear?"

The other man's machismo melts in a puddle. He nods rapidly before leading my brother out of the darkness and to the pisser, before disappearing back into the crowd to compose himself. My brother finally finds the john empty, and makes a beeline for the trough-styled *urinoir* that is indeed filled with crushed ice, just as I'd described. His shaking hand fishes the canister out of his inside breast pocket. He unsnaps the plastic lid and dusts the ice from one end of the trough to the other. *As you wish*, my brother thinks, quoting Westley—our childhood hero from the movie *The Princess Bride*. My brother wanted to be Westley, and I wanted to bed Westley, so neither of us thought twice about watching that movie at least a dozen times until we bonded over this—and maybe this alone. My brother is motionless for a minute at the improvised altar. Suddenly, he is joined by a couple, who stand on either side of him, but continue their conversation through him, as they take out their dicks to piss. William has no choice now but to take out his own penis and . . . is he going to do it? Piss out his tequila on his brother's cremains?

"I think Mary's a little pee shy," one of the two in full piss calls the play by play.

"She has no reason to be shy with that show-er," the other encourages, with a gentle elbow into my brother's ribs.

He winces and opens flow. The three of them have a chuckle as the two bookends to the naval officer cross streams with his. The chuckle only lasts a second or two before my brother realizes the men are getting erections and have pressed shoulders into him and have started to stroke the last of the piss out of their cocks. His own show-er is involuntarily becoming a grow-er—which of course betrays him, just like a man's cock always does.

"Nice," says one in a deep, breathy voice.

"Fuck yeah," says the other.

"Ah, shit," says my brother.

Other uniforms enter the men's room, and nudge their way like piglets to the trough.

I stopped being a choreographer about five minutes ago, and still manage to receive a nicer, more organic sendoff than even I could have imagined.

Thanks, Bro.

NUMMY

RICH IS FIGHTING WITH THE COLLAR BUTTON BEHIND A loosened tie after another suffocating day at work. He stops to press the button on the flashing answering machine before walking into the kitchen to translate the contents of his refrigerator into something that resembles an adult meal.

> Hey bro, yo' baby sis calling from the rez.
> Powwow's happenin', I tell it like it is
> September seventeen, mark it down
> Cause yo' baby sis is headlining da town
> So make a date, I mean it. No excuses now,
> Ya gotta see your sis as she wows the pow!
> Limp Rabbit! It's V'ronica. Remember me?
> I'm your only sister. Don't disappoint me.
> You two better be there!
> Ciao, Cows.

Rich fishes through his briefcase to check the date in his planner. "Shit!" He swipes the screen of his iPhone and dials his sister who lives at home with their father—who he hopes won't be the one to answer the phone. He begins to undress, pinching his cell between shoulder and ear as he waits for an answer.

"Hi Moses . . . I'm fine . . . Yeah, I just got it . . . You know, I can't actually . . . I'm prepping for a major trial that starts the end of August . . . Come on, Dad . . . I don't just defend Indians . . . There are other bad people in this world too you know . . . Yes, I know my sister isn't one of them . . . I know I should be there, alright . . . I know she's gonna be the world's first Native gangsta rapper and I know I'm missing all the important moments in her young life . . . Oh, nice, Dad. Let me just add that one to my list, too: I'm a lousy Indian . . . I don't remember when I was at my last powwow, no . . . That's not true . . . I remind you that I translated several of our people's oral traditions into English for my college thesis . . . That's right . . . I would have had to know more than five words in *Niimiipuutímt* to do be able to do that, now, wouldn't I . . . Yes, let us never forget how I embarrassed you by translating the story of how Coyote used his penis to dam the river . . . Okay, Sorry . . . Yes, I have written it down . . . Tell her I will try to be there but I'm not making any promises . . . No Moses . . . That is not like the white man . . . The white man makes promises . . . He just doesn't keep them . . . Whatever . . . Just tell her I phoned her back please . . . Yes, Dad . . . Yes. We don't have to speak more often for you to know I love you, too . . . Bye."

Rich throws on a sweatshirt and a pair of shorts and quickly sorts through the day's mail. He doesn't know why he still hasn't told many of his colleagues or his family—and especially his sister V'ronica— that I am gone, and have been gone for three months. Wait. That's not right, he calculates; almost *four* months now. He has had his hands full, what with distributing my ashes all over Hell's half acre and managing my mom's sudden need for vital, personal, private information, while having to suppress his own grief during her still weekly phone calls. So as long as he delays telling his sister, he figures, then at least in her mind, her brother-in-law, Ashton Taylor—whom she looks up to and adores—is still alive. It is logic a little twisted but I suppose I cannot be totally gone if there are those who believe I am still here.

Limping Rabbit takes a postcard with the Washington Monument on the front that has dropped out from between advertising circulars, and reads the back. There has been a misunderstanding with one of the canisters he sent to Washington. He taps the card twice on the kitchen counter top, then crosses the living room to the world map where he takes the black pushpin that had been marking Washington, DC, and, with a pause and some study, moves this pin to Baghdad, Iraq.

NEITHER DAVID NUMMY NOR I could remember the year [1984] or exactly where in Albuquerque we'd met [the Albuquerque Social Club], but a decade or two later we settled on this version of our history: we had met in a gay bar pre-AIDS. Bonnie Tyler was wailing "Total Eclipse of the Heart," and we both looked beautiful and virile and relevant, of course. David challenged me to peeling off, without tearing, a gold-foiled label from the bottle of Miller Lite I was clutching. The experiment, as he explained it, was that if the label tore, I was still a virgin, and sexually frustrated. If it didn't, well then, it was because I was one hundred percent, supremely gay, and was getting plenty. So it wasn't enough to just remove the main label. I drove my point home by liberating the neck label from the bottle too, presenting them both for his inspection. Then I lip-synched as Bonnie sang, "turn around, bright eyes."

More than just an illustration of my general competitiveness, my virginity with women—label or no label—was watertight defensible as I hadn't screwed or even fooled around with one. From that moment and for some unknown reason, because I never challenged him back or needed him to prove his own *Perfect Kinsey 6*, I cherished being trusted and loved by David. I guess I also took some measure of pleasure in torturing him, because it was obvious he wanted more from me than friendship and witty conversation. I kept him close but wouldn't capitulate—even courted other boyfriends in front of him. On occasion when pushed, I would recite to him the reasons why it would never work for us: he was too many years older (five); he was only in town temporarily to work on the re-election campaign for incumbent Senator Pete Domenici; he smoked; he was a Log Cabin Republican; he had droopy eyes and jowls (I never actually told him that) but I wasn't attracted to him or in love with him that way. Sometimes I could make the words I used really hurt.

When he pretended to be giving up his pursuit of me, and announced he would be returning to a job in Washington, DC, I did panic a little. I decided that over Christmas break, I would accompany him on a winter road trip in his Datsun 280-Z, taking him back to the nation's capital. But I made it clear I would be flying right back again to New Mexico to continue school and that I would be leaving before Ronald Regan's second inaugural parade (which I couldn't stomach attending, but that ended up getting cancelled anyway due to snow and record cold temperatures—a sign that Hell really had frozen over). The road trip—by David's design—turned out to be a thirteen-day declaration of love and admiration for me. His intentions were already clear on the first leg from Albuquerque to San Francisco, so I was defensive and leery. Unfortunately, in picking the gay-friendly accommodations for the evening, David had made reservations at a place called The Hotel on Harrison Street, which was essentially a gay flophouse. Our dingy room on the fourth or fifth floor had a window overlooking the center courtyard atrium, where there was situated a pair of much larger mattresses than the double bed in our room, and upon which orgiastic heaps of men came and went, but mostly came.

When it was time to go to sleep, I saw that I had a choice between sharing the double bed in our room with a man I wasn't going to give in to, and visiting the open, airy atrium where there was lots of elbow room, or maybe just lots of elbows. So I went for a wander—or maybe it was a gander, since I mostly watched . . . and touched . . . and, well, got touched.

So naïve was I that I didn't know that just eight weeks earlier, Mervyn Silverman, San Francisco's Director of Public Health, had ordered the closure of The Hotel, along with the other thirteen bath-houses in the city—ostensibly to save the lives of gay men who had been dying from a disease that seemed to be transmitted sexually. The bathhouses hadn't stayed closed long. Two had reopened within six hours, and another ten establishments within twenty-four hours, in defiance of the order—you just can't keep a good man from going down, apparently. By the time David and I had arrived a little more than two months later, after sixteen hours on the road, with the Land of Enchantment long vanished from the rearview mirror, it was a brisk business as usual at The Hotel. After maybe ninety minutes of being flattered by sexy, sweaty men, and having smoke blown up my ass— and I mean actually getting reefer smoke blown up my ass—I figured David was either still watching from the window above, or asleep, or at the very least being a gentleman and faking the latter. I returned to the room to find him in bed with his eyes and the curtains closed, but with the lights on—probably so I could see how badly I had hurt him. We never talked about this—not in the car over the next six days, not even six months later when I was absolutely sure I had caught the gay-related immune deficiency virus (also known as GRID), the disease that every gay man in Albuquerque seemed to be talking about and dreading if not already beginning to die from, once I returned from DC.

The road trip continued north to the hometowns of my youth and then cut across the Idaho panhandle just as winter began discovering the punch it could pack if it really tried. The sports car struggled to hang on to the icy pavement, and there was a patch during a whiteout that seemed to last forty-five minutes where we repeatedly began to slide off the highway—off the mountain, really. It changed the atmosphere between us, and by the time we fishtailed into the parking lot of a Best Western motel in Butte, Montana, so very happy to be alive, I looked at the double bed differently. Clothes came off, inhibitions and nerves were fried, and my guard collapsed in a rubble heap around me. David and I had lights-off sex that wasn't nearly as clumsy as I thought it would be—and that changed things too.

We next scooted and skidded north through one of the Dakotas, overnighted in Madison, Wisconsin, and then made it to Manhattan in time to grab a few drinks at a piano bar called Don't Tell Mama, before shoving and elbowing our way into Times Square an hour before the ball dropped on the last night of 1984. We stayed in another double bed at the Empire Hotel, just a stone's throw from Central Park, and we saw seven shows in five days: *La Cage aux Folles, Torch Song Trilogy, Cats, Sunday in the Park with George, Doug Henning and His World of Magic, A Day in the Death of Joe Egg,* and *Forbidden Broadway.*

Even though I had instantly realized that the Butte sex had been a colossal mistake, to show my very sincere appreciation for all David and his American Express card were exposing me to in NYC, he and I had sex several more times before continuing down the highway to Washington, DC, just as a winter storm dumped two feet of snow on my resolve and the capitol. The two of us went apartment shopping; it was as if David thought that finding a nook that I liked and could live with would sway me to stay and keep me from returning to Albuquerque. It wouldn't, and I told him so, which wounded him. By then, I'd become fluent in the kind of mixed messages that involved sex; apparently I had a knack for manufacturing hope and promises every time I ejaculated. I had to leave him. I stated this hourly. I couldn't stay. We'd have sex and he'd try to convince me anew. The Amex card couldn't be blamed for melting into a plastic nugget of ridiculousness with all it transacted in those heady, optimistic nesting days. There had been the acquisition of furniture and bedding and television/stereo equipment, a particular bathroom towel and rug set just because I happened to mention I thought they made for a brighter contrast with the shower curtain I'd picked out the day before—knowing all along that none of this was for me. David set traps of opulence and temptation everywhere, and I tripped clumsily from one into the other until my ankles bled but still my heart could not.

I took a cab to Dulles during Regan's second inaugural speech, when I knew David would be preoccupied, and since the Datsun 280Z could not be sprung from the subzero snow bank anyway. Genuinely remorseful, I cried my way back over the Dakotas and stumbled back into university and my class-work-bars-repeat routine in the no longer enchanting Land-of-Without-David.

For months I was karmically convinced that I had somehow caught GRID in San Francisco (simply by observing unsafe sex), and also that I'd probably given it to a dozen others since. So I sat down and began to plan for the coming death I thought I deserved. I would notice a mole for the first time, or watch a cut that seemed slow to heal, and sink deeper into my mortality. I worked out this plan in searing detail around how, where, and by whom my cremated remains were to be distributed. I no longer saved money or banked vacation days. I spent every dollar or day off that I earned. I stopped talking in terms of "five years from now," because foolish notions wouldn't have time to come to pass. I essentially dropped out of college—because why the fuck would it matter if I had a degree when I was dead and unemployable? I was sort of stuck in this morbid funk for the next several years before meeting Limping Rabbit. But as blood test after blood test came back negative for the human immunodeficiency virus, I was forced to go on a hunt for something else to kill me dead. Turns out it would be a trick ventricle—something I had never seen coming.

Despite (and maybe because of) the miles between us, David and I managed to remain lifelong friends, but never talked about San Francisco or Butte or those very first clumsy months when he had wanted more from me than I could comfortably give. And I saved those beer labels too—pressed them in the back of an architectural address book from the Metropolitan Museum of Art that David gave me, where they still exist in situ, even though I no longer do.

Ashton Taylor, *Last Will and Testament*, page 7

Nobody travels the world like you do, David. Beats me what you do for the State Department, exactly. When you told me you were a Republican, and a Log Cabin one at that, I didn't ask you why. I didn't ask questions. Oh, I had them. I just didn't ask. When your career for the next twenty years tackled one high-profile Grand Old Party gig on top of another, I didn't ask questions. Well, I did ask you once if your brain was right when you told me you had been named the treasurer of the George W. Bush presidential campaign, but that wasn't so much a question as it was my non-clinical diagnosis of your acute insanity.

Anyway, now it's your turn to not ask questions. I didn't get to see the world—not like you did. Where did you get to? I think I had postcards from something like sixty countries. This is my chance. Here's what you do. Go to Kinko's with a couple of your business cards. Ask them to make them into laminated luggage tags, but first make sure you sandwich some of my ash between the cards. Not the big chunks of course. Use a glue stick. It's not so messy. You'll figure it out. You're a smart Republican (which even you must admit sounds kind of an implausible combination). But be a doll and let me "tag" along again, will ya?

A two-tone bell sounds in the slowly depressurizing business-class cabin. The shade of an airplane window is raised by a pair of Camel-stained fingers to reveal a brilliant sunrise tracing the scarcely curving Tigris. His nicotine patches, one on each shoulder, lost potency maybe forty-five minutes ago—somewhere over the Balkans—and he's drumming sixteenth notes into the carpeted floor with his right foot. The two tones signify the plane has just passed 10,000 feet. David Nummy's next cue will come when the landing gear comes down, and the plane suddenly banks to the right to begin the corkscrew landing procedure directly above the runway at Baghdad International—formerly known as Saddam International. Commercial flights have landed here in this spiral manner since November 2003, when a DHL Airbus Cargo plane was hit in the fuel tank by an SA-7 shoulder-fired missile from outside the airport perimeter. Airspace above the airport has a higher probability of being secured these days but it's still one of the most dangerous approach procedures in the pilot's manual.

The only reason any of this matters is that David's first cigarette in eleven hours and fifty-five minutes is roughly twenty minutes away—that is, if the plane doesn't get taken out by a shoulder-launched missile, turning him (almost poetically) into a cigarette himself.

His last trip to Baghdad was just over a dozen years ago. This trip had been hastily put together primarily to commemorate the last; a courtesy check-up by the US Treasury Department on the Iraqi finance ministry personnel that David had hand-selected from a corps of shocked and awed civil servants, to jump-start the new government after Saddam Hussein had been deposed. On March 23, 2003, David had been one of almost one hundred senior advisors from the US Office of Reconstruction and Humanitarian Assistance who were moved into Baghdad from where they had been staging in Kuwait City.

Even though he has a sealed carton of Camels in his suitcase—diplomatic privilege—he plans to make a nicotine dash to a street vendor outside the terminal for a pack of unfiltered Miami-brand cigarettes, just as soon as he clears customs. He presents his black US diplomatic passport at the Customs and Immigration Clearance kiosk.

"The purpose of your visit, please?"

"Meetings with the Iraq Finance Ministry."

"You here to raise our interest rates?"

David chuckles. "That isn't really up to me."

"No?" The officer clearly does not believe him. "The hotel where you will be staying?"

"The Babylon Warwick."

"Oh, fancy." The officer, who wore a razor sculpted and closely cropped beard, raises an eyebrow that had quite possibly been threaded.

David admires the Arab's long fingers, senses a fellow smoker, and drops a hint. "I like being able to smoke on the roof balcony of my club room, overlooking the Tigris."

"I see. Well, that explains the carton of cigarettes in your suitcase. What is your explanation for this, then?" The long fingers gingerly display the black plastic 35mm film canister that David had rolled inside a pair of dress socks in his carry-on.

David's eyes rise from the container to the dark brown eyes of the officer, understanding in that gaze that his first cigarette has just been delayed. Having been involved in the crafting of the Disposition of Remains policy in the event of American soldier fatalities, he already knew that cremation was extremely rare in Iraq, and that local burial almost always occurs within twenty-four hours. He also knows that conveying a uniquely North American fascination with cremation and the ceremonial keeping or scattering of remains was not going to translate well. So he lies. "It's my personal ashtray. I am not one of those messy smokers who stand around a disgusting public ashtray reading their phone. I need space and privacy."

The officer's face is frozen in a look that could only be categorized as blank. Those eyebrows have definitely been threaded, David thinks again, during the eternity that comes next.

"Welcome to Baghdad," the officer eventually says, handing him the film canister.

David smiles and says, "Shukraan."

The officer tips his head in a manner that almost suggests pre-conflict nobility, though he couldn't have been born before the Gulf War. After walking several yards, David looks back at him just before reaching the exit doors that lead to the waiting taxis, and catches the officer in a lull, texting on his iPhone. Such is the modern state of Mesopotamia.

Not forty minutes later, David, in a traffic jam on the Arbataash Tamuz Bridge, and sweat-drenched by the unfathomably sweltering late-July temperature, talks his cabbie into letting him step out of the car to quickly snow the leftover ashes of his dearest friend over the railing and into the Tigris River. (The do-it-yourself baggage tags had hardly required any of the cremains he'd been sent.)

"Rihlat amina, sadayqaa," he yells, drowned out by honking cars. "Safe travels, my friend," he translates in a whisper to himself.

Ashton Taylor, *Last Will and Testament*, page 8

Rich Dreadfulwater, you don't have a single mark on your beautiful brown body. Not a scar. Not a birthmark. Not a tattoo. Not a piercing. Not a childhood scratch or scrape that didn't heal properly. Not an acne scar. Not a mole. I know because I spent twenty years surveying your every perfect centimeter. As a contrast in canvases, consider that I had four tattoos, six major surgery scars, a Big Dipper Constellation of moles under my left armpit, an alarmingly healthy crop of age spots on my shaved head, and that birthmark at the top of my ass crack.

Now at last, and for the record, I'd like us both to acknowledge that I left a mark on you. Though not fatal for you, and certainly more symbolic than corporeal, we left fingerprints and footsteps and DNA and impressions and even the occasional bruise on each other. I would like you to consider taking this one important degree further.

There is a company in Illinois called LifeGem, and they turn ashes to diamonds. They can make you one from the carbon found in my cremains with just eight ounces of my ash. I was thinking you could select their green diamond to remind you of the color of my eyes, and I was also thinking that you could get it mounted on a stud to pierce that proud, broad nose of yours so that you could at last truly be Nez Perce'd.

A .25ct diamond will set you back about three grand, so use one of my 401ks. Here's their website for easy reference: http://www.lifegem.com

NEEDLES HAVE NEVER BEEN HIS THING. IF HE'D EVER HAD A rabies, rubella, polio, or mumps vaccine, it must have come in the form of a sugar cube, because he doesn't remember it. Well after dark and one really hellish long day of witness prepping, Limping Rabbit is at the very busy Fenix Tattoo Parlour in Pioneer Square on the recommendation of one of his clients not usually known for impeccable or discerning taste. But if word on the street was that "Tackle Boxx," who worked there, was a master artist and a genius at pain moderation, well then, that and a $5 off referral card was good enough to get him across the threshold.

The really spectacular emerald-colored diamond, made from the carbon of my ashes, had been FedExed overnight in a plastic bubble pack quite unceremoniously arriving at his office on Wednesday just before noon. It had taken every minute of the fifty-five hours since to gather his courage for the piercing appointment that would tie up this detail of my elaborate wishes. His voice cracks into falsetto when giving his name to the receptionist, who invites him to take a seat with half a dozen others whose previous ink and piercing work is alarmingly on display. To give his amateur self a little extra street-cred—and maybe some wiggle room when it gets to the pain part—Rich thinks about dropping the name of the client who recommended this place to him. When Tackle Boxx—a man the size of a double refrigerator—appears at the counter to retrieve him, Rich fortunately thinks again and catches himself before speaking, just in case there happens to be money owed or revenge pending where his client is concerned.

"I should tell you," he begins, with a voice that trembles, "that I'm not good with needles." He tries to deepen his tenor register as he goes.

"I should tell you I'm not good with wimps," is the reply delivered without a smile. "Have a seat."

Rich reorganizes his strategies and decides to produce a business card. "I could use a friend right now," he says. "Maybe you could use one in the future." So smooth, my operator.

"And what would you need this friend to do for you?" Tackle Boxx asks in a calmer voice, like one that belongs to a prince in a Walt Disney movie.

"I would need my friend to not let this hurt, not let me see the needle, and not tease me for being less the man than I appear."

"Demanding, much?" The man—who has three nose piercings, ear lobe hoops the size of paper towel tubes, and a *Gray's Anatomy*-styled tattoo of his own musculature curving up both sides of his neck and behind his ears—finally breaks a smile. It is a pleasant smile, with evidence of really great dentistry and oral hygiene. They are both just working stiffs at the end of a long day, having a moment together that at least one of them hopes will not turn sadistic.

"I have a few options you might find soothing," Tackle Boxx says, producing a bottle of *Patron Añejo* and two Dixie cups from under his work table. He pours a healthy splash into each. "You're my last appointment, and then I'm off to Zihuatanejo for a week." The two jerk the Dixie cups back and Rich feels the medicine dispatch heat and courage through his capillaries. "And this is for your Trypano-phobia." Rich's disappearing pain magician displays a nearly fresh tube of EMLA ointment in his oversized palm that he just knows grips a Harley Davidson throttle on weekends. "A delectable combination of lidocaine and prilocaine. I only bring it out for friends," he says, tapping the lawyer's business card that lays on the half table between them.

Rich nods consent and turns himself over to the Master. "I need to sterilize the rock we're putting in there," Tackle Boxx prompts. His client's blank face indicates that he doesn't follow. "The diamond," he clarifies. Rich fishes the box out of his suit jacket breast pocket. Tackle

Boxx springs the hinged lid with his thumb, and his sort of permanently squinting eyes grow larger. "Not a petite number, is she?"

"*He*," the prosecutor is quick to supply. Now it is the tattoo artist who doesn't follow and who looks as though he might need some clarification. Rich removes his suit jacket, unbuttons then rolls up his shirtsleeves. "The diamond is made from my dead boyfriend's ashes. The diamond is a *he*." The tequila is now doing all of his talking for him.

"Well isn't that some crazy shit?" Tackle Boxx chuckles, but respectfully. "That calls for a toast, I'm afraid." More Patrón waterfalls into the paper cups. "To the boyfriend," Tackle Boxx booms, with a voice that outs Limping Rabbit to the other clients and artists in the tattoo parlor that opens through the portion of a removed wall to the laundromat next door. He next fishes out new latex gloves from a box marked XXL. "May he rest in peace," he offers, with a softer tone, snapping the air out of the first glove.

"To Ashton," Rich echoes, momentarily forgetting what is about to come next.

Tackle Boxx gloves the second hand and uses an art brush to place a dot just above the end of the crease where Rich's right nostril curves away from his cheek. "That look about right to you?" he asks, extending an LP-sized hand mirror.

"Does it make a difference, right or left?" Rich has been thinking all day to remind himself to ask this question.

"Well, given that the diamond is named Ashton, I think it's really up to you."

"Right. Just wanted to avoid that awkward *left ear buccaneer, right ear queer* trap." Rich laughs at his own sort of stupid rhyme.

"Yeah, I don't think that really matters anymore. I marked your right nostril because your left eyebrow seems the more active of the two, which can give your left eye the appearance of being larger. Placing the stud on your right nostril will lend some visual balance and symmetry to the face."

"Okay then. You're the boss. Let's do this!" Rich is embarrassed by how sexualized that just sounded. Tackle Boxx just grins, disinfecting the outside and then the inside of the nostril with a long Q-tip.

He follows this step with the EMLA crème, outside, then in. He fiddles a little with an eighteen-gauge needle and attaches the sterilized diamond on the end of an L-shaped bar that will follow the needle through the hole it makes in the nostril. Rich can hear these tinkling together like chandelier crystals but cannot see what's happening without making an effort. Instead he closes his eyes as his nose begins to tingle—though whether that's from the crème or the tequila he isn't able to discern. Tackle Boxx takes an instrument that clamps both sides of the nostril and centers the art brush dot in the middle of the instrument's circular guide.

"Okay," he says. "Here we go. I am going to count down from five . . . four . . . three . . ." and in the needle goes through the recipient's nostril, with a bolt through nerve endings the tequila couldn't touch.

"Fuck!" Limping Rabbit yelps.

"I always mess up counting backwards," Tackle Boxx confesses. "And we're done," he announces, dabbing more antiseptic, and cleaning the traces of blood. When the area is all cleaned up and color has returned to the lawyer's face, the hand mirror is extended again with a squeeze to his shoulder.

The diamond looks ridiculously large, and the color starts to escape Rich's face again. Tackle Boxx laughs, loving this joke most of all. "Flip the mirror around . . . you're looking at the magnifying side!"

With relief, Rich exhales, tilting his head to let the diamond play a bit in the light. It is perfect. It is really tiny, he thinks. More importantly, it is done. Rich extends his hand in thanks. Tackle Boxx grabs it and the two shake. "The name is Rory," he says, "so you'll know who I am when I call for a friend."

"I mean it. Anytime," Rich replies, looking him square in the eyes, studying to see if one of them might be larger than the other. He stands up maybe too quickly to access the wallet in the back pocket of his pants, and sort of crumples back into the chair when his boozed up legs can't yet support his weight.

"Apple juice!" Tackle Boxx hollers to the receptionist minding the front counter.

GREG

ODDS CERTAINLY WERE, GIVEN MY OBSESSION WITH MAN-love in my early twenties (a phase that lasted in one form or another until my DOD: March 19, 2016), that I was bound to fall in love with a straight man I couldn't have. His name, for the record, was Greg Barton. When we met at a University of New Mexico campus orientation for exchange students in 1983, he was a wavy-haired blond who was mustached, blue-eyed, and pushing six feet tall. He was a diver and a gymnast and a tennis player, and he was from Oakridge, Oregon, transferring from OSU. I had just transferred (read: escaped) from the University of Idaho. He had the legs of a speed skater and the smile of an actor in a Dentyne chewing gum commercial. We were both the same age, both from the Pacific Northwest, and both new to the desert, and in this, a super-adhesive bond sort of chemically happened—at least in my mind. Plus, he had his own car—an olive-green Opel GT with bright golden-yellow Oregon plates.

We lived in different dorms, but not more than a scorpion toss from each other, and shared the same cafeteria and meal plan, which secured a three-times-a-day togetherness on which I became immediately dependent. We had already registered for classes before arriving in the Duke City, and academically our schedules or declared majors did not overlap. I was taking level four Spanish Lit, introductory

Portuguese, and introductory Russian—all part of my quest to become a post-grad, Cold War diplomat. I honestly don't remember what Greg's classes or discipline were at that time, or even what degree he graduated with some years later. For me, the time we spent together in this new environment took priority over studies and vocations. I had a boner of a crush on this boy.

We made a bet to see who could land a job first. I won by a Whopper with cheese, having secured my first shifts at Burger King a solid day before he got hired by Whataburger. All dressed up in our fast-food uniforms, we posed for a photo in front of the window in his dorm room that opened onto the roof of his building, where we would sunbathe between classes and burger flipping. We double dated to the New Mexico State Fair. This was Greg's idea. I asked a beautiful Latina woman with Pantene auburn hair that tumbled off narrow shoulders to plunge well below her itty-bitty bottom. She sat right in front of me in my Spanish class—or I sat *atras* from her, I don't remember her position exactly. I wouldn't have noticed her at all, if I was being honest, had it not been for Greg's challenge that I find a female date to give his someone to talk to while he and I enjoyed the fair together. That's what he meant, right? Anyway, her name was Andrea Urrutia and she truly was a pageant-worthy beauty. She certainly would have been ranked well out of my league had I not already signed for the gay team. Greg found her gorgeous when I pointed her out to him on campus, and thought one of us should jump all over the chance to ask her out. So just like with the burger challenge, I was first to score—ridiculously so considering my heart and other parts just weren't in it to win it.

Fortunately, Andrea was saving herself for marriage, and even kissing wasn't on the table, so this worked perfectly for my charade. How could it have possibly turned out that neither of our dates liked carnival rides? Squished together by gravitational pull on the Octopus, the Tilt-o-Wheel and the Ferris wheel (okay I faked it on the last one), Greg and I became closer and closer.

At Burger King, just off campus on Central Avenue and Route 66, I had met another woman named Julie Ruderstadt. She was no beauty contestant, about eight years older and weighing more than me. She worked on the Tuesday and Thursday late nightshift to supplement her daytime credit counseling job, which didn't pay much. Turns out she had taken this extra job at BK to save money to record a demo tape, and had middle-aged dreams of becoming a singer. Why she didn't go to her own father, who had a mansion on Pennsylvania Street in the southwest hills above the runways of Kirkland Air Force Base, and who owned the six store Arby's franchise in town, was sort of an estranged mystery I never got into with her.

I told Julie one night in the drive-thru box that I was also a singer, and that if she needed someone for back up, either in the studio or at gigs, I'd be interested. I couldn't resist pitching to her that Greg also played the piano. That came in handy a few weeks later, when into the recording studio the three of us went. We recorded three songs that afternoon—two she had written and arranged, and the sappy Warnes/Cocker duet from *An Officer and a Gentleman* ("Love Lift Us Up"). It was on the latter number that Greg played the piano, and it was to him that I sang and hopelessly felt the lyrics of this song.

The demo tape got Julie and I a few singing gigs at the air force base, with a band of studio musicians she could throw together for any occasion, from a funeral mass to a Quinceañera. Singing on base led to appearances at the enlisted's weddings, with Greg sometimes playing the piano for what became our go-to, most requested song—"Love Lift Us Up." Sometimes when we got to talking to customers, Julie or I would even shamelessly toss a demo tape in with the odd bacon double cheeseburger combo with extra *pee-kuls* and *oh-nyons* handed through the have-it-your-way Burger King drive-through window.

For Halloween that year, I talked Greg into reprising a costume that had just blown everyone away the year before at the University of Idaho, when I'd talked Roberta from the theatre department into doing full body make-up on me as a Bengal tiger, in nothing but a black speedo. That sounded really spectacular to Greg, who looked fantastic in a Speedo and wanted to be a leopard.

So we linked up with this black makeup artist named Benjamin Lamb, who had been recommended by Jeffery Forestell, the flamboyantly hilarious one of three gay BK managers who rotated their shifts between the restaurants located on Central, Menaul, and Juan Tabo Avenues. Jeffery had boasted on Benjamin's behalf that he was reported to have done Penny Marshall's makeup for a number of UNM theatrical productions pre-*Laverne & Shirley*. This turned out to be not at all true, since Penny studied math and psychology at UNM, got pregnant by a Lobo football player, had a daughter, and didn't get into acting until after college, when she moved to LA. What Benjamin did do was transform the two of us into jungle predators. Sure, unapologetically gay Ben was clumsy with his elbow and forearm and sometimes a knee, all of which regularly found themselves resting on, rubbing against, and trying really persistently to arouse the restless contents of each of our Speedos. Greg would deny it, but he was getting turned on. There was absolutely no physical way I could deny being turned on by a nearly naked Greg in spots, so I pounced out his dorm window onto the roof to cool off, just about the time the rest of me pounced out of the leg opening of my Speedo.

We had no problem getting into our characters, and very quickly it was all about the prowl. After the campus costume and zombie walk up Central Avenue, we made tracks downtown, and were particularly well-received at the annual Halloween blow-out fourplex party co-thrown by the same Jeffery who had hooked us up with our makeup artist.

Now I had personal, very extensive knowledge that Jeffery was gay and suspected the other three building residents would be as well, and so I briefed Greg on our way downtown, and his reaction was beautiful: along the lines of *what in the hell does that matter?* What neither of us knew in advance was that one of the other tenants, whose name was John Williams, was a career mortician, who had scattered really lifelike medical school cadavers in the kitchens, on the dining room tables, and even submerged in bathtubs. It was like walking into the bloody middle of Manson's Helter Skelter.

Hands were all over Greg and me, to the point that I became concerned about the integrity of our make-up. In one particularly crowded and poorly lit red stairwell, I took complete advantage of the group grope, and for the first time, right about half past ten, I quickly laid my hands on what I thought would be Greg's bulge—except someone else on the stairs had just hiked his Speedo down onto those speed skater thighs, and Greg was already out of his leopard cage. In the commotion to get his Speedo back up, and the unknown hands—actually much more known than he knew—off his very lovely genitals, it was sort of decided on the spot that we should probably get the hell out of there. We were expected later anyway at the mansion home of Julie Ruderstadt's parents, where she was house-sitting and had invited us for an all-ghouls sleepover. As we drove up into the hills above the flashing lights of the combined passenger airport and air force base, I couldn't stop thinking about the impressive body of evidence I'd just encountered in the four-plex stairwell. It was the same spotted body that sat one bucket seat away behind the Opel steering wheel. This got me worked right up into an animalistic frenzy that desperately left me wanting to mount said evidence, in a very Tiger-like way.

Bouncing around Julie's parent's driveway like Tigger, Greg and I role-played around a bit, jumping onto and off of the landscaping boulders, chasing each other around yucca and cacti, exorcising the last of our wild spirit animals before the inevitable, erasing shower that followed, where we would have to assist each other in getting that stubborn greasepaint off our bodies. Julie had to come outside to tell us to stop growling and roaring, as we might be disturbing the wealthy neighbors. We went inside, regaled our den mother with stories of the evening's exploits. Greg didn't mention the groping incident and *why in the hell did that matter*? Soon we were downstairs in the guest bathroom shower, steam clouding the mirrors and a luffa abrading away inhibitions. We lowered our Speedos a daring inch below our tan-lines, and, armed with soap and washcloths, we tenderly scrubbed the fierce jungle off each other. And then we went to bed—two twins separated by the largest nightstand I think I have ever seen.

Not even a month later, toward the end of that semester, Greg and I made plans to drive his Opel GT up through Utah and Idaho, to deposit me at my parent's house before he continued on to Oakridge to spend Christmas with his family. It was to be an epic road trip, made even more so by the announcement that Julie was going to reward me for helping her with her demo tape by giving me the pick of a litter of St. Bernard puppies that had just been born on a family friend's ranch north of the city. I had softly expressed the desire for a dog and my preference for that breed—which of course meant I would have to move out of the dormitories, and, opportunistically for Julie, into a pet-allowing rental house I could share with her for the next semester. Greg had wanted a ticket out of the dorms too, and was seriously considering the invitation to make it *Three's Company* with us. The deal was sealed for all of us by the roly-poly and irresistibly adorable St. Bernard puppy we would name "Kenji," after the drummer in *Earth, Wind & Fire*. Julie would get great looking and younger roommates who would split the rent and make her feel a fraction of her age. Greg would get out of the dorm into a place with a garage large enough for a dog house, his Opel, skis, bike, golf clubs, and running shoes. I would get a puppy and Greg, and would then spend the rest of my university days researching which of them was cuter.

There was just one problem, and it was becoming bigger by the day. Ever since the "Night of the Tiger" (and leopard), I had a case of blue balls that just wouldn't go away. At first, I sort of walked around gingerly, as though I was carrying a badge. When the swelling of the right nut made it difficult to walk normally at all, I began to worry, but of course couldn't really say anything about the delicate matter to anyone (though the idea of showing Greg my testicles for his opinion had its appeal). I decided I would wait until I could see my family doctor in Idaho.

After each of us wage earners had worked one last fast-food shift, we smuggled the St. Bernard bundle of adorableness from my empty dorm room (where she had peed on the floor and on the mattress, and pooped in a corner under my desk) into the already tightly packed Opel, placing her in a back-seat kennel that we nearly had to use a can opener to load. Greg and I checked our maps and headed out of ABQ on Interstate 25 at around dusk.

We managed to leave the Interstate as planned, to take a shortcut northwest on Highway 550, but then somehow, a few hours later, with a hungry, thirsty puppy whining in the back seat, we became confused under that pitch black desert sky, somewhere near Farmington. Without knowing it, we began heading due west, toward Shiprock. The massive, multi-spired shadow of the monolith of rock jutting out of the desert floor like the largest Mormon Temple I'd ever seen began to puzzle me the closer we got. It didn't feel like we were traveling in the right direction anymore. That's because we weren't—and we went even more off-course after turning left onto Highway 491. Without realizing it, we were heading back in the direction of Albuquerque, but it took us nearly all the way to Tohatchi to figure this out, and another six lost hours to get back on our preplanned northwesterly track.

After snow, ice, road detours, and St. Bernard farts that were anything but dainty, we were all most anxious to get out of that sports car by midnight of the second day, when we finally pulled into my parent's driveway. Before sunrise, after sleeping with Kenji tucked between us on the double bed of my teenage years, Greg continued on his way, so that he could reach his parent's place by dark and before the snow started to swirl.

Later that same morning, I sat in the waiting room of my childhood family doctor, waiting for a break in Dr. Rockwell's appointment schedule so he could get his ancient paws on my right testicle, which now dully ached and was about three times larger than normal. While this created an impressive crotch package in any pair of jeans or pants I wore, I was suddenly only comfortable in jogging pants—and in fact I had been wearing nothing but for about a month without clueing into the more sinister reason why. Even then, the bulge was hard to conceal. I was surprised and even a little disappointed that my sudden attributes had gotten me nowhere with Greg. But then Dr. Rockwell drew my blood, shone his flashlight through the thin wall of my scrotum, and scheduled me for emergency surgery the following afternoon. So far, Christmas was not bringing me great tidings of joy; instead, it left my swollen ball sack swaddled in worrisome gauze.

At no time in the next twenty-four hours did anyone inform me that there was a chance the surgeon would take my testicle. I was really so bewildered by the flurry of sudden medical activity that I didn't register what exactly the hastily scheduled operation would entail, though

I could assume there would be some draining of the fluid that had made me gargantuan and lopsided. At St. Joseph's in Lewiston, they put me under general anesthesia for the third time in my life. Where there is a first, there is often a second, and sometimes a third—but in my case, in which a testicle was but the tip of an iceberg, it would take a fourth, fifth, sixth, and seventh major surgery to correct my many ills, and make me either human or Frankenstein again (it was a tossup).

I underwent a partial inguinal orchiectomy. Don't bother with Google—I'll tell you straight out that I was half-castrated; made a candidate for the Future Eunuchs of America; robbed of the better half of my royal jewels; nad nabbed; de-nutted; emasculated; and, for a budding homosexual, cut off at the functional knees. I sobbed for the next forty-eight hours, waiting in a recovery bed for the results of more bloodwork, biopsies, and CT scans, and wondering how I would ever be able to hold my gay head (either one of them) high again. I absolutely had to know as soon as I could take the pain whether I was still able to get an erection and cum. I could and I did—though undoubtedly I stretched some sutures in the experiment. For the life of me I can't think of any masturbation fantasy I could have conjured in my newly handicapped reality to make any of this really fucked up situation seem sexy or hot.

And just when you knew it couldn't get any worse but was about to anyway, I was given the news that the results were cancer—and not just testicular, either. The scans were showing a large mass, maybe the size of a deflated Miami Dolphins football, behind my stomach and intestines, so large that had I not been obsessed those past weeks by the truly impressive immensity of my crotch, I might have noticed that my belly had started to protrude and ache, making room for a whole new tenant in the guts condominium.

I don't know how the things that happened next even came about, but I was released from St. Joe's in Lewiston to hobble home and reunite with a new puppy who barely knew me and a post-Christmas-scrooged-up-reality I could not have imagined or wished on my worst enemy. Curiously, my very first boyfriend—this real Venezuelan sexpot named Miguel, who I met in the summer of 1980 while staging the *Up with People* show at the University of Arizona campus in Tucson—showed up at my parent's house to cheer me up. His week-long visit was followed by Greg's. Even though Greg had been informed I wouldn't be returning to Albuquerque or university or to our *Three's Company* crashpad with him, he drove five hundred miles out of his way to visit me on his return. Miguel and I cried together. Greg and I cried together. Crying was the only thing that I could manage, but it didn't take me long to realize that it didn't fix or change anything, so I stopped sort of cold turkey and didn't cry again for a decade.

Within days of the new year—my own personal *1984*—I was scheduled to meet with an oncologist in Spokane, who would perform a series of tests to determine just how many toxic chemicals I could withstand in a single session. He proceeded to schedule a series of hospital appointments in which my body would be chemo-assaulted over the next four to five months—or for as long as it took, or as long as I could survive. I lost weight. I lost my hair. I lost my ability to fight off the stupidest of infections. I lost all of my lymph nodes in major surgery number four. I lost everything in this episode but my will.

And I survived to be cancer-free for the next thirty-two years, and by then who knows what my heart-hobbled body was harboring. I didn't die from cancer, and that is something.

Ashton Taylor, *Last Will and Testament*, page 9

> This isn't a particularly elegant request that I'm making of you, Greg, but if there was a single regret in this life I've lived, it's that I didn't honor your need to explore that question you asked me on the eve of your wedding day, when we were both just jabbering on because we couldn't fall asleep. You had asked me to stay the night with you on those camping foamies that your dad had positioned two feet apart on the rec room floor in the basement of your parent's house even though you knew I had already paid for a motel room in Corvallis. You asked me to stay because you wanted to talk.

I was there to sing that fucking "Love Lift Us Up" song at your wedding, at your request—one of six groomsmen to match Joanna's six bridesmaids at the talk-of-the-town event of the decade. I wouldn't let you examine your doubts; questions that were completely natural to have. You asked me, you'll remember, how I was absolutely positive that I was gay if I had never been with a woman— almost as though you were begging me to flip the question on you. In that moment, I panicked. I was afraid if I asked you that question back, it would provoke some clumsy attempt for you to experiment on the gay side, on those foamies, with me, so that you would know without a single doubt that you weren't gay, and so that you could be positively sure you were straight in time for you to say "I do."

I thought my job in that moment was to make sure you said "I do" and that you said it to Joanna, and not to me. Devastating and difficult for me as this certainly was, I didn't see any other way but to deny you this.

You've been married all this time, Greg—almost as long as I was cancer-free. You have a lovely wife who is the mother to your three beautiful children, and so you didn't need me to help you figure out the answer to your question. It seems you figured it out just fine on your own.

So now for the not-so-elegant request: I figure it isn't much more than a five-hour drive for you from your home in Prescott, Arizona, but I'd like you to drive me again to Shiprock, New Mexico. Let's see it during the daylight this time. Hike in, off the road, and leave this part of me behind—who knows, it may be my behind! But then you've seen that before, trying to scrub the Tiger make-up from where I purposely couldn't reach. You were so beautifully gullible and I was so simply hopeful that really, we didn't have a chance to hurt each other.

That, I cannot regret.

ANGELES

"HERE. PUT THESE ON."

"What are these?" I ask.

"They are 5D glasses. You've started the process of evolving to the only dimension we need here—"

"And that's the soul dimension!" Byron gleefully interrupts.

Scotty continues his explanation. "The glasses help preserve the other dimensions while you transition. Think of them as your training wheels," he explains.

"Plus they make us all look fabulous!" Miguel adds with a snap.

I put on the glasses and wow was Miguel ever right. Everyone, their outfits, hair, eyes, just everything looks so vivid and exactly the way I remembered. Since I was the one who had convened this meeting, I begin. "When I conjured up the distribution plan for my worldly ashes, all of you were still alive. All of you at one time had your own little black 35mm film canisters in the back of my file cabinet with your names on them. All of you were still living, breathing, walking proof of my ability to love. But one by one, you managed to get out of participating in my grand exit, and this is why I have called you together, today, here, on this particular cloud." For some reason, I think to add, though it is hardly important, "The Cumulus Meeting Room was already booked . . . some Auschwitz non-survivors reunion." I pause to sip a drink of rain from a glass and pitcher that had been pre-set at my lectern.

"They meet in the Cumulus every Tuesday and Thursday at this time," James adds. "The only meeting room big enough."

I can only nod, having so many things to learn. "So this is heaven? Ba dum bum!" I insert my own rimshot. "Seriously, though, my dearly beloved pre-deceased—Miguel, Byron, John, James, Mark, and Scotty—my gods, you look as fresh as a boy band!"

"You can give that up. Only Miguel and I can dance and none of us can sing," Byron strikes a pose, unable to help but sound bitter and bitchy.

"At least I can act," John argues.

"Please," Byron begs. "Surely you don't think we believe your guest-starring roles in such classics as *The Cockeyed Eagle*, *One Night Stands*, *Fetish*, *Hard Moves*, *Open House*, *Big Ones*, *Songs in the Key of Sex* and *Tattoo Love Boy* could actually be classified as acting, do you?"

"I won the Grabby Award for Best Newcummer in 1990, and followed that up with Best Supporting Actor for *Stranded* and Best Sex Scene in a Gay Video for *Fetish* in 1991."

"Well, three cheers for the porn actor, Jason Ross!" I intentionally use his stage name, trying to sound supportive and to defuse some of this bitchiness.

"Thank you, Ashton," John says, acknowledging his fan base. "Thirteen movie credits on my IMDb profile, so thank you all very fucking much for taking my career seriously."

Something Byron just said isn't sitting well with Miguel. "You jumped up and down inside a Fozzie Bear costume during *The Muppet Show on Tour*. This is not dancing, really," Miguel suggests in his Venezuelan accent, trying to bolster the argument that he was the only real dancer.

"Maybe it's just me, Byron," James suggests in his Oklahoma drawl, "but I would think that your black body appearing naked with that white ten-speed in *Inches Magazine* in July 1985 makes a claim like ten times more brag-worthy than dancing, Honey."

Laughing out loud, John the former porn star says "Ha! And I suppose ten is the operative number in that statement—and I'm not talking about the bike!"

"Hello! All of us knew you weren't talking about the bike." Mark sounds as though he might be growing impatient with the topic.

"Jealous, much?" Byron bites back at John with a lips puckered grin.

"Okay, but I have to ask—" Scotty, the gentlest of these souls in life and apparently after, moves closer to Byron. "With that, er—" he looks downward, "attribute" he gets his smiling mouth around the word "why did John get the porn career and not you?"

"Because John wanted it, is my guess," Byron answers. "And look who's calling the dancer black, Miguel—never mind that I am black. You seem to be hanging your dancing creds on a yearlong tour with that *Up with People* show; scarcely the big time in a dancer's world."

"Hey," I interrupted them. "Don't anyone go knocking the *Up with People* show. That's where Miguel and I met and tumbled into love when we were just eighteen years old. And that's where I became a dancer too."

"Not to mention where you met me," Mark reminds me.

"And tumbled into love all over again," I reassure Mark.

"Whoa, I wouldn't go that far," Miguel counters. "You were a singer, maybe, but choo were never a dancer, no' really. *Tambien*, I was nineteen when we met."

It was true, I knew. I had wanted to be a dancer, but didn't have the quick brain for memorization. Miguel is still reflecting. "My God, at nineteen years old, who could have guessed that my life was already more than half over? *Muerto* at thirty in 1991."

"Yeah, me too," Byron agrees. "Dead at thirty in 1992."

James clears his throat out of polite, southern habit—since, it turns out, there is no phlegm in Heaven. "Thirty-five in 94."

"Me—thirty-five in 95," Scotty offers.

"Just miraculous, when you think about it," admits John, "but I made it to forty-six in 2008."

"Forty-nine in 2010. Does that give me the ironic longevity award?" questions Mark.

"Well, no. No, it doesn't, Mark." I consider my own numbers. "Not quite fifty-four in 2016—and, I might add, the only one of us not to die of AIDS."

"Oh, right. You're dead. It's just that you don't seem or act dead cool like us—not yet, anyway." Mark tries to bend a dig into a compliment, but doesn't quite get there.

"Another way to look at this is that I had to survive all of you; live each day and all these years haunted by my memories of you and your love, and having to deal with the blunt reality that I was alive and the six of you weren't." I pause. "It was harder than it may seem; much harder. I struggled with it nearly every day."

"Remind me again," Miguel starts. "If you didn't die from *el SIDA*, then what?"

"Guilt, maybe—but technically from a ventricle malfunction brought on by aortic regurgitation that caused a backflow of blood into my left ventricle, essentially swamping my heart."

"Qué?" asks Miguel who understood nada of that explanation.

Scotty reaches a hand to my shoulder. "Your heart just drowned in too much love; the love you gave out and the love that came back to you like a tsunami—from me, from others."

"From all of us," the six say, in heaven-perfect unison that almost sounds boy band rehearsed and even *Up with People* cheesy.

"And now here you are—a flawless, gorgeous creature laying your testament before us." Byron adopts an authoritative voice that sounds like James Earl Jones.

"Without blemish or baggage or worldly motive," James adds.

Mark glides forward. "Gloriously naked, curious, innocent, and ready for your ascent."

"To party like a porn star with us, to be a hound in our pack, and to be the god you've become, for eternity," John bellows, holding open his chiseled arms as Miguel shakes his no-jointed hips like Shakira to punctuate the invitation. The Nimbus Meeting Room brightens, as if someone's concealed hand is on a dimmer switch. We begin to bathe in glorious luminescence.

"Ah, come on you guys. That's just the 5D glasses talking," I protest a little. "Can all be forgiven just like that? I'm an instant angel? I am pretty sure I hurt every one of you, let each of you down—and at each of your ends, I could not save you from dying."

"Listen to you," Byron snaps. "Nobody gets saved from dying, Jesus."

I was really sort of speaking nonsense. Of course I couldn't have saved them from dying, any more than I could have saved myself. "Do you remember the very first thing I said to each of you?"

James looks at each of the others, then speaks for the group. "I don't, but Gideon does."

"Who's Gideon?" I ask—and then, just like that, Gideon appears, hovering inches off the cloud like a really hot genie—like the love child you'd get with a protein semen smoothie of Mr. Clean and Disney's *Aladdin*, turkey basted high up into Penélope Cruz. I raise the glasses off my nose to see that Gideon is just really pleasant multi-colored beams of light, like the rest of us. I lower the glasses. They are so lightweight and comfortable, after all.

"I was the first," Miguel elbows his soul to the front of the cloud.

"Ashton Bernard Taylor," Gideon booms, not quite able to pull off the James Earl Jones voice. "You encountered Miguel Angel Paredes Lobo on 7 July, 1980, standing at a Tucson bus stop at the corner of Speedway and North Campbell streets. You said, '*Hola*. My name is Ashton. I come from Idaho. I can speak Spanish.'"

"*Guapo* you were, but you couldn't speak Spanish, no' really," Miguel revises. "Those weeks with you, man . . . wow . . . *muy intenso*."

"Remember when we read the different cast groupings and tour lists posted on the gymnasium windows in the middle of staging the *Up with People* show in Tucson?" I ask, knowing full well he remembers the moment too. "We learned that we had been placed into different tours and were going to be separated. I found it hard to breathe. I don't think I ever cried so much in my life."

"You were my *primero* love, Ashton," Miguel confirms.

"And you were my first boyfriend; my first heartbreak, too."

This is getting too sappy for Gideon, who was supposed to be giving a report in the Cumulus Room five minutes ago. He hurries things along. "Ten months later, on 24 May, 1981, you met Mark Tischler after one of your *Up with People* performances in an ice arena in West Orange, New Jersey. You said 'Hey, my name is Ashton. I'm from Idaho. Did you like the show?'"

"And I did," Mark confirmed. "I couldn't take my eyes off you for two hours as you sang and danced your way across that stage and into my heart. I had just been hired by the *Up with People* folks to manage logistics for the next season, and I was assigned to your tour for the last three weeks of it, so I could learn the ropes—when really, your rope was all that I wanted to master. Every moment I got to spend with you was fantastic and confusing. I didn't really know I was gay, but I was pretty sure I was falling in love with you."

"I don't know who took the photo of us that captured the moment at JFK airport when I was saying good-bye to you; probably that guy in my cast named Igor. There was so much pain and confusion and sorrow on our faces and at least for me, it was all about the love I was feeling for you."

"It was Igor who took the photo," Gideon adds impatiently. "You next met John McCutchan behind the front counter of a Burger King in Albuquerque, on the evening of 28 September 1983."

"I simply couldn't resist you in that brown, orange, and yellow polyester uniform top," John teases.

"Well we couldn't all be assistant managers who got to wear khaki slacks and a dress shirt and tie of their choice. I worked with what I had," I tell him.

"The first thing you said to John that night, as you were trying to work out a mustard stain on your shirt with some spit, was—and I quote—'I think the carbon monoxide coming through the drive-through window is making me sick.'"

"To which I said, 'Seriously?'" John testifies.

"And then my eyes locked on yours and yours on mine . . ."

"Now hold on. What happened next was I told you to get some fresh air while breaking down the salad bar."

"Right," I offer sarcastically. "And then we moved in together, broke up three months later, and got back together three more times over the next five years—each time I believed you had reformed and were ready to settle down."

"And each time, I disappointed you, because I just couldn't settle or stay still."

"Or keep from disappearing on me," I add.

"The problem was you were too sweet and I was too corrupt. We were as star-crossed as Lucifer and Archangel Michael—hopelessly attracted to each other but preordained by opposing magnetic forces to repel each other for eternity."

"Is that even true?" I look to Gideon, who is fidgeting with the golden binding of the ledger book he's brought along. He slowly wags his head from side to side.

"Well, you know what I mean." John flashes that slaying smile of his that of course now only works with the glasses. I do know what he means.

"Josephus Byron Burnside," Gideon says, rushing out the next bullet point on the gilt-edged page of his fat ledger book when he senses an opening. "On 1 November, 1985, during a travel stop with *The Muppet Show on Tour*, you spotted Ashton from the dance floor at the Albuquerque Social Club, where you were dancing off your post-performance adrenalin. You thought he was staring at you as if you were a circus sideshow, and in fact, you were about to become the first (but not the last) black man with whom Ashton Taylor would engage in sexual relations."

"Really?" Byron asked in a voice register approaching soprano. "Tell us, Gideon," he cross-examined, "How many black men were there, in total, after me?"

You don't blush in the afterlife, since you have no blood circulation, so I allowed the question.

"Five." Gideon doesn't have to do much calculation. "But you were the most endowed, Josephus."

"Thank you," Byron offers with finality, resting his case.

I don't have to do much calculation either. Nuts down, Byron had been the largest *down there* of all the men I had been with, regardless of skin color: black, brown, yellow, red, or white; hence that four-page photo spread with the ten-speed in *Inches Magazine* that hit the stands four months before we met.

"And Ashton, when you met Josephus coming off the dance floor, the first thing you said to him was, 'You can't possibly be from around here, or I would have flirted with you before tonight.'"

"That certainly sounds like one of my pickup lines," I admit freely.

"Well, it worked," Byron admits.

"That time, maybe," I say, "but I didn't have any clever lines when I surprised you by showing up at your hotel room in Kansas City two Muppet Show tour stops later."

"And it was me that ended up surprising you with the news that my ex-boyfriend was in my hotel room with me that night—that we were working through some things."

"Devastating," I remember out loud. "Between your rejection and John's rejections—*plural*—I was back to feeling pretty puny about myself."

"But these heartbreaks developed your character, expanded your emotional repertoire, and made you a bit more thick-skinned," says James, "which I eventually found intriguing."

"Intriguing?" I probe.

"Well, yes. I was always attracted to mystery—mostly maintaining a sense of mystery about myself to others. This is perhaps minor, but it's noteworthy here, and Gideon is likely not going to bring it up: I am the only one of us you didn't sleep with."

"That's true. We did not have sex." I know the reason why, and realize that with the revealing 5-D glasses and omnipotence draped all about this place, everyone else knows why too. But James speaks the words.

"Because I had AIDS."

"Because WE had AIDS," everyone echoes.

"I was scared."

"And you think we weren't?" James exclaims more than asks. "But I was still one tainted-blooded, horned-up man, and I wouldn't have been able to stop you if you had been brave enough to start something."

"But I wasn't brave enough—not nearly as brave as any of you."

"You couldn't save us," Scott says bluntly, "despite your cute and acute Messiah-God-Savior complex." It is then that I realize that Scott has taken off his glasses.

"Your loss, though," James smiles that crooked smile of his, and tosses a mop's worth of blond hair back from his eyes and forehead. "You only thought Byron had the biggest who-haw." He accentuates his angel bulge by smoothing his hands over the glistening satin that strains to contain it. I adjust the glasses on my nose, and lo and behold and knock-me-over-hallelujah, the shaft of rainbow-colored light that doesn't arch quite like a rainbow but is emanating from his root chakra as he levitates and arches his back, compels me backward a step.

"Well, would you look at that!" I exclaim, as the others laugh. Nobody comes forward to dispute the winner. Gideon steps behind a turntable and begins to tear a club anthem.

"Work it, Papi!" Miguel encourages. "Work it!"

While the others dance and gyrate around the celebrated James, I move closer to Scotty. "You don't wear the 5-D glasses."

"I find you all to be so much more beautiful without them," he said, in that soft voice that calms me now as it soothed me then.

I remove the glasses for just a moment and see his point—or make that James' point, now flopping to a disco beat a few feet away. Because I had grieved the loss of each of these people individually but also as a collective and so intensely, I still need the glasses to take them all in as I remembered them, and to see for myself once again why I had fallen in love with each of them. In this, Gideon is indispensable, providing facts where most of us could admit that the gymnastics of memory might have gotten the best of us.

"You two first spoke by telephone on July 18, 1992," Gideon addresses the two of us. "Ash had phoned the San Antonio AIDS Coalition for assistance with tracking down Byron's cremains."

"I remember how your New Jersey way of talking was bumping up against your adopted Texas mannerisms and the mash-up was so adorable it had me inventing ways to stay on the telephone with you longer."

"Ashton, the first thing you said to Scott—and you were in and out of crying when you tackled this long-winded introduction—the first time you had actually cried in about a decade. You said, 'I'm here in San Antonio in this enclosed carport of an apartment of a former lover—well, boyfriend actually, who died last week. His name is—fuck—his name was Byron Josephus Burnside, and as far as I know he didn't have any family to uh, take care of this for him so I'm doing what I can, you know, to pack up his things and take care of the bills. I say he had no family, but there was this Aunt Pookie he talked about in . . . I don't know . . . Memphis, maybe? But I can't find a phone number. Anyway, I also need to track down his body, which I think and hope by now must be ashes in a box somewhere.'"

"You were one beautiful mess, Dear Heart, and that came across loud and clear on the phone," Scotty gushes. "In those years, working the AIDS Help Line, I handled dozens of phone calls just like yours every single day—nearly every one of them with sobbing or sniffling on the other end—and I had never before or after felt more helpless, but there I was running a Help Line. It was all I could do to hold myself back and not get personally involved each and every time."

"But you did help," Byron says, overhearing us from the makeshift dance floor. He stops dancing and joins us. "You found my ashes at the unofficial San Antonio AIDS funeral home out on Culebra Road, since most other mortuaries refused the AIDS dead. And for the record, we all got cremated because no official wanted any residual AIDS virus to survive what we couldn't."

"And you did get personally involved," I remind him. "You went beyond your call of duty and helped galvanize for me my resolve to become more actively combative in our common fight against AIDS. I went back to Denver where I had been living, coping with the crisis from the sidelines. I quit my hotel management job to become the Director of Volunteers at the Colorado AIDS Project, and I worked the next two years in one of the most difficult occupations of my life . . . and through your coaching and your letters and our telephone calls, I started to fall in love with you—my comrade in arms with a really nice butt and legs too, battling together on the same front line, but—" I trail off.

"I hadn't told you I had AIDS," Scott completes the sentence.

"You thought I already knew."

"And I thought," Scotty pauses, "that you were infected too. You'd just scattered the ashes of your lover."

"Well technically Byron was a lover from years earlier, but I never mentioned that, I guess."

"No," Scotty shakes his head. "I wouldn't have had sex with you in Denver—especially the unsafe sex we had, when I went up there for that caregiver's conference—if I didn't think you were already infected."

I don't tell him that I slept with him on purpose, knowing he had AIDS, and I don't tell him that I had quite secretly hoped he would be the one to infect me, partly so that we could stay together in love and become closer through tragedy, and partly so that I could shed the anxiety and guilt from all the waiting and blood testing, and just become another one of the walking infected like everybody else I knew and cared deeply about. The PWAs (Persons with AIDS) were having sex, with each other, for crying out loud! I missed sex. I wanted in. It seemed every gay man I had ever loved, including Scotty, was testing positive, had died, was dying, or would shortly be dying from it, but somehow I didn't have it, yet. In the worst years of the early 90s, after losing Miguel and Byron, I did not want to be left behind in a world without them; without the hundreds of thousands and even millions who would eventually comprise the dead.

I don't tell Scotty any of this, like I never admitted my fear and resignation about getting AIDS to anyone. Instead, I stick with telling the story of Byron's wishes, as they truly inspired me to come up with a pretty damn good detailed plan of my own—the execution of which is now well underway.

"So yeah," I continue. "I returned to San Antonio not even four weeks later, and I tracked down and then drove Byron's ashes in a rental car down to Corpus Christi." I turn to Byron "because you had left instructions to be scattered on the surface of the sea at sundown, with Wagner's *Tannhauser Overture* playing in the background."

Byron's head begins to nod. "I had left you a Wagner cassette tape and instructions on my kitchen table—well, not *you*, precisely, because I didn't know who was going to end up taking care of my mess, to be honest. You had just been to San Antonio three weeks earlier when the doctors, you, and I all thought I must have been nearing the very end. I didn't know if you'd be brave enough to return to San Antonio a second time, especially after I spent our whole time together begging you to smother me with a pillow to the face to get it the hell over with."

"Yes. *Tannhauser* on one side and *The Flying Dutchman* on the other." I don't acknowledge that Byron pleaded with me to suffocate him or to raise the level of morphine he was not getting in his IV drip, and I try to ignore any reference to my lack of bravery.

"So I get to Corpus Christie," I go on. "I find a place outside the city limits where I can get the car right down to the beach. I unseatbelt the square cardboard box in the passenger seat, I pop in the cassette and set the car radio volume as high as it goes. I start a procession toward the surf, tears already gushing. And then everything just starts going wrong. I was a West Coaster by that point, so had fully expected the sun to be setting in the water, but there it was going down behind me. By the time I reached the sea, I couldn't hear *Tannhauser*, and it was really breezy. Of course, I didn't yet have any experience with cremains and I hadn't reconciled how Byron could have possibly fit inside the box I was carrying. I opened the flaps to find a thick, clear plastic liner inside. I unfolded the plastic, looked at the ashes, and then looked down at the little waves that were coming on shore, and I realized Byron didn't want to be on shore." I turn to Byron. "You wanted to be scattered so you'd drift out to sea to mix with the oceans, right?"

He nods. "You see, I had spent the last years of my professional dancing career performing on Royal Caribbean cruises. I loved the oceans."

"So then I decided I needed to get into the water beyond the surf break," I explain. "I kicked off my shoes, stripped down to my underwear, and waded until I was about waist deep in the Gulf of Mexico."

"Then the breeze changed directions," Gideon is trying to speed up my story because he has other cloud groups expecting him. "And you could suddenly hear the music blasting from the door speakers of the rental car as though you had ear phones on your head . . ."

"And I started sprinkling the contents of the box onto the surface of the water, but between the breeze, my tears, and getting splashed wading into the sea, half of Byron's ashes were sticking to me—to my stomach and chest and arms and face. Ashes clung to me like Byron wasn't letting go."

"You didn't know whether to laugh or freak right out," Byron exclaims with a giggle.

"The last of the box emptied," I continue the story. "I remember I removed the plastic liner and set the box adrift on the sea's surface. I filled the plastic bag with seawater, flushing it out again to mix some of the last traces of my one-time lover with this watery grave he had chosen. Then I faced my body into the sunset and, as if I were being baptized in the River Jordon, I slowly fell backward into the water, until I was completely under it—one with Byron, and one with the sea. For that moment, I was at peace with the reality that I had been selected to survive this; all of this, and *you*."

I look around at them, then defiantly take off my 5-D glasses and hand them to Gideon. I put my arms around the brilliant shafts of light that would have been Scotty's and Byron's shoulders, and say, "I am one with you all again, and you have never looked more beautiful to me."

V'RONICA

JUST WHEN I WOULD HAVE AFFIXED A BRONZE STAR TO THE
report card of his recovery, Rich has had another setback. My Limping
Rabbit is slumped, sobbing in a seated position with his back against
the pullout freezer door of the refrigerator. He's just come across a
Ziplock bag with the yellowed plaster molds of my upper and lower
teeth, from when I was fitted for a night guard to stop my snoring,
and my teeth grinding while I slept. I had obviously forgotten them
under the blueberries and precooked shrimp, in the freezer where the
dentist had instructed me to store them a few months, just in case
the guard didn't fit properly. Well, now nothing fits properly, but the
good news is we've fixed the snoring and grinding—forever. With the
molded teeth out of the bag and a death grip on the plaster remnants
of my former smile clenched in his fist, Rich Dreadfulwater struggles
still, almost five months on.

The phone rings, and he lets it. It seems there is a ridiculous
number of rings before the answering machine does its thing, rescuing
him from having to do his.

"Hello, Rich. It's Carole Taylor phoning from my cell phone. Ash's
father and I are on our way to the Oregon Coast now. I have a kite
and my instructions for when we get to the Heceta Head Lighthouse,
so will do my best to honor Ashton's wishes." She pauses. "Oh, we're

likely going to take the 405 south to avoid Seattle traffic, so I don't think we'll have the chance to stop in for a visit this trip. We do hope you are well. Please stay in touch. Okay. Bye for now."

He can't blame them for not knowing how to deal with him. He doesn't know how to deal with himself. His iPhone sounds next, which pulls him up and off the floor. He heads toward his desk, placing the set of molded teeth on top of the Nez Perce mat next to the octagonal Carr's Biscuit tin that still holds the measurable balance of my cremains that hadn't fit inside the diamond, the judge's gavel, or the eighteen film canisters that he's dispatched around the planet.

He sees on his phone that it is his sister V'ronica calling.

"Shit!" he says out loud, only to have the sound of his voice snap back at him in the empty space atop Queen Anne Hill that had become his personal grief-a-torium. While Rich is debating in his head whether or not to answer his sister's call, the sun that streams in from the living and dining room windows reveals that nobody has dusted the place in—he almost thinks he doesn't know how long, but catches himself. I had been in charge of all the flat surfaces, so *that* is exactly how long. He lifts the phone to his face. "Well, hello there, Sis." He places her on speaker phone.

"What the frick is up with you, bro? You haven't called in weeks. Your's and Ash's Facebook pages are as boring as Aunt Vida's cooking—and I know that better than anyone, since our father has been on his hunger strike."

"Hunger strike? What's the cause now?" Rich grabs a pair of boxer briefs from the back of his desk chair and begins to dust his desk, starting at ground zero around the Nez Perce mat. Maybe a long catch-up chat with his sister is what the flat surfaces need right now, he thinks, throwing himself into the sorely neglected chore.

"He says he won't eat until the wild salmon return to the reaches of Mission Creek around Slickpoo."

Laughing at the futility in that demonstration, Rich says, "We should just live capture some in a bucket at the hatchery, and move them into pools, then take him there for a picnic feast—then he'd eat."

"Oh, he's eating—behind our backs, but he's eating. It's really a cooking strike, mostly because it's too hot in our kitchen."

"Yeah, I figured." He moves toward the bookshelves that I had knick-knacked out with Native stuff from our travels—things from conferences Rich attended, or conferences at which he gave the keynote. He needs to pick the items up to dust under them, but instead he navigates circles around everything; such a novice. "Say, how did the rummage sale work out for you?"

"A hundred and seventy bucks." She doesn't want to talk about the rummage sale. "So is Ash around? I was really phoning for him. I've left like a thousand messages and he doesn't call me back." Rich stops dusting, lowers the underwear and slumps back down to the floor at the base of the bookcase.

"V'ronica—I . . ."

"No excuses. I want to talk to him," she insists.

"V'ronica, so do I." He can't disguise that he's started crying, or that he hasn't stopped crying for more than an hour in the past five months.

"What?" her voice climbs.

"There was an accident. No. Wait. That's not the right word. It wasn't an accident."

"Oh my god!"

"He, uh . . . well, it was his heart, V'ronica. Part of his heart sort of exploded. We couldn't get him to the hospital in time to, uh, fuck, sorry, uh, save him. He's gone from us. He's been gone from us for five months." Rich is reduced to blubbering now. There is silence on the speaker phone. He scoots back to the desk on his butt to pick it up. "V'ronica?—"

"I'm here. Jesus, Limp Rabbit. Jesus Christ!"

"I wanted to tell you. I was going to tell you in a few weeks when I come home to see you at the powwow."

"You're coming then?" she almost seems to perk up since that is the reason she had been calling for me—to put pressure on her brother to climb off his fancy, big city lawyer horse to visit them, reconnect with where he came from. Then instantly she gets back to processing what her brother just told her. "You're coming alone," she states.

"I am alone," Rich confirms for both of them, scanning the

apartment for any sign to the contrary. "I am trying really hard to come to terms with this. But look, do me this favor and do not tell Dad right now. Is that clear, Ron? The last thing I need is Chief Dreadfulwater to find a reason to think that I'm a free agent with no emotional ties to Seattle now. I just don't need his special brand of pressure; you know what I mean? He'll want me home to head up the tribe's legal council and start acting like the new chief in waiting. I just don't need this. Not now."

There is another pause on the phone, which gets Rich thinking he might be talking way ahead of his sister's readiness to move on from the news he has just delivered. He's had a five-month head start on her, though he sees this as no advantage. Then she breaks her silence to say this:

"How can you be in that apartment without Ash? How do you even go on? He was the only cool thing about you."

"Thanks."

"I mean, through him and this love he has." She stops cold in the middle of the sentence. "Oh my God. Had! Through this love he had for you, you became actually pretty awesome to be around. Ever since I was little kid, the two of you have always been together, and this is what I liked most about my family." She speaks freely, with wisdom her older brother will always think is beyond her years. She handled the death of their mother with this same even keel. Her ability to receive information as fact, process what has occurred, accept it as irreversible, and then to move on to a revised reality without dramatic smothering, astounded Rich when their mother was killed. He's picking up from his sister now that they should both be approaching this loss the same but how can he? This is so not the same.

Rich is searching for the strength to stand up to face the responsibility of being an older brother and answer this sudden challenge to survive the un-survivable. He takes a long breath in through his nose, tickling his new piercing as he finds his strength. "Almost twenty years, Ashton and I were together, and that gets to win over these hundred and forty something days we have been apart." Limping Rabbit snatches the underwear from the floor and returns to his dusting, defiantly. "Yes, V'ronica. I am coming to your powwow in three weeks, but you know what? I won't be coming alone. I'm bringing home part of what's left of Ash with me, and I am going to need your help in finding the right special place for him. We need to scatter his ashes and commit his bones to the earth and assist him on his journey to the Spirit World."

"I could write him a rap," she offers, confidently. I can rap and drum him to the Spirit World—make sure he gets there with good rhythm."

"That sounds perfect. Okay, sis. I have to start cleaning my house. I've let it go since . . . Let's just admit I wasn't the cleaner here. I'll see you in a couple weeks—and remember, not a word to Dad."

"September 17, Limp Rabbit. Write it down. No courts, no trials, no clients, no excuses. You have to be there."

"You're right about that. I have to be there. I am proud of you and I love you. Now you're the only cool thing about me, so don't go screwing that up, you hear?"

"For sure. You got that right!"

The call disconnects. Rich throws open all the windows that open, and the Old Seattle High School condo on the top floor is filled with sea breeze, the breath of the living planet. He takes it in and lets it out. He does this again and then again. He gets to keep doing this, and the look on his face tells me he has just realized how very lucky he is.

THE HOUSE CLEANING THAT follows is thorough and revealing. Returning first to the bookshelf to continue dusting, Rich pauses to pick up the bound copy of his thesis: *A Modern Translation of Nez Perce Oral Traditions*. I've left him a bookmark there—like the teeth in the freezer, I had not remembered until this moment. The bookmark was a note in my handwriting, morosely scribbled on a sheet torn from a John L. Scott Realty notepad that had been delivered with our junk mail. It marked his translation of the Nez Perce fable of how Coyote lost his penis. Limping Rabbit reads the note from me out loud:

> Hey, wouldn't this be cool? You'll argue—cause that's what you do—but I am going to the Spirit World first, and I want you to somehow incorporate me into a Nez Perce ritual for the Dead. I'm not naïve. Every tribe has gotta have one. Then I want you to take the last of my ashes to the place—you know, where Coyote had his penis hacked off. When you get there, tell me again the Nez Perce story of how Coyote's penis becomes a dam. I just love that one! Release the last of me there and find yourself again in the traditions of your people.

PATTI

RICH IS MANIPULATING SMOKED SALMON CARPACCIO ONTO his fork with a knife, but the capers keep rolling away. He is sitting in a padded circle booth that's lost most of its stuffing over the decades, next to Patti McCaleb, my literary agent, who is in Seattle from LA, attending a booksellers' show. She sips rosé from her glass.

"I was only his agent, Rich. I was not his confessor."

Talking around a glob of crème cheese too big to swallow whole, he says, "But he might have given you some idea of whether or not he felt I neglected him in the last months. Maybe?"

"Look, Honey. Ash and I talked. Sometimes we talked about his books or his writing. Sometimes we talked about home life—mine and his . . . yours."

Rich kept chewing, sucking the cheese ball into a more manageable size, pointing with his fork. "Go on."

Sipping rosé more frequently now, she shortcuts the conversation. "He was madly in love with you. That's what you want to hear, isn't it?"

Rich nods, reveals a smile.

"He sometimes didn't think you took him seriously enough—not about his writing so much but more about his health issues and his obsession with dying young." She squints a question mark with her face just in case her honesty has cut too deeply.

Rich pounds a fist onto the table. "I knew it!" His voice is loud, and it surprises them both. The waiter strolls up to their booth with both hands clasped behind his back.

"Is everything to your satisfaction?" he asks. Both Rich and Patti nod, giving somewhat insincere smiles.

Whispering loudly now, Rich continues. "He thought I didn't take him seriously? Seriously! Surely you knew Ash was the original hypochondriac. Pharmaceutical companies would tail him, you know, observe his behaviors, listen in as he told absolutely anyone within earshot of his ailments—and the next thing you knew, there was some three-minute, side-effect-laden infomercial about a pill fabricated in a lab that could take care of that. The stuff Ash was coming up with was . . . was better than any of the manufactured psychoses they've invented in this century. Social Anxiety Disorder? Come on! *Ash* invented that! Restless Leg Syndrome?" The lawyer presented his evidence. "Lactose Intolerance? Celiac Disease? Erectile Dysfunction? Adult Attention Deficit Disorder? Irritable Bowel Syndrome? Uh, Post-Traumatic Stress Disorder? All brought to you by the great, late, and altogether paranoid Ashton Taylor. Didn't take him seriously? You tell me."

Patti conceals the raising corner of her mouth behind her wine glass. "My, my. We are just a little bit touchy about this, aren't we?"

"And with good reason." Rich washes down the last bite drinking half the glass in front of him. "You see, Ash had started snoring in the months before he, well—before he, uh, stopped snoring, shall I say? He'd never snored before in his life—not even when he had a head cold. I thought he had invented another way to get my attention—that is, until he had a specialist confirm his sleep apnea."

"His what?"

"Sleep apnea. It's more common than you'd think, in men over forty, anyway. The soft tissue in the back of the throat collapses or closes during sleep and sometimes the brain forgets to signal the muscles to open the passage back up to breathe. Sometimes, breathing stops for up to a minute, but usually the brain kicks in." He takes one final bite of carpaccio and nudges the plate away. Patti is holding her wine glass in front of her mouth but not drinking from it. "Yeah, so

Ash talks me into playing night watchman, and a couple times in the beginning, I was side-poking him every other night or so to get him to breathe again. I'll admit it was scary at first. Of course I didn't want to lose him. But when the snoring started and I began losing sleep, and especially when that took its toll at a trial in the courtroom the next day, well, I decided to take the snoring as a good sign; a sign I could usually hear all the way from the living room, with a pillow over my head, by the way."

"So what happened, in the end? I never got the full story."

There is a real pause; a long one, and not just because Rich is still chewing. He pours more rosé for both of them. "Neither of us knew it, but the apnea was masking these mini aneurysms his heart had started having—you know, like tremors before the big one." A tear appears at the edge of his eye. "When the big one came, I was on the sofa in the living room, with my head under a pillow." Now his nose has started running, and he begins to break down. Patti sets her wine glass down and scoots closer to put an arm around him.

"You couldn't have known, Rich. You couldn't have known."

"Oh yes, I could. If I took Ash more seriously, I could have."

Patti holds on, tears now testing her mascara. She starts quaking right along with him until his breakdown subsides. He eventually reaches inside his blazer pocket and sets a film canister on the table, pushing it toward her.

"Is this—?" she starts to ask.

"It is." Rich says, involuntarily sucking in two rapid breaths. Patti puts her trembling hands around the canister. "You know what to do, right?"

"Yes, I know," she replies. "Can you believe that after five months and shopping in three states, I still haven't found the right dress? Anyway, I have another few weeks to go before the anniversary of Rudolph Valentino's death on August 23. Don't you worry." She pats his hands. "I'll carry out his instructions to the letter."

"Ash knew you would." He wipes his nose with the back of his hand. "He knew we all would."

Raising her wine glass to toast, she says, "To Ash, and to his third novel, getting published this Fall, now posthumously." Rich taps her glass with his, and then taps the film canister.

"Just like he probably planned it—you know—for dramatic impact."

Patti smiles uneasily, and then taps the plastic canister with her glass too.

STEPHEN

RICH'S HAND HOVERS ANOTHER BLACK PUSHPIN LIKE A helicopter over the one-dimensional terrain of the map, zeroing in on the Tuscan part of Italy, north of Rome and southwest of Florence, pushing it through the canvas to mark the town of Siena. He fastens a pencil eraser to the back of the map, holding the pin in its place. He doesn't know this Stephen fellow that I had traveled to Europe with in the early 90s, because it was before we got together—but Rich cares that I cared about these memories and about this man, so he's relieved to get postcard confirmation that another canister has found its mark. There are a lot of missing details not included in the one sentence scribbled on the postcard with an image of the *Palio di Siena* on the front, but Rich is getting used to tending this new, barren garden of missing information as he wanders a cobbled path of unanswered questions.

Obviously, I am not able to turn back the clock. But if I could, here's what Rich missed, and exactly what transpired eight days ago in Sienna—information the postcard mailed by Stephen does not convey:

A pair of short-toed eagles circle high above the fortressed hilltop town on a sun-bleached afternoon as the taxi carrying Stephen Christopher winds through the Tuscan hills on a back road from Monteriggioni. From the eagle's vantage point, which incidentally is also mine, the car approaches the main gate of the walled city, leaving behind a plume of dust longer than the train that had brought the late, middle-aged, blue-eyed Canadian from Florence that morning.

The son of British immigrants to Ottawa, Stephen had gone west to revolutionize vegetarian cuisine in the late 80s, and was running the kitchen at a social enterprise restaurant called Picasso Café when I met him in Vancouver in the early 90s. My old friend David Nummy was visiting me in Seattle from his latest State Department post in Budapest when I suggested we go cross-border shopping for a couple Royal Canadian Mounties one weekend; mine was going to be red-headed and green-eyed and at least six feet—make that 1.8 meters—tall. I don't remember what was on David's shopping list but I could presume it was still me, since he always seemed to pay a visit anytime he caught news on the wire that I might be single again.

In a bar off Granville Street called The Underground (which wasn't), I'd spotted the nicely bicepted Stephen in a tank top, half-sitting, half-posing on a barstool next to the DJ at the edge of the dance floor. His head was keeping beat with the song that was sending sonic booms out of the speakers. He had rhythm, so I asked if he danced. He didn't. He asked if I was American. I answered that I was. Either this, or the hemp-button vest I was wearing without a shirt (the vest had thematic elements of the USA flag mis-stitched together in a crazy quilt pattern) instantly turned him off. At about that moment, someone else who wasn't David and who wasn't my Mountie asked me to dance, so I pivoted away to face new music.

As it got closer to two in the morning, and all those picky Canucks had to become less so if any of us was to have a chance of getting laid before sunrise, I realized that I was suddenly being vied for by several of them, though not one could be considered Mountie material. One of these was Stephen, who had decided he should probably try getting off on a different foot with me, or he wasn't going to get off at all. "I normally don't care for beards," he told me. (For the only time in my adult life, I had one.)

He had climbed off his stool perch and crossed the dance floor to tell me that. I could have responded, "And I normally don't care for dwarfs," since he wasn't a shot glass taller than five foot. But I didn't. I went home with him instead.

Ashton Taylor, *Last Will and Testament*, page 10

Dear Stephen: So that year-long, cross-border fling you and I had in 1994-95 technically qualifies you as my last boyfriend before I met my husband, Rich. You and I had a wonderful week in Siena once. I will say that memory has stuck with me much longer than you ever did. That's okay, though. I don't blame you, anymore. I'm dead! You win.

Look, I assume you're still going to Spain and maybe Italy once a year, because you're the original Anglo-Saxon creature of habit, and too chicken to visit anyplace new— so next time you're in Rome or Florence, would you mind taking this canister of my remains to the top of the Torre del Mangia above the Palazzo Publico in Siena? And I mean to the very top. Say, Stephen? Do you still suffer from vertigo, I wonder? This could very well be my payback.

When you get to the top, find a chink in the stone wall, mix some of your spit with my ash, and with one of your credit cards, apply my bio-mortar to fill the hole or crack. This way, I can perch, sun-cured, high above the Piazza del Campo in this ancient Tuscan Hill town forever. Thanks for the memory, Stephen. And thanks for your spit, I suppose, now, and then.

The driver is finding it difficult to deploy a clutch on these steep streets. The taxi rolls to a lurching stop, and idles while the payment is transacted. Soon Stephen gets out, hoisting onto his shoulders a small backpack with a Canadian flag patch sewn visibly but crookedly on the top flap. He walks down Via Salicotto, passing under a stone arch between two ancient buildings and down some stone stairs. Everything is stone, including Stephen's stupid, stubborn heart. He suffers from early-curmudgeon syndrome, never smiles, barely speaks, deplores the extroverted—usually American. Steps later, this Canadian emerges into the remarkable and expansive *Piazza del Campo*. It's mid-afternoon, and the shadow of the 290-foot-tall bell tower throws itself across the salmon-colored stones of the scallop-shaped plaza, like a bridge to the other side. Stephen's head tilts to evaluate the tower looming before him. There is a priceless look of panic on his etched face as he begins to breathe, quick and shallow. He is obviously still affected by heights, but determined to grant this final wish in time to catch a cab back to Monteriggioni for the 5 p.m. train back to Firenzi—so he strides toward the tower, jutting out of the Cappella di Piazza. Inside, he pays the fee, which the cheapskate doesn't remember paying the last time. He proceeds to a locker room where he has to pay another euro to stash his backpack, since only cameras are allowed inside the tower now. He tucks the film canister in his waistband, where there is lots of room, since this errand comes at the end of his Spanish holiday, during which he completed, in thirty-two days, the 500 mile walking journey along the famed Camino Santiago de Campostela. Finally, nine euros lighter, he enters the stone staircase that wraps around the inside wall of the Torre for the next 150 vertical feet. He is self-coaching now while the occasional and overweight tourist—likely American or German—squeezes past him on their way down the stairs.

"I can do this," he says out loud, over and over, to keep from hyperventilating. "This tower has stood for seven centuries. I can do this, for Ash. I would *only* do this for Ash. Do you hear that, Ash? I have a feeling you're watching me now, and having one holy giggle, if they allow closed circuit where you are." There is sweat on his flushed face and on the back of his neck as he continues climbing. "I owe you this, I suppose, if this is what you want. I didn't treat you the best, and I took you for granted. The greatest favor I could have done for you was to leave you when I did. At least I knew that much."

Stephen emerges from the closed stairwell onto a day-lit resting platform halfway up. He sees his elevation for the first time, and panics. "Holy fuck!" Grabbing the stone wall, breathing rapidly through his panting mouth, he closes his eyes. "I can do this. I can do this." He continues climbing. "God, my mouth is so dry all of a sudden. I don't know if I can come up with the spit it's going to take to make your cement. I guess I could use sweat." He takes two stairs and stops. "I can do this." And he takes two more steps.

A stair-descending, southern-speaking American gives him a few rapid pats on the shoulder. "You're almost to the top, pardner," he encourages, exuding his American superiority from every gland.

"Fuck right off," Stephen whispers to himself, his legs having turned to lead and each step requiring a colossal coax. Nine more stairs, and Stephen steps from the staircase onto the wooden floor at the bell level. Oh the tricks Stephen's brain and stomach are playing on him in this moment. He looks across the ten-by-ten foot landing toward the edge, where some old wood timbers form a railing to keep tourists from falling out of the stone-framed openings in the wall. He doubles over and grasps his legs above the knee.

To the very top of Torre del Mangia, I try coaching him from the Beyond.

Just then, Stephen slowly pans his head upward to see that he has another fifty or so stairs to go before he is above the bell and at the top of the Torre del Mangia.

"I can do this!" he blurts out. He straightens his posture just as the bells begin to toll 3 p.m. He hits the deck in panic, and lays face-down on the wooden floorboards. They vibrate with each clang of the bells, whose swinging seems to be causing the whole tower to sway. After the last bell is silenced, Stephen still lays there, motionless. He speaks loudly into his arms, his voice muffled.

"I cannot do this. I cannot do this!" He begins fumbling for the film canister in his waistband, to discover it has dropped into his underwear and lodged behind one of his nuts. He's fishing it out of his pants, whole fist in, while a couple of nearby parents and their young daughter look on with an edgy tourist shock. He liberates the container and slowly works himself to his knees and hands. The young girl, excited to peer over the edge, breaks from her mother's hand and rushes toward the wooden railing. Stephen is sure she is going to break through the flimsy railing and so buries his head in his arms. When she gets to the railed edge, she cuts loose an exhilarated scream that trails off and sounds to Stephen as though she is surely falling. The mother adds her own scream to the audio madness. This is instantly followed by the most primal of groans from Stephen, as his head arches up to vomit—ejecting the morning's deep fried eggs and croissant. His nerves have just decided to fuck it.

Oh god! Oh god! This was not in my instructions, but Stephen is improvising by scooping the vomit into the open canister with his Mastercard.

The young girl spins around to stare at the vomiting man next to the cast iron bells and has an impulse reaction—she begins to vomit over the railing. There is discernable Italian cussing from the plaza 150 feet below. Meanwhile, Stephen uses a toothpick he finds on the ground next to him to mix his vomit into the ash until he has a cement-like paste. He crawls toward the stairwell in search of a bloody chink. The mother hurries her daughter into the stairwell, thinking the sick man is after them—or worse, that he wants them to help him. Stephen feels his way around the stone wall like a blind man. With his fingers, he finds a gap between two ancient stones, and, grimacing at the smell of his own vomit, he plasters the cement into the crack, smoothing it into place.

I said SPIT, I want to tell him. *SPIT!*

KRISTA & CAROLE

A BABY BLUE MASERATI GRANCABRIO WITH ITS TOP DOWN IS driving off a Washington State Ferry and up the steep ramp at low tide. The female driver has long, wavy blond hair with suspect roots; it is getting tussled in the wind as she picks up speed. This is my sister, navigating her fiftieth birthday sports car through the small island town of Orcas.

Ashton Taylor, *Last Will and Testament*, page 11

My dear sista-Krista. I don't know how you'll manage this mission of mine, given your high society calendar as a plastic-surgeon's wife and all, but perhaps between hospital foundation meetings and your next tuck or Botox injection, you can whip up to the San Juan Islands and do me this one last favor. Now, you probably won't remember, thanks to your decades of regression therapy, but our parents took us camping once at Moran State Park. Horrifying as it will sound to you now, we were, for at least forty-eight hours, exposed to Nature; some of us more than others, as you would know if you could remember your interrupted streaking incident down to the lake and back. How were we to know you would be intercepted, in all your glory, by Our Father Who Art Always in Fatigues blending into the background?

Krista's face reveals a smirk that almost but not quite turns to a grin as she tries for her blessed life to remember anything about the last time she was here. She raises her sunglasses to the top of her head to wipe a tear from her eye. Not to worry, though. It is caused by velocity, and not some deep-seated emotional pang from her childhood. Besides, she can't really show any range of emotion beyond general disinterest with all the work she's recently had done—and by recent, I mean during the past three decades she's been married to the Edward Scissorhands of the Mercer Island jet-boat set. You name it—breast lift augmentation; rhinoplasty; cheek enhancement (both pairs); eyelid, brow, and neck lifts; tummy tuck; and a punchcard's worth of liposuction—she's had it done. In many cases, she's had it *re*done, courtesy of her live-in Fellow of the Royal College of Surgeons, my brother-in-law, Dr. Hollis Lucky. He's a nice enough guy, and just as gentle as can be, but he's transformed and transfigured my sister into an anesthesia junkie who more often than not acts as though she's sedated even when she's not. She's having a good day, though; bright-eyed, sutures dissolved, alert, off her post-procedure antibiotics—the world, her outlook, and this top-down day could not be any more gorgeous. And she's on a mission.

> Here's my request: Have yourself a weekend away from Mercer Island, the surgeon, the kids, and the anti-depressants, and bring my ashes to Moran State Park. Release them from the lookout tower atop Mount Constitution. I'd say that I'd like you to camp by the lake, like we did all those years ago—but I know camp is a four-letter word, and you will have already booked yourself into the Rosario Resort and Spa before ever leaving the driveway.

Krista speeds the Maserati through the white arched entryway into Moran State Park. Passing the lake on her right, she ponders some more, but still can't recall a memory, then unbuttons her blouse to feel the sun on her breasts. She shakes her hair like Sophie Loren might, and commences her version of cutting loose. Madonna is blasting Krista's personal theme song through the custom Bowers and Wilkins speakers, and she can't help but sing at the top of her lungs and honk her horn as she drives topless past the campsites and tents on her way to the top of the mountain.

She's driving too fast and spills in and out of her lane as the song pitches to the chorus. A truck-camper with Alberta plates honks her back to her side of the road, which earns its occupants a flamingo-pink-nailed bird.

Suddenly, there is this orange diamond sign in the gutter that indicates a flagger ahead, and as she rounds a curve with both tops down, she bench presses her chemically injected lips into a smile and comes to a stop at the hand-held sign attached to the bronzed and pumped arm of a summer student wearing only his safety vest, faded levis, and steel-toed boots. She's just made his day-eh, and she knows it, and makes no apology. He smiles down at her widely, to let her know one is not required. As a train of cars pass by, traveling downhill in the opposite direction, a few hoots and honks inspire the flagger to lower his stop sign so that it covers, and in fact makes contact with the driver's architecturally enhanced breasts. Krista, whose married name—no irony lost with her—is Mrs. Lucky, takes this song break to reapply lipstick that matches her fingernails. Then, while she is still detained there, she launches back into the song.

"Some boys try and some boys lie but I don't let them play-eh."

"No way?" the flagger asks, on cue and in rhythm. He's getting a sizeable boner that he proudly presses into her baby blue side mirror. The smell of fresh asphalt has apparently got them both going, but traffic has stopped traveling in the opposite direction, and the flagger's radio squawks:

"Get 'em moving, Hormone Bag!"

"You have a break coming up?" Mrs. Robinson purrs like the purebred cougar she is. "You can either come find me on top of the mountain, or later tonight at Rosario's." And if that didn't seal it, she says the magic words every teenager dreams to hear: "I'm past my ovulating years, so I don't get pregnant."

"Uh," he stutters, "we're based in Anacortes and I leave with the crew on the last ferry."

Krista fixes her eyes on the boner in his Levis, and decides she isn't taking "last ferry" as an answer. "Tell them you're staying on the island tonight; that you have a smoldering campfire to put out." Car and RV horns behind her start honking, and the flagger stands back from her car, reluctantly removing his stop sign from her breasts and flipping it around. "Cause the boy with the cold *hard* cash, is always Mister Ri-hight," she coos as she edges the car past him, re-buttoning her blouse. She checks herself in the rearview mirror and sees the flagger just standing there in the middle of the best day of his entire summer with his Carhartts bulging and his mouth hanging open. My sister enthusiastically launches into the final chorus of "Material Girl" *voce piena*, providing her own back-up vocals as she motors past the remainder of the paving crew—not one of them the looker that her flagger is.

Spoiler alert here: Nobody is getting laid on top of the mountain today, nor later tonight at the resort, but the two star- and generation-crossed misfits have already given each other the gift that lasts longer than a dozen boners, and that's a quenching and re-playable fantasy to get them both through their droughts. Now, if my sister can just manage a lucid moment and recall the reason she's driving up Mount Constitution on Orcas Island in the first place, I might be the one to get lucky.

MEANWHILE, 596 MILES TO the south, G.L. has parked my parents' silver 2002 Toyota Camry in the parking lot of the Heceta Head Lighthouse Bed and Breakfast, even though he has no intention of paying those prices when he can stay the night at the Best Western in Florence, where they will let him combine both his AAA and AARP discounts. My mother, Carole, is in the passenger seat, wearing oversized sunglasses, even though there hasn't been sun on this foggy stretch of the Oregon Coast since last Tuesday. Ever mysterious and set in their ways, these two.

"It's a long way up there, Carole," G.L. offers sternly. "I sure would prefer to go with you." From the front seats, they can just see the red top of the Heceta Head lighthouse, high on the cliff in the near distance. It is a chilly, windy day, and rain is spitting intermittently.

Gathering the kite and string spool with mittened hands, she says, "I need to do this by myself, Jerry." She can get away with calling him that though his actual name is Gerald, but if it were up to him, he wouldn't respond to either, since the initials "G.L." get the job done with half the fuss. "It's the way Ashton wanted it to be. I'll be fine." She bites her lower lip and then makes a declaration. "I'll be with my son." They have had this discussion and sometimes debate and sometimes argument for the last seventy-five miles. In her vision of how this will play out, she is alone at the lighthouse. In his vision, it is too dangerous. She unfastens her seat belt and momentarily gets the kite and string tangled with it. G.L. holds out his hand. She grasps it and gives a squeeze. They both fight back a tear they would never cry in front of each other—out of some learned and mutually reinforced stubbornness that only metastasizes when they try to meaningfully communicate. She pushes her door open and then pulls her frail self out of the car. The wind slams the door closed much harder than she would have had she been in control, leaving her husband of fifty-six years inside his Camry. Cane in one hand, kite in the other, she begins walking up the service road to the lighthouse.

Ashton Taylor, *Last Will and Testament*, page 11

We've been to Heceta Head Lighthouse together a few times. I know how much you love the Oregon Coast, Mom, and it has always been a special place for me because it seems to draw you there. Since I was a small kid, probably around the first time you brought me to the ocean, I knew I would have to die before you did. Accepting this order of things was easier for me than figuring out how I would ever carry on if you died first. I'm sure this doesn't help you.

> You're definitely stuck with the hard part now that I've kept
> my end of this arrangement.

She pauses to take off her sunglasses, as they have become nearly impossible to see through, with the heavy mist that is threatening to organize into an all-out rain. She is crying, of course; her face wet from tears and salt spray and a lifetime of loss and heartache. She's lost her parents, her brother, and now her first son. She went through several rehearsals for this, she reminds herself—thinking she'd lose me to cancer in the 80s, then AIDS in the 90s, then terrorism or texting-while-driving after the turn of the millennium. Regardless, really, of how I'd be taken out, she has to be admitting to herself right now that she always understood she would survive me. That doesn't mean she ever accepted this order of things, or her struggle now might have been less fraught. She is finding it ironic to feel this lost while heading straight for a lighthouse designed to show the way out of hardship, danger and darkness. But this is my passion play and she will act her part. Sobbing still, she closes the distance. She is determined to do this.

> You've always had the hard part where I was concerned.
> You made my life so very easy, you know? Whenever it
> was shitty, by ordinary standards, you rushed in to make it
> less so. It's clear now I didn't have enough time in this life
> to give you all the love I had for you. By leaving you early
> I've had to take so much of it with me, so you can bet I'll
> be saving it for our next lives together—when you are a
> humpback whale and I am maybe an albatross.

The lighthouse is getting closer. She was right. She could do this by herself.

> I was so fortunate to be your son for more than half a cen-
> tury now—but even more so to know you as a woman, a
> fellow human being on my journey. We were friends; good
> friends who lived and loved at the same time in human
> history. Of the billions of people who came before us

and those who will come after, we were able to share this too-brief section, this passage of the human experience together. That's something.

She raises her caned hand to touch the base of the red-crowned, white lighthouse, knowing she just has to cross the grass lawn between the lighthouse and the white pipe railing at the edge of the cliff.

> Your whole life, you've loved flying kites. We've flown a few together, each of us wondering what it must be like to be a kite on the wind, secure in knowing the string would always reel us back. I don't want this to be the last kite you ever fly, but I want you to take a cheap paper kite and attach the canister of my remains and I want you to fly it high over the cliffs at Heceta Head Lighthouse. When you reach the very end of the string and I'm far over the ocean, I want you to let me go. Close your eyes and let go of the string. Don't be surprised if the kite falls from the sky like a rock. That's just the enormous weight from all the love I carry for you, that I've always felt for you, Mom. Let me go.

Her eyes and nose running, her face red, she clutches the kite (with the canister duct taped to it) to her chest—so hard she nearly breaks the kite's spine. Thinking about her husband now—a man who has the patience of Job but the bladder of a hummingbird—she steps up the pace, takes the kite, and kisses the canister. She holds the kite into the wind and lets out a little string. The kite catches the wind coming off the face of the cliff, and crinkles and pops as it is lifted high above her. *Wait*, she thinks, panicking. Was she supposed to remove the lid from the canister first? She couldn't remember this step in her instructions. *Carole! Think this through*, she nags. *What would Ash have intended?*

As the kite jerks her arm around, she decides I would have wanted my ashes to mix with the ocean, so she starts reeling the kite back within reach—but it is a struggle, as the kite, now wet, begins to dive at her erratically. She holds her cane against the railing with one hand to steady herself, but her other arm is beginning to ache from being elevated, so she starts to switch arms, but the spool slips out of her mitten in the transfer and bounces down the cliff far below her at the same time the paper kite rockets to the sky. When the string snaps taut, it is beyond the reach of even her cane. The spool has gotten tangled around an exposed tree root, so the cliff seems to be flying the kite now, but the kite is not heading toward the sea. It is veering back toward the lighthouse and the trees. Of course the wind would be coming off the ocean and not carry the kite over the sea, she realizes. *Why didn't this occur to Ashton?* she wonders. I am wondering the same thing. This kite is not going to cooperate with her nor her son's final wish, but as it is also just homemade from lilac bush branches, tissue paper and hairspray, the flight will not be long. And it isn't. The kite crashes into the top of a coastal Douglas fir tree—upslope from and nearly as tall as the lighthouse.

"Carole!" her husband calls from less than ten feet behind her. "I think your job is finished here." Of course he has followed her to the lighthouse. Of course he is right. In that moment, they reveal to each other their real tears as he takes her mitten and the wedding-ringed hand inside it and slowly walks his bride of fifty-six years back down the service road.

WILDE

BY THE TIME I'D ENTERED HIGH SCHOOL, I HAD AMASSED A
string of sex-related priors with neighborhood kids, the neighbor's
dog, a pound-and-a-half of raw hamburger, and a step-cousin once
removed. Most of this revolved around your typical run-of-the-mill
crotch grabbing, different experiments with masturbation, and jerking
off the dog, but by age fourteen, I was ready for something more sub-
stantial, more carnal, more adult, so I set out to stalk the one high
school teacher nearly everyone agreed had to be a faggot—just like
I secretly was. His name was Evan Knight. There were five or six
other high school teachers I would have preferred to stalk, don't get
me wrong, but it was pretty clear my chances of succeeding would be
higher if I lured a sure bet out of the herd.

But even before I get to that, I should mention there had been one
other adult man before him, about three years earlier in Missoula. The
last name was Tate—I can't remember his first name, so I'll just call
him Stan. Stan was into airplanes and the airport and exposing me to
activities one would do with a son—had he had one, which he did not.
Mother thought he was odd, and felt a little uncomfortable loaning me
out at the time. But she talked with Stan often in the evenings, when
she was lonely and would sit on the front porch, hoping that some
neighborly adult or even a salesman would come along to talk with

her. Stan usually did. My own father was away on forest fires for weeks at a time, and she reasoned that exposing me to another adult male was for my own good. It was, probably.

Stan took me to see a matinee of *The Poseidon Adventure*—which was cool on one level, I suppose, since at ten years old I was way too young to be seeing a movie like that. On another, more psychologically damaging level, it left me emotionally fouled up, since Shelly Winters and my mom were built roughly the same, and Shelly's character Belle Rosen was a medal-winning champion swimmer, and my mom was a swimmer too. When Belle didn't make it, it was the first indication that maybe my mom wouldn't make it either, in similar circumstances. From that moment forward, I became clingy and protective and vigilant. None of this was really Stan's fault, and honestly I had forgotten all about him until Limping Rabbit one day asked me who had taught me about the birds and the bees. Stan, that's who.

I'm pretty sure I wasn't even eleven yet, and already my feelings for this next-door neighbor were jumbled. We'd sit in his car at the end of the runway and watch firefighting retardant and smoke jumper planes take off and land; planes probably headed to the same fires my absentee father was fighting. That summer, I think I easily spent more time with Stan than with my real dad. Once, we were standing at a urinal trough after a pancake breakfast fundraiser for something downtown. Stan was explaining to me how babies get made, and how when I was ready I would use my penis to plant a baby seed in a woman.

"How will I know when I'm ready?" I asked, staring at Stan's penis.

"Your penis will grow, like this—" he said, stretching his out really long. "And it will get hard as a countertop. That's how you will know." He nervously put himself back in his trousers when he realized I was getting a baby erection.

Next thing I knew, we were moving towns again; and so back to north-central Idaho my family went. I wasn't catching a break here, and my father's government career kept the stone always rolling so that moss wouldn't have a chance to attach. By the time I started seventh grade, when lots of other boys my age had plenty of moss—like Dirk Armstrong and Steve Bednorz and John Baffico—even though

I could grow pretty long and countertop-hard, I couldn't grow moss to save my life. I became desperate for pubic hair, and obsessed by those sprinting, dribbling, tumbling, and dodge-balling chia pets in the gymnasium and swimming-pool change rooms, who seemed to have more than their fair hair share.

Then there was Donny Lerandeau, from my new neighborhood. He was in most of my classes, and I was pretty certain he had been held back a grade—maybe two. Anyway, he demonstrated in a ditch behind our government housing complex that not only was he growing hair down there but that he could get white stuff to spurt out of his penis. For about twenty minutes, we gave our friend Harry Boxleitner's Irish Setter a much needed rest from our attempts to jack it off, and gathered like scientists around the furiously pumping John, who turned out, in the autumn days that followed, to be as predictable at gushing as Yellowstone's Ol' Faithful. If it weren't for the arrival of winter that shut down our exhibition ditch, we might have had real problems in our hands, so rubbed and friction-blistered our penises had become from trying to match John's skill level.

Finally, by the end of junior high school, I could sport some landscaping of my own—just a small hedge, really, but it gave me unstoppable confidence to finally start looking like a man, you know, down there. So I started looking for a man elsewhere too. And with the acquisition of my driver's license and permission to drive my father's Volkswagen beetle, I was ostensibly free to go after a sexual mentor, someone in the adult department, who could usher me into gay adulthood.

The previously mentioned high school teacher, Evan Knight, made an easy target, really, in his navy blue sweater vest, wide ties, and permanently pressed polyester slacks. It wasn't his wardrobe that set him apart from the pack, since that was the official faculty uniform for all male teachers in Idaho in 1976–80. It wasn't his sideburns (which plunged an inch below his earlobes) or the oversized wire-rimmed glasses either. It was his take-no-crap attitude, even when I saw lots of crap being hurled his way. It was also his earned status as a lone wolf: no wife, kids, denomination, or particular agenda. All this made him interesting and huntable. With those credentials in that tiny town, and living solo in an apartment above a garage, he absolutely had to be as fucking bored out of his Idaho potato-skin as I was. That's what made him my round-the-clock obsession. When my plan ultimately succeeded, as I predicted it would, we would be able to save each other from desperation, repression, and genital atrophy. Step one: set the snare.

In a time two decades before caller ID would reach the Gem State, and using a pay telephone outside of the A&W just in case I was being tailed, I phoned his apartment after dark one evening. When he picked up, I nervously said something like *you don't know me but I get a hard-on thinking about seeing you naked. I bet you'd get a hard-on too if you saw me naked. If you're curious, come alone and meet me at the baseball diamond in thirty minutes and we can check out equipment in the dugout.* And yes, I had already mastered the double-entendre by age fifteen. Then I hung up the phone and sprinted the ten blocks to the high school at the edge of town.

Whether or not he sensed an ambush, I didn't have to wait long before a pair of headlights appeared at the top of the high school parking lot and then flashed off with the engine. Whether or not I sensed an ambush by the sheriff he might have called, I didn't move, lying flat as a night crawler just beyond the pitcher's mound. Five minutes later, when he walked from his car through the gates and onto the field, I still didn't move. Turns out, I didn't have a step two. He tried to flush me out with a friendly "hello there," lobbed into the darkness, but I couldn't even summon a twitch. Paralyzed, I let him walk away, get into his car and vanish back into the night.

Step two, when it finally took shape in my barely post-pubescent brain, wasn't as clumsy as it could have been. I phoned Mr. Knight again a few nights later and said I had just been too nervous. . .that I needed to be sure I could trust him. . . that I still wanted to meet. He suggested if I were ready, I could present myself at his apartment. He said that this would be safest for both of us, especially if I arrived after dark. We could talk freely. I told him I knew where he lived and that I would come by a little later. I ran home from the phone booth at the A&W and lied to my parents that I had to go to the Idaho Motel for a get-together with the Foreign Language Club. My Spanish Teacher and her husband owned and lived at the motel; their living room doubled as a teen drop-in center on any given school night, as long as you didn't mind singing repetitive folk songs in Spanish or French—and even German the year Wolfgang came up the winner in the central Idaho foreign exchange student lottery. The smoke screen would prove foolproof for the next two years, as long as I arrived home in a great mood, humming some foreign ditty.

I wasn't yet sixteen, so I hadn't earned my night-time driving license, though I had been legally allowed to drive in broad daylight for two years because of a provision that enabled youth to climb behind the wheel of farming equipment during harvest.

As the Idaho Motel was located at the bottom of South E Street, I started out walking without raising suspicion. When I was out of sight of the house, I started zig-zagging blocks through town, sprinting every five minutes or so to get to the five-hundred block of North A Street as expeditiously as I could. I already knew my mentor lived in an apartment he rented up the stairs and behind the house belonging to relatives of my afterschool, weekend, and summer grocery-store employer—so I had to be extra careful to get in and out undetected.

I almost undetectably knocked on the door and it opened. Mr. Knight smiled and whispered in hushed tones, "Well, hello there," he greeted, holding out his hand to shake. He knew me, of course, and the handshake wasn't the first time he had touched me. As a freshman, I had played Abraham Lincoln for some bicentennial skit that presented two hundred years of history in maybe six minutes, and as the drama club advisor, Evan Knight had helped me apply the fake beard with spirit gum, and then roughly helped me scrub it off using rubbing alcohol—or, more likely, paint thinner since kids were tougher then. He didn't act the least surprised by my revealed identity on his porch, and had probably recognized my "four score and seven years ago" voice calling from the payphone. My fifteen-and-a-half-year-old heart was drumming something right out of a John Philip Sousa score, so it was all patriotism and bombs bursting in my head, and it was several minutes before I could have been considered to have been breathing normally again.

He invited me to sit on the couch. I sat. He plopped down in a reading chair opposite wearing jeans for the first time that I'd ever seen and said, "So, here we are. A lot more comfortable than a baseball dugout, wouldn't you agree?" He had this remarkable chin that jutted out like Wayland Flowers's Madame puppet (the one you'd see in the center spot on the Hollywood Squares after Paul Lynde vacated) and he had this flop of brownish hair he'd part on one side to swoop dramatically across his forehead to the side opposite. His shirt was unbuttoned at the top—easily the first time I had seen my mentor not wearing a tie too—revealing that he had significant moss, just like Rock Pamplin had moss. (And I mean *the* Rock Pamplin of May 1976 *Playgirl* cover fame—that was one of the very first *Playgirl*s I had stolen from the top shelf of the magazine rack at the grocery store where I would eventually get a job two years later. And remember, where there is a first, there is a second—and, in this case, a few years' worth of issues.)

Little brass incense burners churned out East Indian scents that made my head spin. Colored silk scarves were draped over lampshades to toss warm hues about the small room, with its impossibly angled ceiling of dormers and cubbies. Samuel French one-, two- and three-act plays with yellow and light-blue covers were stacked and strewn, and I could see at least two different film projectors from where I sat, with corresponding 8- and 35-mm canisters scattered like Easter eggs on the bookshelves and tables around me. I could see the open kitchen in one corner, the door to what must have been the bathroom across from me, and the opening of a hallway that must have led to a bedroom, unless he slept on the sofa.

"You like films," I must have said awkwardly, because he answered in the affirmative and offered to show me one.

"I answer ads in the back of movie magazines," he said, "and send for short films, and they get mailed to me from all over the world." My mentor scrambled into action, grabbing the small projector and setting it up on the coffee table. He rifled through the film canisters until he found the one he was after. "This is called *Un Chien Andalou*, and it's by this Spanish filmmaker, Luis Buñuel—a contemporary of Salvador Dali." The projector lamp illuminated a lopsided square on the wall opposite, and he bounced onto the sofa next to me, our legs touching while he threaded the Super-8 film through the gears. He wasn't wearing shoes or socks, which gave me the chance to study other places where he had visible dark hair. Even without the little extras that overloaded my senses—the clicking of the projector, the turning off of the closest floor lamp, the incense, his leg still touching mine, Rock Pamplin below the neck, flow of blood not bothering to travel to my brain anymore—it was truly remarkable I didn't just let loose and go *Lerandeau* all over his place, I'd been waiting so long for this adult moment.

I held it together through the opening sequence in the film, where this straight razorblade slices through a full moon but turns out to be slicing across the eyeball of a woman, and by the time these dead horses on top of two pianos get dragged across the floor, I was confused and had sort of forgotten why I was even there. Even though the whole film had only lasted sixteen minutes and I'd been in his home less than thirty, I was immediately concerned about the lateness of the hour and fretted about getting home—and I said so. This prompted him to offer me a ride there in his car, a bronze Volvo, suggesting we use the back road through the town dump so as not to draw attention to my arrival at the family home on the very edge of town. We didn't really say much in the car. He thanked me for coming over, suggested we should get together whenever I felt like it. I crouched down, making myself as small as I could under the Volvo glove compartment. He let me out about a hundred yards from my home, then turned around and drove away back through the dump. I walked through the front doors of the house singing "*Dominique, inique, inique s'en allait tout simplement, routier pauvre et chantant . . .*" and nobody, except for me, was the wiser.

These platonic but still secret film nights lasted through the deep snows of winter—so for another four months or so. Mr. Knight cast me as one of the Mechanicals, Nick Bottom, in *A Midsummer Night's Dream*, and our one-act version took first place at the Idaho State

Drama Festival in Pocatello. I shared a motel room there with Puck, Oberon, and Snug, wondering if my mentor was hoping I'd sneak out to his room at some point. I didn't. I would have been embarrassed by any evidence of an affiliation, and in fact, joined enthusiastically in the regular and relentless group taunting that Mr. Knight endured from all of us who respected him but were embarrassed by him at the same time. It wasn't an overt effeminacy about him, but more the odd way he walked and carried himself, like all his bone joints were full of helium. He didn't shy from the teasing and in fact seemed to divine the attention—especially from the sporty types he'd convinced to take a run at acting and theatre. I didn't one bit mind being in the company of jocks either, as it seemed to diminish, for a while, the teasing they would have otherwise directed at me.

The moment I turned sixteen, it was as though my mentor had checked my school records and cross-referenced them to the Idaho statute for the legal age of consent. The playbill changed, quite overnight, and the covert movie nights at the upstairs apartment in the five hundred block of North A Street became deliciously racy. A dream library of pornographic gay films and magazines from around the world were suddenly available for my perusal—sometimes three nights in a week. On one of those nights with a miniature lap-held projector with a built-in screener, we were sitting tightly together on the sofa, watching a black man make his noteworthy phallus disappear into the throat of an eager Boy Scout. I had been a Boy Scout. I watched my mentor's bulge balloon, which made the projector's image slowly crawl up the wall and partly onto the ceiling. Noting the Boy Scout's enthusiasm, I suggested, "Why don't we try that." When he registered no objection, I undid all five of his 501 buttons.

He moved the projector to a side table. I touched his mossy stomach. Inside my head, I switched out Evan Knight's goofy-chinned face for Rock Pamplin's, and between my imagination and the peaty forest-floor smell that sweetly emanated from deep inside those jeans, I struggled and fumbled to hold on, to keep from passing out from sensory overload. I followed the main tributary of dark hair into his madly distorted bikini pouch briefs, and unleashed the beast with a *boing.* I smelled him up one side and down the other, burying both nostrils deep in his underbrush. Irish Spring—I would have bet my part-time, minimum wage ($2.65/hr in 1978) paycheck on it. Not one to pass up a chance to earn an easy merit badge, I stuck out my tongue, then opened my world as wide as I could to take in a whole new age of adult possibilities.

EVAN KNIGHT WAS A gentle and in many ways perfect teacher. That's not so much another double entendre, as it is a nod to the benefits of his double curricula. Never pushy, insisting or even leading, he didn't take me anyplace I didn't want to go and where we went— well, I was often already there just waiting for him to find the nerve to catch up to me. But he became more confused in the end than I was in the beginning. Idaho will do that to you. Just ask Limping Rabbit. After high school, out into the world I went, and in this world I met all kinds of men that I didn't have to lie or covertly sneak around to be with. This left Mr. Knight in a lurch as he'd started believing we had a relationship thing going on and that I'd either return to Idaho or he'd relocate to wherever I finally landed. I know I hurt the man with my serrated astonishment when he revealed this to me. I hadn't matured to the point of being able to camouflage all of my feelings at that point, nor could I express then how grateful I was that he had carried me on his back across the roughest spot in my adolescence. I might have meant to say thank you but botched it by stating that I no longer required or lusted for his tutelage. After walking away—running actually—I didn't once pause to wonder who in this world—in north-central Idaho, where he was abandoned and stuck—was going to carry Mr. Knight across the roughest spot of my rejection. It wasn't the first time I couldn't reciprocate but I am not going to bother boring you with the second, third, and who knows how many subsequent times I let people down with my inability to quid pro quo at an emotional level. Just know where there's a first . . .

That's him now; my mentor, Mr. Evan Knight, in the back seat of a taxicab turning off Quai Saint-Bernard onto Pont d'Austerlitz. He would have taken the more direct route on Rue du Chemin Vert, but the taxi driver said this would be quicker because of some manifestation clogging the rue.

His hand slaps the back of the driver's seat. "Ici! A gauche, ici!"

The taxi driver dismisses him with a "Merde."

In nearly flawless French, my Mentor says "J'ai dit Père Lachaise. J'habite ici. Je connais Paris. Je ne suis pas un touriste."

Again, the driver just mumbles, "Merde."

My Mentor won't let this go. "J'aurais pris le métro si cette merde de ville n'était pas en grève. Hey! C'est la deuxième fois que l'on passe par la Place de la Bastille! Arrète de me faire chier!" His hand suddenly brandishes the silver blade of a brand-new garden trowel.

The driver is neither impressed nor threatened. "Merde," he says again, making a sudden maneuver that is met with yelling inside and an orchestration of the French horn section of car horns outside. The driver rudely gestures out the window and continues driving in silence—at least now in the right direction—on Rue de la Roquette.

Ashton Taylor, *Last Will and Testament*, page 12

It doesn't have to make one lick of sense why I've decided to contact you after all these years and why I've chosen to wait until I'm dead before I dare ask you another favor. Before I get to that, though, I just want to say, for the record, I never understood why you flipped out like you did. Your self-imposed exile to France twenty-five years ago seemed then to be a bit reactionary and it seems all the more so now that a whole lifetime has passed.

I never regretted what happened between us. My memories from those years, juvenile and undeveloped as they were, are numbered among the most intense and favorite times of my life. I realize that the publishing of my first novel took fiction across enemy lines to confront the truth of my pubescent seduction, and yes, I was underage at first and you were my high school teacher, but Jesus! I confessed in that novel that I consented. I mean, if we're going to get technical, I went beyond giving you permission. I think I even begged you—but that's not the point now, is it? It's not like I was drugged, abducted, held against my will, tortured, or abused in any way at all . . . well, except that one time I was home from college and you got me stoned, and I ended up streaking though your neighborhood at three in the morning with a small bouquet of pink tulips clenched in my teeth . . . that I later ingested . . . that I later threw up. The point is, I didn't get caught. We didn't get caught.

You can come out of hiding now. I'm dead. Our dirty little secret sort of died with me. I say "sort of died" because now my Husband knows about you and about the "early us" (if indeed this canister of my remains has found its way to you in Paris). But you don't need to worry about my boyfriend. He's not the suing type of lawyer, and besides, I'll keep my eye on him—unless, of course, that's what you've got in that little canister there!

The taxi driver slams on the breaks, as a woman with an enormous poodle darts into the street.

"Merde!" he shouts out the window.

"Ici. C'est bon." My mentor signals that he can be let out here. Euros exchange hands across the front seat, and he gets out of the cab, one fishnet-stockinged stiletto at a time. He slams the car door and crosses the street with relatively little difficulty, and enters the cemetery with purpose.

About that favor . . . I've heard that Oscar Wilde is buried in a cemetery there called Père Lachaise. I adored his writing and his plays, thanks to you. Wilde liked boys too, as you well know. In fact, he also self-exiled to Paris when one of the boy's fathers, who happened to be the Marquess of Queensberry, freaked right proper out about it. Oh, the parallels here will not be wasted.

I want you to dig a hole just under Wilde's gravestone, big enough to dump my ashes in. Get me in good and deep will you? That shouldn't be too hard for you, if memory serves me correctly.

Too soon for jokes?

Already six feet tall before adding heels, he cuts though the mausoleum and ducks under a stone portico to get to the other side of the cemetery more quickly. But he is stopped from behind by a policeman who takes him for an American and a man.

"Ze cemetery closes in five minutes, monsieur."

Without turning around, the man formerly known as Evan Knight—who now goes by Évelyne—corrects him using a higher registered voice than was required in the taxi. "Madame. Merci. Je quitte."

"Pardon," he says to her. *Ce n'est pas passable*, he says more quietly to himself. The transvestite—for she has no intention of pursuing the circumcision to end all circumcisions—hurries out of view, clicking and clacking in half time on the cobblestones. Within a few more turns Évelyne is standing fake-boobs-and-face-to-face with the flying naked angel carved in relief along one flank of the massive gravestone with Oscar Wilde's name emblazoned on the side. Her manly hand brushes the new tempered glass that has been installed on all four sides of the restored gravestone to protect it from the thousands of lipsticked lip prints that had been kissed onto the stone over the decades, in memoriam. The chemicals in the cosmetics had begun corroding the stone, which must not have been good publicity for the companies assuring the public their products were safe on the skin. Oscar Wilde once wrote "A kiss may ruin a human life." Well, apparently it could also ruin Jacob Epstein's opus—this daring memorial, sculpted from a twenty-ton block of Hopton Wood stone imported to Paris from Derbyshire, England. The monument to Oscar Wilde had seen far worse affronts than cosmetics during the last century—like when cemetery officials first plastered over the angel's genitals, which were deemed to be an unusual size; or when, later, officials installed a bronze butterfly to cover them after the plaster was chipped away; or when, in 1961, a vandal hacked and then made off with the stone jewels altogether.

Évelyne starts her dig at the front corner of the glass box, which is itself now covered in lipstick kisses, beneath the face of the flying angel. She isn't two trowels in and one of her false nails pops off. "Merde," she says, then hears footsteps nearby, crunching on gravel. She fumbles for the film canister tucked in her handbag, and dumps the ashes in the shallow hole, hastening to replace the dirt as two black pant legs with a vertical gold stripes walk into her wig-obstructed view. There is a throat clearing, followed by a loud policeman's whistle.

"Je peux vous expliquer," the obvious man in neo-cosmopolitan drag says, looking up, and busted.

While the gendarme is writing Mr. Knight a citation for *in flagrante delicto*, which comes with a fine of €9,000 that nobody pays ever, Évelyne recovers her character and reads out loud and smoothly with expression from the epitaph—a verse from Oscar's poem, "The Ballad of Reading Gaol":

> And alien tears will fill for him
> Pity's long-broken urn,
>
> For his mourners will be outcast men,
> And outcasts always mourn.

VALENTINO

"WE'RE GOING LIVE, PEOPLE, IN FIVE, FOUR, THREE . . ." THE producer finishes his count silently. The news anchors are still grinning, not able to recover before going live on camera.

"This next story comes from the file of the bizarre, as we go live to Hollywood Memorial Park, where our man on the scene is Steve Holzer. Steve, what can you tell us about this afternoon's strange turn of events?"

"Well, Anderson, what I can tell you and what you'll believe may be two different things. I'm standing about ten yards from the crypt here in Hollywood Memorial Park that houses the remains of silent film legend, Rudolph Valentino. Now, Valentino, as some of our viewers will know, died on this day, August 23, 1926. Since his death, ninety years ago today, a mysterious, veiled "Lady in Black" has appeared every year on the anniversary of his passing, to present a single red rose at his crypt. This woman was once believed to be grief-stricken Polish actress Pola Negri—but when Negri herself died of pneumonia in Texas on August 1, 1987, the Lady in Black once again appeared at Valentino's crypt, right on schedule, twenty-two days later. And she has every year since. What makes today's anniversary unique is that not one Lady in Black arrived at Valentino's crypt, but *three*. They all appeared at roughly the same time, so a bit of a territorial scuffle ensued. At the moment, police have one Lady in custody in the back of the squad car over my shoulder to the left, and one appears to have slipped away."

The cameraman pans his camera to the left to show a Hollywood police car with its lights flashing. The reporter continues off screen.

"The third Lady in Black, whose identity we have just learned, is one Patti McCaleb from Yorba Linda, who works as a book editor and marketer for the publishing house of Brownell & Carroll. We have some earlier footage from before we were pushed back to our current position by West Hollywood Police. It shows that McCaleb is no longer in black. We learned a few more details of this strange story from McCaleb herself, whose arm continues to be wedged between the wrought-iron bars of the crypt, despite the arrival of paramedics and their Jaws of Life in the last ten minutes."

The station cuts to the earlier footage, showing Patti with a bloodied nose and apparently topless, as evidenced by the sloppy censor job in the form of a blurred rectangle bar jiggling beneath her chin. She seems to have already found the situation laughable, though she is in pain. "When I arrived," she says, "a little before noon, I was surprised to find another Lady in Black already here—but she wasn't a lady at all."

"Not a lady at all—what do you mean by that?" the reporter asks.

"I mean she was a West Hollywood drag queen, and a bad one at that. That's who the police have in their car over there." She points with her chin.

The reporter starts to reveal the makings of a smirk, but narrows his eyes in his trademark "smize" (smiling with just his eyes), trying to look serious. "Now, while you are giving us the details of the afternoon, it's important to point out to our viewers that not only are you naked from your rather torn underpants up, but your arm is wedged between the bars of the crypt. Can you explain?"

"I'm in a great deal of pain here," she replies, "so your rather insensitive grin is not appreciated." She shoots the reporter a squint-eyed glare, and then continues. "When I saw the drag queen at the crypt, I politely waited for her to pay her respects and move on. After ten minutes, I was getting a little hot in my black dress, just standing there, so I decided to move in. When I got to the gates of the crypt, the other one says, 'There's only one Lady in Black, bitch!' So I said it was quite obvious that only one of us was a Lady at all, and I stood my ground."

A male paramedic moves into position, and into the camera shot. "We're going to need you to twist your torso slightly," he says. It is clear that he is enjoying the topless aspect to this rescue.

Patti does manage to twist her torso slightly, and the rectangle censor bar struggles to keep up, but she doesn't break stride with the interview in progress. "About that time, a third Lady shows up, claiming to be the daughter of some Polish actress, and then there's a bit of a shoving match between her and the D.Q."

"D.Q.?" the reporter asks.

"Drag queen," Patti decodes. "While the other two went at each other, I moved over to the crypt, because I had something to deliver . . ."

"A red rose?" the reporter asks.

"Not exactly. I had a film canister of ashes that I was placing inside the crypt, as was requested of me by the late author, Ashton Taylor, who wrote the definitive biography of Valentino, published two years ago by Brownell & Carroll, and just last month screen optioned by Paramount."

Patti looks directly into the camera for the first time to make her marketing plug.

"The book, titled *Val*, has done very well, and is available in bookstores and at Amazon.com."

The reporter tries to short-circuit her infomercial. "So we're to understand that your arm became stuck while you were trying to place these ashes inside the iron gates of this crypt?"

"Yes. I was trying to reach the shelf inside with the canister, but my arm wasn't quite long enough. My shoulder, it turns out, went through the bars, thanks to the shove I received from the D.Q. But it didn't come back out. That's when the other two turned real nasty and began ripping off my black dress."

"And your bra?" The reporter's smize was back.

"I wasn't wearing one," she admits, just slightly embarrassed. "It's the crypt of the World's Greatest Lover, for god's sake."

"And you were trying to what, make an impression?"

"I tried kicking the two of them off me, but by that point they had completely shredded my dress." She again looks directly into the camera. "I paid a good chunk of change for that dress, by the way. Before I knew it, they were going at each other. That's when I started screaming for help, and finally got the attention of a couple gravediggers on the other side of the hill. When they arrived, the D.Q. and the Polack made a run for it in opposite directions. I guess the D.Q. twisted her ankle stepping into a flower vase holder, because she went down with a manly thud and a few choice cuss words unbecoming a Lady, if you know what I mean."

The camera is once again trained on the reporter, as the sound of the air compressor powering the Jaws of Life can be heard in the background. "So apparently the World's Greatest Lover," he says, "is still turning heads, twisting ankles, and causing women to bare their, uh, *souls* in Hollywood. Anderson?"

"Thanks for that rather revealing report, Steve. Steve Holzer, live from"—the anchor starts to break into a laugh—"where else? Hollywood. When we come back . . ."

Rich mutes the television by remote control from his perch on the edge of the ottoman, his hand over his mouth and his eyes still wide in disbelief. He goes to his desk, retrieves a black pushpin, and walks across his apartment to the world map, shaking his head.

MEANWHILE, UP IN THE Nimbus Room, something amazing is happening right now. Listen:

"Still making headlines, huh, Rudy?" I have finally gotten the opportunity to meet my idol in vivid—thanks to the glasses—five dimensions.

"Yes, you and me both," the angel of Rudolph Valentino reaches out a hand to elaborate on his Italian-accented greeting. Gideon is grinning like the cherub he is behind the silent film star, tickled at the opportunity to introduce the two of us. "Now, about that biography you wrote about me."

"Did I get it right, I hope?"

"Some things, yes. Some things, well, I will never tell—though Gideon might, the sainted devil." Valentino constantly changes the tilt of his head to achieve a better angle and I can see in his robotic movements that this conversation is really just a set of poses, like photographic stills. "Say, who do you think will play me when Paramount starts casting the movie version? I hope the guy does a far better job than Anthony Dexter or Franco Nero or Rudolph Nureyev did."

"How about that Finn Wittrock?" Gideon suggests. "He's playing you right now in *American Horror Story.*"

Valentino says nothing, but with a hand checks his own slicked back helmet of hair and has to admit Wittrock certainly has the hairline.

I happened to have spent a good chunk of my adulthood thinking about this question, on the assumption that my first published novel might someday be made into a movie. "My casting money would be on Omar Sharif, Jr. Woof, Woof!!"

"Who let the dogs out?" Gideon raps uncharacteristically, then adds "I'd happily pretend to *be* that casting couch."

"Really?" Valentino says incredulously. "I was really thinking more along the lines of Adrien Brody or Colin Farrell."

"The World's Greatest Ego, is more like it," I half-mumble and half-joke while all-smiling.

"What was that?" The legend says with widely opened eyes.

"Oh nothing, Rudy. Just making notes to myself out loud."

He then turns the question on me. "And who do you think should play you in the movie version of *this* book?" Valentino asks, opening his arms to signify he's talking about my own real life, and my post-death drama in progress.

I look to Gideon for guidance and Gideon lowers his 5D glasses to shoot laughing auras back at both of us. It takes me a few seconds, but then I blurt it out.

"Well, Ryan Reynolds, obviously!"

LAMAR

"YOU'RE RUNNING BEHIND, SUGAR." THE NORMALLY CHATTY stage-door security monitor at the Richard Rodgers Theatre notes the three clocks on the wall that she can see from where she sits behind glass as she checks in Lamar Smith. "The curtain can now go up on Act I," she chides.

"In thirty-six minutes from now," Lamar says back. "Just picking up my dance shoes. Don't ride me, Malificent."

"Ah yes, we all know that rawhide saddle has Anthony's name stitched in gold cord around the horn. And don't call me that!"

"Whatever, Elphaba."

Lamar, six feet tall with muscle-padded, broad shoulders, moseys past her and ducks sideways into the narrow passage leading to the principal dressing rooms. Inside his, which he shares with Anthony, he plops onto the makeup table the shoes, a container of made-to-order sashimi he picked up at *Sushi of Gari 46*, and a store-bought bottle of green juice. He takes a quick, habitual glance at maybe the seventh large-faced clock he's passed since entering the stage door—this one on the baby blue wall between the mirrors with his name in all capitals and Anthony's identical set-up to Lamar's right; both ringed with caged light bulbs. Anthony is costumed and coiffed, fiddling with his forehead mic, which is just visible below his thick black hairline, having already threaded it from the waist pack, through his vest, out the top of his collar, through the knot of his ponytail, and through a series of three toupee clips.

"Shit, shit, shit." Lamar sits down in front of his mirror and realizes how late he is running when he sees how far along Anthony is.

Anthony pipes up. "These wouldn't, by any chance, be the modified boots with the cremains of your high school boyfriend polybonded into the heels, would they?"

"You know they are, so don't give fuss. I don't have time ta argue with yo' right honorableness right now."

"Testy, testy, Hercules." Anthony stands up to stretch his mic cord, checking to make sure it isn't bunching up in the wrong places, and that he has freedom of movement for the opening number. "Let me help you get set," he offers.

Lamar strips out of his street clothes. "I can only hope the actual remains are from his heart, since he certainly danced a few numbers on mine in his day. This is my chance to make things even. It's what he says he wanted. I don't know."

"Those grapes sound sour."

"Those grapes are dead." Lamar does not equivocate, pulling on his knee britches in his break-a-leg ritual of performing this show commando. His co-star and not-so-secret lover attaches the waist pack and holds the cord away while the puffy shirt and then the vest find their shoulders. The blue doo rag is the next step in his preparation, but not before the forehead mic and cord get clipped into his short mat of hair. He has to get it just right. Lamar is particular about this, so Anthony knows well enough to stand back. "Yeah, so I'd all but forgotten about those feelings until this film canister arrives in the mail with the instructions. In an instant, it brings everything right back to the surface; the dates, the clumsy sex."

"Did this Dead Grapes Guy ever see you dance?" Anthony is stretching and exercising his mouth, facing his mirror while at the same time making some guttural noises that do not sound human.

Lamar knows the answer to the question is *yes*, but because he's strategically left the amateurish *Up with People* show off his headshot

C.V. and out of professional performance conversations, he invents a workable alibi. "I danced and acted some in high school—quite amateur—and you know he always promised he would get to New York, even bring his Native American husband backstage after a show. But . . . well . . . he never got around to it."

Over loudspeakers embedded everywhere backstage comes the announcement: "Fifteen minutes, children. Fifteen minutes to curtain, five minutes to green room."

"Shit, I cut that close," Lamar acknowledges, taking a swig of green juice.

"Taylor Swift is in the audience tonight," Anthony sings as part of his vocalization.

"So is Oprah," Lamar sings back.

"Again!" they both sing in unison. Lamar tilts his head back for a kiss, and Anthony is there to plant one on him. They both put on their tailed waistcoats. Lamar adjusts his black self in his pants.

"I really wish you wouldn't do that," Anthony says for maybe the three-hundredth time since the show opened.

"Do what?" Lamar snaps back for the three hundredth time, too.

"You know what!" Anthony exclaims, and their pre-show ritual is complete.

Twenty-six minutes later, four numbers into Act One, Lamar leaps from a table onto the stage, landing his one hundred and ninety-seven pounds with such force that the left heel of his modified boot sails off like a hockey puck. Ricocheting off a dancer's foot for the assist, the heel sails past the conductor's right ear and into the orchestra pit. It's hard to tell whose eyes are bigger in that moment—Lamar's or the conductor's—but the show must go on, and it does.

Ashton Taylor, *Last Will and Testament*, page 13

I'm of course sad that I didn't make it to New York to see you live—and by "live," I selfishly mean while I was living—but I want to be in that theatre with you now. I want this part of my cremains to be sealed inside one of the heels of

your favorite dance shoes. I cannot think of a more exhila-
rating after-life than this. I want to be with you as you leap,
twirl, tap, stomp, and fly. You've made it to the Big Time,
beautiful, gentle Lamar. You never lost your trajectory from
the moment you set your mind to it. My job, it became
clear, was not to get in your way—and that was harder than
you know. I should be credited in that Playbill for saving
your career by letting you pursue it, and this is how you
can thank me: with seven Broadway performances a week.

FIREWORKS

HOME LIFE WASN'T PERFECT BUT IT WAS DARN CLOSE. There were great weeks and sour mornings and idyllic weekends and passionate arguments and silent treatments, both maintenance and makeup sex (neither maybe as frequent as I would have liked) and a relatively equitable distribution of domestic chores. But the kitchen was our battlefield. We were normally content—sometimes even militant—vegetarians, but we dropped our preferences and pretenses whenever company was coming up for dinner. Rich didn't cook, but he thought he did, which was enough to make him dangerous. And neither of us cooked on weeknights, which meant two things: we consumed a lot of takeout garbage that made us cranky—most of it was Vietnamese or Thai—and culinary clashes were almost entirely likely to happen on the weekends, when the carnivore beast within Rich would stir and rub and marinate and grill until whatever the meat was too well done to be chewable, really. I wasn't raised on deer jerky, like apparently he was, so I didn't have the mandible for it.

It was this past New Year's Eve, seventy-eight days before my heart would give out for good—and according to Gideon, on its 2,268,403,198th beat. Because it was Rich's and my annual civic obligation to host friends for dinner, drinks, shock and awe at our front-row bench to the Space Needle fireworks display at midnight, we were having Bret, Kendra, Colin, and Murray over to help us usher in 2016. Bret, you might remember, is an attorney friend and semi-regular gym partner of Limping Rabbit's. Kendra is Bret's other half. I worked indirectly with Murray at Fred Hutch; he is in Grants and Contracts, and I was in Development and Fundraising, and Colin is Murray's partner. Kendra was the sweet and mostly innocent bystander who got dragged along—to Seahawks games, BBQs, half-marathons, and, every other year or so, group camping trips to the Olympics—with the men (and those pretending to be more man than maybe they could pull off convincingly when adventuring beyond the electrical grid—not naming names here, Murray.) But she managed to remain neutral and generally good-humored without losing sight of her primary duty, which was to keep the four of us from turning her husband gay.

Oven-baked and Panko-crusted halibut with sharp sauce had won the menu toss, since a driving rain was sure to douse the rooftop BBQ grill, and probably along with it the hundreds of thousands of dollars' worth of fireworks already sitting in cannons packed in crates and wired to detonators on the Space Needle. I was trying to find a parking space near Pike Place Market; landing my Saturn on the lunar surface would have been the simpler maneuver. I ended up backtracking to Belltown on account of the holidays, which had dispatched anyone with a day off and out-of-town visiting company to the tourist magnet that was Pike Place.

I was cutting through the stalls of statice floral arrangement sellers when my Grindr app chirped with a chat message from *happyhungnhorny*. It was Murray's Colin, also at Pike Place Market, grabbing a bouquet of dried flowers to bring to our New Year's Eve dinner party later that evening. Colin was easy to spot—with that surfer-blond hair, and at six-foot-three, he towered over the mostly Asian crowd. He flashed me that gap-toothed smile of his, with raised eyebrows that made his blue eyes look like laser tracking beams that momentarily stunned whatever they focused on.

"What are the chances?" Colin asked as I approached.

I held up my iPhone and said, "I see you're out shopping this morning."

"Well aren't we a little overdue for a transaction?" he flirted, squeezing his dried, chapped fingers into my left deltoid. Colin owned (and still owns) a landscaping and nursery company which kept him tanned, ripped, and gorgeous, but with laborer hands that always looked like shit. There was a secret handshake and a solemn vow of silence—a foundation for flirtation between us. We'd fooled around on the side—mostly outside at Kinnear Park—for the past few years. It started out almost harmless enough at a small party where Colin had served me magic mushroom tea. When the elixir kicked in, we found ourselves alone on the roof of their house, checking out the Perseid Meteor Shower. Colin was campaigning for a three- or four-way with Murray, who had a *#sexcrush* on my Limping Rabbit. It was a flattering notion, and I was pretty stoned but I knew my husband and soul-mate well enough to assure Colin that with Rich's articulated sense of law and order this would never happen, since Rich didn't break rules, even with permission. That's when the ever-adaptable Colin switched tactics to forwardly announce that even though it had not yet been scientifically verified, I might be interested to know that he had a pair of the largest testicles in all of Cascadia. It was a dare the mushrooms left me defenseless to resist, and down his board shorts my right hand probed. I was no scientist in such matters, but within the first snug seconds I could ascertain no reason to dispute his claim—nor his Grindr handle. Of course, neither of us could muster a boner on shrooms anyway, so that first show-and-tell ended rather uneventfully, unless you counted the shower of shooting stars over our heads. Where there is a first, there's a second . . . and when it came to Colin there was probably a half dozen times we'd find the opportunity to sneak away from the others to satisfy our quest for more science on the matter.

Colin mock-offered me the chosen bouquet and repeated his offer that we grab our baskets and head someplace else quiet for shopping.

"I'm on a different mission—here to score fresh halibut—this morning."

"That's kinky," Colin judged. "Okay," he said, coming in for a kiss on the lips. "We'll see you tonight, Stud Muffin."

OF COURSE, AS WE now know, thanks to the app, Grindr and Rich's discovery of the account on my phone after I died, he and Colin had come within feet of discovering new knowledge the day my husband agreed to meet up with *happyhungnhorny*. It had been his intention to get to the bottom (or top) of things when he set out walking across Queen Anne Hill for sex and answers, but by the time he got there, his determination and needs had changed. From a distance, he had spotted Colin's blond head sticking high above some salal bushes before it ducked into a side trail just as Rich entered the park. Afraid that Colin might recognize him on the hunt in this notoriously cruisy park, he made an about-face and got his cottontail right out of there. Colin had, in fact spotted him. But because he didn't yet know I was gone—since Limping Rabbit hadn't figured out yet how to tell anyone—and because Colin was expecting to hook up with me but spied my husband instead, he too hightailed it into the undergrowth to avoid a revealingly awkward confrontation. Less than a week after that, Murray had brought home the news from work that I had died.

THE OLD HIGH SCHOOL condo kitchen was large enough for both of us to be in there at the same time, but we'd worked out this divide-and-conquer choreography to keep the domestic peace. You'd think after almost twenty years, we would have liked our morning coffee the same way and that we'd eat the same foods, or dice vegetables with the same technique . . . but you'd be wrong. While I was at the fish market, Rich had boiled the golden beets, roasted the pine nuts, and washed the arugula for the side salad. He was funneling the balsamic, honey and Dijon mustard dressing into a cruet when I returned with the halibut and my turn in the prep kitchen.

"Have you thought about a playlist for tonight?" he asked as I set the reusable Trader Joe's insulated refrigerator bag on the counter. "Kendra doesn't like jazz."

"Well, that makes two of us," I said, doing the math. "You could throw something together with a measure of Guy Lombardo—maybe even a little Holly Cole mixed in—whatever you feel like, Bunny." (I didn't always call him Limping Rabbit). I walked up behind him, threaded my arms under his, and embraced him with the pressure from my whole body, grinding him against the kitchen counter. "Happy New Year, Love," I whispered into his ear with a kiss for punctuation. "Are you ready to start Year Twenty with me?"

"Do I have a choice in the matter?" he asked, while sort of fake wriggling out of my body trap before turning around in my confines to look me in the eyes. He linked his arms in a ring over my shoulders. "I'm ready for Year Thirty with you, Ash."

I looked in his hazelnut-brown eyes as mine watered up. "You silly man. I won't last that long, and you won't want me to anyway. It wouldn't be pretty." I kissed him on the lips, grabbing his lower lip in a soft clench with my teeth. "How about we just take each year that we're given and make a lifetime out of it?" I proposed on the spot.

A single tear raced past the gates before Rich could call it back.

"Deal," he said.

WILL

RICH IS ON THE PHONE, AND PACING BACK AND FORTH. HE is upset. He pauses at the world map, and then hits it with the back of his hand and continues pacing. "Bret, Bret! It wasn't like that . . . Ash told me he was going to die within the year. He was convinced of it, and actually I think he was at peace with the whole thing . . . Well, yeah—he was frustrated the doctors couldn't pinpoint what was really wrong with him, but he didn't fight what he knew . . . You know, I didn't take his dooming and glooming that seriously until—oh god, I don't know about six months ago—maybe right after New Year's just two months before he died, when all of a sudden he'd just stop breathing in his sleep . . . I'd lay there at night, dog-tired myself, you know, thinking I had to stay awake to monitor his breathing. Toward the end, when I was too tired to keep up the routine, I used to test him, to see how long I could wait before nudging him to breathe. His heart would start racing madly, and every time, without my help, he would somehow catch himself and start breathing again."

Rich belly-flops onto the chaise length of the sectional on the Union Bay side of the living room, and reaches an arm to open the left side of one of the arched windows. He scootches his body toward the open window and cantilevers his head and shoulders outside to a sort of plank, like Superman in low-altitude flight over the Seattle skyline at night. He does this because he'd watched me do it on those evenings when I just needed to inhale the salt air or the smell of the rain. He used to tease me that the building didn't need to have some ugly gargoyle sticking out of it and that I should get back in before I fell out. In mimicking this, he finds some measure of calm, but this shield can't hold back the legion of grief demons. "Yeah, I'm still here," he tells his buddy on the phone after a sentimental pause. "Ashton's not . . . but I am."

Bret has to remind him where he'd left off in his telling of the story of how I died.

"Right" he continues. "I swear I'd never heard a heartbeat like that before, and it made me worry and then wonder if his heart'd give out before his lungs or brain did . . . Well, a few weeks went by and I eventually convinced myself that Ash didn't need me to monitor him; that his brain would always send the signal to resume normal operations . . . The doctors hadn't come up with anything, so I didn't see how I was going to solve the mystery of his medical problems . . . Look. I'm sorry to lay all of this on you, and I'm sorry for calling so late."

Rich pulls himself back inside the living room, at the same time he pulls his shoulder-length black hair back, and holds it in a hand knot.

"No, I know," he continues. "It's just that I haven't really worked through this—you know, weighed all the evidence to determine"—he makes quotation marks with his fingers—"beyond a reasonable doubt, whether or not I could have, you know, saved him." Rich stands, then moves from the feature windows and returns to pacing a well-worn loop about the fourteen hundred square foot space. "With my case-load these past months, when I finally made it to bed, you know I was so exhausted, I didn't notice his struggle any longer." He suddenly sits on the back of the sofa, facing away from the view, and fixes a stare through the doorway to our master bathroom. "And then, one morning, he just dies on me. Turns out he had a bad heart valve that had pretty much been disintegrating the last couple years of his life. This, plus he became plagued by this disorder they call sleep apnea, and his body . . . his valve really . . . well, it just gave up."

Tears now race each other off the cliffs of Rich's brown, high-boned cheeks. He wipes his face and walks to the desk adjacent the world map. He picks up a black pushpin and toys with it, testing how far he can push the point into his thumb before withdrawing from pain, and before he breaks the skin. "I know that. It's just . . . Jesus! I miss the little fucker! We were twenty years together. I miss his laugh. I miss his routines that kept me on mine. I miss his symptoms and his conspiracy theories. I miss his smells. I miss his strength, his warmth, his corniness. You name it, I'm missing the hell out of it. I'm missing him. I'm missing life. I'm just going through the motions, now. It feels like I'm just waiting to die. This isn't living . . . I don't want another boyfriend. It's not that . . . I went to Aruba a few months ago. It's not that either. My father has a theory that what I'm missing is my Indian. According to him, that's the part of me that I am denying, and I'll never be at peace until the two parts of me unite again."

Rich inventories the eight black pushpins already stuck in the laminated canvas roll-down map. "How should I know?" Surprising himself, he chuckles. "He wants me to come home next month to participate in a powwow . . . I should go. Ash wanted the last of his remains used in a traditional Indian ceremony, whatever that is anymore." He pauses. "I should go . . . You're right. Hell, my father's probably right too . . . Maybe I just need to find my Indian."

He picks several stapled pages off the desktop next to the Nez Perce mat. He chuckles some more. "You'd think in the pages of instructions my husband left me, he would have told me how to find my Indian, but no . . . I guess that one's up to me to figure out." He says, "Yep, talk soon" to his lawyer buddy from another firm across the lake in Bellevue. He presses the red circle on his phone to end the call and then sees he still has a voicemail he received earlier that morning while he was at the law library. He'd listened to the message from Ash's nephew in the car on his way back to the office, but didn't erase it so that he'd be reminded to mark the map when he got home. This prompts him to plunge the pushpin he's been fiddling with through the dot marking Middlebury, Vermont.

172

AS IS REQUISITE FOR a first week in September, it is an eye-orgy vibrant and crisp early autumn day from where a lanky, nineteen-year-old Will Taylor—the spitting image of his father, my brother—sees things. He is dragging a borrowed yellow canoe to the marshy bank on the outside bend of this stretch of Vermont's one hundred and twelve mile long Otter Creek River. The already meta-morphosing oaks and maples and elms project their newly acquired colors onto the river's surface as a brilliant blue sky with a cirrocu-mulus lace tries to hog the mirror.

Is it even flowing? Will wonders. Almost impossible to tell. It is among his first days as a returning sophomore at West Point, and his first chance to break away from drills and classes and pressures too daunting to bear without the occasional break. Dressed in classic L.L. Bean, with a very severe and formal military looking haircut, it took hardly any charm at all to convince the riverfront homeowners to let him access their property and borrow their canoe. It helped that the lady of the house thinks she remembers his uncle, which is the whole reason he is here.

Will pauses at the edge, on terra not exactly firma, water already percolating up around his boots. He looks up, then down the river, not able to tell that it is flowing north to Lake Champlain. He removes the black backpack he is wearing. His hands liberate the flap and reach inside the bag, and he extracts a black film canister with his name lettered on the side: JEFFREY WILL TAYLOR. He spins the canister slowly. He places it back inside the bag, next to a large navel orange he didn't eat on the morning train up from West Point. He secures the flap to the sack and flings it over his shoulders and onto his back.

Will steps one foot and then the other inside the canoe, lowers his six-foot-three frame to the seat like he's on hydraulics, positions the backpack between his legs, and pushes off shore with the tip of his paddle along with a giant lean forward. He glides into the center of the river and allows the current to take over, but in this particular bend, it really doesn't. He sets the paddle in a cross brace position and floats leisurely around the eddy. He extracts a folded piece of white paper from his pack.

Ashton Taylor, *Last Will and Testament,* **page 14**

> We were never close, Will, thanks to your father, who I'm certain was afraid I'd corrupt you. I think you and I both know that I wasn't that kind of uncle. Now he has you tucked away at military school where the only undue influence comes from your weaponized, war-mongering government, so you're safe to become what your father needs you to become—a carbon copy of him.
>
> I won't say this is what sent me to my grave—first, because I don't have a grave, and second, because I generally had other things to obsess over besides how my brother raised his children—but you always have choices, Will. It may not seem like you do, but no decision is without at least one other option. You can become what your father wants you to be, or you can be yourself, whoever that is. But love yourself.

Will lowers the paper to his lap and looks up into the sky, daydreaming.

> You're at that age where you'll rush to deny this, but I've always had this sense about you, Willy—that you were maybe more like me than your own father. If I'm right, you and that Dad of yours are in for some battles ahead and you're going to need this military training. I'm afraid, despite every effort, I've toughened him up for you instead of worn him down. I could never get through that tank armor-grade skull of his.

Satisfied he has the gist of the instructions, Will folds up the note from his dead uncle and tucks it in the pocket of his backpack. He retrieves the canister from the pack. He leans on the paddle that is resting across the canoe. He takes off the plastic lid and examines the ash with a stare he can't seem to break.

I figure the Otter River, just beyond the town of Middlebury, Vermont, is about a seven hour train ride from West
Point. It will take a weekend to get there and back if you
can manage it. I fell under the trance of this river one fall
while traveling cross-country on tour with that group I was
in when I was the age you are now. I stayed with this couple
in a magnificent farm house from the late 1800s that they'd
modernized with a glassed addition. I know with your smile
and good looks, they will easily let you borrow a canoe
to get this little task accomplished. Part of me, when I'd
daydream, went back to this peaceful, simple place often
whenever I felt the world closing in, so it seems appropriate that part of me should return there now.

Will recites the last bit out loud: "In the middle of the river,
sprinkle my ashes in a circle around the canoe, and let that circle
freeze forever in your memory, as the love and protection of your uncle
always around you." With that, Will dusts two wide half circles, as far
as his basketball point-guard arms can reach, and for just long enough,
the thin circle stays with him. Will folds at the waist and then leans
his upper body to rest on top of the cross-braced paddle. He gazes at
the reflection of his own handsome face looking up at him, just as
one tear and then another jiggles the surface. Just like Narcissus, he is
smitten by his reflection, and begins to smile and then pose into it. He
postures ridiculously, to catalog just how handsome he is—just as his
uncle used to do, I might add. Will becomes so carried away with this
self-worship and the out-of-rank headiness of his liberation from the
Academy that too much of his upper body moves outside his center
of gravity. He tips the canoe and empties its contents into the Otter
Creek River. He emerges from under the water a new and baptized
man, laughing and shouting.

"Thank you, Uncle Ashton! Thank you! Thank you."

ALL OUT

THE "THEME FROM MAHOGANY" WAS PLAYING ON KORT radio that autumn afternoon in 1978 and I didn't know where I was going to, frankly—just that I would be going, someday that wouldn't come fast enough. I lay on my double bed, allowing the lyrics to substitute for the therapist I probably would have benefited from seeing but who hadn't thought to hang his shingle in Grangeville, Idaho (population 3,636). I had just rearranged my downstairs bedroom to better accommodate the in-room practice stage that I'd built from cinder blocks, orange bricks, and some shelf-unit boards. Christmas lights were crammed inside each of three holes in each of the bricks and spider-plugged into an already overloaded outlet. The amps I must have been drawing from Bonneville Power to meet the high production values of that basement bedroom performance space, must have made not only the meter spin, but my father's head as well each time he got the monthly utility bill or overheard me rehearsing. I kid you not. A single outlet powered my component AM/FM radio-stereo, a strobe light, a multicolored revolving ballroom light, at least six strings of Christmas lights, and an electric view master that sat in the opposite daylight basement windowsill, to either spotlight my almost daily rehearsal schedule or to lob some National Park scene behind me so

I could replicate outdoor as well as indoor live performances—all the while honing an impeccable and commanding stage presence.

I was on my bed, staring up at the ceiling tiles, listening to the lyrics, and thinking about what life was showing me. I'd recently started fooling around sexually with one of my high school teachers—the aforementioned Evan Knight. In the years leading up to that, I had wrestled, compared attributes, made out, and got my industrial strength nuts off with a statistics-defying number of regulars for a small town that size—boys who were either my age or a year or two younger. I had agreed a few weeks back to taking a night drive on a country road with an upper classman named Dean Colburn, who sat next to me in our mechanical drawing class, and we jerked each other off in the back of his canopied pickup truck. Then there was the mad crush I had on my new best friend, a half-Guamanian beau-hunk named Patrick who arrived with his family from Kuna, a town in southern Idaho. I was dating his older straight-laced sister, Donna, for cover, and had joined his family's tongue-speaking, holy-spirit-filled Pentecostal church on the prairie, just to be closer to my god. Pretty much everything life was showing me indicated that I was going to be a homosexual man when I finished growing up. I looked for any signs to the contrary, but everywhere I turned, my gayness just got rebar-re-inforced by my boner-fied attraction to beautiful men.

Case in point: just that week, Mark Hewitt, a blond senior who had transferred with his family toward the end of the last school year from California to north Idaho of all available options—for reasons I didn't know—had showed me plenty. Now I debated whether or not I should masturbate for maybe the fourth time that day. Whether he did it by accident or as a personally unwrapped gift to me, Mark Hewitt, that blond, center-parted, bad-boy-looking senior from California, our prized running back on the varsity football team, wore gloriously holey jeans to Mr. Smith's algebra class. And he did this, bless him eternally, without wearing underwear. The whole seamed crotch basket was hanging by a denim thread, which allowed his other attributes to hang on either side of that thread too. And hang out they did—all out. The many blessings that spilled forth from that cornucopia between his legs left me lightheaded, and the jerk-off tear I had been on since his open house in algebra class rendered my divining rod positively raw.

If he did it on purpose, then it was because he wanted me to see his junk. He didn't bust me for staring—drooling, really—nor did he make a federal bullying case out of it, so I concluded that he must have done it on purpose, and maybe could be encouraged to do it again. I was in the row of desks to his right and staggered maybe a half-desk behind him. It is where I had sat in that class from the start of the second semester, so as to not be too near the front chalkboard, where I might get called upon to reveal how little I was absorbing the fundamentals of algebra. I mean, he almost had to turn his lower body to the back of the room to give me that open-legged view that capped off my adolescence like a cherry; and then he stayed like that for long after a normal body would have had to correct from cramps. Maybe if I'd paid more attention to the Uri Geller television special that came on after the back-to-back Mutual of Omaha's *Animal Kingdom* and the *Wonderful World of Disney*, I might have been able to focus my concentration to mind-snap that last denim thread to smithereens, emancipating the wild horse that surely yearned to be free. (If you didn't know, Geller was an Israeli-born illusionist and psychic who became a North American television phenom in the late 70s.) But I was too flushed to concentrate—too suspicious the whole set-up might be a sticky-tacky fag trap that would trigger my lynching by the football team—to be caught completely off my guard.

On any other Tuesday or Thursday afternoon in the period that followed lunch, I would have just daydreamed I was a choo-choo train traveling on the track of his puka-shell necklace where it disappeared into the tunnel formed by his shoulder-length and feathered blond hair (just like Shaun Cassidy's) to emerge on the other side blowing my whistle and hugging to a trestle that perilously rounded his pronounced Adam's apple. During a normal algebra class, I might have taken a reality break, in my fraction- and variable-induced boredom, to note and momentarily pity this Adonis his pug nose and lack of kissable lips—since these were his only imperfections, but I had already decided to overlook them anyway.

But this was not just any ordinary day. It was a whole new born-again birthday—my coming out marked by Mark's coming all out. Yes, Diana Ross, thank you. I'd just gotten what I'd been hoping for; do you know?

I needed no further evidence thanks to the clumsy but necessary workshopping I had already done with practically every neighborhood kid I could corner in three towns. I did already know I was a homo, so seeing Mark Hewitt's dong alongside a ball sack divided probably wasn't the epiphany I'm making it out to be, but it was a significant mile post (not to miss another phallic pun) and a journey that had begun long before algebra.

Mark Hewitt, with his hefty accolades, graduated from Grangeville High School a few months later, and I never saw any part of him again after that, except when I closed my eyes and undid my pants.

"The Hustle" played next, launching me off the bed and onto my stage: step back, together, step back, touch . . . step forward, together, step forward, touch . . . rolling grapevine right, clap . . . rolling grapevine left, clap . . . quarter turn left, step back, together, step, touch . . . step forward, together, step, touch . . . four counts of the Travolta . . . then the egg beater . . .

There was a knock on my bedroom door, which was always closed. I opened it an unrevealing crack and my sister fed a short, white envelope through. "Love letter from your boyfriend," she said, not even trying to smother her bullying squeal with a whisper. I snatched the envelope and slammed the door shut with a *whoosh* that caused all but one of the suspended ceiling tiles to jump in their tracks.

The tile that didn't budge was weighted down with a stack of seventeen *Playgirl* magazines—the beginning of a collection that had been growing since I'd started working weekends as a box boy and meat department assistant at Vern's Food City. But that wasn't the only porn I kept in my bedroom. In the closet where the main sewer pipe cleanout jutted through a jig-sawed opening in the painted plywood, I kept stashed a plastic Polaroid film cartridge. Inside the cartridge, I had reinserted photographic evidence of my Herculean development; most noticeably apparent in a series of erection shots where I am straining the engineering of a toilet paper tube that cannot contain me. Oh, yes. I stashed this cartridge behind the wall in my closet, and forgot about it, leaving home for world travel and college and life and not thinking about it again until years after my parents had sold the house and moved to Moscow. [Post-mortem note: This house at the edge of town has since sold again twice in thirty years—with my not-so-little time capsule still presumably asleep in the wall.]

But back to the handwritten and postage-marked letter that my sister had just delivered. My fingers traced the blue-lined stationery of the envelope, and I raised the Seattle Seahawk logo to my nose in case it was scented or perfumed—and faintly, to my surprise, it was, with either Brut or Paco Rabanne. My name and address were handwritten in flowing cursive on the front, and the sender's name, Doug Long, was squeezed in handwritten all caps above the team logo and return address.

I'll be damned, I thought! Doug Long was writing me. Doug Long, one of the most decorated football players in the entire pantheon of Whitworth University, and a two-season free-agent defensive back and special teams player with the Seattle Seahawks, had sent me a hand-written letter. It was only fair, since I had sent the same to him after meeting him and hearing him speak—provide his testimonial, really, six weeks earlier at a weekend church camp for teens at Gonzaga Prep University, outside of Spokane. He'd spoken about his personal relationship with Jesus Christ, how he took Jesus into the locker room and onto the field with him, and I thought, hell, I want that gig, so I wrote to him to tell him how touched I was by the personal story of redemption he had shared, and how much it had inspired me—in my tiny farming town in North Central Idaho—to serve the Lord. It was all back-pasture bullshit, of course, and it was my first brush with someone famous, so I would have said just about anything to get his attention.

Without a KORT Radio disk jockey transition, "The Hustle" faded out and "Grease" by Frankie Valli faded in.

> . . . We got a lovin' thing, we gotta feed it right
> There ain't no danger we can go too far
> We start believin' now that we can be who we are

I carefully opened the gummed back flap of the envelope, already knowing that what I held in my hands had the makings of one helluva prize, and would give me an excuse to phone Patrick and sit nearly in his lap while we read the letter together. But then what if I called and his sister Donna answered the phone—the girl in my class that I was pretending to date, while pretending to be Christian and pretending to be straight. I'd have to tell Patrick when I saw him next in person and since we had church like three times a week, my news could keep. But I couldn't wait until then to read the letter. Inside the envelope were four single-sided handwritten pages, folded in half just once. Again, I ritualistically brought the stationary to my face, breathing in the genuine man scent I had imported as stealthily as if it were white rhino horn powder. It certainly had the same vexing powers. I sat on the edge of my bed, knowing a light-headed faint onto any of the sharp corners of my practice stage would draw blood and likely leave a scar.

> Dear Ash (I hope it's okay if I call you that):
>
> I received your letter last week and I wanted to write you back right away to tell you how very proud I am of you and the path you've chosen to serve Our Lord. I certainly do remember meeting you and thought then that your intensity must have been a calling from a higher power. Your letter tells me that I was right about that. You struck me as an intelligent kid with a special appeal that will draw others close to you to witness your love for Jesus Christ.
>
> I am doing well. Thank you for asking. You probably watched the game on TV last weekend where we had a glorious 27-7 win over the Oakland Raiders. Through the power of Christ, I was presented with the game ball for my performance during this game—this was such an honor for me, and of course I give it all over to the Glory of the Lord my God. We have eight games left in the regular season, so I am working hard, but praying harder

that the Lord will use me as an instrument to bring others to know Him like I do—like we both do.

I am very involved in the Fellowship of Christian Athletes and I serve at least once a week giving testimonials with the Pro Athletes' Outreach Team in the Seattle Area.

Thank you for the photo you sent me to remember you by. It makes me grin because we seem to have the exact same hairstyle—long and not very manageable. What can you do about it, right? At least I get to wear a football helmet half of every week. Keep in touch, keep the faith and let me know how things are going for you in Idaho. If you and your Dad can make it to Seattle for a home game, let me know and I'll see about getting you some tickets.

Your Brother in the Lord,
Doug Long

He had autographed it.

I read the letter like twelve more times. "Grease" merged into "Afternoon Delight."

Thinkin' of you's workin' up my appetite
Looking forward to a little afternoon delight
Rubbin' sticks and stones together . . .

I stared nearly cross-eyed at the photo I was holding with the letter in my left hand as my right hand tugged my pants open to liberate my sky rocket in flight. I had to grab lower than I normally would, as the under cap of my damned circumcised penis head was scabbing over nicely and I wanted to let it heal, you know—but between Mark Hewitt, Patrick, Evan Knight, and now Doug Long I had too damn much material, and it would have been a sin to be idle. I applied some Polysporin and then pig-in-a-blanketed it with a hot washcloth compress. Of course, Carole, this setback wouldn't have happened in the first place (or ever) with foreskin.

Unlike the Polaroid cartridge stashed in the wall of my childhood bedroom closet, I was coming out—and just like Mark Hewitt—all out, just not then and not all at once. But I figured out young that I was going to live my life a proud, out gay man, and that I would definitely have to leave Idaho the first chance I got in order to accomplish this—and, well . . . anything, really. Limping Rabbit would have to leave Idaho too. We could not have met each other there, given the circumstances under which we were raised, and that divided state of backwardness. We had to leave to find our new home in each other.

RUSSELL

IT WAS WHILE WORKING AS A CLERK WITH THE SEATTLE/ King County Department of Public Health's Community AIDS Services Unit that I encountered the sublime Russell Connor, who calmed my ocean and lowered my spinnakers and taught me how—and that it was okay—to drift after a decade of unrelenting headwinds that had left me tattered. Just weeks before, at the end of August, 1995 (a little less than a year before I would meet Rich Dreadfulwater at an AIDS fundraiser), I had moved from Denver, fleeing a soul-crushing job with the Colorado AIDS Project, to be back home in the Pacific Northwest. Totally immersed in the nasty business of this plague, and weighing my own ridiculously irresponsible behavior, I had become certain that I would sero-convert at any second. I had felt this irresistible imperative to come home to die.

The tidy, almost systematic acceptance of my morbid reality had been borne on the heels of a wicked stretch of whoring while traveling solo through South America, where my attempts at accelerating the end had me recklessly collecting and leaving globs of DNA in six countries (Brazil, Venezuela, Colombia, Argentina, Chile, and Uruguay), with about twenty different men in a compressed period of just about three weeks. I didn't even bother learning the first names of half of these hombres, but of course, they were all uncircumcised, so it was as if they were Ashton Taylor-made. I had become a foreskin addict on a jizz junket, fornicating recklessly out of control. I had joked with confidantes that I was doing this in the name of science, and that I should have applied for grants to underwrite my *1996 Brown Uncut Research Tour—B.U.R.T.* for short—as it would revolutionize modern thinking and bring about the informed end to the medical mutilation of North American boys. Like Simón Bolívar, I would become forever-venerated in future uncut circle jerks as "El Libertador."

Behind the curtain—or under the hood, if you will (pun intended)—I had grown clinically anxious over the moment when that ultimate test would return positive. I truly wanted to get that part over with in order to have something definitive and constructive to focus on, because waiting for the inevitable was killing me. My *B.U.R.T.* was subconsciously designed to speed the plow, cut to the chase scene, and pretty much get on with it already. This was my second down cycle in the fourteen years of the AIDS crisis up to that point—and by "down," I mean really, resigned-to-die down. I was never suicidal about this or anything else in my life, but every seven years or so since beating cancer in '84—call it my itch, I guess—but I would become impatient with my lifespan when it didn't jive with my premonitions of croaking young.

I wouldn't test positive, not ever. And I would meet the greatest uncut man of my life within the year that followed my rigid research. But first I needed to risk my luck and travel to extreme lengths beyond rational boundaries exorcising demons and testing fates to prove I was alive and worthy to be so. And because everyone and everything in my life came to me only when I was ready for it, I had to encounter Russell Connor who laid his giant hands on my soul to recondition me for what needed to come next in my life if it wasn't going to be death.

We were workmates in the same health unit. At the time, he was six years younger and about six inches taller, with shoulders that could get stuck in a doorway. His eyes were flaming arrows, so light brown they were nearly orange, and he shot them clean through me. I was pierced and delightfully wriggling, like an earthworm on a hook, too dumb to know it was mortal. When we met on my first day as a new employee on the unit, Russell's black-skinned hand wrapped around mine, like a much larger boa that wouldn't let go, ever. He smiled, revealing dimpled cheeks and braces on already perfectly straight and equally sized teeth, and I remember wondering in that moment if maybe I could fall in love with him on the spot.

In the seconds that followed, he introduced me to Niles, his skinny, tall and beautiful blond boyfriend—also in the unit and technically reporting to me as his supervisor. My internal scream would have shattered the sound barrier and blown out all the windows of the hundred-year-old Yesler Building, but consummate professional that I was, I held it together so that the building and all its inhabitants could be spared. Then I began to plot the destruction of Niles and anyone else who dared to place themselves between me and my new obsession—*Dear Jesus, let him not be circumcised*, I prayed and then preyed.

As flirting contests go, I'd have to give this one an "eight." Bystanders might argue another half-point for unbridled deviousness, but I began to hold back as I got to know (and, surprisingly, like) Niles. Then, in a rapid double play, I met Limping Rabbit at an AIDS Research Fundraising art auction at the SAM, where, not even twenty minutes earlier, Russell had innocently yet disqualifyingly revealed he was circumcised, during a conversation I'd intentionally steered in that direction. The spell was broken. In that instant, this Cupid took aim at a new and even more exotic target—an authentic American Indian. I'd never been with a Native man, which, given my statistics, came as a shock to me—and, later when we talked numbers, to Gideon as well.

Rich Dreadfulwater and I were both after the same painting by a British Columbia artist named Lyle Shultz, and in a delicious tango we took cutting turns toward the bid sheet, our eyes fiercely locked in a pact . . . to the death, as it turns out. The fancy-pants defense lawyer had deeper pockets—all of which I suddenly wanted to get into—so the painting went to him, but I pledged in that defeat to make the painting ours. We shook hands in a truce that commenced all new terms of engagement while Russell stewed in a corner behind a sandstone sculpture. There was an exchange of business cards, a furtive embrace, and a plan to meet for a late lunch downtown during a break in his trial schedule. There we would discover we'd both been born in '62, and that we had grown up 58.4 miles apart. Russell, relegated and not at all happy about it, began to see or manufacture (it was hard to tell) incompatibilities with Niles that caused a fair bit of cubicle friction on the Unit that I tried to deflect by gushing more and more about the singularly spectacular Rich Dreadfulwater in front of both of them. That didn't save their sputtering relationship but it did wonders for jumpstarting mine.

I became Russell's confidante, which seemed like the perfect role for me in his life, and for him in mine. For twenty years, we were the first call, text, or cross-town sprint either of us would make, no matter the challenge. He became my best friend, and I worked really hard to never let him down. This included being his best man when he married Donovan in a civil union ceremony; playing uncle to their adopted beauties Le'liana and Zander; encouraging him to give his lesbian friend, Natalie, the black Russell seed she needed to grow a mixed-race Simone; and sitting enthusiastically through all three acts of his Tacoma Musical Theatre production of *The Wiz*.

On the other end of this balancing act, Russell talked me through one AIDS test after another; practically held my dick out of the way as I had that fake nut threaded through my groin and popped into my scrotum (surgical procedure #6); gift wrapped for me the best job I'd ever been offered working at the Fred Hutchinson Cancer Research Centre; convinced me it was overkill to keep HIV testing long after I'd been mostly monogamous (96.8%, thank you for that fidelity report card, Gideon) in my almost completely non-anal relationship with Limping Rabbit; and worked really hard—sometimes around the clock—to convince me that I wasn't going to die young, despite my paranoid belief to the contrary. And hey—I practically made it to fifty-four which isn't that young, right? Sure, it's a quarter century shy of the mean life expectancy of a North American male but it isn't young. Dying from cancer in '84 would have been dying young. Dying from AIDS in the 90s? Marginally young. Dying in my early fifties doesn't seem old. Still, that Russell did a pretty decent job of keeping me real, all things considered.

But now I'm gone. His watch is over. Aside from remembering, there's just one last task.

Ashton Taylor, *Last Will and Testament*, page 15

To my dearest friend for almost the past twenty years in this life I've led, Russell Connor, I entrust with you this film canister of my cremains, just as I trusted you with my secrets, my panics, my conspiracy theories, my delusions, my life, and my love. Our crazy dance together was syncopated with a drumline of what-ifs, so please take comfort in knowing that I have died wondering how things could have been different for us; how life might have turned out, how long I could have held on in this life if only you had just been uncircumcised. Ha, ha, ha!

Here are your instructions: To honor my memory and anything about me that might have been honorable, please celebrate again the wonderful time the four of us had together at Mardi Gras in '98. Donovan and Rich were so preciously embarrassed when you and I decided to show our dicks for a few strings of plastic pearls on Bourbon Street, weren't they?

I want you to take my cremains to the top of that hotel we stayed at; I think it was the Westin. You'll remember— the one with the pool on the roof overlooking the French Quarter and that crooked bend in the Mississippi River that reminded you of Juan or José—that Latino guy you picked up in the UW change room. Now I bet he was uncut!

My memory of that weekend in the Big Easy is sketchy; obviously heavily influenced by a blood-alcohol level that I'm certain rivaled my body weight. But I'd like you to spread these ashes on top of those big, blue-neon letters on top of that hotel so that I can perch on that lookout with the peregrines and the pigeons and experience every Mardi Gras and every sissy hurricane yet to arrive, foolishly thinking it can quash NOLA's spirit.

Speaking at the 12th Annual Women & HIV International Clinical

Conference (WHICC), Russell is in New Orleans again. Next up for him: the 2016 National Latino HIV/Hepatitis Conference, in South Padre, Texas. Then it's off to Durban, South Africa, for the 21st International AIDS Conference.

It's not easy to determine what his career might have been had it not been for a sexy blond flight attendant for Air Canada named Gaëtan Dugas, who got shackled for eternity to the moniker of "Patient O," and an erroneous but institutionally supported theory that he alone had introduced the acquired immune deficiency syndrome to North America. In talks given around the world, Russell would often include a few PowerPoint slides dedicated to this poor dead man, trying to correct what history, the CDC, and current affairs writers like Randy Shiltz had gotten hysterically wrong about him. In fact, Dugas was not the first individual to present HIV Positive outside the known infection area (though that was the reason for his unusual label, as the "O" in "Patient O" stood for "outside California"—not "zero," although it would often be misread that way). He was not the index patient for this plague, Russell knew, and should no longer be villainized as such. Russell's most oft-quoted lines—the ones that prompted him to raise his voice dramatically, and drew applause and media wherever he presented—went like this: "AIDS came from Zaire to Haiti in 1967, from there to NYC in 1971, and then to San Francisco around 1976 . . . It did not arrive sipping champagne and nibbling caviar on crackers in first class on Air Canada. In fact, Gaëtan Dugas was not even hired by the airline until 1974, at the age of 21. This lovely man did not—I repeat, did not—give AIDS to America."

Now killing some time until dusk, Russell has wandered into the French Quarter to people watch; a film canister snuggled up in his front jeans pocket, riding shotgun against his package. He could get into some serious trouble in this city if he were a single man, the fantasy of which makes him grin in an almost evil way. He could even get into more trouble too as a married man, which makes him hyperaware of the creatures that lurk in these surroundings. A man his size, with those eyes and that smile, tempts humanity. And humanity tempts back with a vengeance that sometimes makes it difficult for Russell to breathe. But tonight, he has a date to FaceTime with his kids at 10 p.m. CST, which is bedtime PST. This keeps his stroll brisk.

He thinks as he walks down Bourbon Street that this city had been through hell and back since the last time he'd been here—and by this, he means the destructive force of AIDS, and not Katrina's dervish through the streets eleven years ago. He walks past the Bourbon Pub & Parade, pokes his head inside Napoleon's Itch, and finally decides to use the john at Oz. Because he is a born Southerner from Florida's panhandle, and because he is a researcher and a scholar, Russell knows his stuff—namely that Louisiana's modern-day HIV problem is a direct consequence of its social conditions post-Katrina. Not that they were swanky, prior. He knows the statistics in Louisiana are dismal, with nearly 18,000 people living with HIV, and maybe 2,000 more who don't yet know they have it. As an African American, he knows the stats are disproportionately affecting black people, and next week in Texas his colleagues will discuss how Latinos aren't lagging far behind.

In his work, he can't just be somewhere, using the toilet in the stall of a club. AIDS took his very first boyfriend, Michael, from him in 1994. AIDS takes several hours of his every single day, and AIDS has never, and probably never will stop taking. Even though the world has moved on to SARS and Ebola and the Zika virus, Russell is stuck and still sinking in AIDS, and is HIV-Negative.

He steps to the sink to wash his hands, and is ambushed by a white guy—my height, my build, with the same green eyes and shaved head—who has been standing idle at the urinal just waiting to pounce on the black man he'd tracked across the wide open dance floor into the toilets. Russell thinks he's seeing a ghost and pinches his fingers around the outline of the canister in his pants.

"No, go ahead," Russell offers with an outstretched hand.

Grabbing Russell's hand and pulling him to the sink, my doppel-ganger says, "No reason we can't wash our hands together; conserve a little water."

The act is not something Russell refuses, finding the tandem hand washing to be more sensually loaded than some of the sex he's had at home lately. "I don't think my hands are that dirty," he volunteers with a giggle after a minute without withdrawing them.

"Filthy, I think." The white man pauses at the ring finger. "Accessory or wedding?" he asks, spinning the titanium band.

"Married, father of three," Russell responds with his orange eyes and that mouth of perfect teeth.

"Very lucky kids to have such a sexy daddy."

"Thank you," Russell says with a southern gentility. He would be blushing if he could, but instead uses that reminder of his responsibilities to cut things short. He reaches for enough paper towels for both of them, and takes a step back from the sink. "Thank you for your attention to my hygiene," he says, more firmly.

"It was my pleasure. Now, would there be anything else I could take care of for you? That's just how caring I am." His eyes fixate on the film canister, which suggests that Russell is hanging much further down his quadriceps than he does. Russell hesitates, which of course proves fatal, and the predator hunches for the kill. With his six-foot-four-inch wingspan, Russell braces an iron cross between the bathroom door and the toilet stall, as the buttons of his jeans are viciously torn open. *Am I going to allow this to happen?* is the question in his mind, and in the mind of his seducer, possibly on the mind of his husband at home with the kids; hey, even I am wondering where this is headed—maybe you too.

"No. I'm sorry. I can't do this."

The other man protests, "You don't have to do anything!"

"I have to leave." Russell releases his brace, guides the man to a standing position with big black hands cradling both sides of the stranger's jaw, and then redoes the front of his pants. "Thank you again for the very thorough hand washing."

Back on Bourbon Street and back on track for the Westin Hotel, he turns left at the corner of Rue Iberville, and heads now toward the diked and mighty Mississippi. He has managed to focus his intentions in the middle of this city full of distractions. Just past North St. Peter's Street, he ducks into the lower lobby at One Canal Place, and nods a racially coded look to the equally tall doorman. The look says: we're black, better-than-cool, equal, invincible, important, potent African brothers, and we know it. The doorman gives him the exact same look in return. The whole exchange has taken less than two and a half seconds.

Russell uses his room keycard to summon an elevator. A few minutes later, he emerges into an expansive two-story lobby with floor-to-ceiling windows and oversized flower displays the size of Volkswagen beetles; the latter sit atop vintage Louis the Fourteenth furniture. The view out the windows shows a serpentine river squiggling off into the distance toward Lake Pontchartrain. For ceremony and just because it is antebellum awesome, Russell ascends the grand semi-circular staircase like he owns the place, or at the very least has earned the right to be able to afford to stay here.

Outside the hotel's ballrooms, he checks his watch, sees he has a good 20 minutes before Faceatiming his kids, summons another elevator—perhaps the same one he had the option to stay on had he not needed to make his grand entrance—and he presses the *POOL/ROOF* button. Surely it has become dark enough outside to carry out Ashton Taylor's scheme.

Russell walks up the slight ramp to the open air and astro-turfed pool deck. Perfectly alone on the abandoned roof, he canvasses the surroundings, planning his task in real time as his eyes move from the reflection on the pool's surface to the source of the blue light: the Westin insignia, followed by the four-foot-tall, baby-blue letters spelling out CANAL PLACE on the fascia of the elevator tower that still rises another story above him. Though a tall man, Russell determines he needs a pool deck chair to be able to reach the top of the letters.

He tower-cranes a white, plastic-ribbed chair onto the other side of the pool deck railing, setting it down on the gravel-topped roof membrane. From a standing position, he hurdles the railing, thanks to his DNA-generous inseam, and steps onto the wobbly chair, hoping the plastic weave can take his weight. He begins to crawl his hands up the wall to see if he can reach the top of the blue letters to deposit the ashes. He can't, but maybe, he thinks, if he steps onto the chair's arms that will give him the clearance.

Discovering a leg-quivering balance thirty-one stories above Rue

Iberville below, he moves first one and then the other leg onto the chair arms, holding rather precariously onto the letter "C" as he rises, lifting his 230 pounds into a manageable levitation. Just as his fingers confirm success, there is a dull, hollow drum percussion sound of metal that is starting to bend in increments, raising his blood pressure to new levels of danger. Trying to determine if the sounds are emanating from the flimsy deck chair or from the letter "C," Russell stretches his neck just as the chair crumples in on itself, leaving him hanging from the top of the over-sized letter. Before he can make the decision to let go and drop the four feet to the graveled roof, the top of the "C" pulls out of the angle iron it was bolted to, then flickers on, then off, then on again, and—"shit!" Russell yells—off for good. He holds his breath and drops to the roof with a two-footed thud. For miles around, and certainly from the Sheraton two blocks away, the building's sign no longer reads CANAL PLACE.

MONICA

Ashton Taylor, *Last Will and Testament*, page 15

I don't want this to seem like an oversight or a snub since you and I have known each other since we were eighteen and saw some amazing places together while we toured with the *Up with People* show and on several world expeditions after. . . Portugal, Germany, Spain, Belgium, Holland, British Columbia . . . any one of which would make a handsome and appropriate repository for the bits of me inside this canister. I know how sensitive you are, Monica, and how prone you are to leap beyond the world long-jump record to obsess over an action, an email, a voicemail, something that was said, or a behavior that might be construed (mostly only by you) to be hurtful or devious. So let me be really clear and go on record that in this request, I am using you. I won't disguise this. I won't fabricate a whole other backstory. Plain and simply put, I need a mule, Monica.

IT HAD TAKEN HER two months of calculating before she could successfully bid and hold a Denver overnight. Though she now flies for American and has a crazy twenty-seven and a half years of seniority accumulated with four different airlines that all got swallowed up into mergers, it was surprising to her just how difficult it was to find a series of flights she could nab and cobble together to build this twenty-two hour layover in the middle of the country. She could have just done this on her own time, flown non-rev, or deadheaded and sprung for a hotel room . . . nah, she really couldn't. Monica doesn't pay for anything she can get for free—or, at the very least, half-off with a Groupon.

Of course, you're thinking—because when it comes to me you are all-knowing—this request must have something to do with a guy; that it couldn't have anything to do with the depth of our friendship or the times you were there for me, the boundless love and respect I have for you, or the lifetime of travel we accomplished together. And though you've heard me say this before too, he wasn't just any guy. His name was Cornelius, something like six-foot-thirteen, surely kicked out of the pantheon of alarmingly handsome Greek gods for being too beautiful. He went by Neil, though I could never bring myself to abbreviate any-thing about him. So picture this: there he was, looking up at me from the tunnel of the automated baggage system between concourses A and B, four stories below the earth, this swaying, swaggering Paul Bunyan-esque construction specialist who worked for BAE Automated Systems. He had come with his company from Texas, where everything is enormous, to help build the Denver International Airport that replaced Stapleton in 1994. I was on a V.I.P. tour of the construction site as a personal guest of the General Man-ager of the closest hotel to the sprawling fifty-two square mile airport; his hotel lobby was about to see a massive seven-days-a-week public tour program hastily organized to counter the mounting public criticism for a public works project running billions over budget and already a year behind its promised opening. Cornelius was in charge of installing the actuators that were designed to move luggage from belt to belt, but which instead sometimes fire-launched the bags out of the system and against the unforgiving walls of the tunnel.

Cornelius and I had this colossal fling, and just as I realized I was falling in love with him, he disappeared. 224 pounds of all-American, Grade A sir-loin, he walked into the tunnels beneath this airport and vanished.

And because you also know that just as I fervently believe 9/11 was an inside job, that Oswald didn't kill Kennedy, and that Armstrong, Aldrin, Conrad, Bean, Shepard, Mitchell, Scott, Irwin, Young, Duke, Schmitt, and Cernan never left astronaut boot prints on the surface of the moon, I know also that Denver International Airport is certainly built on top of a secret government underground bunker city that may or may not harbor reptile-faced hybrid alien-humanoids. I want you to get under that airport and into the baggage tunnel. You've got credentials on a lanyard around your neck. Use them! I want these remains to rest near the spot I first encountered that divine creature, Cornelius. And PS (really stressing the P part): I love you.

Compared to the difficulty of landing the layover, it had been a wide-body stretch easier for Monica to get a tour into the bowels of the airport, for her and the other attendants (Brian, Johnnea, D.B., and Secorra), who were all on her outbound to Philadelphia later in the day. Gathering at a Seattle's Best Coffee outlet forty-five minutes before the official tour time, Monica, just as prone to hop on top of a conspiracy theory as I had been, conducts her own, quite adequately researched, guided tour of the airport's more blatantly displayed *objets d' confusing art.* She starts with the marker in the floor of the main Jeppesen Terminal that at the time dedicated the airport with the inscription "New World Airport Commission." The engraved plate also lists the two Grand Freemason Lodges in Colorado, and features the Knights Templar symbols that form a diamond around a letter "G" out of a compass and a square. Monica informs her entourage, in her deepest tour-guide voice, that "I read that this capstone was actually placed here by Free Masons in a ceremony, and as you can see." She points expertly with an open hand toward the floor. "There is a time capsule underneath that is not to be opened until the Year 2094." This elicits the requisite *ooohs* and *aaahs*, as though she were reading aloud from a Dan Brown fiction thriller. From this starting point, Mama leads her navy-blue uniformed and brass-winged ducklings to the escalators that take them to Level 5 of the main terminal. Here, she interprets the murals by Leo Tanguma that may or may not depict the end of the world. She points to the gasmask-wearing soldier holding a sword and a machine gun who appears in different murals, and asks, "Like, what the fuck is this supposed to mean?"

"You are not allowed to swear in uniform," Johnnea points out, as she checks her Facebook on her iPhone.

"Fuck that noisy noise," D.B. says. "What the living hell is that supposed to mean? And this citation about *Hanus*, the fourteen-year-old who died in Auschwitz in 1943? This shit is crazy!"

"You too," Johnnea warns, wagging an index finger without looking up from her social newsfeed.

Monica takes the opportunity of their height on the second-to-uppermost levels of the Teflon-coated and woven fiberglass-tented terminal, to walk her group to the south-facing windows, where she doesn't have to point out the eerie, thirty-two-foot-tall statue of the blue horse outside. It is reared up on its back legs—either greeting or warning those who approach the airport, depending on your level of cynicism.

"It's called *Blue Mustang*, but some locals refer to it as *Blucifer*, though I can't imagine why; maybe for its beaming red halogen headlight eyes, its obvious thirst for blood, and its Four Horseman of the Apocalypse vibe. But then again, maybe that's just me."

"Did anyone else notice the dong on that donkey driving into the airport from the hotel this morning?" Brian asks seriously, possibly missing the point of this stop on the conspiracy express.

"You know I did without even asking, Sugar!" D.B. trails off to snap a photo of the statue's hind quarters. "Made me pop in my polyester!"

"Well," Monica regains control of her tour spiel, "did you two size queens know that the sculptor, Luis Jiménez, actually was killed after a large section of this horse fell on him, severing an artery in his leg?" Eyes around the semicircle grow larger.

"It was probably that phallus that fell off." Brian's comment sends the boys into giggles.

"Seriously?" Secorra asks. "You two think that's funny? How infantile, honestly."

Monica notices the time. "Whoa, we gotta go!" She pats the film canister in her front blazer pocket.

"*Whoa.* That's the sound a horse rider makes. Now, *that's* funny!" Johnnea looks up to discover she has to catch up to her already-departing group.

As arranged, Monica and company head to the sixth level, walk to the opposite end of the main terminal and just to the left of the A Bridge security checkpoint, and report to the Administration Office right on time. It is their tour guide who shows up a minute late—but when he does arrive no one seems annoyed.

"Hi there. So sorry to be running behind," says the gorgeous hunk of man, who is holding five extra hard hats with hands that could slow pitch the planet through the galaxy. Reflective vests are draped over a forearm that makes Popeye look like a wussy. "My name is Cornelius, but you can call me Neil. I will be taking you deep inside the airport today."

Atta girl, Monica!

Woof! [That was Gideon. Not me.]

SAM

THANKS TO A TEXT HE'D RECEIVED EARLIER IN THE DAY from Russell, a black pushpin now finds its place sticking through the world map at New Orleans, Louisiana. It is followed by a second pushpin that pierces the dot marking the location of Las Vegas. Rich is cradling his iPhone with his right shoulder as he moves to the back of the map to attach the pencil erasers.

"I don't think Ash resented you, Sam. He did express to me once or twice that he was confused why you made puppets in the likeness of all your other friends, but you wouldn't make one of him, even after he asked you."

There's a pause.

"You even modeled a puppet after me, and you'd known Ash long before I came along." Rich emerges from behind the map. "Yes, I know you needed an Indian for your Lewis and Clark sketch, but I don't think it would have been unreasonable to write a clinically, middle-aged hypochondriac into the expedition party." He examines his reflection in the evening window. To look possibly more Indian, he simulates two braids by grabbing his hair and pulling the bunches forward. He thinks it makes him look like Sacajawea Longstocking.

"Well, I wouldn't say he developed a whole separate complex over this, but you know how Ash was," he goes on. "Every symptom, ailment, and insecurity had its fifteen minutes of fame on his pay-at-tention-to-me scale, before he moved on to something else that was *definitely killing him.*" He releases his hair. "Thanks for telling me. Now, so I'm clear, you encased his ashes in the head of the puppet, right? Then I'm certain Ash is pleased with your rendition of him." Rich starts to wish Sam good luck, but remembers that is not appropriate for theater. "Uh, break a puppet leg, with the premiere. Goodbye, Sam."

By rote, Sam disconnects the call and puts his phone on vibrate, cues the track with the medieval roundelay, then plugs the puppet box audio system into the headphones jack. On the backstage side of the giant puppet theatre, he's taped a printout of a fairly decent photo of me he could have grabbed from Facebook had he been quick about it. As my appointed Legacy Contact, my husband recently deactivated my Facebook account after coming clean with his sister about my conspicuously stalled status. Deactivation had always been part of my exit plan from the World Wide Web as I didn't want my profile memorialized so people would feel obligated to creep around my timeline all sad-like, posting crying emoticons and leaving morose, epitaph-like messages—or worse, Bible scriptures about how much I'd meant to them or how close they thought we were. It had always disturbed me when FB would remind me of a dead friend's birthday. *Why not wish Steve a Happy Birthday*? UH, MAYBE BECAUSE HE STOPPED HAVING THEM THREE YEARS AGO! (And yes, all caps because it needed to be shouted!) I wanted the world to face it: Facebook isn't an appropriate platform for the non-living; so when the ol' timeline is no more, get the hell offline already because we could really use the bandwidth. Besides, nobody wants to see a selfie of you where you've stopped aging when they haven't; pisses people off. Anyway, Rich had just delayed following through with this deactivation task for a few months as a symptom of his greater communications crisis around my absence.

As Sam studies the photo and contemplates me, the puppet he's finally fashioned in my former likeness animatedly pops up next to the photo, and the resemblance is obvious. Sam's other hand fixes a king's crown to the puppet's bald head, which contains my ashes. He then ties a royal robe around its neck.

"It's showtime, King Barticus!" Sam sings quietly to himself before taking a long, deep breath and pressing the play arrow on his iPhone. A mostly strings ensemble crescendos out of speakers that ring the kiva-like sunken theatre space that he talked the DLR Group into letting him create during a retro-fit of the mall about six years ago. Children begin applauding on the other side of the curtain, some seated and others standing in the much-heralded Meadows Mall Atrium Puppet Theatre, situated in the triangulation of open space between the entrances to Dillard's, The Disney Store, and Peet's Coffee and Tea.

The volume of the royal music diminuendos and the curtains are tossed open to reveal a delightfully crafted miniature castle set, complete with throne. The puppet that looks like me makes his debut sauntering onto the puppet stage with his puppet hands on his crowned puppet head. The children applaud enthusiastically.

Sam delivers King Barticus's commanding voice: "Oh my head! My head is splitting in two! I am certain the palace chef is trying to poison me!" The children scream, thinking absolutely everything is funny.

A second puppet, Queen Constance—modeled after a mutual friend, Kate—follows behind him into the castle set. It should be noted that this puppet has been a longstanding member of this repertory troupe, with a character dossier as long as the arm up her dress. Kate didn't have to beg to get a puppet made in her likeness.

Sam changes registers to broadcast Queen Constance's voice: "If anyone wanted to poison you, it would be me. Now, help me button the back of my dress."

The children squeal as the queen turns her back to the king, who ignores her anyway. Sam props the queen puppet in a holder that keeps her visible, with her back to the audience, so he can manipulate a third puppet. The king doesn't attend to the queen's dress, but instead walks to the shuttered windows, throwing them open with his puppet arms and shouting, "My kingdom for an aspirin!"

Simultaneously, courtesy of a contraption modeled after a foot-operated snare drum, there is the sound of a rapid knock at the door.

"Come in!" shouts Sam, in the king's voice. A wooden door at the back of the set swings open, and in walks a villager puppet. Sam parks the villager in another holding notch in the castle floor, spins the queen's head so she can look at who has just entered, and turns the king around from the window and moves him toward the villager. The villager, who looks remarkably Native American—with braids on either side of his head, a headband, and two red bars painted beneath each eye—is nevertheless dressed in medieval garb. He bows his head reverently.

"Your Royal Majesty, I have heard your decree, and I have brought you an aspirin!" the Indian-looking villager exclaims, holding out a velvet pillow on which every child in the audience can see is propped something else entirely. The atrium erupts in howling.

"That is not an aspirin! That is a cinnamon roll! Do you take your king for a fool?" Sam snaps the king's head around, drops the villager's chin to its chest and moves the queen a little closer in.

"King, my King, calm down," Sam says, in the queen's voice. "Mind your blood pressure!" Sam props her against the throne.

Sam switches to the villager's voice, but perhaps not as cleanly as rehearsed, and says: "Your Highness, I was assured by the wizard that this was an aspirin, sure to cure the worst headache in the kingdom."

"Say . . ." the king says, walking closer to examine the villager. "You're not from around here, are you?"

"Is it my accent that gives me away?" Sam makes the villager's voice ascend into soprano. There is scattered adult laughter since it is obvious from the puppet's ethnicity that he came from someplace else.

The king turns away. "Yeah, that must be it. Look here," he commands. "You have exactly one hour to bring me that wizard!" The villager starts to leave. "But leave that cinnamon roll here!" the king bellows.

The villager drops the pillow with the pastry onto the throne, and then rushes to leave, sort of hitting the doors with his face before actually exiting them. The children in the audience go wild. Sam pauses to let them get it out of their systems, because he wants the next exchange to get a chuckle out of the scarcely supervising adults, whose faces are in their phones.

Sam delivers the queen's voice: "Surely, you are not going to eat that cinnamon roll, are you? It could be poisoned!"

"Surely, I am not," says King Barticus. "But surely you are! I command you to eat that cinnamon roll!" The queen protests loudly but the king shoves the cinnamon roll into her face. "Eat it!" the king shouts, almost demonically. The audience laughs, clapping at the farce.

Suddenly, the queen stops struggling, and is still a moment. The king holds her in his arms, thinking her dead, and shouts "Just wait until I get my hands on that wizard!" The audience sees and hears Queen Constance drop to the floor with a thud (courtesy of the snare drum). The king goes to the window and shouts, "My kingdom for a cinnamon roll!" Almost simultaneously, there is a rapid knock at the door. The king spins around. "Yes, who is it?" he demands.

The villager returns through the doors at the back of the set. "I have returned, Your Majesty, with a cinnamon roll, as you have decreed." The Villager displays a new red velvet pillow, but on it is a tiny white tablet.

The puppet that looks like me lowers his crowned head to look at the pillow. "Why, that's not a cinnamon roll! It looks like, like . . . this is an aspirin!"

"No, your Royal Highness," the villager corrects the king. "I assure you, it is indeed a cinnamon roll, as you have decreed."

The king looks out to the audience raising his arms, looking for their support, and the children detonate. He looks down at the pillow, then back at the audience. More laughter.

"And this was given to you, I am to gather, by that same wizard?"

It is the now the village Indian puppet's turn to look at the audience. He looks down at the aspirin, then up at the King. "Yeah, well, about that . . . I made up the *wizard* part."

The king puppet begins to lose it. "You what? You made it up?" The king butts heads with the villager. "You just made it up? Now, see here. You've killed Queen Constance. You've lied to your king . . ."

"She's sleeping."

"Who's sleeping?"

"Queen Constance. She's only sleeping. She finds you boring, so she has decided to take a nap." The villager gets the biggest laugh yet. Sam finds children very sophisticated.

The music amplifies as the king's tirade grows. Sam purposely knocks the king's crown off to reveal his bald head, which gets a laugh. He just continues screaming and flailing his arms like a lunatic, chasing the double-crossing villager around the castle set. The king begins demolishing the set. The children are screaming with hilarity, as some of the adults in the audience have started to look up from their Facebook and eHarmony and Instagram and Grindr apps, thinking that maybe they should be concerned and perhaps even horrified by this sudden violent outburst at the Meadows Mall Atrium Puppet Theatre.

Sam almost feels like he isn't controlling what is happening above him in the theatre box. He withdraws the villager puppet from the chaotic scene with his left hand, but when he lowers his right, King Barticus is no longer attached to the paddle. Children in the audience are screaming and shouting. Given the sounds of thumping and the shadows being tossed around in the lights above the puppeteer's head, the king seems to have gone rogue and off script, destroying the castle set. In desperation, Sam tugs on the curtain string—but it breaks. He tries to ad lib while jabbing with his hand, trying to get the king back under his grasp, but the puppet in the royal robe keeps jerking just beyond his capture.

He decides to reintroduce the sleeping Queen Constance. Up she pops, back into the plot, on the end of his left hand, which is concealed by her royal dress. This resurrection comes as a complete non sequitur, without attending dialogue, and it does not calm the king down nor resolve the plot. Sam, now sweating under the scene, becomes more impatient. He plops Queen Constance on the throne and tries to get his head under the castle floor to get a better look at what the hell is going on up there—and that's when he sees it: a child's hand coiled around King Barticus' royal waist.

"What the . . .?" Sam says in his own voice before changing it into the queen's.

"So it is you, dirty child!" the queen says. "You must be the wizard that sent the cinnamon roll that made King Barticus crazy. I command you to let the king go, or I will call mall security—uh, I mean, the palace guards." The queen is clearly in no mood for this slapstick.

Then, with the magic of puppet theatre, a mall security guard arrives, lifting the trespassing (and likely autistic) child back from the box. King Barticus is dropped from great height and hits Sam in the forehead. Sam grabs the puppet from the floor, to see it is now missing one side of its head—the fall has caused the casing to crack open along the seam where it had been glued together to contain my ashes, which are no longer contained and have been strewn about like a Depression-era dust storm backstage. Where to take this twist in the plot, Sam doesn't know, but realizes it is up to Queen Constance to resolve the puppet play, as she is the only puppet left standing. Parents have started to drag their children away from the theatre, as the real drama has shifted to the kicking and screaming child who had been daring and masterful in outsmarting the palace guards and the village Indian by storming the castle to kidnap King Barticus. *Dig deep, Queen Constance, and pull us out of this*, thinks Sam as he prepares his voice to let her take a run at it.

"Children, my royal subjects," she starts out, getting at least half of their divided attention back. "Can anyone tell me which might be better for a king with a headache—an aspirin or a cinnamon roll?"

"ASPIRIN!" the remaining children scream, almost unanimously.

"Ibuprofen won't rot your stomach!" yells the autistic kid, still under detention off to the side. *He is quite possibly more advanced than any of them, and certainly more advanced than this plot*, thinks Sam.

"I think it is time for my royal nap, before I am the one with a headache," decrees Queen Constance from her throne. Sam contorts under the puppet theatre on his back, reaching his hands high up into the wings to shut the curtains manually. There is clapping and music—and most importantly, twenty-five minutes before his three o'clock show.

I guess that's what you get for waiting so long before sticking your hand up my ash. Get it, Sam? *Hand up my ash?*

BEAR

"I'M TELLING YOU, RICH, IF YOU DIDN'T ALREADY KNOW better, you'd think there was flat nothing to Cheyenne, Oklahoma. I can't figure out why the dickens Ash would have wanted any part of his remains to come here to this creepy place. Do you even know what happened here . . . in history, I mean?" Barry Marlow's deeply resonant baritone voice travels into falsetto to ask the question.

Rich turns up the volume on the home phone he's answered on speaker so that he can continue folding the laundry just out of the dryer. "No, I have no idea." He has never met the caller in person, though he remembers wandering into the frame and saying hello to him once during a Skype call the two of us were having, probably to plan an upcoming *Up with People* reunion. That's how I knew Bear.

"Well, aside from the place where Ash says his great-grandfather, Heritage Howerton married his great-great-grandmother, Molli Curby on October 16, 1898, I can tell you that nearly thirty years earlier, almost to the date, this place was the location of the Battle of Washita River. Some history books call it the site of the Washita Massacre, since this is where George Custer's 7th US Cavalry attacked the village of Black Kettle while the Cheyenne were asleep."

"Well, that's not surprising, since the US Calvary made a decade-long habit of attacking Indians while they slept. You know, my own great-great-grandfather, Chief Joseph, surrendered to the Calvary after General Howard attacked the teepee camp where several hundred of my ancestors were sleeping on October 5, 1877."

"You're kidding," Barry exclaims, a bit automatically.

"Not about that, I'm not." Rich doesn't mean to snap, but it's a touchy bit of history for him. "When he surrendered, Chief Joseph sent Howard a letter." He recites it from memory as he folds his boxer briefs into a neat stack:

> I am tired of fighting. Our chiefs are killed. Looking Glass is dead. Toohoolhoolzote is dead. He who led the young men, Ollokot is dead. It is cold and we have no blankets. The little children are freezing to death. My people, some of them, have run away to the hills and have no blankets. No one knows where they are—perhaps freezing to death. I want to have time to look for my children, and see how many of them I can find. Maybe I shall find them among the dead. Hear me, my chiefs. I am tired. My heart is sick and sad. From where the sun now stands, I will fight no more forever.

"Wow," Barry says, using his southern drawl, KBEZ radio voice—since DJ-ing Adult Hits is what he does for a living. "That is so profound. I'm pretty sure some of the Nez Perce were relocated to Oklahoma—this place, perhaps."

"That's right." Rich had momentarily forgotten that part. "My great-great-grandfather and his people were taken first to Kansas, but later to what is now called the state of Oklahoma. They were kept there in Indian Territory for about eight years, before being allowed to return to small reservations representing a fraction of their original lands."

"Hey, it's a stretch, but maybe Ash's great-granddad crossed paths with your great-great-granddad here in Oklahoma."

"It's a nice thought, Barry." Rich figures he knows why Barry has called, but isn't completely sure until Barry tells him.

"Anyway, I have just mixed some Oklahoma dirt and Ashton's

remains together here at the bank of the Washita River. It floods here every year, so Ash won't have to endure this desolate place for long. I wanted you to know that I hope I've done what he wanted me to do." Barry's voice trembles in a way that tells Rich this wasn't easy for him.

"The way I have had to cope with this, all of this, is to believe I am doing what he wanted me to do, too," Rich says, not knowing if he is consoling Barry or himself. "I do appreciate you telling me, and I know what you meant to Ash. He would sort of light up like a Christmas tree every time he talked with you or about you. He always threatened he was going to drag me kicking and yelling to one of those *Up with People* reunions you guys keep having every few years. He was always saying I needed to meet Barry Marlow in person one day."

Barry can't speak; not in his charming drawl, not in his DJ baritone, not in falsetto. The phone is silent, prompting Rich to think he's dropped the call.

Finally, a feeble "Thank you" breaks the silence. "You go ahead and take good care of yourself, Rich," Barry says, in his southern, well-meaning way.

"You be well, too, Barry. Thanks for calling." Rich disconnects the call.

Who were all these men who got to spend so much time with me, Limping Rabbit is probably wondering now. Most of the film canisters went to men. Sure, some of them he had heard me talk about over the years, others he had met before—but several were new to him. Since his time with me has run out, I suppose it is natural for him to feel a bit of latent jealousy for the time and attention—and, in a few cases, affection—these other men had received from me. Then there were all the men from my life who somehow got away, who didn't receive a film canister with their name on it—like Daren Sparks, the UNM college football player who developed a crush on me but whose love for himself was so pure that I knew I would either taint it or not be able to compete with it. Or Mitchell DiBisleglie—the bar manager of Nines, the gay dance club on Albuquerque's Louisiana Avenue that I got emotionally tangled up with, it seemed, every time I got dumped again by John McCutchan. For that matter, what about all those other men I could have loved, maybe tried to or wanted to love, who maybe thought they loved me in return, but who likely don't even know I am dead now?

Rich doesn't know of most of the men who came before him in the first place to know he needs to inform them in the second. I didn't make any provision for this task, which, in light of all the other details, strikes me as shoddy and irresponsible. Rich could go to my address book, and maybe he will someday, and send a note or a Christmas card with this news to everyone listed there. Some of these men might even try to contact him when they can't reach me to ask why I am no longer on Facebook, retrievable in a Google search or just to find out what I'm up to or how I'm aging. Then he can tell them that I am not. I am not—that is still weird—says all the failed anti-aging creams, serums, exfoliators, emulsifiers and hydrating face oils that still sit on my shelf above my sink in this house, humiliated by my defeat.

It is hard to tell what is going on in that complex brain of his right now. He's just leaning against the kitchen counter, his eyes fixed in an unfocused stare on the mounting collection of wine-of-the-month bottles across the counter from him. He drags an index finger through the dust on the oldest of these. He really needs to cancel my subscription. That's what he's thinking, I'm sure. Then he takes the bottle, fishes through the drawer for a corkscrew, and cries through the first glass of a bottle we were meant to enjoy together.

When in the hell is this supposed to start getting easier? is what he is really wondering.

DOOGIE

TOPPING THE SANITY CHARTS AT NUMBER SEVENTEEN ON my ash distribution Hit Parade, Rich has walked to Queen Anne Hilltop Dental on McGraw Street for his appointment with long-time friend of mine, James McIntyre, D.D.S. The two of us had dated very briefly in the mid-nineties, about the same time I had been flirting with Russell at the health unit, and just before meeting Rich—but it didn't take.

James had been one of the youngest dentists ever to graduate from the University of Oklahoma School of Dentistry, and because he had specialized in a graduate program for oral surgery at UW, he decided to open his own practice on the top of Queen Anne at the age of twenty-seven. He actually looked a little like Neil Patrick Harris, and so I began referring to him as the Doogie Howser of dentistry. Dental Doogie had too much ambition for me, and it was an open-and-shut case from the start that I wasn't as smart or driven as he was, and so therefore I knew we couldn't make a believable match. He went on to woo and marry Christian, an architect from Quebec. A dentist with an architect equaled a believable match. I was a best man in their Montreal wedding as this was a more appropriate role for me.

It was shortly after that that I chased and then squarely tackled my lawyer. (Doug Long of the Seattle Seahawks would have been proud of my prowess . . . horrified by my homosexuality . . . but impressed with my skills on the playing field.)

Now, a novelist-slash-biographer paired with a summa cum laude law school graduate equaled a believable match. It doesn't have to make any sense how my brain worked—even less so now—but I stumbled over that believability quotient most of my life. It was probably a throwback all the way to *Ferdinand the Bull*. Ferdinand could not have anymore been a snorting, fighting, man-charging bull than I could have been a dentist's boyfriend, so I called us what we needed to be— friends, and we settled into that definition like a pair of fine leather shoes that needed to be broken in before they felt comfortable.

Doogie had done the crowns on my upper central teeth, in what was by then just the latest attempt to mask the discoloration that had resulted from a pogo-stick accident that had happened when I was a ten-year-old in Missoula. Back then, I had already broken the Dixon Street consecutive jumping record, when the handle broke off, discharging the spring to sucker punch me under the chin, which laid me out cold on the driveway. The blunt-force impact caused me to bite clean through my lower lip (stitches would be necessary), and severely loosened my secondary teeth. Some weeks later, after the swelling had gone down, my teeth had stabilized, but still showed permanent signs of trauma. Through junior and senior high school, I'd vainly gone through more porcelain veneers than a typist goes through fake fingernails—and never did one of them pop off at an opportune time. My mother was always on standby to spirit me across the prairie and down the canyon, to my orthodontist in Lewiston, for any number of emergency repairs. World tours and university pursuits meant I didn't have any down time or money to address a permanent solution for my two beleaguered front teeth, so I retrained my smile, started bodybuilding, and opened my green eyes wider, providing my suitors with nicer things to look at. I suspected Ferdinand had probably done the same thing when he posed to show off his nose ring—or, more likely, his ginormous sack of bull testicles. But Dental Doogie went to work on restoring my smile. He also flawlessly filled a cavity that had drawn the envy and awe of every dentist who climbed inside my mouth thereafter. Even though I already knew we didn't make a believable match, I let him get really good at his trade by practicing new skills in my mouth—and over time, my smile had never looked brighter.

Dr. James walks into the exam room, where Rich is already aproned and reclined, watching *The Ellen Degeneres Show* on the television embedded in the ceiling tile above him. "Hey," Rich says.

"Hey," Doogie answers. "Say, thanks for signing that release, Rich."

"Not a problem. I expected you'd need to have some kind of bulletproof consent in place before agreeing to do this procedure, which is why I had it drawn up for you."

"Appreciate that. It's just that the new bondable fillings that are non-metallic are way too technique-sensitive at the cure stage to be attempting this. I'm going back to my old school days to fashion a silver amalgam with some of the material that you've brought me." James holds up the re-appropriated contact lens case in plain view, without turning around. (Rich has run out of black film canisters). When the dentist does turn around, he does his best to conceal a cotton ball full of numbing gel, followed a bit too quickly by a needle juiced with Novocain. Rich Dreadfulwater's dental chart is plainly coded pink, which stands for DOES NOT LIKE NEEDLES, so James works quickly, without commentary or warning.

Rich winces, shouts a muffled "fuck me!" around the needle and fist in his mouth and then speaks when the needle is withdrawn. "I know it's unorthodox—but, well . . . that's just the way Ash was."

"You're telling me? Don't forget that he and I attempted coupling, somewhat catastrophically."

"Yeah, thanks again for bweaking him in." Rich is already having trouble coordinating his lips for speech.

James places a latexed hand on Rich's shoulder. "You know what I meant." He swivels away on his stool, returning to the compound he's mixing. "This is pretty chunky stuff."

"I know. I was hoping you could use a sieve or one of those gold-panning dishes to sepawate out the finer stuff for this pwocedure."

"Well, it's grittier than I'd prefer, but it might give your tongue a curious place to visit and remember. Shall we get started?"

Rich nods. The drilling starts.

Ashton Taylor, *Last Will and Testament*, page 18

Not that this will ever happen, since the Nez Perce are evidently blessed with flawless teeth and aerodynamically perfect cheek bones and jaw structure from centuries of bareback horse riding, but should you ever need a tooth filled or capped, it would be cool if you reserved a bit of my ashes to be mixed into the filling. You know you can talk Doogie into doing this for you. He has a crush on you—a surprise to absolutely nobody.

One of my all-time greatest pleasures was getting my tongue and other bits inside that mouth of yours. This way, I can always be there, inside you. It may sound creepy, but trust me when I tell you that's where I want to be.

Rich opens his mouth wider to gasp for a breath and some suction, which he is operating himself. It's a Saturday, and Doogie didn't call in any of his other staff, since the pro-bono experiment was neither standard procedure nor one for the billing charts.

"Okay. So what I'm going for here is a two-layered filling. I'm going to start with an ash-filling mixture that I will seal and cure with a more traditional resin-based material on top." Again, his latexed hand squeezes Rich's shoulder.

"You doing alright on your own?" he asks sincerely, letting his hand linger while his fingers assess the lawyer's musculature. Rich nods.

"What's it been? Five, six months?" Rich nods again.

The dentist lets go of his patient's shoulder and begins to compact the ash into the bored-out micro-cavity. "So, do you think you'll start dating again?"

Rich's brown eyes focus on the dentist's blues, showcased by eyelashes that are so gorgeous they should be attracting pollinators. Rich couldn't decide how to play the question. He starts out looking as though he is shocked by the brashness of it, but then he smiles. "Awe you asking me out, Doctow?" He forms the words around the suction tube candy-caned over his lower, deadened lip.

"Try not to talk." Doogie smiles at his patient deviously, lifting only one side of his mouth. "It's a secret not kept very well that I've always been jealous of you as the man Ashton chose to spend his life with. The real secret here is that it wasn't jealousy at all . . . it was my attraction to you. I admitted to Ash once that I had this crush on you and he laughed it off—you know, saying something like he was going to die young without any notice so I should just be prepared to move in. He joked, or maybe it wasn't a joke, but he was enormously proud to have snagged you. Who wouldn't be?"

"Snagged?"

"Shhh! This is my monologue. Open." He inspects the first compound, making sure there is enough of a margin for the outer layer. "I don't want to rush you, but maybe when you're ready, we could grab a movie or something."

"Snagged?" Rich asks again. "Anyway, awen't you a mawwied man?"

"I'm not a prisoner. I am allowed to go to a movie or dinner. If you ask me . . . if you ask anybody, you were Ash's greatest catch. Ash certainly knew it. Open wide." Doogie applies the second compound, which will harden into the outer shell. Next, he holds the dental curing light over the area for about a minute, for a complete polymerization of the resin-based composite he's blended to match Rich's other teeth perfectly. "Okay, I think that should do it. I imagine the one unknown here is just how sensitive the tooth will be to hot and cold, so you'll have to let me know." Rich nods. "It's a bit more extreme than a tattoo or a piercing," the dentist points to the emerald diamond in his patient's nostril. "Is that new, by the way?" Rich nods. "But now you can carry a bit of your boyfriend with you wherever you go." Rich tries to smile without drooling, thinking the dentist doesn't know the half of it. "Alright, then. I'll just clean you up and get you on your way."

There is a bit of buffing and polishing, followed by a warm washcloth and a bit of awkwardness when the dentist seems to be coming in for a kiss. "I need to rinse!" Rich says, scrambling into a seated position, reaching for a Dixie cup and holding it under the waterspout of the spittoon. Doogie taps a foot pedal and the cup fills. Rich rinses and then explores the modified tooth with his tongue. "Nice job. I think that's definitely worth a couple hours of legal advice any time you need it." He negotiates his way out of going on a date by offering his own professional services, quid pro quo.

"I'll have to come up with a quandary, then," Doogie returns.

Rich stands. They hug.

"Take care of that mouth. You've got a passenger in there now."

"I will," Rich promises, waving as he shows himself out.

He's walked two blocks, tongue massaging the urn his tooth has just become, when tears began to fill his eyes like someone is still pushing a pedal on the floor. "See? There isn't anything I wouldn't do to get you back," Limping Rabbit says out loud, wiping his eyes and trying to suck a gulp of air past the sensitive filling into his lungs. "Anything."

ARMANDO

IN 1985, I HAD MY HEART SET ON IT. I'D WORKED THREE JOBS and skipped classes to take extra shifts just so that I could afford to get there, to be in position for the automatic big break I was going to get simply because I was white, good-looking, spoke decent Spanish, and knew Miguel. He had been my first boyfriend four years earlier when we met in Arizona to stage the *Up with People* show—and he was also the brother of the beauty pageant actress who was starring in Venezuela's upcoming telenovela, *La Salvaje (The Savage)*. I'd been smuggled the synopsis of the script, so I already knew there was a role for a womanizing son of an American ambassador, and that an actor hadn't yet been named or discovered—that in fact this *pequeña problema* in casting had even delayed the start of production. I'd scrambled to Fed-ex a series of 8 x 10s with my extensive acting and modeling resume printed on the back. By "extensive," I mean that I'd been in a fashion show at the age of eight at the Buttery Suburban Grocery Store in Missoula, that I'd performed with Karen and Richard Carpenter in a live concert. Oh wait. I already mentioned that part. And also that I was an extra in the 1974 Charles Bronson/Jill Ireland western railroad mystery *Breakheart Pass*, because it was shooting about forty minutes from my home, and my mother had gone to high school with the assistant to the continuity director who, incidentally, should have been fired and banned from working again in the industry for all the mistakes and flubs that ended up in the final cut. I included a list of my leading and bit roles in high school and university theatre productions, and casually mentioned I had just begun dancing with an amateur company in New Mexico that had been recently featured in a televised community cable access telethon at around 1:45 in the morning.

I was assured by the brother of the actress that these were excellent performing references and that his sister would hand-deliver my headshots and resume to the director at Canal 2, with her professional recommendation that I be screen tested and signed on to the cast, so that taping could finally get underway and everyone could start getting paid. On this lark, I had quit my three decent-for-a-university-student jobs. I flew from Albuquerque to Miami and on to Caracas with the wickedest hangover from the going-away party that had washed me and my well-wishers right up to the boarding gate at ABQ International. I'd heaved up at least five pounds of chips and guacamole into the airplane toilet somewhere over the state of Georgia (epiglottal episode #2), since those stomach contents had been the foundation of my six-week preparation diet for the Speedo scenes I was sure to be begged to do.

It is pertinent to mention here that at the time, being down a testicle had its Speedo-packing advantages as I appeared mannequin-perfect and package-forward in all sizes of skimpy swim and boxer brief underwear. I would eventually cave to Russell's friendly prodding and opt for the insertion of a prosthetic testicle in 1995 (surgical procedure #6 requiring anesthesia). Not that I'm bragging, but it was sized large by the smirking surgeon to match the real one that had probably gotten pretty used to riding solo in the baggage compartment. I road-tested my all-weather superball during the B.U.R.T., and I relationship-tested it just a couple months later when I began dating Limping Rabbit. It was maybe our third or fourth date when he first inquired why one of my nuts was Silly Putty hard. I told him it was bionic and he'd best stand back a safe distance when I got excited. Then I gave him the true explanation. His brown eyes turned watery as he pulled me into a naked hug before he lowered himself in the bed to kiss both my balls, then each of my scars, then both of my nipples—even though there had never been anything wrong with them. Then he kissed my lips, and then both of my eyes for everything sad I had ever seen, then each of my ears for everything sad I had ever heard. Then he shrugged off my medical trials, for they were in the past, and we never really talked about cancer again.

The fake nut did give my cremation technician some pause when it didn't render to ash and then gummed up the Cremulator. It was ultimately discarded as foreign anatomical matter—which is good, since it wouldn't have fit into a film canister anyway—just like my adolescent penis couldn't be contained by a toilet paper tube—just like my ego probably doesn't fit between these covers.

I landed in Caracas that summer (1985), sporting my untanned American skin, my nutrition-starved waistline, my involuntarily flexing pecs and biceps, and my stomach, which I perpetually sucked in until abs and directional groin muscle lines could be detected under the silk T-shirt by a gentle touch. Since my light olive skin tanned so readily, I had adopted all measures to avoid the sun—not easy to do in Albuquerque—and took to eating my chips and guacamole (for protein) in the shade. I couldn't risk the role by showing up dark and pudgy as a local *mestizo*. I was scooped up by Miguel and a couple of his friends named Andrés and Beto, who reminded me of Don Quixote and Sancho Panza from *Man of La Mancha*, so that's what I called them. We drove straight from the beachside airport up and into Caracas that sat in the bowl of the mountains where I was deposited at a disco—curiously named *New York, New York*. There we met up with the famous sister—Yajaira, the actress—along with about a dozen actors and actor-handlers and studio hangers-on from *La Salvaje*. Each and every one of them fell madly in love with me on the spot. How could they not? Yajaira, thrilled that the unknown Yankee pushed on her by her brother was such a hit with her fellow thespians, became my credibility agent, introducing me to everyone as her personal find. And I'm sure some of the star-struck fans shoving and kicking to get closer to us on the dance floor must have thought I was her new or latest boy toy as well. She had been something like a Miss World Runner-up not even a year and a half before, so I did not mind the affiliation, and in fact, used her to advance my Casanova acting audition, which began the moment I took her hand.

Oh, I played the part. That, after all, was what I was there to do. Freddie, *La Salvaje's* Assistant Production Manager, didn't need to be hit on the head with an adobe brick to recognize that I was "all that" and *mucho mas*, and within the first twenty-five minutes, he pronounced with a darling accent that I was *positivo perfecto para el papel actuando del hijo del embajador.* Freddie would take care of the screen test and the paperwork in the morning, but tonight it was decided we would dance shirtless until the sun came up. I may have been the one that proclaimed that last bit, anxious as I was to show off my other *atributos* to seal any deal I could get.

I was just naïve enough to believe that Freddie could do all that because he said he could do all that—just as I had banked my summer and sacrificed my class load on my connection to the brother of the actress who would change my life. How my silk shirt ended up in Freddie's back pocket, and how I ended up in the backseat of a limo with a fold-down mirror with two-inch cocaine letters that spelled F E L I Z   C U M P L E A Ñ O S when it was nobody's birthday, are mysteries I never solved. But the sun did come up, and as it did, Yajaira remembered the studio was being fumigated that morning, though she didn't remember for what. We weren't supposed to report to work until the following day. Freddie floated a rumor that the studio furniture must be full of *chinches* since everyone and their schnauzer fucked on the set. And Yajaira announced we—meaning her entourage—would all be going to *la playa* instead.

At some point overnight—but likely within seconds of Freddie heralding his discovery of the actor who would play the American ambassador's son—I'd become separated from Miguel and Andrés and Beto, who no longer had anything to do with the telenovela career I had just launched, except that they had my suitcase in the trunk of Beto's car. I shuffled out of the limo that I saw nobody pay for, and into the passenger seat of Yajaira's Renault Fuego, headed for her family home to grab swimsuits. That mission hinged on me hopefully reuniting with my suitcase, since the home of her parents—the entire sixth floor of the *Edificio Oriente* apartment building on *la Avenida Los Proceres*—was also to be my crash pad for the summer.

The plan—which I clearly didn't know the half of—had been for me to sleep on a trundle bed in Miguel's bedroom. Miguel had only baited his hook, and craftily so, with the long-shot mirage of an acting job, just so that he could hook up with me on the trundle every night, thinking he would rekindle passions we'd only scratched the surface of five years earlier.

I didn't know how much of the random birthday greeting in that limo had gone up the perky little nose chimney of my co-star, but neither of us had gotten any sleep nor eaten anything of nutritional benefit—plus, we were still inebriated. We were heading to her parent's house on one direction on *la Cota Mil*—the elevated expressway that circled the city—when suddenly, with a jerk of the steering wheel, a squeal, a skid, and at least one-and-a-half revolutions, we were facing the opposite direction, with our hood crumpled and emitting smoke under the back end of a school bus.

Yajaira was sort of slumped over the steering wheel where she moaned—not surprisingly—a bit dramatically. I first-aid assessed that the hand with which I'd braced myself against the now-shattered windshield was cut and bleeding. I heard sirens, and kept hearing them for possibly the next forty-five minutes, as we were transferred from the Fuego into separate ambulances heading to the same hospital—the Policlinica Metropolitana—where we were isolated in separate rooms on a private floor. I sat on a small sofa in my room, clutching a washcloth, as there wasn't anything really wrong with me. Yajaira was across the hall in a hospital bed in a neck collar, and it wasn't ten minutes before studio heads began hovering around her.

Eventually, Freddie walked into my room with a lawyer from Canal 2. The lawyer asked Freddie to translate for her. Freddie told her that I was an American who spoke Spanish. The message she delivered and that Freddie bolstered, whether he liked it or not, was that Yajaira was hurt, and that it could be serious enough that the start of *La Salvaje* was now in limbo, if not in jeopardy of being scrapped. The studio had a duty to manage the information that would be getting out about the accident, and it wasn't convenient for them that drugs and alcohol had been involved nor that the passenger in Yajaira's car was both unknown and an American.

The studio had decided to write me out of the accident, and substitute Yajaira's boyfriend for me in the car. "Yajaira tiene novio?" I asked. I was sort of surprised, since she'd been partying with me as though she were a free spirit.

"Si, tiene novio," was the response from the lawyer—and on cue, into my hospital room walks Karl, a skinny, well-dressed kid who looked like a model, with long, curly, blond hair.

"Soy, Karl." He reached over to shake my hand, and I showed him the blood-pink washcloth.

"Karl is the lead singer of the popular Venezuelan boy band, *Chévere*," Freddie said, filling in the blanks. "He's been dating Yajaira off and on." He leaned close to my ear, and added in a whisper, "Mostly for publicity."

"Okay," I said, tentatively giving my consent, I guess. Freddie asked if I needed a place to stay for a few days while this story made the rounds through the fan magazines, gossip columns, and news channels. Before I had to figure that out, Miguel appeared in the doorway and said I was staying with his family, and that he was there to take me home. Freddie quickly wrote down his telephone number on a Kleenex and smuggled it to me lipping the word *llamame*. Without being allowed to check on or say goodbye to Yajaira—because she was busy posing for staged photos with a concerned and hastily hand-bandaged Karl—I was ushered out of the hospital, as photographers and cameramen poured onto the private floor.

The stars did not really align for me in the weeks that followed the accident, though Yajaira's and Karl's stars continued to rise, inflated by a ridiculous amount of coverage and buzz following their harrowing car accident. Between the beaches, the theatres, the arepas, a few *Chévere* concerts (courtesy of curious Karl), and lots of obligatory sex on the trundle with that first boyfriend of mine, my first Venezuelan summer was compressed, and, after the crash, a bit anti-climactic. As consolation, Freddie did manage to get Miguel and me into the studio to work a couple days as room meat in a discoteque scene which gave me a chance to see the Casanova they eventually signed to replace me in *La Salvaje*. Miguel and Yajaira did organize a robust and star-studded going-away party that sort of tidied up the mess. Lots of cast and crew from *La Salvaje* and all five of the boys comprising *Chévere* stopped in, along with the reigning Miss Venezuela—Bárbara Palacios, who, less than a year into the future, would be crowned Miss Universe. Of course Andrés and Beto were there, along with a bunch of other family friends who packed the four-bedroom and one-*baño gran salon* apartment.

Halfway through a very loud and crowded party, there was a surprise guest that I had been sent down the elevator to let into the building. The elevator at *Edificio Oriente* had already been the scene of two separate propositions earlier in the evening; the first from Yajaira, who stated/asked in her best English, "You want to make love with me tonight, don't you?" and the second from Karl—her fan magazine *novio*—who stated/asked, and by this point in the evening not very originally, "You want make love with me before you say *adios*, don't you?" I had to break it gently to both of them, and since they used the same pick-up line on me, I used the same let-down line on them: "Estas equivocado, somos amigos" (you must be mistaken, we're friends). Because really, at this point I didn't want to make love or have much of anything more to do with either of these professional make-believers. They deserved each other.

When the elevator door opened—and the elevator shaft was so skinny that it only had one door that sometimes opened all the way but usually gave up at half or two-thirds open—I looked across the short lobby through the front doors and tried to see if I recognized the arriving party guest. I opened the door, still trying to figure it out, and this dark-skinned god of a mestizo man said with the deepest voice, "Hola, Ashton . . . Soy Armando."

And I'd be damned if it wasn't, too. Armando, the very first Venezuelan in what would become a necklace of Caracas contenders, who would serve as the heart-throbbing punctuation *de mi vida* prior to tracking and then snaring my Limping Rabbit. There had been Miguel in 1980; Joe Benetar—a fair-skinned, English-speaking fling I'd met behind Miguel's back that same summer in 1984 during Yajaira's film premiere for *Homicidio Culposo*, and who, as face would have it, was the same actor I'd later bumped into at the studios playing my role as the American Ambassador's son when *La Salvaje* finally began taping; Andrés (yes, Don Quixote), who met me for a NYC opera series and other unfinished business five years later in 1990; Victor in 1991, shortly before Miguel died; and Douglas the psychic on that flight from Buenos Aires over the Amazon early in 1996. But Armando was the *primero Venezolano*, and it was on November 9, 1979, in the tiny town of Nyssa, Oregon, near the border with Idaho, that I became fucking *loco enamorado con el*. I had driven seven hours to this town with my father to see and then audition to join the traveling *Up with People* show. This was going to be my one-way ticket out of Idaho. Armando was one of a hundred performers who sang their lungs out and danced their butts off that night, but I was mesmerized by only him in his blue-and-white striped shirt with puffy sleeves—and his afro-styled hair.

I interviewed and auditioned and then talked for several hours in Spanish with Armando, and also the show's cast director, an older fellow with four names—Jose Luis Something Something—himself from Mexico and a veteran performer with the company since 1976. My father sat patiently on the last row of the back bleachers so that he would be out of everyone's way as his first son chased his dream of joining this company of international optimists who were absolutely certain they were changing the world through music.

Landing this audition and an invitation to join the performing company had been my only plan for the previous three years, my Potato State exodous, as I mentioned, but I hadn't factored in stumbling over Armando. I still had to finish high school and turn eighteen, which didn't leave a lot of room for falling in love. Armando's tour still had another six weeks on the road, but we pen-palled this promise that he would come back for another year as a performing staff member, and we would pull every string we could to get into the same touring cast to be together—or so I hoped. We really hadn't worked the rest of that out, but we had fallen for each other quite possibly me more for him than vice versa.

Flash forward three months: I was eighteen, graduated from GHS, and on the first scheduled jet out of Idaho. I arrived in Tucson to begin rehearsing the new *Up with People* show during summer break on campus at the University of Arizona, and to find my Armando, of course. Instead, I stumbled again . . . this time over Miguel, who—surprise, surprise—also hailed from Caracas. So, magically-spell-bewildered, I fall for Miguel, and he falls for me, and we hatched this plan to switch his billeted housing arrangements so that he could stay with me at the quaint adobe-and-cactus-landscaped home belonging to the married couple that was hosting my stay for the five weeks we would be in Tucson mounting the show. But we needed to get an UWP staff person to authorize this change. Miguel knew an UWP staff person, who we then quite truly smacked right into while sprinting through an afternoon monsoon between vocal and dance rehearsals the next day—and it was Armando.

Miguel laid the situation out in rapid Spanish that I couldn't follow and the whole time he was speaking Armando was looking at me with the most wounded brown eyes I had ever seen. I was barely ninety days into my eighteenth year of life, so I didn't really have coping or negotiation or restitution skills yet. But I had a heart, which was apparently really weak for Venezuelan men—well, it was weak *period*, as it turns out—and it was breaking in halves over those two as they stood there, side by side, waiting for me to choose. Obviously, I couldn't foretell the future to know that Armando would be the one who aged beautifully and outlived me or that Miguel would be dead within a decade from AIDS. I was eighteen. I just didn't know. Armando said he would see what he could do. Then he embraced me, speaking breathily into my ear—Hola, Ashton—with that sweet, deep voice of his. I was rendered into indecisive pieces of a fool who needed to get it back together but who felt as though he had just been viscerally bisected.

Armando pulled his strings and fixed the paperwork, Miguel moved in with me and my host family for the rest of staging, and then four weeks later the three of us got split into three different casts touring the same *Up with People* show but in opposite directions. I was out of strings. There were no Venezuelan men in my cast; there was one from Mexico, one from Costa Rica, and one from the Canary Islands, but it was not even remotely the same. My soul had been branded by the descendants of Simón Bolívar—and that scar does not fade, wash off, heal, or in any measure go away.

So there I was, in the summer of 1985, standing face to face with Armando again, this time in the lobby of a Caracas apartment building, and all I could think to do was get us out of there, because I couldn't risk losing him again in the party crowd upstairs. We went for a walk to his car, parked a few blocks away. We both knew I was leaving; it was a going-away party. I was thinking: *Great, I'm headed back to Albuquerque in the morning to beg for at least two of my three jobs back, and here I go again—stumbling all over a Venezolano.* Crying was the only thing my body could manage, and in the front seat of his car, steaming up the windows, I blubberingly confessed that I already knew I screwed up five years earlier, that I chased the wrong man, that our lives could have been different if I would have only had the courage to believe my heart and wait for Armando to reappear. He says, "I'm reappearing now. It's not too late."

And I said, "It *is* too late. I'm leaving in the morning. I can't stay." And with that, I just screwed up all over again.

It would take five years of pleading postcards, letters and telephone calls, FTD Worldwide flower deliveries on birthdays and Christmases and long-distance midnight toasts on New Year's Eves, to address the wound-healing and trust-building and future-setting, before I would have another chance to get things right with Armando. And when he arrived in Denver in December 1991 to spend the snowy Christmas holidays, snuggled up in front of a fireplace with me, what do I do? Of course, I screwed up again. I had fallen for a corporate travel agent named Brent Baranovsky the weekend before, and I spent Armando's ten-day visit trying to keep the two of my Secret Santas from finding out about each other. It all culminated with my telling of a very dire Christmas Future with Armando because I couldn't overcome the distance and the red tape of who immigrated where, while botching up Christmas Present with the travel agent who presented me with two roundtrip tickets to Palm Springs for New Years' in my Christmas stocking when Armando's return ticket wasn't until the midweek that followed. I had to face it. I was Scrooged!

If you can believe it, the travel agent found *me* to be too flighty, and moved to Florida to manage a Hampton Suites Hotel. Armando returned to Caracas and I never again had the chance to stand face to face anywhere in the world with him. The one who got away, you might wonder? No. He was the one who never tried to get away. There is a distinction there. And I missed it.

Ashton Taylor, *Last Will and Testament*, page 18

Armando: ever suave, sophisticated, sensual—and Jesus, so sexy! You were my benchmark, my escape, my obsession—and, on too-few very remarkable occasions, the terremoto, the earthquake that shook me in an epicenter that only you could touch. I was seventeen years old when I saw you for the first time. You showed me patience, which I never mastered. You offered me a love I could never equal. You became a larger part of my life in your physical absence than anyone could manage to become in my presence.

From where I rest, my lifelong pursuit of you—or the tail of you, or my own tail, or an illusion of a mirage that maybe wasn't real or even mine to begin with—I can neither stumble over you nor torment you any longer. This is finally *el fin* for us.

Now, the Venezuelan Postal Service is notorious for being short a mission statement, unless it is this: "To Deliver Nothing Ever." But let's take a wild chance on this getting through. I'll do what I can from my end, seeing as it could very well be my end in the canister.

Ah, mi Caracas. Having spent some wonderful months in this remarkable city, it only seems appropriate—since I left parts of my heart here each time I left—that parts of me are returning in a film canister. I want you to take these ashes of mine to the top of El Avila and sprinkle me there, where I can watch over you. Gracias, Armando, por eso y por todo. Until our next lives, when we will hopefully find a way to be together. At last, I am with you now.

Now, if you were here next to me, standing or floating or hovering (or whatever this is I'm doing), looking out over the modern skyline of Caracas from the hotel roof of what used to be the Caracas Hilton, your eyes would eventually settle on the architectural wonder below. That is the Teresa Carreño Cultural Complex. There. Look! See that attractive man in the beige dress pants and royal-blue oxford shirt with the sunglasses on top of his shortly cropped hair? The one emerging from the main doors of the theatre and striding right now across the plaza? That's Armando. And yes, he is looking twice as handsome for every year I let him get away. Gideon, if he were here with me, would compute this mathematical statement to a sum of seventy-four times handsomer than the day I met him in 1979, and I don't think anyone could dispute that.

With superior eye-hand coordination, Armando's hand is repeatedly tossing then catching the canister as he walks. On the fourth toss, the hand misses the catch, and I can just make it out when he shouts, "Coño!" Now, there he is, kneeling on the cement of the plaza, using a bankcard to corral the ash back into the canister. He is careful to get every particle, despite the platoons of feet and legs of passersby moving around his hunched frame.

Okay, now he is over there, leaning against that light pole at the Parque Central Metro Station, his hands in the pockets of his chinos, looking very machismo, very together, waiting for the next train. I'd better hustle if I'm going to keep up with him today. The yellow line train arrives. Armando boards, and I slip in to hang out across from him, as the city center begins scrolling past the windows. Armando's gaze focuses briefly on the large fountain at the Plaza Venezuela, as the above-ground train sprints through downtown Caracas. I almost miss

Armando jumping off the train, like he was intentionally trying to give me the slip. This stop caught him daydreaming, and he almost missed it.

Armando transfers to a bus that whisks us up La Avenida Principal Maripérez in no time, and then through the gates that proclaim in all capital letters on an ornately brocaded archway that we are entering PARQUE NACIONAL EL AVILA. Our commute has climbed into the foothills of the large mountains that surround the city. Armando buys a ticket at the booth of the Teleférico de El Avila and boards the very next gondola car. He sets the film canister on the edge of the window, and holds it there with his hand as we ascend above the floor of the city. Riding in the gondola car with us are four tourists and a few employees from the Hotel Humboldt, which is located on the top of El Avila Mountain, which we are now ascending. Armando seems transfixed by the view as a breeze coming in from an open window rustles through his hair—still coarse-as-ever, even at fifty-eight—and flutters the collar flap of his button-down shirt. He is grinning ever so slightly as the sun warms his face.

The gondola attendant, a college student, sounds quite robotic as he every so often recites memorized city facts, in a mixture of Spanish and English. In between, he studies from an open book in his lap. He has an earphone in one of his ears, connected to his model of Samsung that has been recalled for a battery defect everywhere else in the world. There is a sudden mechanical grinding, and the gondola rocks to a precarious halt, dangling between two towers, at a considerable height above a deep canyon. But for some troublesome creaking, the motors are silent. One of the other passengers lets loose a scream. The look on the gondola attendant's face isn't going to calm anyone.

Armando, assessing that he is more likely than the attendant to take charge, and that he might be the only local aboard who speaks and understand English, uses his deep voice to cut through the anxiety. "Everybody, please be calm," he says, holding up his arms, the film canister in one hand. "Tranquilo! Estamos seguros." Turning to the gondola operator, he asks, "Como te puedes ayuda?"

Now sweating, nervous, and panic-stricken, the attendant pulls the earbud from his ear, and asks, "Estás un mecánico?"

"No. Not exactly." Armando chuckles to expel some of his own anxiety, wondering if he can possibly offer up any transferrable skills from his career as a stage manager at el Teatro Nacional. "Tienes un radio, no?"

This prompts the attendant to pick up the phone receiver next to his chair. His eyes grow large. "Muerto. Cortado." The attendant lets this sink in for exactly three seconds before jumping to his feet, dropping his book on the gondola floor. "Somos todos muertos!"

And with that, Armando is now officially in charge. "Everybody, sit down on the floor. You too," he says to the attendant. "Siéntese, por favor. Siéntese y no mover." Not everybody follows the instruction, so Armando calmly revises. "Primero, nos todos hablamos Espanol?" There are three American tourists and possibly a German shaking their heads no. "Okay, does everybody speak English?" All eight passengers in the car, including the operator, nod their heads affirmatively.

"Okay. I'll use English. My name is Armando. It is important that we don't panic." He raises his hands again, showing the film canister in one hand and his cell phone in the other. Now, I'm going to use my cellphone to call the Hotel Humboldt on top of the mountain, so they know we are stuck. Does anybody know the number?"

"Just call 9-1-1," suggests one of the Americans, an impatient Southerner. "Do you want me to do it?" he volunteers.

"That only works in North America," Armando explains. "We don't have that here."

"Surprise, surprise," says the American, showing his all-around frustration at the backwardness of the place. "Can we call the American Embassy, please?"

"Here. Maybe the hotel number is in here." The attendant reaches under the fixed seat and hands Armando an emergency manual.

"Estoy llamando mi jefe," says one of the girls. "I'm phoning my supervisor. I work at the hotel," she explains in English. "No respuesta," she reports to Armando alone when her phone just keeps ringing and ringing.

It has only been five minutes since the gondola became stranded halfway between two towers, but the passengers' elevated adrenaline twists their perception of time. Nobody understands why they aren't being rescued by now. Within minutes, one, then two helicopters are circling the scene. Venezuela may not have 9-1-1, but their drama-sniffing writers and photographers and freelancing gossip-magazine reporters can be counted on to be the first responders to any event with the potential to turn disastrous. Like mosquitoes to carbon dioxide, they just know.

I'm eavesdropping now, perfect case in point, on a female reporter in the black and purple helicopter with the CRTV Lion logo on it. She's staring into a television camera that she herself is holding, fully confident in her hovering selfie that she is bagging the top story that will bump the docket and lead the five o'clock Noticias Especial. None of these hard-working professionals would ever be so disillusioned to think their story could interrupt the regular afternoon or evening telenovela programming. It's widely understood that the mere whisper of the sudden death, assassination, or coups of the unpopular Presidente Nicolas Maduro would have to be embargoed until five.

"En el cuatro desventura en cuatro meses hasta . . ."

Here. Allow me. She's saying: "In a fourth mishap in as many months since the Avila Funicular Service was rescued after fifteen years in mothballs, it is believed that seven passengers are stranded, at this moment, between towers nineteen and twenty, dangling sixteen meters above the steep, perilous slopes of Avila Mountain." She pivots the camera to aim at the motionless gondola, reflecting the day's sun. She continues: "We understand that only two of the company's eighty-seven gondolas were being used at the time of the system failure, and that one of these was near the bottom of the mountain, and all its passengers were able to climb down a tower ladder to safety."

Here she already plans to edit in stock footage of the large wheelhouse at the top of the mountain, with smiling passengers getting on and off gondola cars during normal operations, and a *grabando antes* (recorded earlier) news ticker scrolling along the bottom. She continues:

"Un representivo de la compania funicular . . ."

Sorry. She's saying: "A spokesperson for the cable-car company, who was reached by cell phone, said that the top of the mountain, including nearby Humboldt Hotel, has lost all power, and that at this time, back-up generators are malfunctioning. One gondola, normally used for medical emergencies and repairs, is evidently being retrofitted with new brakes, and is not available to participate in this rescue."

Back inside the gondola, our hero Armando is speaking rather impatiently into his cell phone, while other passengers attend to the attendant, who has hyperventilated and passed out on the floor. "Un otra vez, estamos siete personas, incluiendo el empujador, quien tuve un ataque de nervios, has hiperventilado y hace desmayado en el piso." He looks at each of the passengers. "Creo que si. Espera. Is everyone able to climb down a ladder?" He turns back to the window and quickly evaluates how impossibly long the ladder would have to be to reach the ground from their position. "Si, todos con el excepcíon del empujador."

Translation: "Yes, everyone, with the exception of the gondola operator." There is a pause like maybe someone on the other end is figuring out what to do. He's listening to and then acts on the instructions he's receiving. "Sí, sí, sí." From a metal box welded under the operator's chair, Armando extracts a rope and aluminum rung ladder. It takes several armfuls to pile it on the floor. Other passengers help him.

"La puerta, sí." Everyone carefully moves away as Armando releases and then slides open the door to the gondola. A passenger gasps at the height. A whoosh of fresh air does a quick pass through the car. You can't help but watch Armando's scarless, brown, self-manicured hands at work, stretching out of the ends of those bright blue shirtsleeves, as he moves the pile of ladder toward the open door.

Still palming the film canister in one hand, and cradling his iPhone between his shoulder and ear, he searches for the right end of the ladder—the end with the industrial-sized carabineer hooks attached to it. Then he moves to fasten these to the welded rings on the outside of the opened door. Things seem to be going really well until, in one crazy instant, a ladder rung somehow flicks the film canister from his palm into the air. As he shoots his arm nearly out of his shoulder socket to snatch the canister before it can tumble out the open door, his chin involuntarily releases the squeeze it has on his iPhone. Slow motion would be really handy right now. His cellphone and the film canister tumble through the air, just as there is a racket of sound.

The ladder he hasn't finished attaching disappears rung by rung through the doorway of the gondola. From the helicopter's vantage, the reporter/camerawoman watches, but isn't quick enough to zoom in on the fully extended ladder as it spills from the gondola to freefall and then collapse like an accordion as it hits the steep mountain slope below. A dust cloud is quickly and silently carried away by a strong breeze.

There is silence inside and outside the gondola, except for the whirring of the circling helicopters. Armando, now red-faced from exasperation, looks exhausted as he tucks the film canister into his shirt pocket and reunites the cell phone with his ear. The other passengers are either too busy praying or contemplating the lawsuits they feel they have a right to launch, so nobody rushes in to blame Armando for the loss of the ladder. Armando straightens up on his spread knees and gives his upper body a convulsive shake to cast off any further bad luck. With no one else contending to be hero of the day, all hope and the control of this situation still belong to him. He speaks into the phone. "Y ahora?"

From the second helicopter, which has no camera and only a pilot aboard, who is commentating live for radio station *Hot 94 FM*, comes a minute-by-minute account for all the city's taxi drivers and passengers. "Lo parece que los pasajeros fueron tratando a poner una escalera de mano mas abajo cuando . . ."

The pilot is saying: "It would seem that the passengers were trying to lower a ladder to the ground when the ladder suddenly disconnected and dropped from the gondola. I am now hearing in my headset that the Austrian Company who designed and installed the funicular system on the mountain in 1956 has a technician on the phone, advising the controllers at the top of the mountain, who are in turn communicating by cell phone with a passenger in the gondola."

Armando is listening to the discussion happening between the Teleferico managers in the background on his phone, and then new instructions are delivered to him. He lowers the phone to address his fellow passengers. "We are being asked to gather any backpacks, luggage, or purses that are not essential, and throw them down where they will be collected shortly. They hope this will lessen the weight on the cable, so the gondola can be manually pulled to one of the towers."

One of the Americans pipes up. "And who do they expect will do the manual pulling?"

Armando takes a deep breath and quite calmly replies, "They have asked me to do it."

The CRTV reporter/camerawoman is in the middle of a long shot when items begin falling from the gondola to the ground. "Dios mio!" she screams, a bit unprofessionally. "Lo parece que algunos passajeros estan saltando de la gondola . . ."

Incorrectly, she reports that some of the passengers have begun jumping from the gondola in panic. She corrects herself when she sees her pilot shaking his head. "No, wait." She stalls. "We are receiving new information that the controllers are trying to lighten the load on the cable by jettisoning any unnecessary items."

"Podemos ser mas cerca?" She asks the pilot if he can get her any closer. "I think what we are seeing at this moment is one of the passengers climbing onto the roof of the gondola," she says.

That's my Armando, climbing through the roof hatch of the gondola car. He has his cell on speakerphone, clipped to the collar of his shirt, with the volume as high as it can go, and he is wearing a harness around his shoulders that fits under his arms. He slowly, one hand at a time, lifts himself to a standing position, clinging to the main support strut connecting the gondola to the cable. He instructs the American to close the main door and the roof hatch in case things start to get rocky.

There are six rungs built into the strut, and Armando is coached by phone to climb them. His black hair, once an afro three inches long, is now too short to be affected by the strong breeze outside of the gondola. He can hear the helicopters circling overhead, spotting out of the corner of an eye an occasional shadow from one of them being cast onto the mountainside. When his hands reach the top rung, where he could touch the cable if he wanted to, he attaches the harness to a ring on the strut, and then, really for the first time, takes a moment to look down, then up and around.

He can see everything from up here: the top of the mountain, the skyline, even the late-day sun tracing this brilliant freeway of light across a slice of Caribbean Ocean in the far distance to the north and west. He wipes the sweat from his forehead with the back of one hand. He angles his chin to yell into the cell phone. "Estoy arriba."

In the makeshift control room on the top of El Avila, there are six men and a woman in a darkened room using flashlights to pour over rolled-out diagrams and manuals that they compare to a replica gondola car that is in storage about twenty-five feet away from their table. The main man with the cell phone connected to Armando on the other end dashes across the room, grabbing a ladder and scrambling on top of the spare gondola so he can try to walk Armando through the risky procedure. He is handed a flashlight so he can see what it is that Armando should also be seeing. He has plugged his ear buds with the built-in mic into his phone. "Bueno, Armando. First, make sure for me that you are secured to the gondola by the harness."

"Sí, sí," Armando shouts back, tugging firmly on the harness to be sure.

"Okay. Escuchame. There are two levers, Armando. One is the brake and the other . . . the other lever is the release, the mechanism that disconnects the gondola from the cable. Don't touch anything yet! Our problem here is that the two levers look identical." The controllers at the table and those with flashlights pointing at the spare gondola all exchange worried looks.

Armando examines the two levers up close. "Yes, the levers look the same. How can I know the difference?"

The man on top of the spare gondola in the control centre shifts himself as though he were connected to the strut by a harness. "Follow the lever on your left to where it connects with the cable. The system is designed for the brakes to seize on the cable when there is a power outage."

Suddenly the lights flicker on and there is a huge clang of whirring engines starting up in the control room. The real gondola, bouncing on a slack cable between towers nineteen and twenty, jerks violently, knocking the air and some profanity out of Armando: "Coño la puta madre!"

The passengers below don't know whether to scream or cheer.

The cable and the car jerk again, even more violently this time, and Armando loses his grip at the same time his feet fly off the strut rung, his whole body now suspended in the air, at the mercy of the harness. His cell phone, this time in super slow motion, becomes unclipped with the jolt, and tumbles end over end through the air below, deflecting off the edge of the gondola and gracefully arching away like a rainbow.

The man on top of the spare gondola in the control room is screaming as loud as he can. "ARMANDO! ARMANDO! Can you hear me? Puedes me oiga, ARMANDO?" He looks to his colleagues, and all heads sort of bow, defeated in unison.

It's now coming up on five in the afternoon, and the producer in the studio at CRTV decides to pre-empt a series of bill-paying commercials to go live from his "Lion in the Sky"—Cindi Gallegos. ". . . Nos podemos confirmar que este es un hombre passajero quiene tiene el nombre de Armando."

What she is reporting from the chopper is this: "A passenger named Armando apparently volunteered to go onto the roof, to attempt a manual rescue of the passengers trapped inside the gondola. We do not know at this time if Armando has experience at this type of thing, and we cannot tell if he was injured just moments ago when the *teleférico* suddenly started up again. From our point of view, he seems to be hanging there, lifeless."

But Armando is hardly lifeless. He struggles to find the ladder with his feet and hands. He connects to it. The gondola cable goes taut, and they are once again moving slowly up the hill. Armando hangs on for dear life. Inside the control room on top of the mountain, the man climbs down the ladder from the spare gondola, still yelling every few seconds into his phone. "ARMANDO! Answer me!"

His female colleague has an idea. She goes to Google, on the laptop that has just finished booting back up on the table in front of her. "Canal Dos! Pronto!" With a few clicks she finds a streaming live feed on the CRTV website. Everybody in the room scrambles around the laptop to see the helicopter footage of Canal 2's live coverage. On that tiny screen, everyone can make out an image of Armando clinging to the strut of the gondola as it moves up the mountain. There is a volcanic eruption of cheers and whistles from the group of controllers as they celebrate Armando's safety.

Armando, feeling all eyes on him, somehow knows to wave to the television helicopter in that moment, to signal he is all right. The CRTV camera pulls in tight on his uplifted and crying face, and in this close up, completely misses the real story behind Armando's late-afternoon heroics. Off camera, he reaches into his shirt pocket and extracts the film canister. Craning his neck, he can see that the gondola is nearly at the top of *El Avila*. He opens the lid to the canister and flings the ashes into the air.

"Como te deseo, mi Amor. As you wished, my only love!"

HOMEWARD

RICH IS APPROACHING THE FRONT STEPS OF THE OLD QUEEN Anne High School building at 201 Galer Street, testing out, for the last several blocks, his new filling with the probing tip of his tongue. He whistles in and out, bites his top teeth against the bottom ones for fit, and monitors his pain as the Novocain dissipates. Between the two cement lions guarding the first three steps in the wide approach to the front doors of his building, he spots a druggie or homeless person, sort of crumpled in a seated position underneath an oversized black hoodie. It strikes him as a bit random, since it's a serious hike up the hill from lower Queen Anne or the Seattle Center, and five blocks away from the panhandling action you can sometimes see on the stretch of Queen Anne Avenue between the Five Spot and Trader Joe's. Like a bird that suddenly shows up in a place way outside its normal migratory path, this person definitely seems out of place, Rich is thinking. He purposely scuffs his foot to make a noise as he passes, and the startled lump glares up at him, familiarly.

It's his sister, V'ronica.

"Limpie!" she wails, hopping athletically to her feet.

"V'ronica, what are you doing here?" He asks in a strange-even-to-him soprano voice, trying to compute how his brain just went from homeless to related DNA.

"I've been waiting since about 7:30 this morning for your sorry ass. That's what I'm doing here!" She scuffs one of her tennis shoes back and forth on the step. "And I think I must have fallen asleep, which I never do in the middle of the day. Probably looked like a druggie homeless person out here, huh?"

Rich can only smile, and even that is with a still partially frozen lower lip. "But what are you *doing* here?" He will have to repeat this until he gets it answered.

"My mission is complicated," his twenty-seven-year-old sister says, laying it out. "I needed to see for myself that Ash is really gone." She has to stop because the tears have started. Then she continues, through sobs, "And I am here to bring Chief Limping Rabbit home to the *Nimíipuu*."

"Ah, sis." He throws his arms around her in a shock-delayed embrace, and the two have a moment that leaves them both spent from crying. Rich also leaves a bit of drool on his sister's hoodie, since he still doesn't have back full control of that bottom lip. "I was already going to see you next Thursday. You didn't need to take a—what, bus?—all the way here."

"Eleven hours on a Greyhound, and yes, I absolutely did need to come." A sign of her age and perhaps the awkward twenty-nine-year age difference between them, she defiantly stamps the same tennis show on the sidewalk. "Hey," she reaches her index finger to the side of her big brother's nose to flick his piercing. "That's cool."

Their late mother had delivered her chief a son when she was only nineteen. With this solitary obligation ceremoniously behind her— and with their mutually opposing walls of stubbornness the two young parents built up in the decades since —V'ronica was very much the result of a quite accidental pregnancy after their mother had already reached the pasturing age of forty-eight. It had been toward the end of four back-to-back, record-setting parched valley summers, between 1988 and 1991, that she convinced herself she was so hot she must be going through the great change. She wasn't. Those summers were just plain dry, long, miserable, and blistering hot. As V'ronica's arrival would prove in 1991, following what must have been a brief détente between the chief and his Mrs., the Dreadfulwaters would find out they were still plenty fertile and still had parenting work left between them in this life—a life that wouldn't last too much longer for her.

"Well, let's get inside," he says, picking up her small black duffle bag. "Sort this out for you."

The two walk up to the front doors of the Old Queen Anne High School Building and Rich fobs them inside.

"I couldn't remember your apartment number, anyway. Plus, neither of your names are listed on the call buzzer thing." Her voice rattles, as she is still recovering from the crying jag.

"We're unlisted, and you know what?" He answers his own question: "I never use this front door. I always come in through the parking garage. So you could have been homeless tonight."

"I have your cell number, you idiot. I've already left two messages. And besides, it's not like homeless would be a new experience for me."

"Oh, really?" he says, incredulously, as they start up the wide interior school staircase, taking two and three stairs at a time with each switchback.

"Really," she said, already panting. "And why aren't we taking the 'vator?"

"If you must know, it's because I don't like being alone in there, or in any enclosed spaces anymore." He switches her duffle to the other hand. "It's just a new thing." They hit the fourth landing and head left down the hallway to the corner door with the 4-0-2 on it. Rich pushes down on the hardly-ever-locked lever handle, and the sun-drenched condo, with those ridiculously opulent, arched feature windows, sucks them into the open-concept home, which would normally present as welcoming, comfortable, and awesome. But of course, this place has been none of those things since March 19 of this year.

This sad reality seizes V'ronica profoundly. "I don't think I can do this," she says, panicked and breathing heavily from either the stairs or her nerves, or both.

Surprisingly accomplished at sustaining sadness, having endured almost six months in this mortuary realm, Rich reassures her. "There's lots of Ashton inside. You'll see. He's still here; mostly because I won't let him go." He corrects himself. *"Can't* let him go." He takes his sister's hand. "Let's get the gruesome stuff over with first. So-o-o," he says expelling all the air in his chest as they pass the main bedroom and ensuite. "Ash collapsed here in the bathroom in the middle of shaving his coconut."

His baby sister puts a hand to her mouth and lowers herself down to sit on the back of the long end of the couch lined up to face the Palladian windows.

"I found him in there, 'cause I had to pee—and this is random, but I knew the folded laundry I hadn't had time to put away was sitting on top of the toilet and the washer/dryer in the spare. He wasn't talking." He exhales again, big this time. "He wouldn't say anything to me." She watches her brother's eyes burst and his lips begin to quiver. Not enough time has gone by—there may never be enough time gone by to let him talk about this. "I'm—I don't know, lightly slapping his cheeks, trying to get him to come to . . . you know, snap out of this. When he doesn't respond, I race out of the bathroom to grab my phone off the desk, and I'm like dialing 9-1-1 while I'm running back, and it's a combo of three fucking numbers but I can't do it right and I'm crashing into the bookcase and the wall. I press the button for speakerphone and toss it on the floor where it hits the razor that has, you know, fallen from Ash's hand and I straighten him out on his back while the phone's ringing. I tilt his head back, and there's shaving cream sort of everywhere. I wipe . . ."

He stops in the middle of the sentence. He sniffs the snot back into his nose and shakes his head, not knowing how to tell his little sister this. He sucks in a room's worth of oxygen and tastes the salts from crying. He blows out and continues the sentence. "I wipe the shaving cream off his mouth and his, uh, lips . . ." Rich suddenly pulls his own lips in tight, trying to keep these next words from tumbling like a barrel over a not survivable waterfall. If he tells this complete story out loud, he's thinking, then it's out there, beyond the rapids. It might get away, escape from him forever. Right now, the story of their last minutes together is all that he has left. So grief and recovery get magnified in this push-pull struggle to stay put but move on. "Sorry," he says to his sister, though no apology is necessary. He is trying to unsquint his swollen eyes, to stop them from crying, and this sends his eyebrows behind the drawn curtains of his longer-than-shoulder-length hair that in places is sticking in the tear tracks of his cheeks. "And when he isn't responding and I realize he isn't joking around I get close to see if I can feel him breathing, cause I can't see it, my shit eyes aren't working. This guy finally answers on the phone and I just start shouting stuff . . . Ambulance . . . 201 Galer Street . . . top of Queen Anne . . . Old High School . . . unit 402 . . . my partner is on the floor . . . not . . ."

Rich pauses, but it's already coming out anyway. "Not breathing," he says, involuntarily sucking in two short breaths. "So the guy on the phone tells me the ambulance is on its way and he asks me if I know CPR. Well, shit, yeah, I know it, I'm thinking, but just on first-aid class dummies. This is my husband! Anyway, I tell him *yes* and he says then you should start CPR, so he counts out thirty compressions with me as I'm pushing down on Ash's sternum and I just go right out of myself. The guy says *now two breaths into your partner's mouth. Do it now and let me hear you do it.* I press my mouth onto Ash's so hard that our teeth knock and I'm trying to push my breath into him and I want his breath to push back. *Good, now thirty more compressions as hard as you can push.* But I know it's not good, like he's not responding. Ah, I remember fucking shaving cream is everywhere. We get into the teens and I start shouting instead of counting. I say: YOU . . . ARE . . . NOT . . . FUCK . . . ING . . . GOING . . . TO . . . LEAVE . . . ME! And the guy keeps counting, *twenty, twenty-one* . . . I get ready for two more breaths, but it already seems like I've been doing this forever. Then, on the second breath in, Ash chokes out this cough, and then I know we are still in this together, so I go back to the compressions shouting BREATHE, BABY, BREATHE, PLEASE, FUCK! The guy on the phone is counting for me so I don't have to. ASH . . . LIS . . . TEN . . . TO . . . ME, I tell him. I . . . NEED . . . YOU . . . TO . . . BREATH . . . AND . . . STAY . . . WITH . . . ME . . . YOU . . . CAN'T . . . LEAVE. Then the guy asks if I can check to see if he's breathing and—fuck!—he's not, so I give him two more breaths, longer this time, and I go back to pressing on his chest, deeper this time, and I think I might be breaking his ribs, but I keep going. The EMTs sort of show up in the bathroom, both of them sturdy, you know, husky women. I've no clue how they have gotten into the building or the apartment. I've got shaving cream all over my face and in my hair. Ash has shaving cream on his face and head. I've gotten it all over his chest. It's on the floor and the vanity cabinet. The firemen show up next and I move a little off to the side but I'm holding Ash's hand and I keep squeezing this count of thirty over and over and I'm starting to breath funny myself, like this isn't going to work no matter what anyone fucking does. People are asking me questions and I'm answering them but my energy and my eyes and every cell in my body are just focused on HOLD . . . ING . . . HIS . . . HAND . . . AND . . . NOT . . . LET . . . TING . . . HIM . . . GO! The firemen have gelled the paddles of the defib, and the EMTs yell *Clear!*, but I'm not letting go. They shock him, and there's this bounce—not at all like on TV, but then there still isn't a pulse—but I'm still squeezing the hell out of his hand. They shock him again, and one of the gals yells *I've got something!* Then they pack him up on this gurney and I go with him to the emergency room and everyone lets me just keep holding his hand. By the time we get there, Ash has kinda come back into the room, and he's talking to me but we are both just stuck in this fear. "So," he says, "to be honest, I'm a little scared this time."

The waterworks have started up again, but Rich blubbers on.

"And that's when I looked him in those frightened green eyes and I told him *you are not permitted to leave me, ever.*"

V'ronica catapults up from the back of the couch and into her brother's arms, and the two of them have another moment.

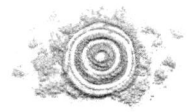

A LITTLE LATER THAT evening, while his sister is taking a shower, Rich is clearing some books from the top shelf, disguising a built-in

Murphy bed in the den that is his office, but that is about to become his sister's bedroom for the next few days. He tugs the bed out of its hiding place and sees that a slightly crumpled white sheet of paper has been tucked under the strap holding the bedding in place. He opens the paper to discover my handwriting:

Don't stay mad. Come back to bed with me.

GERALD

THAT MAN IN HIS LATE SEVENTIES, BUT IN DECENT SHAPE,
is my father—Gerald Leroy, though he prefers to be called *G.L.*, thanks
to a compulsion for abbreviation. He is wearing his weekend army-issue
camouflage pants and a non-matching mostly white shirt with plaid
undertones and long sleeves only rolled up once at the cuffs. Leaning
back on the hood of his silver Camry, trying to summon his courage for
the expedition that is coming, he looks across the raging Lochsa River
through clip-on sunglasses, to a trail sign beyond the footbridge on the
other side. He is back in his old forest service territory, with its familiar
smells and sounds and ghosts. Now, I just happen to be one of them.
He hasn't quite worked up the gumption to address the purpose for
which he has just driven 163 miles. He threads part of his belt through
the reinforced slits in the olive green canvas pouch with the mostly
rubbed off US Forest Service logo; the pouch holds his metal canteen.
He checks the canteen's fit, and checks his pockets—car keys in one,
plastic film canister in the other. If he's to make it back home in time
for dinner—and it's grilled cheese and tomato soup night so not a huge
motivator for him—he needs to get going.

Well, Dad, if it helps, think of this as a daring mission behind enemy lines. Think of my ashes in this canister as arsenic you have to introduce into the enemy's water supply.

G.L. crosses the footbridge and warms up to a fairly fit stride along a heavily worn and rutted path that parallels the creek.

I'd like to be released into one of the rock pools at Jerry Johnson Hot Springs. I can count on your military training to dictate that you don't ask questions of your mission; you just complete it. Still, I think you should know why I choose this spot.

My father encounters a couple of shirtless, giggling young men, walking in the opposite direction. My father nods, extending his chin. "Hello, Pops," one of the kids says, and they both look back at Gerald's ass and make demonstrative signs of approval. My father is oblivious to the attention he has drawn, and remains focused on his mission.

You brought me here once before, you'll remember. You will likely now elect to view this as the weakest decision ever made in the entire history of your fabulous parenting career, but you brought the whole family on an outing to Jerry Johnson Hot Springs in the early Seventies. No doubt, you would like to have dismissed the whole incident as inconsequential to the development, normal or otherwise, of your highly impressionable offspring. But I was taking copious notes in my Book of Memory that day.

Gerald suddenly stops on the path in a spot of sun to let his breath catch up to him. Posing there next to Warm Springs Creek, like a statue commemorating wartime Vietnam Veterans, he can't help but flash back to 1973 . . .

THE TAYLOR FAMILY PLATOON consists of Commander Gerald, as a young father, and likely in the very same camouflage pants; my McCall's-pattern-loving, self-fashioned mother; a not-yet-quite-teen me, in bell bottoms; my younger sister, in ponytails tied up in fat fuzzy neon-colored strings; and chubby baby brother, tethered by a leash attached to a child harness to keep him from bolting—a penal throwback to the one time he disappeared for hours in the neighbor's garage. The platoon comes to a marching halt near the end of the path, where it has encountered a splinter group of the *Rainbow Family of Living Light* that has established a commune camp around the natural stone pools of the hot springs. In this clearing at the creek's edge, there is drumming and tambourines, and, I'm pretty sure, a flute. Some of the women are singing "Abraham, Martin and John." The Taylor family members are the only humans in this encounter in the middle of nowhere who are wearing any clothing, though it is woefully mismatched. The rest of the scene is defined by 100% nudity.

Too proud to beat a retreat, General Taylor presses forward. After all, he's brought his troops this far. G.L. signals the family to take up position in the closest and emptiest pool nearest the creek. I am mesmerized, and have this sort of stoned look of euphoria as my head and eyes follow every movement of every naked boy and man cavorting in my blessed, extraordinary field of vision. I am sort of grossed out and a little irritated by the naked women and girls, because there seems to be so many more of them.

I was self-conscious for exactly eight seconds, thinking that I must have looked pale, maybe even sickly when compared to the evenly tanned and roasted bodies cavorting all about me. My siblings, acting timid and ashamed thanks to their Baptist upbringing, don't dare raise their heads to make eye contact with any parts of anyone. Mother Carole, I am certain, wants to gaze over all the attractions at the summer fair, but doesn't reveal this desire under the General's watch. The Taylor Family, trying so very hard to be inconspicuous, strips down to bathing suits we've been wearing under our clothes since leaving the house a good four hours earlier. We quickly submerge our pasty bodies up to our chins in the pool, until we look like a gaggle of stealthy Russian periscopes, like the ones that had appeared off the Oregon Coast a decade earlier. It is, I think, integral to point out that beneath Gerald's camouflage pants, he is wearing a camouflage boxer-style swimming suit, sourced from a J.C. Penny catalog and tucked under the tree with his name written all over it, several Christmases ago.

The family hasn't been a minute under the murky mineral water when young Corporal Ashton realizes he has an entirely different modus operandi and so peels off his bathing suit, and, completely naked, climbs on top of the biggest rock at the pool's edge, where he is afforded the best view of the Rainbow Family spectacle and has his best chances for adoption. He spends the next five minutes facing away from his biological family, sitting there on that boulder, growing his little boner.

"TAYLOR, get back into the pool this minute!" the General orders.

I may have cocked my head slightly, but I didn't turn around as I addressed him. "As you know, Father, I have an adverse skin reaction to sulfur, not to mention a high risk of *ghiardial infection* if some of this water is accidentally splashed into my mouth."

My father jerks me off that rock and back into the pool with a giant splash. "I'm sure your mother brought ointment! Now sit there and don't move!"

Bruised and indignant, I sit in the pool with my arms crossed and my eyes squinting nearly shut in defiance. Not all shut, mind you, since—duh!—there are still all these naked people about.

Within seconds, a very hippie looking, almost Sasquatch-hairy man, and a not-as-hairy woman, walk up to the Taylor Family tub, and ask to join us in the water, so that our two families, their's Rainbow and our's Taylor, can steep our genes in immersive communion. The man's scrotum looks like it has spent the last month in this geo-thermal wonderland, it hangs so low. The couple passes a marijuana cigarette they've kept above the surface, back and forth. They graciously offer a toke to General Taylor, who is suddenly not the big man he pretends to be, and shakes his head, looking down at his hands below the greenish surface of the water. Only I have the courage to make eye contact with the Hippie Man—and truthfully, I couldn't break my stare with a sledge hammer. He smiles at me and jokingly offers me the stubby cigarette. I smile back suggestively in my sophisticated, eleven-year-old way, my hand already surfacing from the depths to accept, but I end up shaking my head, *no*.

"Okay, troops," my father barks and startles all of us, including the hippies. "We have another four hundred miles to go today if we're going to make the Lewis and Clark Caverns by nightfall. Shall we?" His eyes have narrowed to slits that communicate there is not an option here. The Taylor family scrambles out of the water like they've just discovered leeches. Taking my sweet time, I reluctantly follow, not taking my eyes off the hairy Hippie Man. Sensing my amusement, if not the full, clinically developing obsession, the Hippie Man raises himself out of the water to perch on my rock. The couple had each used only one hand to pass the joint between them. By now, the full-grown evidence that their other hands may not have been idle below the surface, has risen out of the hairy forest to hoist its flag of virility. As this burns like a happy face brand on my retinas, I cannot, will not take my eyes with me as my father barks again and I race to catch up to the hasty retreat in progress. The Hippie Man smiles this toothless grin—not that all his teeth were missing—and waves a super slow-motion wave as the scene blurs like Vaseline has been spread across the lens and cross dissolves to happy faces then fades to black and everlasting joy.

G.L. SHAKES HIS HEAD, emits a half chuckle to himself and continues his trek toward the pools. The trail soon empties into that same large clearing next to the creek. Sun-bleached logs are strewn about, and the place is overrun with about a dozen modern-day hippies in dreadlocks, macramé jewelry, and various states and styles of dress and undress. They are smoking just copious amounts of marijuana, the smoke of which hangs on the branches of the trees like a wet sweater. There is an intimidating and accelerating beat of bongo drums as the newcomer approaches, just in case he's a cop. My father pauses briefly to take it all in, to focus his resolve and assess the scene, before making a bee-line to the closest pool. Once there, he quickly strips down to his camouflage swimming trunks and begins gingerly climbing over the mossy rocks and into the hot tub the stacked rock dam has created.

"Clothing isn't optional here, dude. Lose da trunks!"

G.L. spins around to see a young man and two women, all naked, joining him from behind.

"I beg your pardon?" my father says, as authoritatively as he can.

The speaker, a French Canadian, tries to be clearer. "The camouflage trunks, man. If you're trying to blend in, camouflage isn't the ticket, 'cause war ain't the answer." He motions with his head to the trunks the older man is wearing, but smiles so as not to be intimidating.

Trying to act cool, but blushing, my father says, "Yes, of course," and lowers his trunks, careful to step out of them one foot at a time.

One of the young women is already in the pool, with her breasts bobbing on the surface. She introduces herself and her friends on either side. "That's Jacques taking control of the dress code. I'm Madeleine. This is Jacinthe."

"My name is Gerald," my father says, clearing his throat.

Two other guys jog over from the tree line, genitals flopping. "Hey. I'm Paul and this is Bernard." They splash their way into the pool.

"Cool," Madeleine proclaims. "What brings you out here, Pops?"

"Me? Uh, I came here once back in the seventies. Just wondered if it had changed."

Jacques, the only one lounging out of the water, with just one foot in, says in his accent, "And I betchoo it has not changed, no?"

"No," my father answers. "I can't say it's changed at all."

"But you've changed, I bet!" says Jacques, laughing jovially.

Madeleine rushes to his defense and says, "Hey, he's still sexy as hell . . . in or out of camouflage."

Blushing again, or blushing still, G.L. says, "Yeah, I've changed.

Had three kids of my own . . . older than you all now, I imagine." This catches him off guard, and he pauses to reflect on the recently reduced number of his living offspring, and remembers the canister in his pants pocket. He starts to reach his arm over the rocks for those pants but changes his mind, given the mixed company he is entertaining.

Jacinthe, the younger appearing of the women with the long blond hair that it looks like she's curled around Ponderosa pinecones, agrees with Madeleine. "You must have been quite the looker in your day . . . in the seventies, I mean."

G.L. chuckles uncomfortably. "Like I said, I have changed."

"I bet you still get high though, right?" asked Jacques.

Squinting, G.L. blocks the pre-noon sun with a flat hand, nearly saluting his inquisitor. He stammers some, as though there is still a security clearance in question, and responds, "Uh, I was in the military, then a career in government. I was never high."

"Right," Jacques feigns, not believing him.

The girls giggle to themselves. Jacinthe confesses the obvious, "We're high right now."

It is a struggle for the Commander not to stare at their buoyant breasts. "Yes, I can see that," he concludes.

"Dudes, I'm coming down," Bernard announces, almost frantically splashing out of the pool. "I'll be back." He bounds off, dancing up the rocky trail barefoot, glistening, and naked.

Jacques yells after him. "Don't come back empty-handed!"

"Hey, wait up," Paul shouts, then splashes out of the pool after his friend.

In the commotion, G.L. discovers he's been bookended between the two hippie chicks. He looks down first at one, then the other, then up at Jacques. "So where you kids from?" he asks, as if polite conversation is what the developing situation calls for.

"The Global Village, where else?" Madeleine asks.

"She means Montreal." Jacques clarifies. "We're all from Quebec."

"Except for Paul. He's from South Dakota," Jacinthe volunteers, rubbing her thigh against his leg—nonchalantly or accidentally, G.L. can't tell.

Time to deploy countermeasures. "Look, I need to take a leak. I'll be right back." Gerald makes an awkward, splashy exit, and his fellow soakers watch his aging though still decent white ass hustle off toward the tree line. Jacques only watches until the old man disappears inside the trees, and then he reaches over to the camouflage pants and checks the pockets.

Madeleine protests. "Hey, whatcha doing? He's a nice man."

"Hello?" Jacques says, without pronouncing the *H*. "What's this?" His hand emerges from the pocket holding a film canister. Seeing that the old guy's still pissing on the tree trunks, he opens the lid to the canister. His face lights up.

Jacinthe leans in. "What is it?" she asks, pulling her wet hair behind an ear.

"I tink it looks to be, I dunno, maybe a rough cut o' cocaine. Unrefined stuff, maybe. Pops is o-kay!" Jacques speaks in a loud whisper. His eyes dart around for a flat surface, and he spots a table rock. "Hey, watch da trees and tell me when he starts back 'dis way." He taps a few small piles of the ash out of the canister onto the rock and, using a piece of wood, cuts it into four really rudimentary lines. "Who's first?" The girls exchange looks and pass. Jacques slowly reveals a devilish grin. "I guess it's me." His face gets close to the surface of the rock, and a line of the ash disappears up his nose. He throws his head back, dreadlocks flying, and holding the side of his nose. "Shit!" The girls lean forward, waiting for the review. "'Dat's some whacky shit!" With that, the two girls bump heads getting their noses to the flat rock. Each takes a line. The three of them steal a glance toward the trees and see that the old man is now returning to the pool at the edge of the river. Jacques thinks he still has time to do one more line. With the film canister in one hand, and his stick in the other, he snorts the last line of ash.

"What in the hell are you doing? Hey! That's mine!" My father is making a much bigger deal of this than the kids think he should. Jacques jumps to his feet as his face turns beet-red. He holds the canister out of reach as my father tries to retrieve it.

"Saving it all for yourself? Dat's selfish, man!" Jacques taunts.

Exasperated and panicked and confused, my wise old Dad figures out what they've just done. "You snorted it?" he asks. He looks at the girls. "What? All of you?"

Still thinking he can turn this thievery around, Jacques teases him by holding out the canister and then withdrawing it just as G.L. reaches. "Promise to share, like a good hippie, and I'll give it back to you."

Beyond upset, and now visibly crying, G.L. points to Jacques's hand. "Those," he says, "are the ashes of my dead son!"

The three hippie kids are stunned, and kind of paralyzed. It is clear from their faces that they are each shocked by this information. The girls suddenly begin trying to expel the ashes from their noses, in a most unfeminine manner. Jacques has to save face, and elects to merely wipe the end of his nose.

The girls are nearly hysterical. "Jacques!" Madeleine screams. "You idiot!" The two girls take turns looking up each other's nostrils to make sure they've gotten out what they can. For a minute or two, nobody says anything, their brains too busy processing this. Eventually, the girls calm down and G.L. relaxes his naked stance.

"I can't stop thinking about it," Jacinthe says, almost philosophically. "I mean, what we did amounts to . . . I don't know . . . recreational cannibalism!"

Already starting to calm down, G.L. says, "Don't be so hard on yourselves. My son was very much into experimentation. I'm sure he's amused by this."

This doesn't help. The girls race off to the creek maybe twenty-five yards away to wash their noses out.

Jacques leans forward on his rock, extending the canister, which he presses with both of his hands into the outstretched and quivering hand of my now weeping father. "I am . . . wow!" A tear escapes Jacques's eye. "I am so sorry, man." With his hands around my father's, Jacques tenderly helps a trembling G.L. to a seated position on a rock, then pivots his butt on the rock to face him. "Please tell me about your boy."

My father looks into the Frenchman's bloodshot eyes, and can easily read his sincerity and remorse. "He was smart," he starts. "Ashton, that's his name." His voice is proud, as he sucks in a bunch of emotion that's trying to escape. "Ashton was a smart boy—clever, you know? He wrote books and poems and plays, even a musical once. He was sensitive, like he was too aware of this world. He took on the pain of it and carried it around like a burden I will never know." He pauses a moment before he blubbers through the next part. "My son, from the day he was born, was this beautiful boy that I never felt I deserved. My boy would smile this smile when I knew I hadn't given him a reason to be happy, and he would listen to what I taught him, with the attention, you know, of someone way beyond his years—a worldly scholar, really—and then he would do the exact opposite, every time." Gerald laughs a bit and wipes the snot from his upper lip. Jacques laughs with him and reflexively puts his arm around the bare shoulders of this father, a man old enough to be his grandfather, spilling his guts out into the open. He gives this stranger a squeeze, and my dad looks into his face and they are both crying. There's still ash under Jacque's nose, and G.L. sobs even more.

"Let it out, Dude. Dis is good. Dis is perfect, you know?" Jacques coaches him now as though he'd waited his whole young life for his own father to say this truth.

"Ashton reminded me a lot—at times too much—of my own father. He was sensitive, and just like Ash, he would take on all this suffering that he saw everyone around him going through, and this made it easier for everyone else, but really tough for my dad—just as it was for Ashton, my son. And then there's me; this stone-cold, serious, strict, rule-making and rule-following man, always calculating the bad in people, stuck between these two sensitive souls of the earth, both of whom were only showing me love and joy and an easier road that they in truth had made easier. I didn't know how to deal with this. I just couldn't leave my path."

Clouds appear to be organizing overhead, like the summer day could get interrupted.

"You are shivering a little . . . let's get you into da pool." Jacques leads by example, easing himself in. Gerald follows. The two face each other as a giant thundercloud eclipses the sun overhead.

"When my Father died—when he probably killed himself," G.L. revises, "Ashton was only seven."

"Why did he kill himself?"

"He was sad . . . just very sad. The pain of this world broke him. He took some pills and he went to sleep forever in the bathtub." G.L. sniffs, and exhales big. "And even this, he did to make it easier for the others around him."

"Easier, how?"

"Well, there was a life insurance policy that took care of the financial matters. My mother, I guess, had this thing for my dad's best friend, who was a widower. They were married less than a year after my dad died. I have always sort of felt my father took himself out of the picture to make it easier for her to be happy. I think that was his true love for her."

"Jesus."

"And Ashton . . . well, Ashton decided very young that he was going to be different from everyone else; and not just different but special about it. He set out to make a difference in the world and ended up being the difference. Does that make sense to you?"

"I tink so, yes. He sounds pretty amazing."

"He knew he was going to die young—before me, before his mother, before his brother and sister, his partner, and many of his friends. He knew this and it didn't scare him. When he was twenty-one years old, he was home for Christmas from the University of New Mexico. He said he wanted to see the family doctor; that something didn't seem right. We made the appointment for him and that's when we learned he had this cancer and then a week later we learned it was bad . . . worse than they thought at first. He insisted we not be sad, not around him and not when we were alone. He was determined that this was not going to ruin the lives around him. In the months that followed, he would get so sick from the chemotherapy that would have probably killed a horse, but he would just joke and tell us how boring we were when we came to be with him in the hospital. When he went into this isolation tent contraption because he had no white blood cells left, and the doctors said we couldn't visit him for about a week, he made us promise him—in notes that were radiated and sent back and forth—that as soon as he could build up his resistance and bust out of there, the whole family was going skiing together. He kept that promise and so did we. The whole family, just scared to death and crying our eyes out, loaded gear into the car and drove to the ski hill and put in a half day. His doctor had advised against this, of course. A normal cold could become pneumonia overnight in his compromised state. We were so nervous that he would have to go back into isolation again, and in our panic somehow the only keys to the car got locked in the trunk in the parking lot below the ski lodge, and we ended up having to call and then wait for a locksmith to come up the hill. I thought I was going to lose my son to cancer, but then he recovered and I thought I was going to lose my son to AIDS. It was always going to be something I would lose him to—he'd convinced me of that, so I tried to be ready; you know, walking around half-prepared and waiting to find out how my son was going to die before me. It wasn't the order of things, but it is how Ashton said it was going to be. And damn it all, he was right."

"What are you supposed to do with the rest of the ashes?"

"I'm supposed to spread them here, on top of the water, after I have finished remembering."

"I'd be okay with dat," Jacques tells my old man.

The two strangers sit in the thermal pool in an understood silence, as parts of me settle to the bottom, and work their way through the nasal and digestive tracts of three Quebeckers. The sun finally emerges from the thundercloud undefeated, to bathe their upwardly tilting faces in an unworldly warmth brought to them by me.

TUKEYÚ·TPE

IT JUST MADE SENSE TO RICH TO GIFT MY PIECE-OF-SHIT plastic car—that early 2000 black Saturn Vue—to V'ronica. A young, independent woman her age should not ever have to take a Greyhound bus to know her freedom. And so after a stop at the DMV to take care of the transfer paperwork and get her insurance prepaid for the first year, the car he is following over Snoqualmie Pass belongs to and is being driven by his sister, V'ronica Dreadfulwater. He is the caboose of a two-car caravan heading home to Spalding, Idaho.

The drive was never very interesting to him after passing Ellensburg, and it always became worse after crossing the Columbia River at Vantage to travel the two-lane agricultural waistband of Washington State on dusty Highway 26, past roadside onion, potato, and fruit stands, and towns with names like "Othello" and "Washtuccna" and "Colfax." He tries to fuse with the excitement that surely must be the party theme in the car keeping to the posted speed limit ahead of him, as his sister drives the first wheels she's ever owned. But even then, drafting behind was a dull affair through these barren parts.

Rich had been reluctantly planning this pilgrimage even before his vagabond sister showed up on the old high school steps to deliver in person her version of a no-escape guilt trip. He had even made this iTunes playlist of the songs he wanted to hear; music that would condition his soul for its re-entry into the atmospheric and sometimes backward culture of his childhood—of his people, of the *Niimíipu*. This soundtrack has been playing for the past two hundred miles through the ten speakers of his BMW Z4 Roadster, and is programmed to transport him through all five hours and thirty-seven minutes of the journey if he needs it to. The playlist includes every song from the *Smoke Signals* soundtrack, except "John Wayne's Teeth," and by extension, because the group is on the soundtrack, every song by the American Indian trio of female a cappella singers known as Ulali, and by extension again any song by Ulali's lead singer Pura Fé and her cousin Jennifer Kreisberg, who sometimes perform as Twolali; then of course there was a healthy smattering of Cher; *Four Nez Perce Peyote Songs* by a group calling themselves Indigenous Sound; absolutely everything ever recorded by the Chickasaw composer Jerod Impichchaachaaha Tate, and by extension the entire CD *Documerica*; all fourteen songs off the Wild Sanctuary album called *Music of the Nez Perce*; some but not a lot of Wayne Newton; a few tracks from his own sister's demo tape; a little Buffy Sainte-Marie; some hit and miss rap by Litefoot; Radmilla Cody's album *Spirit of a Woman*; and "We're All Alone" and "Higher and Higher" by Rita Coolidge.

By the time he'd sped past Uniontown and was nearing the very edge of the Palouse Plateau on Highway 195, he could admit to himself that after five hours, he was all-but-Indianed-out, so he switched over to Beyoncé—but only the artist after Destiny's Child, and of course, nothing from *Dream Girls*. If he had to get technical under cross-examination, he could posit that Beyoncé's mom was of Louisiana Creole and Acadian descent, and therefore, the indigenous criterion for his road trip soundtrack had not been compromised.

A half hour ago, when his sis had pulled the Saturn over for a pee and a Slurpee in Pullman, he hopped out to set the trunk to receive the automatically retracting roof, so that he could drive with the top down for the last forty-five miles home. There, next to his Coach leather travel bag, was the pillow from our bed, from the side I always slept on, covered with the woven Nez Perce cornhusk mat. These cradled the rose-adorned biscuit container with the rest of my ashes, like the queen's crown jewels on a red velvet cushion. My Limping Rabbit is getting there, having made good with the task of sending what's left of me madly off in all directions. And so it comes down to this, whatever "this" is going to entail. He bends his torso inside the trunk to kiss the Rubaiyat red rose depicted on the lid of the container. He can't really deal with ashes right now, though he's been coping with Ash and everything I've thrown at him for nearly twenty years. It is bound to come to him shortly what is supposed to happen next. But just for insurance, I have reminded him:

Ashton Taylor, *Last Will and Testament*, pages 19 and 20

And now comes the final instruction, Limping Rabbit. You were always so secretive about your Native ways; so much so I was often left feeling more ethnic than you, and we both know what white trash I was.

Nineteen and a half years together and you never introduced me to your parents, or let me see where or how you grew up. I don't think it's because you were ashamed, either of me or where you came from, but because you never reconciled what you've become—which, you have to admit, pretty much embodies a rather privileged, monolithic white ideal. Face it. You're rich and successful, and until very recently, you had the best-looking trophy husband this side of the Continental Divide.

But there's a problem in your paradise. All these adornments of achievement—the fact you've crashed through the cultural glass ceiling and all—hasn't made you happy. It's made you angry, Limping Rabbbit. You have to ask yourself, why is that? What's missing? And you have to find whatever that is and build it back into your life.

You can die with your six-figure income and your BMW and the envy of everyone around you, but don't die with the regret of not being true to yourself. If you don't get it right this lifetime, you'll be sent back to do it again, and with your damned Indian luck, you could end up with the same nagging partner of yours a second time around.

So here it is. I want you to somehow incorporate me into a Nez Perce ritual for the dead. I'm not naïve. Every tribe has gotta have one. Then I want you to take the last of my ashes to that place, you know, where Coyote had his penis hacked off. When you get there, tell me again the Nez Perce story, "How Coyote's Penis Became a Dam." I just love that one! Release me there and FIND YOURSELF in the traditions of your People.

This is the last recorded wish of Ashton Bernard Taylor. I promise. Now humor me and know in that crazy heart of yours that I have loved you with my life. It is now time, Limping Rabbit, for you to get back to living yours.

Back in the driver's seat and clocking fifty-five, he's thinking there was something erogenous about the sensation of his thick black hair being held back by the Roadster's velocity. He supposes this might be genetic, having more to do with his Appaloosa-riding ancestry than his BMW. (My Rich has never personally experienced the sensation of horseback riding—bareback or otherwise—so he is going strictly on gene memory here.)

By the time the twin cities of Lewiston and Clarkston come into view near the top of the ridge at the edge of the Palouse, he already knows he is entering the homeland of his people. It spreads out before him across an immense valley floor more than two thousand feet below, bisected by the confluence of the Clearwater and Snake rivers—the latter of which also divides modern-day Washington from Idaho further south. He doesn't need a soundtrack for this. He doesn't need to see the sign for the Nez Perce National Historical Park or read Idaho State Historical Marker #294 about the Nez Perce War of 1877. Limping Rabbit automatically knows he is home. This homing instinct, or navigation by magnetism, is in his genes; it has been floating around in amniotic fluid of his ancestors in these reaches of the map for the past 11,000 years. Everything, for as far as he can see, and to places beyond

the curve of this earth that he cannot—from the treed tops of the Bitterroot Range, carved by the Lochsa and Selway; to the rocky teeth of
the Wallowa Mountains to the west; from the Snake River hissing out
of Hells Canyon; to the Clearwater River Valley giving rise to the Big
Camas Prairie—this is the traditional territory of the *Nimíipuu*. And
whether he likes it or not, and whether he acknowledges it or not, it is
the home of Rich Dreadfulwater.

Each of his ears pops as he follows V'ronica's car, now bombing
down the four-lane, mostly 7% grade of the Lewiston Hill stretch of
Highway 95—a one-switchback engineering marvel that forty years
ago replaced the Spiral Highway, retiring its sixty-four hairpin turns.
Down they go, dropping two thousand feet in elevation so steeply in
eight minutes that they whiz past five separate (and frequently used)
runaway truck ramps, down to what was once the ancient flood plain
of mighty rivers that ran thirty feet lower in the thirteen million years
before the steelhead- and salmon-stopping monoliths of cement and
greed killed the rivers and turned them into stagnant and putrefying
reservoirs. The highway veers to the left in a banked turn that would
send a matchbox car off the orange plastic track if you tried this at
home and then levels off along the river. This river will reclaim its
floodplain again, Rich firmly used to believe, when *Hanyawat* becomes
bored with us and restores what once was, his father used to prophe-
size. Limping Rabbit used to think he would live to see that day, but he
doesn't believe in much of anything anymore.

He thinks to tune the BMW's radio to station KIYE, 88.7FM—
Voice of the Nimíipuu—in time to hear the last five minutes of the
classic rock and oldies mix before the Saturday afternoon programming shifts to "*Voices from the Circle*, with today's special guest—Chief
Moses Dreadfulwater." *Well, what would be the chances of that?* Moses'
son, behind the wheel in the BMW Z4, thinks sarcastically to himself,
knowing that his father is an on-air fixture at KIYE. V'ronica toots the
Saturn's horn three times to signal to her brother that perhaps she is
tuned in and listening to their father, too.

"It's nice to have you on the show, Moses. I understand that before we get into today's topics, you'd like to give a shout-out for the powwow that starts tonight with the Grand Entry?"

"That's right, Ben. Tonight kicks off the annual Chief Joseph and Warriors Memorial Powwow at the Lapwai City Park. As you know, tribal members on the Lapwai reservation and other surrounding tribes get together to watch powwow dancers compete, and to honor those lost in the Nez Perce War of 1877 led by Chief Joseph—and in fact, to honor Native American veterans of all wars."

"It is really a family event, isn't it?" says host Ben. It's a statement more than a question. "We play host to families that travel here from across the Nez Perce nation too."

"We sure do, Ben. I am particularly proud that both of my children are traveling home right now to participate in the singing and dancing tonight. The powwow is about the family and about remembering those we've lost and those who came and went before us."

"Is there anything in particular that you are looking forward to at this powwow, Moses?"

"You know, my daughter is going to perform a rappin' song she wrote, and I'll tell ya, if we can get all the weyekins to cooperate, I might even get my son to exhibit his famous pow-wow-winning Duck and Dive dance."

"That would certainly be a treat, wouldn't it, Moses?"

"It would . . . it would." Listeners might suspect the Chief is getting emotional now.

"It would *not!*" Rich yells, slapping the dashboard. He hears V'ronica tooting the horn again, waving her arm out the window supportively.

"Okay. So today we're here to talk about Washat, the Seven Drums faith, and what it has in common with Christianity . . ."

Rich had gone to elementary and high school with KIYE radio host Ben LeDuc, who had been given the Indian name of *Broken Killdeer Wing* because he'd been born with his left arm shorter than the right. He had mostly grown out of this deformity by the time he was a teenager—unlike Limping Rabbit, who still walks with a slight hitch in his step if you watch closely. They should have gotten along like native brothers on fire, given that both of their Native names had involved handicaps and overcome-able shortcomings and they were just a year apart in age. In grade school and halfway into high school everyone assumed the two to be best friends. But then there was this crack in the firmament when Ben lost in a heated tiebreaker at one of the last powwows before Rich left home, where the two of them ended up competing against each other. They barely spoke to each other after that. It all came down to this dance-off between Rich's Duck and Dive technique and Ben's interpretation of the same traditional dance. Ben took issue with the judging that night. He had always been secretly resentful that Rich—who seemed to him to be a reluctant Indian, who had always insisted on playing the cowboy instead of representing what he was, and who had these frequently pronounced plans to leave the reservation the first chance he got—was in line to be chief. It must have slipped Rich's father's memory, or he wouldn't have brought up such an insensitive topic on Ben's radio program. *Maybe Ben's wing had healed and he was big enough to get over it by now*, Rich thought. Then again, maybe Ben was just using the wing to fake that he had gotten over it.

He and his sister zoom past the Nez Perce-owned and -operated Clearwater River Casino and Lodge on the left side of the highway. It appears to have doubled in size since the last time Rich was home. That and cultural tourism were key generators for the largest tribe in Idaho, and he had played an early legal role from his high-rise Seattle office tower in negotiating terms and approvals. Gazing to the right, across the Clearwater River, he begins watching for the waterfall that looks like a horse's tail, which had been created millions of years ago through fault uplift, basalt lava flows, glacial carving, and floods. He'd been told as a child that this was *Tukeyú·tpe*, the site of the legend where Coyote lost his penis. Rich is thinking about the oral tradition of this story as he pivots his head to keep his eyes momentarily locked on the waterfall, when he nearly rear-ends the plastic car in front of him, which is signaling and slowing down to move onto the shoulder.

What the . . .? he thinks, and then he remembers: she's stopping at the spot where their mother was plowed off the road and killed in April of 2003. Rolling to a stop at a replaced section of guardrail still too shiny to be missed or mistaken as original, he turns on his hazard lights and waits to see what his sister is going to do. As difficult as it is for him—for either of them, he imagines—he turns his eyes to the life-giving and life-taking river, running deep in this bend between the highway and the slowly cutting channel it creates with Hog Island.

V'ronica gets out of her car, checks for traffic, and then walks back to climb in the passenger seat of the Roadster, to confer with her older brother. "Nice shout-out from Dad on the radio, eh?"

"I'm not performing that dance tonight!" The river here makes him grumpy, he's decided. "What prompted you to stop here, anyway? This place gives me the creeps."

"I've been thinking about it the past couple hours, and have decided that I want to add my portion of Ash's remains right here, at this spot in the river, so that I can make this a happier place to think about every time I have to drive by it. When I think about Ash, I can't help myself. I just start smiling inside and out."

Rich thinks about this plan and knows it is a good one. It reminds him though that he still hasn't formulated his own "native ritual" for distributing what still remains in the container, which is a surprising amount even after he made the decision to fill and gift the last remaining unlabeled canister—the nineteenth—to his sister. "Do you want me to go down the bank with you to the river?"

She nods her head, yes.

This river, which the Nez Perce called *Koos-koos-kai-kai*, flows for seventy-four winding miles, has coursed through Rich's life just as it flows through Idaho's panhandle from Montana to Washington, through this reservation, and through the centuries since creation. It has sustained salmon, deer, elk, waterfowl, pheasants, grouse, wild grasses, berries, and the *Nimíipuu*. In 1805, it brought the Lewis and Clark Corps of Discovery expedition—lost, dispirited, and near starvation—to a place not far upriver, where Rich's ancestors nourished them, cared for their horses, and guided them on their way to where this river joins the *Ki-moo-e-mim* before flowing into the *Nch'i-Wàna* that carries salmon to and from the great ocean beyond. The Clearwater River brought them the French Canadian explorers and traders who gave them the exonym *Nez Percé*, even though they didn't pierce their noses. It brought other white men and their diseases, both of which stealthily reduced the number of *Nimíipuu* from around 6,000 to 1,800 in less than the century that followed. This is the legacy, the bounty, and the pain of the Clearwater River. Swallowing whole the mother of Rich and V'ronica and the wife of their father, Moses the Chief, was just one thing more that got factored into the love/hate relationship the *Nimíipuu* have with this river.

On the far side of the guardrail, the brother and sister sort of accidentally ski down the highway embankment of dust and pebbles to the larger rocks at the river's edge, each grabbing fistfuls of shrubs and grasses to slow their descent. The noise of the highway mingles in their ears with the sounds of the river, which still flows in this spot before getting stupid and lazy, just about even with the casino, in slack water backed up behind the dams downstream. V'ronica looks long at her brother, and thinks the transformation from city slicker back to Indian must be happening and all according to her plan, which was really my plan first. He stares straight down through the clear water to the boulders at the bottom of the river while a whole separate river seems to start flowing from his own damned eyes. No question: he had been his mama's little Indian boy, and he had enjoyed her all to himself for twenty-seven years before his sister came along. He had not been able to find his way in this world since losing her, and this is the place she had left him, slipping through a whirlpool leading from this world down a drain to the next.

"Hello Clara Peo-Peo-Hix-Hiix," his sister announces, greeting the water with outstretched arms, palms up. She has been here plenty, Rich realizes now. She uses the *Niimiipuutímt* language for Whitebird, as their mother, Clara, had been descended from the great medicine man by the same name. "Look who's here," she grins as she speaks, knowing this would please their mother's spirit. "Together, Limping Rabbit and I bring someone else here to meet you; someone I don't think you ever knew, but someone we are all tied up together in a love lost."

Rich bites his lower lip. His sister must have been thinking about this since leaving Seattle. She was going to beat him to the delivery of

Ash's native ritual, and she was probably going to do it better than he could, too. This and just being at this place makes him scream on the inside and bawl on the outside. V'ronica produces the film canister for her brother; he looks into her eyes to find out what to do, and then he does it. He removes the lid from the canister.

"To keep your spirits company until we can be all tied up together in love again in the afterlife, or the next life, or whatever . . ." She sort of doesn't know where to go with this part. "We commit these remains of the body of the man named Ashton Bernard Taylor to your care, Peo-Peo-Hix-Hiix." Together, the children of Clara and Moses sprinkle the ashes from the canister onto the surface of the Clearwater, and just as they do, in that magical instant in a place prone to legends, a steelhead trout the size of two of their arms leaps open-mouthed through the ash and out of the water, frightening both of them so that they fall backwards on the river bank, where they nearly laugh themselves to death.

RICH IS STILL SHAKING his head in wonder and disbelief another three miles down the highway at the junction very near the *Ant and the Yellowjacket* monument, where another legend has it Coyote punished the two insects by turning them into stone because they wouldn't stop quarreling. From here, V'ronica, Rich, and Highway 95 veer to the south over a bridge spanning the Clearwater. He passes a hayfield on his left, where a sawmill once stood with this giant, smoldering, belching teepee burner that churned out smoke and carcinogens for most of his young life. By this time of year every year, since a very long time before he was born, these fields and hillsides have been broiled lighter than a beige crayon by the sun that Rich figures *Hanyawat* must be using a looking glass to focus extra intensely on this valley. His father, Moses the Chief, used to say—before it became impolitically correct to use reverse-racism—that *it needs to be this hot so no more white people will want to come here to live with us. And if that means we have to sweat it out a few of the hotter months, we'll just plunge our brown bottoms in Lapwai Creek up to our chins to tough it out.* (This always got an Indian laugh, no matter the audience.) Rich chose to believe that these summer temps without precipitation were necessary to purify the lands of the *Nimíipuu* for the centuries of atrocities that befell them here. He looks up toward the sun through his roofless car—even the sky is bleached to a washed-out periwinkle.

When his sister doesn't signal or turn left off the highway at the Nez Perce National Historical Park Visitor Centre, Rich suspects she is up to something new. Why else would she miss the shortcut to the family home off Watson Store Road unless she wasn't leading him home? Rounding the curve in the highway, the two cars drive right past the second turnoff for Spalding. Rich looks back at it in his rearview mirror: the oasis from which he had sprung and the only patch of green for miles and miles, courtesy of the grove of Cottonwood trees that congregate where Lapwai Creek tumbles out of Winchester Canyon and into the Clearwater River. Henry and Eliza Spalding only did what those shade trees had done before them when they too chose a slightly cooler spot to establish their Presbyterian mission one-hundred-and-eighty years ago.

Her right signal light comes on, just as soon as the speed limit sign announces the change from fifty-five to thirty-five. She turns onto North Main Street. They crawl through a school zone so slowly that Rich has time to read the Thunderbird IV Convenience Store sign which someone has cleverly spray-painted over the spaces just under the Pepsi logo that used to hold the gas price numbers. The modified sign now reads:

Gas, Diesel, Discount Cigarettes
Unleaded: Arm
Midgrade: And
Super Unleaded: Leg

Even if he missed this sign; or the fireworks stand on the highway; or the Kmart blankets printed with animal designs and hung up in half the house windows in lieu of curtains; or the empty parking spaces at Valley Foods, which closed early or the Moccasin Flats Trading Post that didn't bother opening today at all; and even if he failed to note that North Main Street had just turned into South Main Street in the middle of a block for no logical reason, Rich Dreadfulwater would still know he was home. It's when he spots another sign that a corner of his mouth lifts into a knowing smile; this one hand-painted with three balloons stapled on each corner: POWWOW TODAY, PUBLIC INVITED.

The parking lot next to the city park is jam-packed. They must have commandeered every lawn chair within a 200-mile radius to form the two half circles on the grass lawn under the giant green military parachute tent, which spokes out from a center pole, lending the illusion of tree shade. Rich hears the drum circle before he can see it, of course, while still hunting for a parking spot. V'ronica has claimed hers. *This is pretty crazy*, he's thinking. He would have appreciated a creek-cooled beer on his father's back porch if his re-entry plan had been up to him. He was hardly festooned for a powwow in his ratty Green Lake Rowing Club t-shirt, but clearly the event had already started. He did have a faux black-and-white cowhide vest in the trunk. He could have tossed it on, but it was hardly the weather for a layered look. He grabs it anyway as an implement to show a smidgeon of respect.

His sister yells at him to "just leave it in the road already and come on!" Well they both know he can't just leave a BMW Roadster Z4 in the middle of South Main Street in Lapwai. He closes the roof and elects to park in an empty spot at City Hall; the one normally reserved for the dogcatcher—which is sort of a reservation running joke, because there never has been a dogcatcher here.

Veronica drags Rich by the hand back across the street to the ceremonial circle in the park. By the number of cars and the age of the children now dancing, Rich can calculate that the powwow is maybe already forty-five minutes underway. Two smaller children are in the center of the circle now, doing a basic dance as Rich and his sister travel around the outside to reach their father and several of their relations, all sitting in lawn chairs except for Uncle Percy, who is half napping but all drooling in his wheelchair. Their arrival causes a commotion that nearly drowns out the drumming and singing, but quickly everyone settles down.

From a standing position behind the lawn chairs, the youngest generation of the Dreadfulwater family watch the children dancers as V'ronica clings to her brother. The children finish, and the next set of young dancers, a few years older, file into the center of the circle, with prods and encouragement from their parents. The dance, with some technique, becomes a bit more complicated—the drums louder and the singing more intense.

"When did you decide to come?" Rich's father shoots the question over his shoulder without turning around.

"Oh, I imagine I made my decision about the same time you sent my baby sister into the big city to stage her helpless, homeless tantrum to make sure I'd be here."

Rich can't see it, but his father is smiling at that. "I don't think I am that clever and I know I'm not that conniving. But you did the right thing. You did the Indian Thing. I am pleased to have you both back home."

"Aw," Rich acknowledges, a little patronizingly. "But I have to drive back on Sunday. Got a trial starting Monday, first thing." Limping Rabbit is already casting around for his way out of here.

"Of course you do," his father says, then adds, "I understand"— though he didn't.

Rich embraces his father along with a bit of the lawn chair from behind.

"Now, wave to your Aunt Vida over there by the buffet tables. She can't see this far, but wave anyway, so she knows you've arrived."

Rich waves to the far end of the circle, where the food is being prepared, just as his aunt turns away to tend to a pot of pork and beans that have just arrived from Sweetwater up the highway. A man in a baseball cap—who looks older than Rich but is in fact a little less than a year younger—assumes that wave is for him, and sends a sort of macho nod back. Rich recognizes him as 88.7 FM Ben, and knows he's just stepped in something squishy and is about to get uncomfortable. *Don't you go falling for that broken wing*, he reminds himself. The radio host is now on the move and heading his way—but being a local celebrity, he doesn't get even a quarter of the way around the circle before he is stopped by fans.

"I have to go get ready," V'ronica suddenly announces, planting a freshly lip-glossed kiss on her brother's cheek, which he casually rubs off. Her departure reminds the cousin sitting in the lawn chair next to his Dad that he was supposed to relieve one of the drummers—another cousin—so he could mix the turntables for V'ronica's number. Like a tuxedoed seat filler at the Oscars, Rich slips into the emptying lawn chair.

"So this is to be a short visit. We better get started. How are you doing?" his father asks, studying his son's face. It has been as many years as he has been a widower since the last time he saw it.

"I've been better." Rich pauses to politely applaud the youth for their dancing. "I've definitely been less stressed out, and I don't think I've ever been this sad, that's for sure." He crinkles up his face to keep from losing it, raising a hand to rub one side of his head, and then diverting it to pull his hair back into a ponytail he holds in a fist.

"Well, you've never been more handsome. That's what your mother would want me to tell you."

Shrugging off the compliment, Rich says, "I could look like horse shit and you'd say that."

"Well, as a matter of fact, you do and I just did." His father waits a comic's beat, always cracking himself up first. "Oh, you know I'm joking!" The drumming and singing continue and it's the teens' turn to enter the circle. "So, V'ronica told me about Ashton before she got on the bus for Seattle. I was real sorry to hear that news. I imagine you are still in mourning, and why wouldn't you be?" His father wouldn't know how to beat around a bush; he'd never in his life been any way but direct.

"With my workload, I don't have time to love or mourn or put my life back together. I miss my Ash like hell and I can't just get over loving and losing him. But I also don't have any energy to do anything about it. So I'm stuck. Like you must feel about Mom."

"I met your boyfriend once, you know."

"You did not!"

"I did. Your mother figured out that we were about five hundred frequent flyer miles from getting two free tickets to Hawaii, so she drove me to the airport and put me on a plane to Seattle and back in the same day. I phoned to tell you I was coming and that I had a couple hours at the airport to kill, but you were in court or something. Your boyfriend said he'd give you the message in case you called and then he surprised me himself! Just showed up at the airport and we had a beer together. He even treated!"

Rich's eyes are starting to swim. "That devil! He never told me that."

"We had a good laugh about some of your eccentricities."

Protesting now, Rich asks, "Mine?"

"Then your boyfriend asks if I have a traditional remedy for acid indigestion. I told him about Arm and Hammer baking soda." Rich and his dad have a strong belly laugh over that.

The drumming and singing stop. Aunt Vida picks up the microphone that is attached to a single amplifier speaker sitting on the ground with the front edge propped on top of a river rock. She clears her throat with the microphone already in front of her mouth. "Hello, everybody. The food tables are ready for the elders to go through. A message to the elders: leave some salmon for the rest of us!"

"Your sister's group is up now," his father announces as he gets up to head over to the food. Rich watches his sort of square-shaped father as he shuffles along, cutting straight across the grass circle.

The drumming starts up, and V'ronica's group of young women begins to dance. Rich of course focuses on his sister and the seriousness with which she takes her dancing, their traditions. The well-earned creases of this lawyer's forehead begin to smooth out—possibly melting in this heat—and his eyes open wider, seeing more, understanding more as the drumbeats and the singing enter him traditionally, making love to his tired soul. His head begins to automatically bob in time with the drums. He closes his eyes and is greeted by the worried faces of his ancestors and those who have gone before; his mother is there, too, and she hold hands with everyone else, absolutely living again in that moment inside his eyelids. A grin slowly overtakes his face, where twin tributaries of tears have begun their course as rivulets that will soon form a delta under his chin. He doesn't want them worrying about him. He will be fine, he wants to tell them, but he has to believe it himself first, or it won't arrive in the other world as authentic.

With elbows on the exposed knees that show through his torn jeans, Rich lowers his heavy head onto his open hands. If he opens his eyes, the ancestors will disappear again. If he keeps them closed, he can hold them his prisoners. Then there is an unsteady, almost arthritic, grip on his shoulder and a familiar voice in his ear.

"Welcome home, Limping Rabbit." It is his Aunt Vida's voice. He doesn't need to open his eyes to know this. She sounds precisely the way her sister, his mother, sounded. His shoulders now quake with sobs, because he can see his mother's face and he hears his mother's voice, and the two together slay him. "My knees don't bend anymore," Aunt Vida says, not seeing him cry. "So you will have to get up to hug me, ya big lug." The beautiful old woman tells it like it is. Rich stands up from the webbed lawn chair like he's Ray Charles getting up from the piano, to embrace his mother, who has taken the form of her sister. He grabs on, but doesn't yet know how to let go. He rocks her back and forth there, wearing ruts in the grass, until the drumming stops.

"Hey," she says. "You should go and say hello to Ben LeDuc over there. You two were in that movie, *Breakheart Pass*, together."

"We were all of us in that stupid movie," Rich counters, still unable to let go of his Aunt Vida, who is already patting him on the lower back, signaling she's ready to be released. She shouldn't be away from the food tables this long, with a hungry crowd this big. Finally, he lets go and reluctantly opens his eyes.

"What's this?" Aunt Vida asks him as she tries to coordinate her vision to guide her bony index finger to the green diamond in the side of his nose. "Looks like a booger."

Rich has gotten used to answering this question. He smiles. "It is a reminder," he says. "A reminder of who I am, who our people were, who I should be, and who I loved."

"That's one mighty powerful booger," Aunt Vida says, seeming satisfied. "Welcome home, Limping Rabbit." She pats his shoulders with both hands as she glances anxiously over her shoulder toward the potluck line-up. She excuses herself just by turning to attend to her duties. Rich raises a hand to his face to wipe a brand new tear that he delivers on the tip of his finger to the diamond stud in his nose. This has become ritual for him, as he seems to be destined to produce at least one tear every day.

Older teenage boys in traditional warrior costumes have entered the circle, and the dancing and singing elevates to a new level. The young men, with their torsos bared, dance themselves into a controlled frenzy as Rich plunges deeper and deeper into his heritage. His father is returning to his lawn chair by walking straight through the dancers with a paper plate not engineered to carry what he thinks he can eat. He is admiring his only son, who has become a fine-looking and successful man. Moses tries to put on a smile, having had to accept many years before that the hereditary line of chiefs, centuries old and unbroken, stops here, with Limping Rabbit. The music and the dancers suddenly halt. There are hoots and hollers from around the circle.

Once Chief Moses settles into his favorite sagging lawn chair, he says to his son, around a mouthful of Aunt Vida's potato salad, "There's something for you over there inside my camper. Go, but don't miss your sister singing." Rich looks into his father's hazel eyes as though he needs to ask them permission. Moses motions for him to go. Rich starts to trot toward the parking lot, but stops short. The drumming has been juggled, mixed into black noise and scratches that come out of the speaker, as a woman's amplified voice sends the sonic booms of "Yo! Yo!" to bounce off of the surrounding hills. It's V'ronica! This is her song.

Rich dashes back to stand in one of the openings to the circle. His baby sister has quick-changed into a muscle shirt and sweat pants, and is wearing more jewelry around her neck than Aunt Vida; perhaps it is Aunt Vida's collection she's got on. Rich lobs his proud smile into the circle like an emergency flare, so that she can see he is there. V'ronica sends him a big brother microphone salute back, in time with the hip-hop. And then she raps:

So, yo, yo, yo
What do I know?
Just a girl who
Never left the rez
'cording to my TV
Real girls are white
But that ain't how it is

That bitch Britney
Ain't singing 'bout my life
I said that brat
Ain't talkin' 'bout my dreams
I say bad act . . . and curtain
Bring it down!

Oops! I dissed her again

This last line is sung to the melody from Britney's tune. Suddenly, the powwow grass circle has transformed into an MTV-styled music video, and the Native women from V'ronica's traditional dancing group file in behind her to knock out a few smart dance moves under the parachute.

That Justin T's
Too skinny for me
I'm no size four
Squeeze through the door
My skin's red-brown
I'll paint the town
Streets need color
That's what I'm rapping for

That bitch Britney
Ain't singing 'bout my life
I said that brat
Ain't talkin' 'bout my dreams

I say bad act . . . and curtain
Bring it down!

Oops! I dissed her again

There is another really well-practiced dance break, this time with some of the younger teen dancers joining his sister's crew. Rich is laughing in amazement as his sister launches into the bridge of her song:

Who yelled fire?
I'd like to know
I look around
Where'd they all go?
The rez sits quiet
No brave or bow
Run off forever
Chasing buffalo
I mourn my race
Conceal my face
Know my place
I'm trapped in scenes
I act eighteen
As though I'd seen
Life from fast lanes
'stead of magazines
Hair's not in braids
I don't wear beads
Can't ride a horse
My hide's not raw
I move to drums
This much is true
News for the world:
My name's not squaw!

That bitch Britney
Ain't singing 'bout my life

I said that brat
Ain't talkin' 'bout my dreams
I say bad act . . . and curtain
Bring it down!

And with the last word, all the dancers drop to their knees with heads bowed and right fists pumped at the same angle into the stale valley air in perfect and defiant unison. Everyone, even the elders balancing plates on their laps, break into applause, and all the focus is on V'ronica. Rich can't help it. He leaps into the circle to toss a giant hug around his bad-ass little sister.

The drummers, bathing in their own sweat now, need to take a break. It's their turn to fill plates at the buffet tables, so the powwow shifts easily to the visiting phase.

Rich slips away to his father's camper. The vehicle is unmistakable: it's the one with the staggering collection of AIM bumper stickers seeming to hold its rusting backside together. The camper door is unlocked. Rich climbs inside, letting the flimsy aluminum door slap against the dented alloy frame. He smells his childhood like an ocean-returning Chinook who smells each river and every creek to know it is home. It is sweltering inside this box, and he wants to minimize his time here, but that was not the plan that was laid out on the foam mattress bed where the dining table on its support pole had been removed. There, in anatomical order, from the porcupine and eagle feather headdress known as the porky roach to the rabbit fur and rabbit-feet-fringed ankle bands, is the ceremonial dancing costume of his young adulthood. The headpiece, had been handed down to him from his great-great-grandfather—alive in the era of white missionaries Henry and Eliza Spalding. He had hand-tied each of the guard hairs of the porcupine after ordering them from short to long to short again, and then sewed this bundle around the curved portion of an elk antler to get them to spread and stay open. The elk antler bone was attached to a deer hide braided base, which tied with cords under the chin to give the dancer an appearance of being taller than his cowardice.

Each generation after him had added to the finery of this ensemble.

Rich didn't know the origins or age of the beaded waistband and woven cedar-bark breech cloths, arranged here in the middle of the bed. Rich, when he turned sixteen, had added the rabbit-fur belt with about—he was guessing now—maybe twenty rabbit feet that relatives would give him on his birthdays and for Christmas. He had attached them with single cords so that they would bounce when he danced. To commemorate the birth of the son who had guaranteed the survival of the lineage another generation, Rich's father had contributed to this ceremonial costume in the biggest and flashiest way. His addition had been the always crowd-pleasing, double-bustle tailpiece, which consisted of forty-eight eagle feathers that had been ingeniously attached inside cylinders with spinners on the ends. These caused the feathers to twirl independently as the wearer danced—or even when he walked or stood still, as long as there was the slightest of a breeze. This was worn like a low-hanging backpack on extra-long straps, through which the rabbit fur belt was looped to hold the bustle tight and low against the body. On a long lanyard worn on one shoulder and under the opposite arm, was a draw-stringed rabbit-hide satchel, full of tiny bones scavenged by his ancestors from beneath eagle and osprey nests, he'd been told, along with some seashells from the coast that must have been traded here when the rivers flowed free to the sea—all this and one warrior-honoring, bare-chested brave to fit inside it all, and the assembly of a Duck and Dive dancer would be complete.

By now, on this hot late summer night inside this tin kiln of an unintended sweat lodge that served as his father's four-star hunting camp come the first snows of every October, Rich is slowly expiring. He peels off the vest he is wearing but quickly discovers he can't stop until he is down to his boxer briefs. He is being taken over, compelled by the will of his ancestors and the spirits of the *weyakins* to adorn himself with these implements. His normal, impenetrable shell of stubbornness and denial has cracked in this heat, and the shards began falling away to reveal an authentic, hard-baked, and fire-cured Indian at the core.

He knows it would be frankly unbelievable to report that the components laid out on that mattress had levitated in place and onto his willing body—and yet Limping Rabbit cannot remember getting dressed. Neither can he recall having anything to do with the decision to emerge from that camper in full regalia, or to walk across the street to the City Hall parking lot. Once there, he sort of snaps out of it—but by then it is too late, isn't it? His intention has been set into a motion that won't stop until he'd done what he doesn't yet know he's come here to do. He dumps out the contents of the rabbit skin satchel—the tiny bones and the seashells—into a cup holder between the front seats of his BMW, and then moving to the back of his car, he refills the pouch with all the ashes that remain of the body of the man that was me, his boyfriend and husband, from the biscuit container that has traveled here in the trunk of his car nestled on the pillow from my side of the bed, covered in the woven mat of corn husk and dogbane.

He walks straight to the grass circle under the green parachute, drawing a gasp from the visiting phase of the powwow with his dramatic entrance, tail feathers spinning. He alerts the drummers. About a quarter of the circle of lawn chairs away, 88-FM Ben LeDuc, in his baseball cap and the plaid shirt with the missing sleeves that might not have been able to contain his impressive biceps anyway, gives Limping Rabbit two thumbs up and a dimpled smile—all the while wondering, suspecting, and certainly hoping that the wink he's just sent to *Pathos69* without a profile pic—who shows up on *Grindr* like an Eastertide miracle, and only 100 feet away—might somehow have just gotten delivered to Rich Dreadfulwater. Limping Rabbit gives Broken Kildeer Wing an upward jut of his chin and a wink back in truce, having no idea that 88-FM Ben has just sent a hook-up wink to my iPhone, buried in Rich's bag in the trunk that is not so coincidentally about 100 feet away.

Continuing his scan around the circle, he easily finds his father holding court with a group of elders, either griping about the dismal salmon runs or not enough revenue coming out of the casinos to support youth programs. His father listens and offers to do what he can—but he can't create more salmon or magically grant them wings to fly over the eight hydroelectric dams between here and Astoria. Casino revenue, on the other hand—now *that* is how the magic really happens around here. But he quiets them all down, because he can plainly see that his son is about to honor him, their ancestors, and every warrior from every war the *Nimíipuu* have ever been forced to fight.

And look: there's Aunt Vida, waving a Kentucky Fried Chicken drumstick as she talks—just like his mother, she can't communicate without using her hands. Narrowing his eyes, he thinks that if he squints until his vision is as bad as hers, he can make believe in this moment that he is about to dance for his mother's enjoyment, which is really the only reason he did anything growing up; the only reason he hasn't given up still.

When V'ronica spots her brother in his Duck and Dive costume, both her hands fly to her mouth like a pair of snow geese, and her eyes grow large with wonder, and marshy with sudden emotion that up until now she's held back like Dworshak Dam, just a short ways upriver; or Lower Granite, Little Goose, Ice Harbor, McNary, John Day, The Dalles, and Bonneville dams—all downriver.

Rich gives his signal to the drummers, and they interrupt the visiting around the circle by starting a synchronized and elevated heartbeat that rises and ricochets around, bouncing off the hills that surround them. On cue, a cool evening breeze rolls off the parched hillside to lift the parachute with a rustle, focusing every pair of eyes on the already bouncing rabbit's feet and spinning eagle feathers. The high register singing begins. Rich's moccasined feet give the appearance that they are making the drums beat and not the other way around. They work the grass, and every few beats, Limping Rabbit ducks, sort of collapsing in on himself while he spins 360 degrees. He does this so the white man's bullets miss him. With this dance, he is depicting the great and final Nez Perce battle that occurred with a surprise attack by Colonel John Gibbon and his 206 soldiers at around three in the morning on August 9, 1877.

Limping Rabbit squeezes his eyes together while he dances, forcing himself to picture the more than seven hundred *Nimíipuu* under Chief Joseph who had refused the US government's insistence that they be relocated to reservations, all of them exhausted by the month-long pursuit by the military that had chased them off these lands and over the Bitterroot Mountains into Montana. Most of these seven hundred were women and children, sleeping in eighty-nine tee-pees along the north fork of the Big Hole River. Only two hundred were warriors, with several of these sleeping, tucked away a short distance from the camp in the hills. Rich concentrates his respect on the warriors now as he continues to dodge the bullets being fired into the teepees of those deep in their dreams of peacefully crossing over into Canada. He dances now to the mayhem that causes the drum-mers to work harder, beat faster. There are more bullets with more ducking and more spinning and more diving. The rabbit-skin satchel is orbiting the dancer on its long leather cord. The people in their lawn chairs start lending their screams and yells to the singer's panicked voices. Limping Rabbit is only spinning now, down low, for a minute or two until the drumming and the movement and the singing and the shouting all suddenly stops. *I will fight no more forever.* He thinks of Chief Joseph's words while, in his head, his heartbeat seems as loud to him now as the drums.

THE SMELL OF FOLGERS coffee lures Rich off the sofa where he spent the night—oddly, because Folgers smells right but tastes like crap—and into the kitchen. His parents had sworn by Folgers *Mountain Grown* ever since the Christmas he and V'ronica had pooled allowances to get them a Mr. Coffee, in an attempt to wean them off of Nescafé.

Moses, whose insomnia has had him installed on that squeaky barstool since about four this morning, is the first to speak. "Whadya think of that sister of yours?

"Quite the rez-pop sensation, I'd say."

"She's going to put us on the map all over again! It's a new pot." He nods at the Mr. Coffee that has just beeped. "I saw you talking with FM Ben last night. You two kiss and make up?"

His father's frankness and bull's-eye accuracy catch Rich off guard. "Not exactly," he too quickly responds without turning around from the coffee pot, lest his face betray him. "Ben did concede that I am probably the best Duck and Dive dancer of all time." He fabricates this on the spot, since Ben did not. But his father isn't all that has caught Rich off his guard in the past twenty-four hours—since actually he and FM Ben did kiss last night, standing in the shadow behind the building in the dog catcher's parking spot. They had been chatting about everything and nothing, and Rich had been admiring how nicely his childhood friend had filled out, especially those bulging arms of his, and out of nowhere, Ben—confidence boosted by the Grindr confirmation of a *Pathos69* in the immediate vicinity—came in for the kiss. Rich had been taken in by the old Broken Kildeer Wing all over again.

"Say, son, did your sister introduce you to that friend of hers from Kamiah last night? Her name is Angelica, I think?"

"Really short hair, round face?"

"Really pretty?" the chief prods.

"I suppose she is," Rich concedes, not even really knowing if the two of them are talking about the same girl.

"Your sister says Angelica is on the hunt for a sperm donor—doesn't want anything to do with the man who donates, just has this yearning need to have a baby."

"And you tell me this, why?" Rich looks suspiciously back at his father who suddenly smiles into the newspaper he is pretending to read.

"Well, I did ask the elders about her father last night and everyone's pretty sure that she's full blooded."

Rich pivots the topic to avoid the hereditary lecture. "Dad, I need to stop by that place called *Tukeyú·tpe*. Can you tell me the best way to get to it?"

The chief looks up from his *Lewiston Morning Tribune* and over the top of his reading glasses. "What business do you have there?"

"I have to take care of Ash's last request. It's important I go there."

'Well, it's the waterfall about seven miles down the river . . . the opposite side of the highway; looks like a horse's tail. You know what happened there, don't you?"

Rich gives his dad an eye roll. "Duh, I translated the oral narratives for my college thesis, remember? I know what happened there. So did Ash. This is on his request that I take him there," he says, patting the rabbit skin pouch still strung around his shoulder over his t-shirt, both of which he wore to bed, as he was too exhausted to totally undress when they had finally gotten home last night. It had been near midnight by the time he'd said goodbye and thank you to V'ronica, and by the time he had invited Ben to visit him some weekend in Seattle.

"You must honor the wishes of the dead. No matter what, you cannot neglect that duty, Son."

Wincing at the first taste of his father's coffee, Rich says, "It was good for me to come home, Dad. I'll do it again real soon." His wise father smiles, but says nothing, revealing that he knows better than to believe his son's promises.

NOT EVEN AN HOUR later, after grabbing a shower and slipping into fresh clothes, Rich turns off the highway onto the gravel road that follows the south side of the riverbank. He drives with one hand on the steering wheel and the other hand around the satchel on his left thigh at rest now, after an animated evening.

"You wanted to hear the Nez Perce story of what took place at *Tukeyú·tpe*?" he says, talking out loud to the rabbit-skin pouch. "Well, let me tell you." He begins fluently in the Sahaptian dialect known as Niimiipuutímt:

> ʔiceyé·ye koná hikiyé·yiksene káloʔ kí·met kuʔskihí·x
> hiné·sexne neqé·ykex ʔisí·met neqé·y hitqelú·six titm'a·ý.
> ká· wá·qoʔ hiné·swewluqe "ʔí·hax kála manmaʔí" ka·
> hiʔpċó·qa sí·kstiwa·.

(Once upon a time, Coyote was going around there, and all at once he saw some girls swimming on the other side of the river. He thought to himself, "I wish I could have those girls somehow!" He began pounding his penis, and he tried to see if it would reach to the other side of the river. It wasn't quite long enough yet, so he pounded some more . . .)

ka· hicapá·ʔyahinawiqana káĺa qoʔc wiclé·m kawá hé·nek'uʔ. q'oʔ káĺawnik'aý q'oʔ ʔawá·yixqawna wí·ťec koná ka·kaĺa titolá·t hiwsí·x hitq'elú·six ka· té·q'isne koná peʔénpe.

(Finally it almost reached the other side. The girls were swimming around unconcernedly over there. Coyote entered the oldest girl. She felt something, and she screamed, "He's done something to me!")

Rich parks the car next to an old cow barn. He gets out, and from under a roof he creates with his hand to block out the sun, he looks beyond a closed cattle gate to the skinny waterfall, tumbling out of a narrow opening at the top of the basalt cliff towering before him. He begins walking up a livestock trail, switchbacking up the side of the steep hill to reach the base of the cliff face.

ʔipné·tewyeke tim'á·y "kíyex kuʔús hí·kus kuʔx ʔitú·m." ka· pé·nkesuʔpeńixne. káĺawnik'ay' pankaʔallawíyaʔńixna ka· "ʔaʔsak'í·wkitx." ka· paʔsak'íwkaʔnixna q'oʔ wé·tu kuʔús wax pewitilíxniksene koná le·hey.

(The girls tried to get Coyote's penis off her, and finally the girl became so uncomfortable that one of them suggested "Cut it off!" So they tried to cut it off, but had little success.)

With some effort now, and a lot more risk than he'd imagined, Rich is climbing hand over hand, stepping carefully from one green-slimed rock to another, reaching and pulling his way toward the very top of the cliff. From under this slight overhang, he can see that the water leaves the mountain like a piss stream after a night of beer drinking.

When he looks even further overhead, Rich can see that a giant ring—no, make that several astral rings of unknown origin—have appeared around the sun. For specific reasons he's not smart enough to know or figure out, there is a bizarre haze inside the rings. The rest of the sky is cloudless and blue. Could *Hanyawat* be reducing the sun's intensity today, Rich wonders, so that he can be better able to concentrate on the ceremony that needs to happen here? It must be, he accepts, with new resolve, pausing for breath and perspective. His eyes track the waterfall from the piss slit down to the splash pool below, and then beyond that pool to the creek that meanders through the pasture down to the river, realizing from this height that he could slip or lose his grip and fall to serious injury or even death. This cannot deter the storytelling, mission-bent climber. In a few more minutes, and with a few more grunts, both he and the rabbit skin pouch have reached the top.

He surveys the scene from this remarkable vantage point, possibly eighty or one hundred feet above the Clearwater River. He slowly turns a complete circle on the edge of the escarpment. He can see Hog Island from here, and the Ant and the Yellowjacket. He can see the tops of the plumes of smoke that rise from the Lewiston Pulp and Paper Mill, and he can see over the yellow and undulating wheat fields almost to the Camas Prairie, where Ashton Bernard Taylor grew up to become his partner in this life. He can see the gouge of a canyon cut out by the Snake River. He can see the green triangle where Lapwai Creek empties into the Clearwater.

After staring a half minute into the hypnotizing rings around the sun, he spins around again, like a cameraman panning the scene for the movie version of his story. At last, during this revolution he can magically see that he is not alone. He is now standing here with Hin-mah-too-yah-lat-kekt (Chief Joseph) and two of his four wives—Heyoon and Springtime; Hal-hal-hot-soot; Looking Glass; and Toohoolhoolzote, the Medicine Man. Standing next to Joseph is my great grandfather Heritage Howerton and his bride Molli Curby who, as young Christian newlyweds incidentally did meet Joseph and Heyoon near Cheyenne, Oklahoma and showed them genuine kindness in the Year 1901. This entourage has been joined by anyone who had anything to do with me getting to my final resting places; both the Davids and Stephen; by Monica, Greg, and Patti; by William senior and Will-Jeffrey junior; by Russell and Armando and Barry and Sam and James; by Gerald and Carole and Krista; by Evan Knight and Oscar Wilde and Rudolph Valentino; by Limping Rabbit's mother—Clara Peo Peo Hix Hiix—and his sister V'ronica and his father Chief Moses. Hell, even 88-FM Ben is somehow here, flexing his biceps, in this glorious hallucination.

Not to be overlooked, and overlooking this circle of witnesses, is my new angel A-Team of Gideon, Miguel, Byron, Mark, Scotty, John, and well, of course, me. I am most certainly here.

Limping Rabbit knows this, senses me everywhere—inside and outside the rabbit pelt pouch. He feels me as he inhales through his gaping mouth and the air tweaks a sensitive cavity he's just gotten filled and tickles the diamond post inside his nostril. His tongue darts to soothe the spot on his tooth and his brown eyes open wider to stretch the piercing in his nose. He can see these apparitions and the rings and the haze of the sun, but he can't see his shadow, so it must be noon and it must be time.

> ka· wáqo? le·héype hiná·stiyoxna kínix "hiwí·wki ?ekú·tx" manáma ku?ús hihíce. ka· hiwí·wne pá·?yaqcana ka· konkí pa?sak'í····wka?ysa. q'o? yóq'o? tá·qc kí· konapí hí·wes kí·ka tíkem hanyí·n hí·wes simí·nekem. tukeyú·tpw yóq'o? hí·wes koní·x we?nikí·n. yóq'o? kiwáyl.

> ([The girls] worked on [the penis] for a long time, and after a little while Coyote hollered over to them, "Use the split (that's already there)." The girls found the split, and with it, they cut Coyote's penis. And to this day, there is a waterfall at Lewiston where this incident occurred. The name of this place is Tukeyú·tpe. That is all.)

The sun has bleached all color from this scene, rendering it with blisters of beige and white. Only the emerald diamond piercing Rich's right nostril emits any color at all, and the brilliance of it springs from his face like a lighthouse beam of green arrowing through the dust and doom of all despair. Rich sprinkles the remaining ashes of his boyfriend from the pouch into that trickle of a creek just before the edge of the waterfall, and in that instant, the water astoundingly turns blood red. Rich pops back up, frightened by what has happened; his face, determined to comprehend this, extends on the end of his stretching neck to peer over the side of the cliff as the red water tumbles over the edge to plunge sixty feet into the pool below, mixing there for a minute before bleeding red across the pasture to the Clearwater River, which speeds this crimson spill past the confluence with the Snake to the Columbia to the Pacific to the thunderclouds that will send red rain back down to quench this thirst for understanding.

yóq'o? kiwáyl

That is all.

This is the third published fiction novel for MICHAEL SCOTT CURNES, both WINNER of the 2011 Green Book Awards and named a FINALIST in the 2011 International Book Awards for his previous novel, *For the Love of Mother*. His debut novel *Val* was published in 1996. His writing has also appeared in *The Globe and Mail, Writing the West Coast: in Love with Place* (2008) and *Living Artfully: Reflections from the Far West Coast* (2012). Born in Coeur d'Alene, Idaho, and a dual US/Canadian citizen, he frequently migrates around the region but makes his home in Victoria, British Columbia.